LYDIA

LYDIA: A STORY

(with notes)

Paula Gooder

HODDER &
STOUGHTON

First published in Great Britain in 2022 by Hodder & Stoughton
An Hachette UK company

1

A CIP catalogue record for this title is available from the British Library

Hardback ISBN 978 1 444 79206 5
eBook ISBN 978 1 444 79207 2

Typeset in Sabon MT by Hewer Text UK Ltd, Edinburgh
Printed and bound in Great Britain by Clays Ltd, Elcograf S.p.A.

Hodder & Stoughton policy is to use papers that are natural, renewable
and recyclable products and made from wood grown in sustainable
forests. The logging and manufacturing processes are expected to
conform to the environmental regulations of the country of origin.

Hodder & Stoughton Ltd
Carmelite House
50 Victoria Embankment
London EC4Y 0DZ

www.hodderfaith.com

For Ruth Babington.
The best and kindest companion
anyone could wish for.

Contents

How to read this book

This is a book in two parts. The first part (which is around two-thirds of the length of the book) is a story focussed on Lydia, someone who is mentioned in Acts 16:11–15. It imagines that she left Philippi shortly after the events described in Acts, but then returned many years later. It is a story, but it is also more than that. It is trying to bring to life what it might have been like to live in Philippi in the first century, and to be one of the people who heard the letter to the Philippians when it was first brought to them. It is easy to forget that the New Testament was written by real people for real people, and contained a message that made a difference to their lives. This story imagines who these people might have been, and also encourages you, the reader, to imagine their world for yourself, to wonder what their lives might have been like and to see the letter to the Philippians in a new light.

The second part of the book contains notes that are designed to elucidate and expand on the details in the story. The notes represent what I consider to be the most interesting scholarship written about a whole range of topics, such as who Lydia was, the selling of purple in the first century, Acts 16 and its connection with Philippians, Philippi as a Roman colony, and, of course, the letter to the church in Philippi itself.

How you choose to read the book is entirely up to you. You can read the story in its entirety and, when you have finished, read the notes. Or you can read the story chapter by chapter, turning to the notes at the end of each chapter to help you understand what is going on as you proceed. You might want to read the story first all the way through once and then return to it a second time with the notes. Another option is to read the introduction to the notes before you begin on the story, as it sets the scene and might give you some pointers to help you understand what follows better. You can also opt not to read the notes at all or just to dip into the ones that interest you, leaving the others. The choice is yours. I would, however, recommend that at some point you read Acts 16:11–40 and the apostle Paul's letter to the Philippians, as both of these form the backdrop to this story.

PART ONE

Lydia: A Story

Chapter 1

Lydia was the opposite of joyful. The midsummer sun beat down relentlessly, its suffocating heat leaving her no option but to pant like her father's elderly dog. Sweat covered every inch of her body. Her head pounded. Her vision swam, though it was hard to tell whether this was due to the sweat dripping incessantly into her eyes or to the baking heat shimmering upwards from the interminable Via Egnatia, which snaked onwards as far as her blurry eyes could see. Then, to cap it all, the ache that had lodged determinedly in her hip ever since the cart rumbled out of Neapolis the morning before, began seeping upwards and outwards, heading for the small of her back. Lydia shifted her position irritably, letting out a small, undignified grunt as she did so.

'Let me guess,' the dark brown eyes of the young woman sitting opposite her twinkled mischievously, 'you're too old for this?'

Lydia shrugged her acknowledgement. Even through the fog of her toweringly bad mood, she had to admit that this phrase had hung almost constantly on her lips since their small party had departed Thyatira a few weeks earlier.

Ruth, her brown-eyed companion, became suddenly serious. 'When are we going to talk about the real reason you didn't want to come?'

Lydia sighed. 'I hate it – the travelling, the upheaval, the discomfort . . . all of it.'

Ruth moved to sit on the bench next to her and settled back with an exasperating appearance of comfort on the same hard wooden bench that was causing Lydia so much pain, her fluidity of movement suggesting that she would never be too old for . . . well . . . anything. 'It's *a* reason, but it isn't *the* reason, is it?'

From his position at the front of the cart, John snorted and mumbled something inaudible. The horses picked up speed obediently in response, but Lydia had a suspicion that whatever he'd said was meant not for them but for her.

It was true that she had never felt as old and tired as she had in the past few weeks. The more excited and animated Ruth appeared at what lay ahead of them, the more stifling Lydia's sense of dread had become. Fear crept into every corner of her waking mind and, most nights, her dreams too. Each morning she would wake exhausted, hardly any more rested than when she had gone to bed.

She should have said something all those weeks ago when it became clear that someone had to go to Philippi. Alexander, their faithful steward, who had taken over when Lydia had had to leave so suddenly all those years ago, had fallen ill and died suddenly. Over the years, he had run the business with such a graceful competence that Lydia hadn't had to think much about it. But now he was gone, and with him the much needed income from Philippi's love of all things purple. Someone needed to be there to run the business, and, try as she might, Lydia hadn't been able to think of anyone else who could go. Her father really was too old to travel, and in any case was so deeply involved in the dyers' guild of Thyatira that to remove him from it would have been like losing a limb. After the deaths of her three younger brothers and two sisters in their infancy, and then of her mother in a final ill-fated pregnancy, Lydia and her father had clung together and slowly remade their lives. The reality was that there was no one else to ask. Like it or not, Lydia would have to go. She'd made a half-hearted attempt to persuade Ruth to stay in Thyatira with her father, but her pleas had not worked. From the moment when they'd fled Philippi with only the clothes on their backs nearly ten years before, Ruth had barely left her side. And since Lydia found it impossible to put her sense of foreboding into words, how could she have made a case for Ruth to stay behind?

So she had kept silent, and had – or so she had thought – kept her fears to herself. Now Ruth's inquisitive eyes and John's censorious back suggested that she had been less successful than she had imagined. But how much did they know? John had lived all his life in Thyatira working alongside her father and becoming highly regarded as an expert dyer of purple; Ruth had been only a child when they had left Philippi, and so, Lydia sincerely hoped, remembered little of the events that had driven them out. After arriving back in the safety of her home town and sinking into the peaceful embrace of familiar sights, sounds and rhythms of life, Lydia had never mentioned the turbulent events to anyone, priding herself on a well-kept secret; her status as a brilliant businesswoman safely intact in everyone's mind but her own.

As they had drawn nearer to Philippi, Lydia watched Ruth for signs of the stirrings of memories but there appeared to be none. There was, as far as she could tell, no apparent anxiety to mirror Lydia's own. Throughout the gruelling cart ride to the coast, the boat voyage hopping from Samothrace to Thassos and onwards to Neapolis, Ruth was her usual relaxed self; poised on the brink of this new adventure as if it were the most exciting thing that had ever happened to her. Lydia looked at Ruth again now, but all she saw was gentle inquisitive concern for Lydia's welfare, nothing more.

'You'll be afraid that what happened back then will happen again.' John's gruff tones broke into Lydia's thoughts. It was probably the longest sentence, not connected to the art of dyeing, that Lydia had heard John utter in a long time.

'Of course you are,' said Ruth. 'What we don't understand is why you won't talk about it.'

Lydia looked at her, astonished. She opened her mouth to speak a couple of times, but hesitated. At last she spoke in a tumble of words: 'I thought you didn't know. I didn't want to worry you. I didn't know how. I was so ashamed . . .' She tailed off into silence.

'I was there, of course I know,' Ruth said. 'You just never wanted to talk about it, so I talked to Tata instead.' Although technically no blood relation, Lydia's father – with a character-istic generosity – had gathered Ruth to his heart when they had reached Thyatira, weary after the long journey from Philippi. So it had seemed natural to everyone when she called him Father. No one could remember when she'd started doing it, it was so obviously the right name for him.

'So he knew? Did everyone know?' Lydia said, incredulously, as she attempted to readjust reality in her mind. What she thought a secret so well kept that no one knew of it was appar-ently a well-known tale that people avoided mentioning to protect her feelings.

'Well not everyone obviously, but you must have known that people would wonder what had happened to the business in Philippi and why you had arrived unannounced with a young girl they'd never heard of before?'

Lydia closed her eyes as the memory of those first days back at home in Thyatira came flooding back to her. She had been so numb and tired when she had arrived back home that she had simply not wanted to talk to anyone. The few visitors she had seen had, she remembered, tried to ask her what had happened and whether she was all right, but each time she had changed the subject or sat in awkward silence until, eventually, they had given up and gone away. She had always imagined that this meant she had kept her secret; now she began to wonder whether her silence had been more eloquent than any words.

'Tata tried to talk to you again when we made the plan to come back,' Ruth went on, 'but you just wouldn't talk to him. He is so worried about you. We all are.'

Lydia cast her mind back to the numerous awkward exchanges she had had with her father over the preparations for leaving. Guiltily, she realised that she'd written him off as an old man who was reacting badly to change, when all along he'd seen her panic and had been trying to help. She looked back to Ruth. 'Why didn't you say?'

Ruth threw her hands upwards in exasperation. 'I have been trying to talk to you for *ten whole years.*' Travellers, trudging their way along the road weighed down by their heavy burdens, lifted their heads at the sound of her frustration. 'You just won't listen; you *never listen.*'

Normally, Lydia would have been horrified at the thought of the attention they were drawing to themselves. For once, however, she paid no notice to the commotion they were causing. The story she had told herself over the years of a serene closing of the door on everything that had been so difficult, leaving her reputation intact and Ruth blissfully ignorant of all that had taken place, had been snatched from her grasp. It had been replaced instead by a much less flattering tale of denial and self deceit.

Her emotions must have been written clearly on her face because Ruth threw herself into her arms. 'Dee-dee,' she reverted to the affectionate name she had first used for Lydia before she became too grown up for such childish terms, 'don't worry. None of us want you to worry. I talked it all through with Tata. I'm fine. He's fine. We just want to make sure that you are too. It is so hard when you shut us out.'

'But aren't *you* even a little bit scared?' Lydia was struggling to adjust to this new view of events. 'You're the reason we had to leave.'

Ruth grinned. Her frustration now vented, she seemed to have reverted to her usual sunny self. 'Not the entire reason, there was that moment when you stood in the forum shouting at Caius and Julius in the marketplace so vehemently that you were nearly arrested on the spot.'

'True, that didn't exactly help.' Despite the many anxieties jostling her, Lydia couldn't help smiling at the memory of the time when she had lost all semblance of dignity and shouted as though she was possessed by a spirit. 'So you remember it? And you're still not afraid?'

'I was a little girl, not a baby.'

'But you were so quiet, you barely said a word afterwards.'

'Not speaking is different from not remembering. Of course I remember it. Some of it is a little jumbled, but I do remember my old life.'

'Do you remember us running away?' Lydia asked.

'How could I forget?' said Ruth. 'I've never run so fast or so far since, but surely our departure will be forgotten by now? Alexander has been there all this time tending the business. Surely people will love purple more than they care about something that happened years ago?'

Not for the first time, Lydia pondered Ruth's youthful confidence. Following a traumatic early childhood and the catastrophic incident that had led to their flight, Ruth had been surrounded by people who loved her unquestioningly, and, nourished by that love, she had blossomed into the self-assured young woman she was today. But was she right? Would people have forgotten? Or were they heading back into the middle of the same storm from which she had fled all those years ago?

Her aching bones swayed along with the lurching cart as it headed northwards along the Via Egnatia, its sturdy wheels scattering hot, midsummer dust over the unfortunate travellers they passed on the way. It was, she realised, the shame that still clung to her, its fumes as noxious as her father's dyeing workshop in the summer heat. She had called it fear and, while her stomach still lurched at the thought of that turbulent time all those years ago, what she had never acknowledged was the shame she felt. She had been so successful in Philippi. People across the city and beyond, almost despite themselves, looked up to her: a woman on her own in trade who had succeeded against the odds. She had a great reputation. She knew who she was. She had found her place in the world.

It had been her idea to go to Philippi in the first place. Some traders passing through Thyatira had laughed at the prices they asked, joking with each other about the profit they would make when they took their wares to the gullible Romans. People in places like Philippi, they said, would do almost anything for purple. They were, it turned out, entirely right. In Thyatira, where the madder plant grew abundantly and dye was produced in copious quantities, the price for purple was low and profits small, but in Philippi, a Roman colony, where demand for purple was high and purple sellers were rare, there were great profits to be made. At first her father had been reluctant to let her go. They only had each other, he said, and wasn't that worth more than the profits they would make? But Lydia had set her heart on it and in the end he gave in. The business had grown and grown, and, although she missed her father, her success put all other thoughts out of her mind. There were other sellers of purple, but none so sought after as Lydia. She was a triumph . . . but then she had had to leave, abandoning not just the business but the hard-won admiration she had built up little by little over the years.

Ruth leant over and squeezed her hand. 'We'll be fine, Lydia, you'll see.'

'You'd better be,' said John, 'we're nearly there.'

And he was right. Through the shimmering haze it was possible to pick out the faintest outline of the city walls.

Chapter 2

As the familiar sights and smells of Philippi drew closer, Ruth's delight became impossible to resist. The landscape began to pull memories to the surface in them both. Before long Lydia was caught up in a stream of chatter about remembered trees, the way the road turned at certain points, the smell on the air which differed slightly but significantly from the smell in Thyatira. They were in the midst of an in-depth and animated discussion about which bush provided the waft of perfume that hung above the dusty, sweaty smell of travel in summer, when suddenly the cart was splashing through the stream near the Neapolis gate.

Lydia had spent so long playing and replaying in her mind the shame of fleeing the city, carrying with her the few items that she had had time to gather together, that she was entirely unprepared for the torrent of memories that now flooded through her. Although she had spent most of her time in the city, working from dawn until dusk, selling purple to eager citizens, week after week she had come out to this spot, to a small building down by the stream. She had been drawn there by something; she didn't know quite what. An itch that couldn't be soothed? A restlessness that wouldn't settle? A sense of emptiness that needed to be filled? She had never found the words for it, but whatever 'it' was, it had drawn her week in, week out to hear the story of God's people, to study the Jewish Scriptures, to ask question after question, to laugh and cry, to sing and argue with a band of like-minded women. People thought they were mad – and that was on a good day – but looking back Lydia realised, in a way she had never done at the time, how precious that time had been. They had been companions on a journey, even if they weren't sure where the journey was heading.

The end had come, she recalled – as ends often do – unexpectedly. One Sabbath, four strangers had joined them, fresh off the boat from Neapolis. The fringes peeking out of the corners of their long flowing robes showed that they were Jewish (or at least most of them were; the fourth member of the party, who stood a little apart and seemed to be weighing the crowd up, was dressed in more normal Greek attire). The whole group had greeted them with joy. Maybe a little too much joy. Lydia remembered wryly the momentary look of panic that had crossed the face of the small, bow-legged one. The tall one had stepped in quickly, his calm kindness smoothing the ruffled atmosphere in the room. His name, he said, was Timothy, and he introduced his travelling companions: Paul, the small bow-legged one; Silas – 'you can call me Silvanus, if it's easier'; and Luke, who nodded but continued watching at a slight distance to the rest, as though he were taking it all in.

'May we join you?' asked Timothy, slightly superfluously since Paul was already sitting at the front of the room with the Torah unrolled on his lap. Lydia's twinge of irritation at his presumption dissolved as soon as Paul began to speak. Although later she learnt that Paul could enchant or infuriate a crowd within a few sentences of speaking, then, having never heard him or indeed anyone speak quite like that before, she had been spellbound.

Lydia had been hearing the stories of God's people since she was a child. There was a customer of her father's back in Thyatira – Jacob he was called – who would often come to the shop to discuss dye. The fringes on the corners of his garments were purple; 'Tyrian purple, the best kind', he would tell her with a wink and a sideways glance at her father, inviting the well-worn debate about the relative merits of Tyrian purple over

Turkey red from which they both derived immense pleasure. Over time Jacob had become a friend. His persistence meant that her father had quietly bought some murex dye at vast expense and begun mixing it with madder root, devising their trademark purple that no one else could mimic. On those happy afternoons, when the debates about shades of purple had begun to wane, Jacob would tell the stories of his people – of Abraham, Isaac and Jacob; of Moses and Joshua; of David and Solomon; – and sometimes, when pressed by Lydia, of Miriam and Deborah, Ruth and Esther too. Lydia had drunk it all in. Years later when alone in a new city, she had heard of women who gathered to tell these stories together, and it had seemed natural to join them. These stories were a part of her, after all.

So when Paul began to read Torah, she settled back expectantly, hoping to be drawn back into the world she knew so well. He read Torah and then began to talk. He told the story of Israel – of love and of betrayal, of hope and despair, of David and the longed-for Messiah, but then, the story changed. He spoke of Jesus Christ, Son of God. How he died and rose again, and how he changed the world, newly created, transformed for ever. And as he spoke, all of a sudden something fell into place for Lydia and she knew, with a certainty she had never felt before, that he was right. This Jesus, the Christ, Son of God, made sense of the questions she'd never even managed to put into words. Her questions remained, as varied and as tantalising as ever, but they had settled around a single certainty that this Jesus of Nazareth of whom Paul spoke really had changed the world. As she heard Paul talking about him, she had known more clearly than she had ever known anything that he was what she had been searching for. His faithfulness called faith from her and nothing else mattered much. That very day she had been baptised in the small stream by the place of prayer, and had set her life on a wholly new – and as it turned out, also extremely difficult – path.

The group had felt different after that; and in any case Lydia had fled the city a few days later. What had happened to them? Lydia wondered. Did they still gather like they used to? Whatever had happened, she wondered, to her two particular friends, Euodia and Syntyche? The cart lurched as it came out of the stream and at that precise moment a man emerged from the doorway of the place of prayer. He stood for a moment, allowing his vision to adjust to the bright summer sunshine after the darkness inside. He was tall, towering above the small doorway that had been plenty high enough for Lydia and her friends to walk through without ducking, but his height wasn't what drew the eye – that came from within. He was immaculately dressed, and Lydia's professional eye noted not only the presence of the fringes at the corners of his long flowing robes, but that they were pure Tyrian purple. Jacob would have approved. Their eyes met for the briefest moment before his moved on, barely registering her presence. She was just a woman in a cart bringing goods to the city, and clearly couldn't have been less interesting to him. He, on the other hand, was fascinating to Lydia. Who was he? Where had he come from? What was he doing in their tiny place of prayer?

Moments later the cart swept through the Neapolis gate and they were trundling towards the middle of the city to the forum and the sanctuaries before turning hard right and heading northwards towards her house. What state would it be in? she wondered. Alexander had died months before, so she could only imagine the dust and the grime that would have built up. At Neapolis, she had sent three slaves from the household ahead on foot, while she and John and Ruth had negotiated the careful unloading of cloth and dyes, the hiring of an ox cart, and had then trundled slowly and wearily the short distance to Philippi. The slaves would have had no more than a day to straighten the house and there would simply not have been enough time for them to have prepared everything – and certainly not to Lydia's standards. Before long John pulled the cart to a stop. They were still a few streets away but the further away from the forum you ventured the narrower the streets became. They would go the rest of the way on foot. John stayed behind with the cart and its precious cargo of cloth and dyes that would tide them over until he had time to settle into the dyeing workshop and could begin to work his magic extracting and blending colours to just the right shade. Lydia and Ruth picked their way through the narrow streets until at last they turned the corner and there it was. Lydia's beloved home.

When she had first arrived in Philippi all those years ago she had lived and traded in the ground floor of a tenement building, eking out her existence. It wasn't exactly a hard life, but she had felt a little trapped. Too poor to live in the parts of town frequented by the richest Roman citizens, she could only sell to those who would deign to travel to her rundown tenement block. She had very little money, so could only stock small quantities of cloth and dye, needing to sell them before she could afford more. But she had scrimped and saved, working from dawn to dusk until, at last, she had saved enough to move to a tenement block in a nicer area. There, she would receive the slaves of richer clients, and before long had saved enough money to move to, not exactly a large villa, but a pleasant one, in this much more affluent part of the city. She had opened a shop in the front of her house. Once she was established, she would receive the wealthy clients themselves. They came, their purses bulging, to buy purple bordered togas and tunics; dresses and veils; curtains and draperies. In a Roman colony like Philippi, the love of purple never ran dry.

And now, here they were, standing in front of her house once more. Lydia had forgotten until that moment how much she had always loved it. She remembered the first time she had seen it. It had looked closed up, lonely somehow, a shell of stone and brick waiting for someone to come and breathe life into it.

Lydia had lavished it with all the love she could muster. It was in the days before Ruth, when all she had to love was her business and her house. She poured the fullness of her heart into the place, and all these years later still felt the house tugging on her heart as she stood on the street looking at it.

She peered anxiously through the windows at the front – the cloth shop to the right; the dye shop to the left. She had found early on that the richest clients did not want to stand in the same shop as the slaves sent to buy extra dye to touch up fine garments, and so had split the façade into two shop fronts. From inside the shop she heard a man's voice she didn't immediately recognise – was he singing? He seemed to be; the tune tugged at her memory, taking her back to those long evenings with Jacob, who, when he had finished telling stories of God, would start singing songs. Psalms he called them. She looked in through the window. The man had his back to her and was sweeping, his singing keeping him in an easy, fluid rhythm. As she listened she became aware that he wasn't the only person singing; there was someone in the dyeing shop too, and people further back in the atrium and garden beyond. All singing together.

She looked on in horror. Her beloved house had been taken over. There were people everywhere. In her fevered fear of returning, she had imagined many and varied disasters that might befall them, but not this; not returning home to discover someone else living in her house, sweeping and singing as though they belonged there. She had no idea what had happened to the slaves she had sent ahead. Now she, Ruth and John were alone in a city with a cart of goods, with nowhere to go. Her fears, which had been beaten back an hour or so earlier in her conversation with Ruth, came thronging back. Whatever would they do?

Chapter 3

Lydia closed her eyes, hoping to shut out the bleak reality that lay before her. She had thought that she had imagined in advance – and so prepared herself for – all the terrible things that could happen on her return but had never imagined this. Who could she turn to in this city that had hated her so much they had driven her away? Who would help her to reclaim the property that had somehow been taken over by intruders? She took a deep breath in an attempt to calm her pounding heart and was startled to hear Ruth cry, 'Look, there's Tertius.' Her eyes flew open, and there indeed was Tertius – who, with Rufus and Marcus, had been sent to prepare the house for them. He was standing in the middle of her shop handing a drink to the stranger.

'Tertius!' She had intended a whisper but it came out as a hiss.

Tertius spun around, as did the mysterious but melodious sweeper, whose face broke into a beaming grin.

'Lydia, how we've longed to see you!' he exclaimed.

Lydia shook her head, blinked and looked again, struggling to identify this genial stranger.

Seeing her bemusement, he laughed. 'When we knew each other last I had more hair and much less of it grey.'

It wasn't the helpful description of his greying hair but the tone of his voice that suddenly helped Lydia place him. 'Clement, is that you?'

Clement grinned acknowledgement. 'I was starting to think you had forgotten me.'

'I had . . . well of course I never would, but it's been a long time . . .' Lydia tailed off in embarrassment. There was no way that the sentence could end any better than it had begun, so she abandoned it.

The sound of their voices had drawn people from the far corners of the house. Rufus and Marcus fell into the room, then Alexandra, Clement's wife and after them two others. One whom Lydia didn't immediately recognise, but the other was . . . no surely it couldn't be . . . was that Syntyche, one of her companions from the place of prayer all those years ago? An awkward silence fell as Ruth and Lydia stood outside, looking through the shop window into the room.

'What *are* we thinking,' Alexandra broke the silence, 'leaving you standing outside after such a long journey? Let them in.' Rufus pushed through the press of people to open the street door and let them into the hallway and the cool of the atrium beyond.

'Is John with the cart?' he asked.

Ruth gasped. 'He's going to wonder where we are!'

'Not really,' said Rufus. 'He'll assume you've found someone to talk to.'

Lydia and Ruth exchanged a glance. He was, of course, right. Ruth could fall into conversation with almost anyone. In the course of their long journey, Lydia, sunk deep in her fog of shame, fear and anxiety, had been aware of the constant buzz of conversation that emanated from Ruth as she chatted with travellers on the road, soldiers at the ports, merchants in the towns. It didn't really matter who it was, Ruth could strike up a conversation with almost anyone within seconds of meeting them. And, as she did, John would wait patiently until he was able to continue the journey once more.

'Don't worry, we'll . . .' said Marcus '. . . go and help him,' finished Rufus.

They strode off in the direction from which Lydia and Ruth had just come. Noticing their exit, Tertius scurried after them.

'I missed them,' chuckled Ruth. Marcus, Rufus and Tertius had an unbreakable bond. They had come to the family as slaves when they were young children, shortly after Lydia had returned from Philippi. Lydia's father had gone to the market to buy a slave boy one day, someone to fetch and carry and to train up in the dyeing workshop, but had come back with three. He had found them in the slave market, three young boys, clinging together as though their lives depended on it. Any attempt to separate them had caused such a commotion that the slave trader had left them at the back of the market while he sold his more attractive stock, and Lydia's soft-hearted father, seeing their anguish at the thought of being parted, had bought them on the spot. They were clearly not brothers – well not blood brothers anyway. Between them they represented the full sweep of the Roman empire, with Marcus's deep brown skin, to Rufus's red hair and almost translucent, freckly complexion and Tertius's olive colouring. Together they were a microcosm of life in the empire, and together they faced the world. No one – not even they – knew how they had met in the first place, but it was inconceivable to imagine any one of them without the other two. When Lydia had been wondering who to bring with her to Philippi, they were the obvious choice, and as she watched them laughing and joking their way to find John in the cart, she knew it had been the right one. Now on the cusp of adulthood, they were deeply loyal, not just to each other but to everyone in the household. They loved fiercely, and Lydia felt her need of that. Her household – herself, Ruth, John, Tertius, Marcus and Rufus – might be small in this new beginning, but it was strong.

'Come in, COME IN.' Alexandra's voice broke into her thoughts. 'It feels wrong to welcome you into your own house – but if I don't, you might stand in the street all night!'

Lydia was bustled into the atrium. It had always been her favourite space in the house – neither inside nor outside, a half-way place of fresh air and shelter that suited her character perfectly. The narrow hallway that led to the street door passed the two shops on either side and opened directly onto the atrium. The space, the largest in the house apart from the garden that lay immediately beyond it, was light and airy. The late summer sun streamed in through the opening in the roof and bounced off the pool of water below, casting shimmering reflections on the plain white walls and floor. Lydia looked around her, allowing the familiar sights of her old home to soothe her travel-weary, anxious spirit. As she looked, she couldn't help noticing that everything was pristine. There was not a speck of dirt anywhere, apart, Lydia realised, from the trail of dust that she and Ruth were leaving in their wake.

'It's so clean,' she exclaimed.

Clement beamed. She was reminded that smiling was Clement's resting face; the only variable being what the beam conveyed – joy, contentment, excitement, or, as now, pride. 'We've been looking after the house ever since Alexander fell ill. He and Alexandra always had a strong bond – it began with their shared name but grew into much more. She cared for him in his final days. After he died, we knew someone would come, so we kept on looking after it. When Rufus, Marcus and Tertius arrived and we heard that it was *you* coming back, we – all of us – redoubled our efforts.' Clement gestured around the room, taking in Alexandra, Syntyche, and the other woman.

'But we haven't introduced you,' said Alexandra. 'This is Artemis sister of Epaphroditus, and the best cook you will ever meet.'

Artemis smiled her welcome and broke into what was clearly an automatic – though unnecessary – explanation of her name. 'Our parents had a thing for Greek goddesses – they named my sister Athena. I'm not sure Epaphroditus has ever quite reconciled himself to being named after the goddess of love.'

Lydia felt her tired brain scrabbling to keep up. Who was Epaphroditus? Alexandra and Artemis spoke as though she knew him well. She wrinkled her brow, trying to picture some-one of that name from all those years before.

Alexandra caught her cue from the puzzlement on Lydia's face. 'But of course, you don't know him. He's so important to us, it's hard for us to imagine that you've never met him.'

'He is a deacon of our church,' said Syntyche. 'We sent him with our gift to Paul in prison. The last we heard he had fallen ill, but after that we heard nothing more. We wait every day for news.'

Artemis made the softest of noises, a quiet moan that signalled, more clearly than words could, how painful the wait-ing was.

Syntyche carried on speaking determinedly as though to distract from Artemis' distress. 'You may not remember me, I'm . . .'

'. . . Syntyche.' Lydia completed her sentence. 'We used to study scripture together down by the stream.' A wave of love for an old friend, long put out of her mind but never forgotten, washed over her. 'Whatever happened to the others?' she asked. 'What about Euodia? Is she still here?'

An awkward silence fell. Clement, Alexandra, Artemis and Syntyche suddenly appeared to be fascinated by different details around the atrium. Alexandra spoke first: 'You must be raven-ous. Let's eat.'

Lydia allowed herself to be distracted – for now at least – by the mention of food. In that moment she realised how dusty and tired she was. Ruth, who had from an early age a well-developed gift for reading social clues and easing awkward moments, started chattering to Alexandra about how dusty she felt after the journey. A flurry of activity produced water for bathing and even clean clothes loaned by their generous friends. Lydia and Ruth retired to bedrooms at the back of the house and emerged a little later, bathed and ravenous, summoned by the tantalising smells that permeated around the house.

Their meal was brought to the dining room by Syntyche and Artemis. When Lydia protested, horrified that they – honoured guests in her house – should serve them at table, they refused to listen, arguing that they tried, as far as they could, to ignore constricting rules, at least when dining with other followers of the Way. Lydia subsided. She felt ill-equipped to argue. So when, halfway through the meal, the sound of bumps and scrapes from the front of the house announced that John, Rufus, Marcus and Tertius had returned from the cart, she did not demur when Alexandra summoned them to join them in the dining room. Rufus, Marcus and Tertius, however, hesitated at the door of the dining room, looking to Lydia for permission to breach rules that had governed them since they had joined her household as small boys. They were accustomed to eating with the slaves in the kitchen, not with the family in the dining room. Lydia shrugged and nodded them in. Within moments they were incapable of speaking, so full were their mouths with the array of delicious food provided by Artemis. John, however, stood uncertainly by the door, anxiety exaggerating the wrinkles on his weather-worn face. Lydia could feel his silent plea begging her not to make him sit and eat with them.

It would be easy to imagine John taciturn, since he spoke rarely in company, but to do so would be to misunderstand him. He preferred silence and solitude to conversation and company. He spoke if necessary, but most of the time found it unnecessary. As a result, he radiated the comforting stillness that comes from a person who is deeply and utterly content with who he is and what he does. Dyeing wasn't just his occupation, it was his passion, and he liked nothing more than being locked away in his workshop, on his own, experimenting.

Lydia took pity on him. 'Why don't you take some food and go? There will be many things to set up in the dyeing workshop.' John sagged with relief. The location they had found for his workshop was located well outside the city, on the banks of the river Gangites, where the water was plentiful and the eye-watering stench of urine, decaying molluscs and boiling plant roots wouldn't drive their wealthy clients away. The plan was that he would spend much of his time there creating dyes and dyeing fabric. The three boys would journey backwards and forwards bringing orders and carrying the completed fabric and dyes back to the shop. Lydia and her father had spent a long time discussing whether it would be better to move the dyeing workshop nearer to the shop, even – despite the noxious smell – into the house itself. John had settled the discussion himself: 'I work better alone.' They all had to admit that he did. So they had sent ahead and found a small place to rent, where John could live and work in peace. Lydia had noted that the past few weeks of constant company and background noise had taken its toll on his spirits. He had never said anything – who would have expected him to? – but he had exuded a weariness that increased as the journey went on.

'You go. The boys can stay here with me.' The boys, who had been leaning over their food like hawks protecting their prey, displayed a relief that mirrored John's own. In celebration they shovelled more food into their mouths. Lydia, watching John's retreating back as he departed, could have sworn she saw him do the tiniest shimmy of delight.

Lydia's exhaustion took hold once more and she sat quietly, listening as the conversation swirled around her. Clement, Alexandra, Syntyche and Artemis passed the time exchanging news about people Lydia didn't know. She kept her ears open for further mention of Euodia, but heard nothing. She was about to enquire about her again when Clement, leaning over her to talk to Ruth, said, 'Are you Lydia's daughter?'

'Of course she isn't!' Alexandra broke in. 'Lydia only left ten years ago with no sign of a daughter in tow. And Ruth you must be, what . . . eighteen? Twenty?'

Ruth shrugged. 'I don't know,' she said, a tinge of colour on her cheek revealing that she wished she did.

'The only person Lydia left with was . . . you know. What was her name? That little slave girl?'

Lydia glared at Alexandra, willing her to stop. She was treading on ground that had lain undisturbed, even unacknowledged, for years.

'I didn't have one.' Ruth's voice was barely audible. Having no name – or none that anyone could recall – was a wound that went even deeper than not knowing her age.

Clement and Alexandra gazed at her incredulously.

'That was you?'

'But you're so grown up!'

'So confident.'

'So elegant!'

'And she was so . . .' In their surprise and discomfort, they could barely finish a sentence.

Lydia knew what they meant, even as she wished that they would be less clumsy in their asking. The diminutive slave girl she had rescued all those years ago had hardly spoken when the spirit wasn't upon her. She would avoid meeting anyone's eye if she could. She had sunk deep within herself, a silent shadow of a girl. Lydia readied herself to jump in and answer, but Ruth was ahead of her, her voice now calm and even, though tinged with sadness.

'You don't know my name because I never had one,' she said. 'I wasn't considered important enough to have one. You probably knew me as "pythoness girl", like everyone else. Occasionally people called me "that girl who tells fortunes", but mostly it was "pythoness girl". Lydia gave me so much, but the greatest gift she gave me was a name. On the way to Thyatira, she asked me what I wanted most. I thought she was offering to buy me something.' Ruth looked towards Lydia, her eyebrows raised in a question.

Lydia nodded. She had been. She had wanted to give this quiet shadow of a person something she could call her own, but had been surprised by Ruth's answer.

'I told her – I just wanted a name. I wanted to *be* someone; a proper person that people would see and remember, not just the girl with the pythoness spirit.' Alexandra and Clement shifted uncomfortably, realising that all they had remembered of Ruth was someone with a miraculous gift, nothing more.

'Lydia told me how lucky I was. Most people get given their names and have to live with them ever after, but I could choose. I could choose any name I wanted. So I did. I chose Ruth. Every night on our journey to Thyatira Lydia told me Ruth's story. The more we talked about it, the more it became my story. All those years ago Ruth went with Naomi when her life got too hard and she wanted to go home. Ruth means companion,' she said. 'She stayed with Naomi through thick and thin. I loved those words that Ruth said to Naomi, "Where you go, I will go; where you stay, I will stay . . ."'

'"Your people will be my people, and your God my God,"' Lydia joined in. 'Ruth chose her own perfect name. She is the best and kindest companion anyone could hope for.'

By this time their conversation had drawn the attention of others from around the room. Even Rufus, Marcus and Tertius had been persuaded away from the food for a moment, their eyes wide with wonder. 'Did you really just say that you used to be a snake?'

Chapter 4

The unease, which had hung in the air since Clement and Alexandra's clumsy questioning a few moments before, dissolved in laughter.

'Ruth wasn't a snake,' said Lydia. 'She had the pythian spirit.'

The boys looked at Ruth accusingly as though she might have tried harder. 'Being a snake would have been a *lot* more interesting,' grumbled Marcus, while the other two nodded their agreement. 'What is one of those pythian things?'

'It's a—' began Lydia.

'Let me,' said Ruth. 'It's my story, after all.'

Tertius grinned. 'And you tell the best stories anyway.' They settled down, their chins cupped in their hands – the posture they used to adopt as small boys in Thyatira when Ruth would regale them with stories. It was only now that Lydia realised Ruth had never told the boys anything of her former life. She used to entertain them for hours with tales of escapades at the market, or of dyeing disasters in John's workshop, and uncannily accurate imitations of Lydia's father's customers, or stories passed on by her many friends. None of these stories, however, had even hinted at a life before Thyatira. Clement and Alexandra, Artemis and Syntyche followed the boys' lead and settled down to hear Ruth's story. All eyes in the room were fixed on her animated face. Most people would have found the level of attention directed towards her unnerving, but not Ruth. She was a born storyteller. There was nothing she loved more than summoning people through the open door of a story and into a new world. Taking a deep breath, she began.

'It first happened when I was young. My first memory is the slave market in Neapolis. Even then, I don't know if I remember it or if Caius and Julius told me about it so often that their memory became my memory. Either way I don't remember anything before then. I had been in the market for days. No one so much as paused to look at me as they passed by. I was too small and scrawny; no value to anyone. The slaver was furious. It looked as though he would be stuck with me for ever. I sat very still and made myself as small as I could, hoping he would forget I was there.

'One day, two men walked by. They were arguing. They thought they'd lost all their money and blamed each other. Just like everyone else who had passed by, they didn't even look at me. They told me later that, as they passed, I stood up and spoke with a loud deep voice. It sounded, they said, like an old woman's voice, and it was out of place in my mouth. Apparently, I told them that Apollo would bless their business and their ship would come in. They laughed and carried on, assuming that I was playing a game. The only thing was that two hours later their ship, which was carrying a valuable cargo of goods and which they had feared had sunk, did come in. One of them, Caius, came running back to the slave market, only to find the other one, Julius, already there, and about to buy me. The slave trader, who was wily and still cross with me for not being sold weeks before, sensed an opportunity to make a lot of money and drove the price up. Caius and Julius may have been business partners, but they hated each other. They were always on the lookout to make money, preferably at the expense of the other. That day they were both broke. They didn't dare wait until they'd sold the cargo on the ship that had just come in – but the trader suddenly became alert to my potential for attracting new customers, so they pooled all the coins they had available and did the one thing they had sworn only moments before that they would never do again – they went into business together.

This time the business was me, or more accurately, me telling oracles.

'It turned out that oracles were a lucrative business. Caius and Julius embellished my story to make me more valuable, saying that I had been found in the groves of Delphi itself.'

'And were you?' Even Alexandra had been drawn into Ruth's tale by now.

'Of course not – or at least I don't think so. I was a tiny child on my own – even I don't know where I came from. It was a good story, though, and everyone loves a good story.' The assembled group nodded their agreement. This was already a very good story.

'The problem, though, with having the pythian spirit is that it doesn't come to order. The clinking of coins doesn't summon it in the way Caius and Julius hoped.'

'Was it actually the pythian spirit?' Alexandra asked.

Ruth tipped her head on one side, her face thoughtful. 'How would I know? When it came – when it actually came rather than when I pretended – I felt my mind go numb. I never knew what had happened. One minute I was there, the next it was as if I was asleep. I hated waking up again and wondering what I'd said.'

'I remember that time you followed Paul,' said Alexandra. 'I was in the crowd. One minute you spoke in the voice of a little girl, the next you spoke with a strange deep voice.'

Rufus, the most confident of the three boys, twitched with frustration. 'What's wrong with telling the story in the right order?' This was not how they were used to Ruth's stories unfolding. She smiled at them and settled back into her story-telling posture.

'Where was I?'

'The snake didn't always appear when they wanted it to,' Rufus prompted.

Lydia opened her mouth to remind them again that it wasn't actually a snake, but, seeing the look of near desperation on his face as he waited for the rest of the story, relented and let Ruth continue.

'At first, I think Caius and Julius thought they'd wasted their money. The spirit didn't come again for weeks. No matter what they did, nothing happened. Then one day, Caius was trying to sell a fine lady a piece of elegant pottery and it happened again. I've no idea what I said, but she bought the pottery, and paid him extra – a lot extra. Then the word got out, and before long people would queue for hours to hear my oracles. I became a celebrity. Romans thought I was an intriguing curiosity, and Greeks lapped up the chance to hear from the Delphic oracle without having to travel all the way to Mount Parnassus.

'No one ever stopped to wonder if it really was the pythian spirit. Caius and Julius said it was, and they accepted it – we all did. It was a story people wanted to believe, so they did. Of course, there was still the problem that the spirit wouldn't turn up on demand, but Caius, it turned out, was quite a performer. He would make a show of the unreliability of the spirit's arrival, charging a flat fee for talking to me, and trebling it when the spirit did come with great fanfare and excitement. Before long I learnt how to breathe deeply and make my mind go blank in just the right way that would mean the spirit was more likely to arrive. People kept coming; money poured in. Caius and Julius were delighted. Their moneymaking ventures had always been precarious, dependent on the next big scheme, but I was their guarantee of wealth and status. Their togas became more elaborate; their houses exquisitely decorated. They began mixing with the wealthiest Romans in the colony. Their future looked magnificent.

'I was valuable to them. Not valued, but definitely valuable. Then one day, four men turned up in the forum. Caius and Julius used to take me there each afternoon. The crowds would jostle around me, vying to have their oracles declared. Sometimes fights would break out as people competed for their right to have me speak to them first. I remember a passing Greek trader being horrified by the spectacle of it all. In Delphi, he had yelled at Caius, the Pythia would be elderly, a peasant woman chosen for the role. The temple was a holy place, a place of reverence and awe. There should be, he bellowed in revulsion, a holy atmosphere. Caius shushed him and hurried him on his way – for him, money pouring in was as holy as it got.

'I saw four men crossing the square towards me and right away felt the spirit fall on me. A while later I came to myself again and found that I was far away from the forum, out by the Krenides gate, with three men looking at me in astonishment, and a fourth – a small ugly one – glaring at me in fury.'

Clement chuckled. 'I'm not sure Paul would appreciate being called "a small, ugly man".'

Lydia smiled. 'Oh I don't know. I'm sure he's been called much worse.'

'Anyway,' said Ruth, breaking in before their conversation could distract them any further, 'one of the other men said to Paul, "She's only speaking the truth", but Paul didn't like this. He harrumphed with irritation. "Slaves of the Most High God we may be, but I am not," here his voice rose both in pitch and in volume, "proclaiming *A way of salvation*. I proclaim *THE way of salvation*. Salvation is NOT a selection you can make at a market stall."

'Day after day it happened. They would appear in the forum, and a little later I would find myself outside the city with Paul looking at me furiously. The others would try to soothe him, but as the days went by it became harder and harder for him to contain his rage. I remember him shouting about how it wasn't right. People should hear the gospel and respond to the truth, not have it revealed in a circus trick. I would trail home, heartsick, caught between the rage of this man and knowing I'd meet an equally furious Caius and Julius when I returned. Apparently my oracles about these men were causing quite a stir in the town, but not one that brought them any money.

'Eventually it came to a head. Paul and his companions entered the forum and I felt the usual veil fall over my mind. This time, though, I didn't just wake up like usual – it felt as though the veil had been ripped apart by force. For a moment there was a wild wrestling, and then my mind was clear, clearer than it had felt in years. I looked around me. I was only just outside the forum this time. I hadn't followed them far. The crowd around us was eerily quiet. Everyone was looking at me; their mouths open in astonishment. Paul stood in front of me, his finger still pointing right at me. Horror was written on the faces of both Caius and Julius.

' "What have you done?" they cried almost in chorus. I remember thinking that I'd never heard them agree, let alone speak as one, about anything before. They were, for the first time ever, in absolute agreement. They pounced on Paul, and one of the others with him.'

'Silas,' said Clement. 'This is where my story begins.'

Alexandra shushed him. 'Let's hear the end of Ruth's first.'

Rufus, Marcus and Tertius nodded their earnest agreement while at the same time eyeing Clement with glee, realising there were more stories to be told and heard.

'They dragged Paul and Silas away, and I was left there in the street all alone.'

'Not quite alone,' said Lydia.

Ruth's face split into a grin of pure joy. 'No, not alone at all. Lydia was there with the other two of Paul's friends.'

'Timothy and Luke,' supplied Lydia.

'And Lydia took me home and I've stayed with her ever since.'

Ruth sat back, as though she had reached the end of her story.

The silence that had settled on the room while Ruth was speaking was replaced by a gentle rustling of people shifting their position uncertainly. It sounded like the end of the story, but it didn't feel like it.

Rufus, the usual spokesperson for the three boys, whispered, 'Is that it?'

Ruth grinned at him. 'For me it is. I said I'd tell you my story, and I did. That day gave me a happy ending, but it isn't the end of the story, is it, Lydia?'

Lydia's discomfort flooded her body. Unlike Ruth, she hated being the centre of attention, but more importantly this was a story that had remained untold for years. She had consigned it to the dusty unvisited recesses of her mind and had no desire to bring it out again.

Chapter 5

L ydia steeled herself to begin, but Clement got there first.

'I'll start,' he said, cracking his knuckles dramatically. He adopted an exaggerated narrator's pose and began. 'I was making sure the cells were washed and clean. The blood of the prisoners really got in the cracks of the stones, and the last one who had just been sent to execution had bled a lot. It would have started to fester in the heat. So I made sure my guards gave everything a good scrub. We didn't care that the prisoners had to smell it, but we had to work there too. Some weeks the smell was so bad that I wanted to throw up every time I—'

Alexandra patted his hand. 'Maybe it would be better if I tell it?'

Clement's smile faltered a little, clearly disappointed. The faces of the three boys mirrored his regret. His storytelling might not have been a patch on Ruth's, but they had brightened visibly at Clement's mention of the gore in the jail. Reluctant to let this golden opportunity pass them by, they peppered Clement with questions from behind their hands in whispered tones: 'What was the most blood you ever saw?' 'How bad was the smell?'

Clement cheered up immediately. 'I'll tell you later,' he hissed back, spotting a ready audience for his usually forbidden grue- some tales.

'Clement was at the jail, tidying up,' said Alexandra, looking sternly at Clement, who beamed back at her, his good humour restored – he mimed at the boys a washing movement which, as

Lydia: A Story

he had intended, had the boys sniggering with glee – 'when the magistrates' guards – the lictors – arrived.'

Clement shuddered. 'I'd never liked them, especially that tall one. You know – the big one with the broken nose and eyes too close together, what was his name?'

'I can't remember,' said Alexandra. 'I called them Brutus and Stolidus for so long that I forgot their real names.'

'Why did you call them that?' asked Marcus, who only spoke Greek and had never got used to the more angular sounds of Latin.

Alexandra blushed a little. It was one thing to call people rude names. It was quite another to be required to explain what they meant. 'I was calling them "dull" and "stupid".'

The three boys giggled. This part of the story may not be as well told as Ruth's had been, but its subject matter was not disappointing.

'Between them,' Alexandra continued, 'they were holding up two men in bad shape, leaving a trail of blood behind them as they were dragged in.'

'How much blood?' whispered Marcus.

Alexandra shot Clement a 'look what you've done' glance, which he misinterpreted as an encouragement to chip in, 'Lots, and all over my clean floor!'

'I saw the beating,' said Lydia quietly. 'It was vicious. That big lictor . . .'

'Brutus,' supplied Marcus, his eyes dancing.

'Brutus,' agreed Lydia, 'enjoyed it too much. I remember thinking he looked as though he was in some kind of ecstasy as he brought the rods down again and again. In the end the other lictors had to pull him off before he killed them. I remember thinking, then, that one day he would actually kill someone.'

'Oh he did!' said Clement. 'Not as a lictor – no one would have minded that – but in a brawl, late one night. A year or so

33

later, he killed a Roman citizen – beat him to death with his bare hands. That was the last we ever heard of him. He disappeared overnight.'

'What about the two men?' asked Tertius, always more tender-hearted than his companions. 'The ones they beat that day, what happened to them?'

'Clement put them in the inner cell,' said Alexandra.

'The scariest cell of all,' Clement added to the delight of the three boys. 'It's right in the middle of the jail, pitch black and icy cold even at midday in the middle of summer. We always put the convicted murderers there. They used to say that being in that cell was like being dead already. You would hear their howls of despair echoing around the prison.'

'Were they condemned to die?' asked Rufus agog.

'No,' Clement said, 'I think the magistrates were trying to frighten them, make sure they left the city and never came back.'

'I remember after they took them away,' said Lydia, the memories returning as though it was yesterday, 'I saw Caius and Julius shouting at the magistrates, waving their arms around and pointing back to the place where Ruth had been. I thought then they were up to something, and that they would never forgive Paul for what he'd done. But I'd seen enough, so I hurried away and took Ruth back home, to look after her.'

'I knew something must have happened,' Clement said. 'After we'd put them in the inner cell I got an extra message to put them in stocks. It wasn't necessary. No one got out of that inner cell unless I let them out. The only reason to put them in stocks would be to cause them as much pain as possible.' He shuddered. 'With your feet in the stocks all you could do was lie down . . . and their backs had been ripped to shreds by the rods.' At that, Clement's usually smiling face crumpled. 'I lie awake at night thinking of all the things

I used to do. How am I meant to live with myself? I thought as I shackled them that night they were in such bad shape that the next time I saw them I'd be pulling their dead bodies out of there.'

Alexandra took his hand. The conversation was clearly not a new one. 'You know you had no choice. You did what you had to.'

But Clement shook his head, his kind, cheerful face lined with anguish. The memories of deeds long past holding him in their grip. Alexandra took up the reins of the storytelling once more. This time because Clement appeared to be incapable of speaking.

'Clement fixed them in the stocks and came back home. Our house was right there in the jail in case any trouble broke out.' She shuddered. 'I hated that place. We would lie awake at night listening to the screams of the poor tortured souls in the inner cell. Their screams got into your soul. All these years later I still hear them sometimes in my dreams. We went to bed that night braced for the screams – the sounds of souls in torment – but that night was different, that night we were kept awake by the singing.'

'What singing?' asked Marcus.

'The two men – Paul and Silas – they sang all night.'

'In the dark? With their legs in stocks? And their backs cut open?'

'Yes, we couldn't believe it either.'

'What were they singing?'

'Well obviously we didn't know at the time. The words from inside the cell were muffled. We heard the odd word like "praise", and "God"; and then later on "Jesus", and "love", and there were others we couldn't make out. It was the most beautiful, most haunting thing I've ever heard. We asked them later what they were singing. Paul told us that he was singing out his love of God and his faith in Christ. More helpfully, Silas told us they were singing psalms and new songs about Jesus Christ. Later, they taught them to us.'

'And we've been singing them ever since,' beamed Clement.

Alexandra rolled her eyes slightly for dramatic effect. 'He never stops.' Artemis and Syntyche, who had until this point been sitting listening but saying nothing, nodded and smiled their recognition at this: 'All the time'; 'Day and night'; 'Top of his lungs'.

Lydia noticed that Clement, who despite his unceasing good humour could be easily bruised, looked hurt.

'Why didn't you say? I could have stopped,' he said.

Alexandra reached over and patted his hand. 'We didn't say we minded, dear one. And we know you can't stop, any more than a song bird could stop itself singing. But you must admit you sing all the time!'

Clement smiled again, his good humour restored. He had no problem admitting this.

'So did you let them out in the morning?'

'Oh no,' Clement said. 'By the morning the prison was in ruins. The earthquake had destroyed it.'

The eyes of the three boys got wider and wider. This story had everything: blood and gore, beatings and imprisonments, and now an earthquake too.

'It was the middle of the night,' Alexandra continued. 'We'd just dropped off to sleep, despite the singing, when the floor rippled beneath us. I've lived all my life in Philippi, but I'll never get used to earthquakes – it feels as though a god has picked the world up and is shaking it up and down. When at last it stopped, we saw that every door in the place was broken, hanging off its hinges. We could hear sounds of the prisoners moving around inside the jail. Before I had time even to think, Clement had grabbed his sword and had run across the tiny courtyard to the inner cell. The next minute he'd raised the hilt high above his head, its point resting on his heart. I couldn't watch. I knew what he was doing. If the prisoners had escaped, his life was as good as over. For the time they were in the jail, the prisoners were Clement's property. If he lost any of them, he would pay the price for it. He'd never lost a single prisoner in all his years as jailer, but now he'd lost a whole prison full of them. Not that anyone would have thought it was his fault, but honour demanded that he paid the price. Someone always has to be blamed, and the magistrates would have made an example of him, probably with a long, slow, agonising death. We knew this from bitter experience, so it was better for him to go like this, at his own hand, quickly, cleanly. I hid my eyes in my hands. I knew he had to do it, but I didn't need it imprinted on my mind's eye for ever.

'Just then I heard a voice saying something. Then more voices. Then Clement shouting something. I peeped through my fingers. The other guards were rushing around with lamps, and there, coming out of the jail, were Paul and Silas, blinking in the lamplight, and behind them, all the other prisoners. Not a single one had run away. No one knew why. They just hadn't. When the guards asked them later, the prisoners didn't seem to know either. They said it hadn't occurred to them to go. So they hadn't.'

Clement picked up the story again. 'I fell down on my knees before the two – Paul and Silas – and said, "You saved me." They replied, "No, no we didn't, but let us tell you about someone who can and will." And then they did. We sat there until the dim light of the dawn shone through the open doors, still hanging uselessly on their hinges. They told me all about this Jesus of Nazareth. About his life and teaching, about his death and resurrection. They told me what it meant. They told me how the world had changed for ever. It was the strangest thing – they told me the story of a man I'd never met, and with every word I knew it to be my story. I had never known anything as clearly as I knew that. We were baptised that day, all of us

– Alexandra, me, and the rest of the household – and we've been singing out our joy ever since.' Clement threw his arms wide in one of his loveable but overly dramatic gestures.

'Well . . .' said Alexandra, 'that's not quite true, is it? When you think about what happened next.'

Chapter 6

'What did happen next?' Ruth leant forward, as gripped by the story as Rufus, Marcus and Tertius.

'We lost everything,' said Alexandra.

'But gained the whole world,' declared Clement, looking suspiciously as if he were about to break into song again.

'You can't both be right,' said Marcus, expressing the frustration of all three boys. This storytelling was not going as smoothly as they were used to. They loved the details – especially the gory ones – but the story itself could be improved. They liked a clear account that ran from beginning to end. They especially liked a good ending. 'The end of a story is either a disaster—' he said.

'We like those,' chipped in Rufus, 'especially if lots of people die.'

'—or a triumph. It can't be both. It just can't.'

'Sometimes,' said Alexandra, 'in real life, it can. What happened next was a disaster for us. We lost everything: our house, our money, our status, and most of our friends. We lost it all. But if you gave me the choice again today, I'd make the same one. We lost everything we used to think was important, but what we gained was worth far more. It's been a solid rock to stand on in everything that followed. As Paul left the jail that morning, he whispered in my ear, "Hold fast to the God who raised Jesus from death." It was as if he knew what would happen.'

'What did he mean?' asked Ruth.

'I wasn't sure myself until later. Later I realised he meant that when life collapses in on you, when you lose everything and it feels like hope is gone, then all you can do is hold on. And it's better to hold on to God than to anything else that might leave or be taken from you. If God could raise Jesus from the dead, then God can do anything. If God can bring life where death and disaster reign then you can be sure that somehow, at some point, this is what God *will* do. God will always bring life in some form or other. If you can hold on to that, then you will find a still point while everything else rages around you . . . I think I'd better get back to the story,' Alexandra said hastily as the boys started to huff tetchily.

'Paul baptised us in the river by the gate in the early light of dawn. While we were there I washed their lacerated backs and bound them with healing herbs. We'd only just got back to the house and were about to eat, when the magistrates sent a message with Brutus and Stolidus that we should let them go quietly. We breathed a sigh of relief, Clement and I. Maybe we would avoid further trouble after all. The problem is that we hadn't accounted for Paul. Causing mayhem seemed to come naturally to him. I'm not sure he meant to, but it happened nevertheless. He got to his feet, drew himself to his full height – which brought his nose to no higher than the middle of Brutus's chest – and thundered in anger. He should have looked ridiculous, that small, bow-legged man, shouting at the solid chest of a giant of a man. He should have looked absurd, but he didn't. He was a force of nature. He might have been small, but his fury filled the entire house. "How dare you?" he raged. "How dare you beat us – uncondemned men – and in public? How dare you throw us into jail and then try to get rid of us secretly?"'

Clement, who knew what was coming, started chuckling. 'That moment,' he said, 'that moment will stay with me for ever. Brutus was standing there all muscle and power, looking down at Paul as though at any moment he would swat him like a fly, just like he had the day before. And then Paul said . . .'

'What?' Everyone leant forward and spoke as one. 'What did he say?'

'He said,' Clement replied slowly, savouring the moment. 'He said, "Is that how you treat a Roman citizen?"' Clement chuckled again, caught his breath, and nearly choked, spluttering so much that Alexandra was obliged to take over once more.

'It felt as though all the air had been sucked from the room. Brutus, who had been standing with his arms folded, a look of disdain on his face, had turned a shade of chalky white. "What did you say?" he asked.

'"I said," Paul repeated, "is that . . . how . . . you treat . . . a Roman citizen?"

'"Of course not, it's against the law, we could be punished with death for that. We'd never do that." Brutus had started sweating, the beads of moisture standing out on his forehead clearly visible from across the room.

'Paul mimicked Brutus's stance of a few moments earlier, crossing his arms and glaring at him. "I think you need to take a message to the magistrates, don't you?"

'Brutus and Stolidus turned and fled, almost jamming themselves together into the doorway in their haste to leave.'

'Why didn't he say earlier? He could have stopped them beating him in the first place,' said Ruth.

'I asked him that,' Alexandra replied, 'but he never really answered. He said something about sharing the wounds of Christ, taking up his cross, and something about suffering, but I didn't understand and he didn't elaborate. It was almost as though he objected to the shame of being dismissed privately more than to the shame of being beaten. A few moments later the two magistrates arrived at the door, breathless and sweaty. A crowd had formed outside, sensing an unfolding drama. Paul went out and stood in the street where everyone could see and hear. The magistrates seemed barely to notice the crowds pressing around them. They were beside themselves with anxiety. If word got out of what they had done they would be stripped of everything – their titles, their wealth, their status. Shaking, they apologised and apologised again, begging Paul not to send a message to Rome about what they had done, asking him to leave and never come back. Paul stood there impassively receiving their apologies, but giving nothing in return. Eventually he nodded, said, "I will leave when I am ready," turned on his heel abruptly and headed towards Lydia's house, Silas a few steps behind him.

'Silence fell in the street while the crowd eyed the magistrates, wondering what they would do next. Paul's announcement – made so publicly – was the height of embarrassment and everyone was curious about what they would do. We didn't have long to wait. Someone at the back of the crowd sneezed, breaking the stillness. In that moment the magistrates turned as one on Clement. When you think about it, what else would they have done? We had overseen the jailing of two Roman citizens – even if it was on their orders – the jail was in ruins after the earthquake. Blaming us allowed them to save face . . . and so they did. They berated us in front of the crowd and threatened to turn the lictors on us. Brutus standing just behind them cracked his knuckles with glee. As keen as the magistrates to recover his dignity, beating us publicly would have served this purpose well. We grabbed what few belongings we could from the house and ran for our lives. We ran and ran through the narrow streets not knowing where we were going.'

'Until you bumped into me,' said Lydia. Caught up in the flow of the storytelling, she had completely forgotten her previous nervousness at revealing what had happened so long ago. 'I was coming back from the Krenides gate. I had just said goodbye to Paul, Silas, Timothy and Luke. Paul refused to be hurried, but even he recognised that the time had come for them to travel onwards. So I was coming home when Clement and Alexandra ran right into me, a few belongings clutched in their arms, a wild look in their eyes. They explained what had happened . . .'

'. . . and you took us to your home,' Clement interrupted. 'The kindest, most generous thing a person could do.'

'I'm not sure it was all that kind in the end, after what happened next,' said Lydia.

Ruth laughed. 'I really do need to teach you all how to tell a story. The poor boys over there will expire if you don't get to the end soon.'

Looking over at them, Lydia relented and continued. 'The next day I mustered up my courage and went to find Caius and Julius in the marketplace. I took a big bag of money with me. The whole year's profits. They were there, as I expected, surrounded by a large crowd of people.'

'I offered to come too,' said Clement.

'But I said no,' Lydia said. 'I thought it might make matters worse. Now I look back on it, I'm not sure how it could have been worse.'

'But I came,' said Ruth.

Lydia smiled at her. 'Yes, you came. Though I didn't know it until we'd got to the forum, when it was too late.'

Ruth grinned. 'I was good at being quiet then. It's a skill I lost with age.'

'We pushed our way through the crowd, my heart pounding so loudly in my ears that I thought I might faint. When we got to the middle, we found Caius and Julius, who had been bemoaning their hardship to the magistrates, who themselves were clearly still smarting from the shame brought upon them by Paul. The weight of their grumbles still hung heavily in the air above us. The four of them, Caius, Julius and both magistrates, turned towards us. I knew them all. Each one of them loved purple and had spent hours in my shop poring over cloth and dye, debating shade and depth of colour. They were some of my best customers, often greeting me in the street, so keen were they to maintain my favour. Today they were not so friendly.

' "She's one of them," Caius said, before I could open my mouth. "I've seen her down by the river, with their weird writings and unnatural prayers."

' "Well then," said one of the magistrates, "what have you got to say for yourself?"

'I told them I'd like to buy the slave girl. Angry though they were, they still owned her, and could, technically, claim her back at any moment.

'Caius looked at me, his eyes narrowed, clearly wondering whether I knew something about her that he didn't. Then he looked over at Ruth. "Have you found new powers for her? Got her a new spirit? Did that bloke do something to her that makes her valuable?"

'I told them I just wanted to look after her, make sure she was safe. The more I argued with them, the more suspicious they got. I argued and argued. In the end I just stood in front of them and accused them of everything I could think of, from fraud to dishonouring the god Apollo. I could see the magistrates losing patience and signalling to Brutus and Stolidus to come and drag me off to prison, but I couldn't help myself. I knew I needed to rescue Ruth, and didn't know what else to do. In a last desperate act, I pulled out my money bag full of coins and threw it on the ground in front of Caius and Julius. I don't know why I hadn't thought to do it earlier. That did it. They fell over themselves to sell off their previously lucrative possession to the mad woman standing in front of them. As they counted the coins, I could see them watching me through narrowed eyes, trying to decide if I was stupid or knew something they didn't. I turned and walked away with as much dignity as I could muster, feeling their eyes boring into me as I went.

' "It's people like that who will bring our city down," one of the magistrates declared to my retreating back. The crowd roared their agreement. They might have relished the public shaming of the magistrates the previous day, but they knew where the loyalties of sensible citizens lay and had clearly rallied back to their side. I felt a shiver run down my spine. It wasn't over yet. All through the day, the streets around our house and shop were eerily quiet, in the distance we could hear the occasional roar from the forum. Halfway through the afternoon, Alexander, our faithful steward, returned to the house at a run.

' "You need to go," he said. "A mob is heading our way. You too," he added, indicating Clement and Alexandra. "I'll stay behind and make sure everything is safe."

'We grabbed what we could, clothes for travelling, some food and pots, and ran.'

'Do you remember?' Alexandra asked Ruth. 'Do you remember us running?'

'I do,' Ruth said ponderingly, 'but I remembered it as an adventure. I don't suppose it was, was it?'

'Well, maybe a little bit,' said Clement, always the optimist.

'No,' Lydia and Alexandra agreed, 'it wasn't an adventure, more of a nightmare.'

'We fled to Neapolis. Alexander sent messages about what was going on in Philippi: there was rioting; they tried to break into our house, but Alexander had it too well barricaded. He told us that he and our goods were safe, but that we shouldn't come back yet. Then a ship came in. It was bound for Ephesus. I was tired and frightened, I'd lost everything.'

'Apart from me,' Ruth prompted.

'Apart from you,' Lydia echoed. 'And all of a sudden, the only thing I wanted in all the world was to be at home. I was bruised and shamed and miserable. So we said goodbye to Clement and Alexandra, and left for Thyatira.'

'We really thought you'd come back,' said Clement. 'We never expected you to stay away for so long. Why didn't you come back sooner?'

Lydia knew that saying she didn't know was inadequate, but it was the truth. She had fought for Ruth on a great wave of adrenaline, but afterwards, when they had fled to Neapolis, she had felt more wretched and tired than ever before in her life. Looking back now, Lydia realised she had lost herself for a while and, like a wounded animal, had run for home. Once at home she had locked what had happened away so tightly she had never allowed herself time to reflect on it.

'It just happened. I didn't plan to stay away,' said Lydia, 'but the longer I was away, the harder it got to come back. I think . . . I think most of all I was ashamed.'

Lydia found herself looking at an array of astonished faces. Clement and Alexandra, Syntyche and Artemis, even Ruth, were gazing at her open-mouthed.

'What on earth were you ashamed about?'

Lydia shrugged. 'Everything. Here, I was a success. I had honour and respect. I was invited to the finest houses to dine. I had everything I had always wanted, and then overnight I had nothing. The shame of it was almost too much to bear.'

Syntyche reached out and grasped her hand firmly. 'Let me tell you a different story. The story we tell here. We tell the story of a bold, courageous woman who lived her new found faith with every fibre of her being. She stood up and fought for what was right when she needed to, and saved the life of a small girl who had no one and nothing. We tell your story often, here in Philippi.'

Clement, Alexandra and Artemis nodded their agreement at this. Clement smiled. 'And I sing it too.'

'He does as well,' said Alexandra, rolling her eyes affectionately.

Lydia was dumbstruck. She had spent so long believing in her failure and shame that she found this new interpretation of events almost impossible to process. She had assumed that her version was the only version there was. This new one was so unexpected she didn't really know what to do with it. Ruth came to her rescue, adeptly turning attention away from her while Lydia recovered her composure. 'What happened to you both next?' she asked Clement and Alexandra.

'We waited a few months, and then Alexander gave word it was safe to return. The magistrates had changed. Caius and Julius had gambled everything on a new moneymaking venture and failed, losing not just their money but lots of other people's too. They really left the city in shame, barely able to lift their heads in public. So we went back. We worked with Alexander, here, until we'd earned enough money to rent our own shop. We have the one next door to you. Not the house of course, we don't earn that much, but we rent the front shop from your neighbour and sell buttons and brooches and buckles. It was Alexander's idea. People come here for their purple, and then come to us for knick-knacks. It's a good life.'

'It is,' Clement agreed, 'it's a great life.'

Alexandra suddenly stood up. 'Look at you both, you're exhausted and we've been here telling stories and wearing you out. Come on, it's time for us to go.'

And with a last whirl of activity they were gone. Ruth and Lydia stood in the doorway blinking at each other, watching the retreating backs of Alexandra and Clement, of Artemis and Syntyche. As they walked into the twilight of the Philippian dusk, Clement started singing again. They could hear his voice echoing off the walls of the tightly packed houses long after they had disappeared from view.

Chapter 7

That night Lydia slept more soundly than she had for weeks. Even after so many years away, her house still felt like home, and she slept with the relaxation that is only possible in familiar surroundings. She awoke refreshed and went out into the garden, drawn by the most exquisite birdsong. There on the mulberry tree, which she had planted when she first moved into the house, sat a small brown bird singing its heart out. When it saw Lydia it paused in its song, tipped its head on one side and hopped up to her, as though it expected something from her.

At that moment Ruth also came into the garden. Seeing the small bird, she uttered an expression of delight. 'This must be Philomela. Tata told me about her. Alexander used to love sitting out here in the evening. One day a small brown bird flew into the wall just by his head and broke her wing. He cared for her for weeks until her wing was mended. When she could fly again, she would sit on the top of the mulberry tree and sing her heart out. He called her Philomela after the woman in the story.'

Lydia looked at Ruth enquiringly. The name meant nothing to her.

Delighted, Ruth settled down to tell her the tale.

'Once, long ago, there was a young girl named Philomela. She was brave and strong and sang like an angel. Her sister Procne married a handsome king, Tereus his name was, King of Thrace. But he was handsome only on the outside. He was a greedy, violent man, and soon Procne became sad and withdrawn. She begged her husband to let her bring her sister, Philomela, to live with them.

48

'At first he refused, but after many weeks of Procne's persistence, eventually he relented and gave permission. He travelled to Athens so that he could bring Philomela back to Thrace, but on the return journey he fell deeply in love with her. When, at last, they reached Thrace, he took her to a remote cabin in the woods and raped her. He ordered Philomela to say nothing about what had happened, but she refused. Tereus, anxious at what she might say, cut out her tongue and left her in the cabin. Alone in the cabin, Philomela wove a tapestry that told her story. She sent it to her sister. Procne was so horrified by what Tereus had done that she killed their son. When Tereus found out, he took an axe and tried to kill both sisters.

'The two sisters prayed to the gods for help and the gods heard them. Procne was turned into a swallow and Philomela into a nightingale. Each night, Philomela sings her song of lament at what happened to her. Tata said that Alexander thought this bird's story was happier than Philomela's. He never thought she sounded mournful at all.'

Lydia looked at her amazed. 'How do you know all this?'

'I told you, Tata told me.'

'But why did he tell you?'

Ruth looked at Lydia with affection. 'People tell me things. They know I love stories and so they tell them to me and I add them to my store for when I need them.' She paused thoughtfully. 'I think, as well, that Tata hoped your life might sing again, just like this nightingale.'

Lydia was saved from answering by the sound of crashing and banging in the shops at the front of her house. She left Ruth looking for crumbs to feed to Philomela and rushed to the front of the house. There, she found John in the dyeing shop, carefully rearranging the dyes on offer in incremental shades, from Tyrian purple at one end to Turkey red at the other. John exuded a still contentment that Lydia hadn't observed in him since they had left Thyatira. Clearly time alone had restored his equilibrium.

49

She backed out of the room as silently as she could, leaving him to his work. The crashing clearly hadn't originated in her house. She listened again and heard singing too. She chuckled to herself. It seemed that Clement had begun work next door and was one of those people who did nothing quietly. Her day was punctuated with Clement's singing. He really did sing all the time, only breaking off to answer his customers' queries. Even then, his resonant voice could be heard clearly through their open window. Lydia might not be able to see him, but it felt as though he was there with her nevertheless.

Trade was slow at first, but picked up during the day as word spread around the city of their return and of the vibrant, multi-hued array of purples they had brought with them. Alexander had been a highly competent businessman, but his range of purples was limited to whatever could be shipped from Thyatira. John could hear a description of a shade, then mix it on demand. It didn't take long for people to learn of what was on offer. There were a few faces that were familiar to Lydia. A few people had clearly come simply to see for themselves that she had returned, but most were intent on the serious business of selecting the right shade of purple to enhance their status, real or imagined. Ruth, a natural saleswoman, persuaded more than one person to leave the shop laden with far more fabric than they had come for. By the end of the day, the shelves were significantly emptier than they had been at the start, and there were clear gaps in John's carefully arranged dyes.

'I'll have to start making more,' said John with quiet satisfaction as he left the house to travel the short distance back to his workshop. Lydia understood this to be a declaration that it would be some days before they saw him again. 'Send the boys if you need more fabric dyeing,' John called as he headed northwards in the direction of the Via Egnatia, his long legs soon finding a rhythm that would deliver him to the workshop far more quickly than he could manage in the cumbersome ox cart.

When it became clear that their customers were now safely at home preparing to enjoy their evening meals and would not be dropping by to make any purchases, Lydia closed the shutters on the street windows and breathed a sigh of relief. She had worried about how she might feel once she was back. Would the heavy weight of dread that had sat in her stomach ever since she knew she had to return to Philippi distract her from the task in hand? Would the trickle of fear that ran up and down her spine intrude into her thoughts? The answer, she discovered, was no. In fact, somewhat anticlimactically, the day had felt normal. No fear, no dread, no sweaty panic, just a steady rhythm of greeting and serving customers one after the other.

Ruth called out to her from the hallway, announcing her intention to roam around the streets of Philippi and see how many places she could remember. Lydia stayed in the shops, and was tidying the shelves ready for the next day's customers, when she heard a gentle tap on the outside door. It was Syntyche and Artemis, bearing a pot from which an appetising scent wafted, promising a repast every bit as delicious as yesterday's meal had been. As she saw them, Lydia felt a mixture of relief and guilt. She realised she had not even thought about food for the household all day. She had sent the boys running to the street vendors during the day, but hadn't thought beyond that to this evening. 'You don't have to cook for us every day,' she said, anxious that she was trespassing on Artemis' goodwill, her anxiety lending her voice a sharpness she hadn't intended.

Artemis' face crumpled. 'She was hoping that she might,' Syntyche said, her arm immediately going around Artemis' shoulders. 'She worked for Alexander, caring for the house and cooking, and . . .' she hesitated '. . . she could do with the work.'

This statement seemed to galvanise the diminutive Artemis into speaking for herself. 'After Epaphroditus left, Alexander was so kind to me. He gave me work, took me in.'

'And let our church meet here,' Syntyche chipped in.

'And now Epaphroditus hasn't come back,' Artemis continued, desperation written all over her face. 'We have heard no word for months, and I have nothing and nowhere to go.'

'But we know where he is,' said Syntyche soothingly. 'Surely he won't leave until Paul is freed?'

'Or dead,' said Artemis. 'What if he's dead? What if they both are?'

Lydia vaguely remembered Artemis saying something the previous day about a brother named after Aphrodite, and something else about him going to see Paul in prison, but it had washed over her in the rush of introductions and telling of stories. She remembered now her sense of surprise, which had quickly been sublimated by the volume of information coming her way. But she had been surprised. She had heard back in Thyatira that Paul had been arrested in Jerusalem, and then heard that he had been sent to Rome, but surely he wasn't still there? That was a few years ago. When she had heard nothing more she assumed he had been freed. She opened her mouth to ask more, but closed it again. Syntyche and Artemis appeared locked in a battle of wills.

'You know we'll always look after you,' Syntyche said. 'I've told you time and time again that you can live in my apartment with me for as long as you need.'

'I prefer looking after myself,' said Artemis, the confident angle of her jaw somewhat undermined by the quivering of her bottom lip. 'And you have no space.'

Lydia recognised the impasse of a well-worn argument when she saw it – she'd had enough of them with her father over the years. With sudden clarity she knew what to do. She had in any case been wondering how to manage the domestic side of the house with such a small household. She had intended to look for a new slave, but this was a much better solution. She smiled, cutting into the tension between Artemis and Syntyche by saying, 'It is a great idea. I really didn't know that you used to work here. There's clearly so much I didn't know about Alexander's life.' Her gaze rested ponderingly on Syntyche. The mention of the church meeting in the house had startled her. 'Would you like to live here?' she asked Artemis. 'There's plenty of room.' There was indeed. The house was designed for a large family with multiple slaves, so Lydia, Ruth and the three boys – even if you added John on the rare occasion he would stay over – could never hope to use all the space. Artemis sagged with relief, her face saying the 'yes' that she forgot to utter.

'Why don't you go and get settled in,' Lydia suggested, 'while Syntyche and I catch up?' A few minutes later Lydia heard the crash of utensils towards the back of the house, where the kitchen was. Artemis' idea of settling in appeared to involve being in the kitchen. A few minutes later the delicious smells that had emanated from Artemis' pot had begun to seep around the house. As though summoned from their different locations through the rooms, Rufus, Marcus and Tertius appeared and began drifting towards the back of the house and the source of the smell. Lydia smiled to herself – Artemis was about to find herself with three devoted companions.

She turned to Syntyche and ushered her into the spacious atrium, silently giving thanks for its welcoming elegance. More than once it had lent her a poise she felt she would otherwise have lacked. Today's lack of composure had been triggered by Syntyche's mention of the church meeting in her house, which stirred up an unexpected maelstrom of emotion. As she gestured Syntyche to a chair, she attempted to untangle the threads of her reaction. She'd had no idea that Alexander had been baptised after her departure and realised again, guiltily, how little she had known of what had happened in Philippi after she left. On her return to Thyatira ten years ago, and still so new in her faith, she had discovered a group of Jesus worshippers in Thyatira, and joined them. Most of them, like Lydia, had heard of Jesus elsewhere and had brought their faith with them to Thyatira. Most of them, like Lydia, were new to faith in Jesus, and were trying work out what it all meant. Their community was eclectic. Some had heard of Jesus from his disciples, who had passed through their town. Some from the apostle John, who now lived in Ephesus a few days' journey to the south. Some, like Lydia, had learned about Jesus Christ from Paul and his companions as he crisscrossed his way through Asia Minor and Greece and back again. In Thyatira, Lydia and her fellow worshippers had met in the house of a man named Hector, and prayed and talked together of the man named Jesus whom they all followed but none had met – at least not in the flesh.

It often felt as though they were feeling their way in the dark. Questions would emerge to which they simply didn't know the answers. From time to time a traveller would pass through with a new story about Jesus or a new teaching about how to live. Together they had to work out what it meant and sometimes even whether to believe it or not. Lydia remembered one person telling a story of Jesus as a boy. They said that Jesus had made birds out of clay on the Sabbath day and, when he was chastised for it, clapped his hands, and they'd turned into real birds and flown away. Then there was the child who had bumped into him by accident and Jesus had turned in fury and declared he wouldn't get where he was going, and the child had died on the spot. They'd talked about the stories for days. Many of them had loved them, especially the detail about the clay birds, but Lydia had felt uneasy. This just didn't sound like the Jesus Paul had told her about, or indeed the Jesus she now worshipped. Would this Jesus really have done these kinds of things?

Lydia had often found the whole experience unsettling and disturbing. Faith in Jesus Christ – the faith that Paul had spoken about to her – had given her a firm foundation beneath her feet, something to cling to while her life fell apart around her. She had felt, at the start, that she knew what it was and what it meant. After her years of searching and questioning and exploring, she had found, she felt, what she had been looking for. But then she had returned to Thyatira, where everything was less clear. Most of the Jesus followers there hadn't met Paul, let alone Jesus. They were working it out as they went along. Lydia regularly wished that she had had more time with Paul. She had so many questions. She often felt at sea, uncertain and unsure.

Lydia suddenly realised that Syntyche was sitting looking at her, waiting quietly as Lydia's mind roved backwards and forwards. She remembered with a jolt of thankfulness what a restful person Syntyche was. All those years ago in the tiny house of prayer by the stream, she had been a gentle presence, always more ready to listen than to speak, seeking to understand and not to pass judgement. She smiled at Lydia now. 'It is so good to see you, sister. I've prayed for you often over the years. Did you continue in the Way after you left?'

Lydia nodded, remembering Syntyche's other skill of appearing to read your mind. 'Yes, yes I did. You gave me a jolt when you mentioned the church meeting here. I didn't know that Alexander was a leader. I . . . I . . .' She ran out of words. The thought of trying to emulate Hector, who battled constantly to hold together the different believers in Thyatira while they fought like cats in a bag, made Lydia feel faint with horror.

Her dismay must have shown on her face because Syntyche chuckled. 'Don't worry, no one is asking you to lead anything. I know that in some places that is what happens – you lead the gathering in your house. We abandoned that early on. Having a space big enough to gather people would be an odd way to pick someone to lead anything. What we do is find the best leader in each place. We pray together and then we pray with them. If we all agree, we lay hands on them and pray for God's Spirit to guide them in their calling. It works much better, we think. We call our leaders *episkopoi* – overseers – so everyone knows who they are. I lead the gathering that used to meet here; Clement leads another; and there are others around the city. Remember Euodia? She has a community across the city.'

'So you're just asking to use my house?' Lydia sagged with relief.

'Only if you are happy?' Syntyche's kind face was creased with concern. 'We can try to find somewhere else if you're not.'

'Of course I'm happy.' Lydia had responded with kneejerk politeness, but, even as she did so, realised that she wasn't just saying it. She really was happy at the thought of the gentle Syntyche leading a group of Jesus' followers in her house. Syntyche patted her arm and was about to speak when Ruth burst into the atrium, her face a chalky white.

'What's happened?' Lydia rose to her feet in concern.

'I . . . I just saw Caius,' Ruth said.

Chapter 8

Lydia helped Ruth to one of the benches placed around the edge of the atrium ready for any guests that might visit, watching her thoughtfully. The whole journey here she had been worried that Ruth would find the return upsetting; that it would uncover some hidden trauma she had never mentioned; that once she was back, Ruth's happy, confident outlook would unravel in the face of something she had buried long ago. Throughout the journey, there had been no signs of it at all. Now, after only one day, what Lydia had feared – that Ruth would be sucked back into a world that had scarred her young self – seemed to have come true. She looked at Syntyche questioningly. 'I thought Caius had left Philippi?'

'So did I,' said Syntyche. 'Let me get Clement and Alexandra. We can see if they know any more than I do.'

She returned a few moments later with Clement and Alexandra in tow. She had clearly filled them in as they walked the short distance from the neighbouring shop, because Clement began speaking even before they had entered the atrium. 'Are you sure it was Caius?' His genial face was creased with concern. 'I've heard no mention of him for years. Are you sure you didn't just imagine him?'

Ruth's natural colour had begun to return after her initial shock. 'I think so. Or at least I think . . . I think so. He looked very different. He was so thin and his hair stuck up all over the place. His clothes were little more than rags. He was sitting on the far side of the forum and he stared at me, as if he'd seen a ghost. I just turned and ran home.'

Clement got up determinedly. 'Well then, we need to go and find out.' Lydia looked uncertainly between Clement and Ruth. She felt torn between staying to take care of Ruth and going to find out if it was really Caius, and if it *was* him, to ensure he went nowhere near Ruth, today or in the weeks to come.

Ruth seeing her uncertainty said, 'You go, Dee-dee. I'll be fine here.'

Looking at her Lydia realised with a flood of relief that she would. On one side of her was Syntyche, on the other Alexandra. Artemis, drawn by the commotion in the atrium, had emerged carrying a range of the most delicious looking snacks. Despite her anxiety Lydia smiled with relief – Artemis was clearly one of those people who would try to feed someone out of any problem they might face. In addition, within a mere day of arriving back in what she had thought would be a miserable and hostile city, she had met four new people whom she could clearly trust with her life and, for her more importantly, Ruth's life. In Artemis' wake trailed Rufus, Marcus and Tertius, their growing bodies demanding that they stay as close as they could to the main source of food in the house.

'Come with us,' she said to them, suddenly grateful for their ungainly slightly lumbering presence. There would be nothing they could do if she suddenly faced danger, but she would certainly feel better knowing they were there. The five of them strode off through the narrow streets in the direction of the forum.

Although the sun was already beginning to dip and the shadows lengthen, the forum still bustled with people buying hot food from the many tabernas and stalls set up around its edges. On the far side of the forum near the public offices was a man. He was sitting on the ground, his back to one of the buildings. He looked exactly as Ruth had described. His hair stuck out in all directions. His tunic was in rags. He was gaunt. If it was Caius, he had changed dramatically from the well-groomed, ambitious moneymaker she used to know, with his love of togas and of purple in just the right shade. As they approached, the man turned to look at them, his eyes haunted and sad.

'I used to live here,' he said mournfully, almost as though speaking to himself. 'Look, there is the place,' he said, pointing to the centre of the forum, 'where the crowds would flock to see me. Me and my pythoness girl.' He turned then and looked at them, his eyes seeming to come into focus. 'Today I sat here all day and no one even stopped to greet me. Do we know each other? Caius Livius Fortunatus at your service.'

He looked for a moment as though he was about to stand, but then his eyes grew cloudy again. A moment or so later he appeared to continue speaking to himself. 'I saw a girl earlier who reminded me of my pythoness girl, but she turned and ran away. Here I am sitting all alone . . .'

Clement and Lydia exchanged a glance. Ruth had been right – it was him. Lydia sent the boys running to a nearby stall and they came back in a few moments with food and drink. Caius fell on the food as though he hadn't eaten in days. He ate three bowls, one after the other, with fierce concentration. At last, satisfied, he drew a deep breath and lifted his head. Lydia was relieved to see that his eyes were a little more focussed.

'*Do* I know you?' Caius asked again.

Clement squatted down next to him. 'You used to, a long, long time ago. When you lived here.'

Caius looked from him to Lydia. His gaze lingered on her face, recognition dawning in his eyes. 'I remember you. You sold the finest purple in all of Macedonia, but then you followed that man.' Lydia steadied herself, waiting for an outburst of anger to match the anger that had driven her from the city all those years ago. But it never came. His outburst was of a very different kind. Tears began flowing down his cheeks. 'That was the beginning of the end . . .'

Lydia thought wryly of Ruth's description of him and Julius living from one collapsing venture to another, and wondered whether the beginning of the end could, in fact, be located much earlier, but she said nothing and waited for him to continue.

Slowly, over the course of the next hour, they pieced together his story. Rufus, Marcus and Tertius couldn't quite believe their luck. Close on the heels of Ruth's, Clement's and Alexandra's stories yesterday, here was another. This time a sequel. Caius was no better at telling stories than Clement had been. Indeed, even Lydia, who was no storyteller herself, had to admit that Clement's frequent interjections did nothing to help the narrative flow. Despite this, Caius's tale began to emerge and take shape. He and Julius had left Philippi soon after Lydia had, just as Clement and Alexandra had heard in their refuge in Neapolis. Lydia's sudden exit from the city had offered them an unforeseen opportunity. They had bought a large batch of purple cloth in Neapolis from a passing trader, and sold it, going house to house around all the wealthiest inhabitants of Philippi. But the dye in the material had not been fixed – it took every ounce of control that Lydia had not to expostulate about amateurs who didn't understand the dyeing process – and before long the elite in the city who had been cheapskate enough to buy knock-off purple cloth were all to be identified by the tell-tale streaks and patches on their faces, hands and arms. As it turned out, the dye fixed much better onto skin than onto the original material. Before long they were the laughing stock of the city. They turned their shame and fury on Caius and Julius, who had no choice but to gather everything they owned and flee the city, travelling westwards on the Via Egnatia towards Rome.

One night they had gone to a thermopolium to eat, and Julius had plied Caius with wine and, Caius suspected, something else too. He had slept around the clock and woken with a pounding head to find no sign of Julius or indeed any of his belongings, including the money they had earned from selling Ruth. Everything was gone. Caius had spent the next ten years down on his luck, travelling from place to place, trying to recapture his 'good luck', but his ragged appearance and lack of money meant that he failed over and over again. He had been driven out of more places in the empire than most people had visited. He was here, he said, because he had thought he would return to his old home one last time.

'And then?' asked Clement.

'And then I shall bid farewell to this world and journey onwards to Hades. After all, my life is all shadows now anyway.'

'I have a different idea,' said the generous-hearted Clement. 'I'll bring you home with us and tell you the good news of Jesus Christ. I'll tell you about hope and new life, about love and freedom from sin. I'll teach you to sing it with the whole of your mind, body, spirit and strength.'

Caius looked at Clement, bemused. 'You think singing will solve my problems?'

'What have you got to lose?' beamed Clement.

Caius shrugged his acceptance of this, struggling to his feet. 'Two days,' he said, 'I'll give you two days.' They trailed back in the direction of Lydia's house and Clement's shop, the boys taking the lead, remembering the presence of Artemis and the delicious smells that had emanated from the kitchen area before they had left. Rufus, Marcus and Tertius reached the house and turned in, but Lydia gripped Clement's arm fiercely. 'You can't take him in there,' she hissed. 'We have to help him, I know that, but I will not subject Ruth to his presence. I will not.'

'Don't you think we should forgive him?' asked Clement.

'No I do not!' exclaimed Lydia, outraged. 'I have no desire to see him die, but I will not have him in the same room as Ruth until I know that he has changed. Until I know without a shadow of a doubt that he is trustworthy and safe, he will not set foot in my house. You saw the effect on her of spotting him across the forum. I will not open her to further harm. I will not!'

Lydia's voice had risen and she had, unconsciously, turned to block the doorway with her body, her arms crossed across her chest. She became aware of three bodies behind her. She knew without turning that they belonged to Rufus, Marcus and Tertius, drawn back out and away from Artemis' food by her raised voice. She felt a flicker of love run through her. Her household might be small, but they were strong in love.

Clement, seeing their determination, looked crestfallen. His generous heart wounded by Lydia's vehemence. He tried again: 'But what about forgiveness?'

Lydia struggled to put into words something that was purely instinctive. 'Forgiveness has to be coupled with love. Love for Caius, yes, but love for Ruth as well. You think you are being kind, but kindness to one person at the expense of another is no kindness at all. You look after Caius, and I will look after Ruth.'

Clement shrugged his acceptance of defeat and guided Caius into his nearby shop. Lydia, suddenly exhausted and wondering how she would walk the short distance into the house, found herself surrounded and borne inside by the three boys. As they went, Rufus described in great detail the joys and flavours of the dishes prepared by Artemis; Marcus chipped in with superlatives where he felt that Rufus had not been enthusiastic enough. Tertius, always the quietest of the three, squeezed her arm in rhythm with their descriptions. Unable to articulate their love in any other way, they surrounded her with their world. The sound of contented laughter greeted her inside the house. Ruth, Alexandra, Syntyche and Artemis had settled into each other's company as though they had been friends for ever. Ruth's colouring had returned, and she was regaling them with one of her tales from Thyatira. They broke off as Lydia came in with her threefold escort.

'Was it him?' Ruth asked quietly.

'Yes, yes it was,' Lydia said. She had just opened her mouth to tell them what had happened when Rufus broke in and told them himself. Lydia watched him, marvelling, seeing in him for the first time the man he would be in a few short years.

'Lydia was brilliant,' he concluded, 'a real warrior woman. Just like an Amazon. She wouldn't let Caius set foot over the doorstep. She'd have punched him if he tried to.'

Lydia chuckled, a little reassured. The little boy wasn't quite gone.

'Would you really have punched him?' Ruth looked astonished.

'Of course not. But I wasn't going to let him in.'

Alexandra, Syntyche and Artemis tutted and murmured their agreement.

'Clement's big heart gets the better of him sometimes. He gets so focussed on the needs in front of him sometimes and forgets to think about everyone else,' said Alexandra. 'He means well; you must remember that. Let me take some food next door and see how they are getting on.'

As she got up to go she noticed Ruth's anxious face. 'You don't have to see him unless you want to. I'll make sure of it.' And with that she left the house to deal with her generous-hearted husband and his new guest.

Chapter 9

The next few months passed with, for Lydia, a contented absence of drama, and, for Ruth, a stultifying dullness. The drama of Caius's arrival had faded after a few days. Ruth didn't mention it again and Lydia assumed that that particular crisis had passed. She wondered occasionally if she should ask Ruth about it, but years of not mentioning her own anxiety to those around her had schooled her in avoiding bringing up difficult issues unnecessarily. As she listened to Ruth wondering when anything of any interest was ever going to happen, Lydia thought wryly of the change that the years bring. For her there was nothing more delightful than a contented routine in which the most fraught event was the need to send one of the boys running to John's workshop outside the city to deliver an order, or to wait for their return with vials of dye or newly dyed fabric. News had spread quickly of the new, superior range of purples on offer, and the dyes and fabrics sold rapidly, aided by Ruth's storytelling abilities and Lydia's own deep knowledge of how John achieved each carefully mixed shade.

Days had become weeks, and weeks months as they worked together in what was for Lydia a happy rhythm, re-establishing the business as the foremost seller of all things purple in Philippi, maybe even in the whole of Macedonia. Summer came to an end and the temperatures began to dip slightly. Lydia had become accustomed to beginning and ending her day with Philomela in the garden. She would take with her a few tasty morsels from Artemis' kitchen, and Philomela would come and peck them from her hand, tipping her head this way and that as though taking everything in. Lydia would tell her news of the day, and Philomela would perch lightly on her finger as though listening politely. When Lydia had finished her tale, Philomela would fly to the top of the mulberry tree and sing as though broadcasting Lydia's tale to the world around.

Then the morning came when Philomela was on the tree already before Lydia came out. As Lydia emerged into the garden, Philomela flew down, but almost immediately flew back again as though drawn upwards by something. Eventually she came down long enough to receive a few titbits from Lydia's hand, but she only ate a few crumbs. Then she did something she had never done before: she began singing while still perched on Lydia's finger. She flew up and down a few more times and then took off into the sunlit sky. Lydia watched her go, her heart aching slightly, wondering whether she would ever see the little bird again. Over the course of the next few days Lydia looked for her eagerly in the garden, but with decreasing hope each time. Her small companion had gone and did not return.

Philomela's departure was a small pang of loss in an otherwise full and happy new life. She felt surrounded and upheld by a wonderful community. There was her household: Ruth, John, Marcus, Rufus and Tertius, and now also Artemis and often Syntyche. There were her business neighbours Clement and Alexandra who lived across town, but who were as often as not in the shop next door. There was also the small group of people who met to worship Jesus Christ in her house. Twenty people gathered regularly under Syntyche's oversight in Lydia's spacious atrium to read Scripture, to tell stories of Jesus and to break bread. They were a gentle, compassionate group who often sat in comfortable silence together. Lydia had imagined herself a generous benefactor when she had agreed to let them meet in her house, but now, a few months in, she acknowledged that she had gained far more from them than she had ever given. Their calm reflective presence had become a highlight of her week.

Not everyone in the household enjoyed the gatherings quite so much. Ruth, Rufus and Marcus chafed a little at the silence. They loved the reading of Scripture and the conversation, but when silence fell they would often slide away. Lydia watched them go, saying nothing. They would probably have preferred singing their hearts out with gusto at Clement's gathering, but Caius's arrival had made this difficult, and so they all skirted around this fact, saying nothing. Lydia consoled herself with the knowledge that Tertius and John revelled in the silence. Tertius was always to be found in the centre of the group, and John, despite living outside the city, 'happened' to be delivering new supplies at the time when the group arrived, getting earlier and earlier each time so that he never missed out.

Although Lydia had heard mention of the other gatherings, she hadn't met any of them yet. She had been astounded to discover that, since her departure ten years before, when the followers of Jesus could be counted on the fingers of her hand, there were now over two hundred followers of the Way in Philippi, meeting in different groups around the city. Clement oversaw one in his small tenement apartment; her old friend Euodia, from the days before Paul came, oversaw another in the far north of the city, and there were three other gatherings as well scattered around the city – one even in the place of prayer by the stream where they had first met Paul. A few times Lydia had asked Syntyche about Euodia or about the place of prayer and the man she had seen leaving it when she had first arrived, but Syntyche would become cool and distracted, and Lydia would let the subject drop.

She saw less of Clement than she would have liked. She would hear him singing throughout the day from his neighbouring shop, but since that day when they had found Caius he didn't come to visit as much. Alexandra would still drop in at the end of the day for a chat, but whenever Clement came with her there was a constraint in the air, a 'something' they avoided mentioning. In his presence Lydia felt herself becoming unlike herself: cool and uncommunicative. She was aware of this, but was unable to do anything to counteract it; doing anything else would expose Ruth to potential harm, and that she was not prepared to do. Clement seemed to be uncomfortable too, and bit by bit stopped coming. Lydia missed Clement's big-hearted, generous presence, but decided it was a price worth paying for Ruth's safety.

Meanwhile Artemis had rapidly become an essential part of their household. At any moment when there was a lull in the day's activities, you could be sure to find whoever you were looking for in Artemis' warm, fragrant kitchen. She rapidly found out what food brought comfort to whom, and had it in a ready supply when it was wanted, often sensing the need before the intended recipient was even aware of it themselves. Not only that, she cared for their gathering of followers too. No one went hungry or uncared for with Artemis around. 'We are blessed to have such a deacon in our community,' Syntyche would say with pride.

Lydia struggled to get used to some of the language Syntyche used, and she wasn't the only one. The boys found it particularly hard. They had taken Artemis to their hearts, with a passion and loyalty that Lydia worked hard not to mind about, and objected vehemently every time Syntyche referred to her as a servant. Both Artemis and Syntyche tried hard to explain to them that 'deacon' was for followers of the Way – an expression of honour – but, try as they might, the concept was too radical for them to wrap their minds around. They had imbibed from a young age the idea that there was a hierarchy in life, with the wealthy and powerful at the top and servants and slaves at the bottom. Those at the top received honour; those at the bottom, shame and humiliation. The boys were towards the bottom on this reckoning, and between them shared a determination to rise upwards. Their young minds were incapable, as yet, of grasping a different reality in which serving others involved honour and not shame.

Artemis, on the other hand, not only embraced her role, but embodied it with profound dignity. Taking care of others was not just who she was, but who she was called to be. She shone with pride when Syntyche called her a deacon, and bemused the boys by talking about the honour she felt in being able to serve. She would talk to them gently about the difference between being forced to serve, which brought with it a whole bundle of shame and indignity, and joyfully choosing to serve others, which, she said, was the greatest glory she had ever encountered.

'Better,' the boys would ask, 'than being the honoured guest at a grand feast?'

Artemis would shrug and admit that since she had never been such a guest she couldn't say for sure, but she was pretty confident that the answer was yes. Fortunately, on top of all her other virtues, Artemis was blessed with patience and didn't seem to mind having the same conversation over and over again. Yet, at the same time, there was a deep sadness that emanated from her. In her rare quiet times, she would be found sitting, her mind far away, a look of sorrow on her face.

One day Lydia plucked up the courage to ask her about it, and little by little her story spilled out. Artemis was anxious about her brother, Epaphroditus, who was the only actual family she had. Her sister Athena had died of a mysterious illness while they were still children. Shortly afterwards their parents had died too, leaving Artemis and Epaphroditus alone. They had clung together, and as they grew had forged a life for themselves, with Artemis cooking food that Epaphroditus had sold from a stall in the forum. Artemis' skill as a cook and Epaphroditus's hard work had ensured that they made enough to rent a small apartment on the top floor of a crumbling tenement building. They were a satisfying unit, facing the world together shoulder to shoulder.

Lydia: A Story

One day the sound of singing from the neighbouring apartment had aroused their curiosity and she and Epaphroditus had peered in through the open door. Inside was a small gathering of people, singing together as though their hearts would burst. As she watched them, a yearning swept over Artemis so strong that it made her catch her breath. She loved her brother more than words could say, but she wondered what it must be like to be a part of a group like this. They seemed so at ease with each other, so comfortable in each other's company. She looked over at Epaphroditus and saw on his face a longing that matched her own. Their band of two seemed, somehow, less self-contained than it had a few moments before.

They turned and crept away, but they had been seen. The next day Clement – 'Who else would it have been?' Lydia thought to herself – was waiting for them when they returned from the market and invited them to join the group: '*ekklesia*', he'd called it. Stammering, Epaphroditus explained that they weren't citizens of the town so wouldn't qualify. Clement had roared with laughter. 'Not that kind of *ekklesia*. In this *ekklesia* everyone is welcome. No matter who you are or where you come from.'

'But,' Epaphroditus had tried to explain, 'we can't bring you anything. We have no advantage to offer you. Including us in your group will bring you no honour.'

Clement had beamed at them. 'We, followers of the Way, care about love, not honour. We offer you our love. Come follow Jesus with us.'

'We had no idea what we were doing,' Artemis said. 'We were drawn by Clement's big heart and passion, and by the companionship we'd seen through the doorway. I didn't know who this Jesus was or why I'd follow him. I didn't know if he'd turn up in person or whether we'd find a new temple somewhere and offer him a sacrifice. We knew nothing, and Clement, generous though he is, is not good at explaining.' She smiled to

69

herself, caught up in the memories of the past. 'We had no idea, no idea at all of what we were joining, but it didn't matter. We plunged in and never looked back.'

'But you believed?' Lydia asked, surprised, thinking of her own experience of listening to Paul and recognising the deep life-changing truth of what he had said.

'Not at first, no; then little by little, yes. Clement and Alexandra and their group loved us into faith. We went back time and again because we were so loved and felt so welcome, and then, bit by bit, we believed too. I still don't understand it all, but I do know that I belong. In those days, sometimes, every few months, all the gatherings would meet together here in your house. You're the only one with a house big enough for us all. We didn't meet often, but it was lovely when we did.'

Lydia opened her mouth to ask why they didn't meet together any more, but closed it again sensing the answer would come soon enough.

'We met Syntyche here, and after a few years she asked Epaphroditus to be a deacon for her community. He was so good at it, proclaiming the Word and ensuring no one went hungry. There was nothing he wouldn't do for people.' She sighed. 'I wonder now if he was the glue that bound us all together. After he left, we stopped meeting the other groups. I haven't seen Euodia in months; I barely see Clement even though most days he's only next door; Jonathan down by the stream in your old house of prayer keeps him and his community to himself. It's as though something has come loose and we've all drifted off in different directions. And I don't know if I'll ever see Epaphroditus again . . .' She tailed off, a tear winding its way slowly down her cheek. 'He might even be dead, and I wouldn't know.'

Chapter 10

Lydia sat waiting, sensing that Artemis would begin again when she was ready. She knew Epaphroditus had gone to see Paul in prison, but beyond that knew very few details of why he had gone or of what had happened next.

After a few moments, Artemis began speaking again. 'It all started to go wrong before he went really. We'd heard about what happened to Paul in Jerusalem and how he was being sent by ship to Rome.'

Lydia nodded; they'd heard about that in Thyatira too. Timothy and Silvanus sent letters from time to time telling people news of Paul and what he had been doing. They would be copied and passed from hand to hand around all the churches he'd founded, and, as in the case of Thyatira, those he hadn't founded too. They'd been horrified to hear of Paul's arrest; horrified again when he was sent to Rome, despite Timothy's reassurance that it was what Paul had planned; terrified while they waited for what felt like endless months for news of his arrival; relieved to hear he had arrived safely in Rome, but, at the same time, worried not just for him, but for themselves too. What would happen to them all if Paul was condemned to death? What if, when Paul saw the emperor, he declared faith in Jesus Christ to be against Rome and Roman values? What would they do then? Back in Thyatira they'd talked about it for hours. It wasn't as though any of them, other than Lydia, had ever met Paul, but he represented something even to them, and they weren't sure what they would do without him.

'We were so cross with Paul,' Artemis continued. 'Timothy passed through one day, after Paul had been arrested. He told us not to worry; going to Rome was what Paul had wanted all along. He had taken the good news of Jesus to the ends of the earth – and had plans of even going further, to Spain, once he'd been to Rome – and now was taking it to the centre of the known world. Timothy was usually so level-headed and calm, but even his eyes sparkled as he told us about how Paul was going to speak to the emperor to tell him the good news of Jesus. We were gathered together that day, the overseers and deacons from across the whole city, to talk to Timothy and hear the news. I remember Euodia exploding with rage at Paul's self-ishness, gambling with the safety of us all by going to the heart of power for what she saw as a vanity project. What would happen to us all if it went wrong? What if the emperor Nero took against us? What would happen then? We'd heard stories about Nero, about his mood swings and unpredictability. What if followers of the Way drew his attention? What would happen to us then?

'Euodia gave a long and impassioned speech about the impor-tance of us distancing ourselves from Paul. Putting space between us and him, and then if anything happened, people would know we were different. "We aren't, though, are we?" Epaphroditus had said. "We aren't different. We follow the same Jesus Christ as Paul. And even if we were, the Romans wouldn't see it. Surely you remember how they expelled the Jews from Rome because of arguments about Christ? If they can't tell a Jew from a follower of the Way, how will they tell the difference between Paul and us?" He then scolded us all for our selfishness. He'd grown by then, from my hesitant little brother into a tower of integrity and justice. He was still his sweet gentle self, but he fought for what he thought was right with single-mindedness and passion. He was, he said, horrified by our self-centredness and negligence. Paul was in prison, for proclaiming the Gospel, and all we could think about was whether we would suffer as a result. He seemed to grow a hand's breadth or so in his indignation,' Artemis recalled, 'and we all squirmed in the heat of his fury . . . well almost all of us did. Euodia didn't. She was adamant that Paul had let his pride run away with him and refused to listen to Epaphroditus's impassioned pleas.

'Then Syntyche stepped in. Her gentle presence usually calmed the most vicious of arguments, but not this time. Euodia looked really frightened. She knew what happened when you became an enemy of the Romans, and she was convinced that what she called Paul's vanity project would bring the full wrath of Rome down on us all. She was, she declared, done with Paul. He would get no more help from us in Philippi . . . ever. Timothy left that day empty-handed, a little deflated and chastened. He used all the persuasive powers available to him – and Timothy could be very persuasive when he wanted – but it was to no avail. Euodia and a few others were intractable, and no amount of coaxing would get them to change their view.

'The next we heard of Paul was when he had arrived in Rome and was set up in a small house near the Pantheon, along with the solider that was looking after him. Epaphroditus and Syntyche worried about him constantly: concerned that he had to take care of himself in a strange city where he couldn't go out to meet people; anxious that he would grow weak and tired, kept inside without access to fresh air and good food; troubled at the thought of him running out of money. They wore away people's reluctance with their persistence, visiting person after person until they had gathered a sizeable gift ready to send to Paul in Rome. Euodia never came around and refused to have anything to do with the scheme, but almost everyone else did, and before long we waved Epaphroditus off on his long winter journey from Philippi to Rome.

'I couldn't help thinking,' Artemis said, 'as I waved him off, that if he'd gone when Timothy had first visited, he would have been leaving in June and could have gone by ship in half the time. The delays and endless arguments meant that by the time Epaphroditus was finally ready to leave it was January and far too dangerous to navigate the seas. So he trudged off to Rome down the Via Egnatia, the money bound to his body. In April, we received a letter telling us that he'd safely arrived. After a couple of months, we got another letter. Then just before you got here I got a note from Timothy telling me that Epaphroditus was seriously ill and might not survive. And since then,' Artemis' voice wavered, 'nothing. Day after day I have waited for news, and day after day there is nothing. It's the waiting . . . it's never ending. He might already be dead. I tell myself I'd know if he died, but he's so far away, maybe I wouldn't.' She tailed off, her heartache written clearly all over her face.

Lydia reached for words, but found none that would fit. She wanted to tell Artemis that everything would be all right, but had to admit she had no idea whether it would be. She wanted to reassure her that Epaphroditus was alive and well, but didn't know if he was. She wanted to comfort Artemis with the knowledge that whatever happened she would get through this, but had to admit she had no idea if that were true. In the end she gave up reaching for words and sat quietly next to Artemis, grasping Artemis' hand in her own. She felt useless, frustrated by her own inarticulacy. After a long period, Artemis heaved a shaky sigh and turned to Lydia to thank her.

'But I did nothing,' Lydia protested.

'You did everything,' said Artemis. 'I needed to know I was not alone. Now I do.'

She patted Lydia's hand and got up to return to the kitchen, looking visibly lighter in spirit. Lydia shook her head in bemusement, glad to have helped, but unable to work out what she had done. A moment later, Ruth burst into the atrium, her eyes sparkling. Lydia's gaze flicked instinctively towards the front of the house where the two shops were located – if she and Ruth were here, who was in the shop?

Ruth catching and correctly interpreting her eye movement said, 'Don't worry, the boys are in there. Rufus is telling a Roman gentleman the story of Hercules' dog and the discovery of purple.'

Lydia was only mildly reassured. Rufus's love of storytelling, combined with his equal fascination for gore, loved to turn the gentle story about the hero Hercules, who was strolling along the beach near Tyre one day with his dog, which ate a murex shellfish, turning its saliva purple, into a horror story of the dog foaming at the mouth with red drool before dropping down nearly dead at Hercules' feet. Lydia acknowledged, however, that the shops were in safe hands, and that she could wait long enough to discover what had made Ruth's eyes sparkle so brightly before rescuing the Roman gentleman in question.

'Tell me a story,' she said, slipping into the well-worn question from Ruth's childhood. Ruth had started it when they had first arrived back in Thyatira and had often been left at home while Lydia went to see old friends and business acquaintances. Thirsty for knowledge of Lydia's life she would ask her what she had been doing and when she answered in a simple sentence would object. 'No, a story,' she would say, demanding that Lydia take time to give shape and texture to her tale, to describe the people she had met and the interactions she had had. It didn't come naturally to Lydia, but over time she grew to appreciate Ruth's insistence. She would pay more attention to her surroundings and store up the treasure of a small detail here or turn of phrase there that would entrance Ruth later in the telling.

She was, therefore, doubly astounded when Ruth said simply, 'I've been chatting to Caius.' It took her a moment to form her words, and even then all she could squeeze out was 'No, a story'.

Ruth leant over and grasped her hand. 'It's all right, Dee-dee, you don't need to worry, he's all right, I'm all right.' But then she relented and started at the beginning. Lydia, happily absorbed in her work in the shops, and feeling awkward about her relationship with Clement, had not noticed that Caius had begun working in Clement's shop next door. He was, Ruth reported, a natural. His love of performance and of fancy things meant he could find exactly the right brooch or hairpin for the fastidious Roman ladies who dropped in on the way out of Lydia's shop. He had become quite a draw, and no one, other than Clement, Lydia and Ruth, appeared to have connected him with the Caius who had left the city in shame so many years before. Lydia hadn't noticed his regular appearances in the shop, but Ruth had. Her sharp eyes had observed his arrival day after day, until one day she had decided to go and see him.

'Why didn't you say anything?' Lydia exclaimed. 'I would have come too.'

'That wouldn't have worked. You would have glowered at him and he would have got defensive and I would have said nothing.'

Lydia had to acknowledge that this was probably true. One of the passages from the Scripture that she'd always loved was the prophet Hosea talking about God being like a mother bear robbed of her cubs. It summed up perfectly her emotions towards Ruth. Whenever she thought of the thoughtless, selfish way that Caius and Julius had used and discarded Ruth, she could easily imagine rearing up on her hind legs, a clawed hand ready to rip them to shreds.

'But I was always safe. You've taught me above all to look after myself and be safe.'

Lydia smiled, despite herself. After what had happened to Ruth as a child, she worried that she would become prey for other unscrupulous men looking to take advantage of a young girl, so she had spent hours schooling her in what to look out for, how to be safe in a savage and uncaring world.

'First I talked it over with Alexandra, then with Clement, and today, when the time was right, I talked to Caius. Alexandra and Clement never left me alone with him, I was always safe. Dee-dee, I'm so glad I did.' Ruth turned to her, her eyes sparkling again. 'I told him how he'd made me feel. I told him the effect his behaviour had had on me. I don't think he'd ever thought about it. He and Julius had been so caught up in the money and the excitement, they'd forgotten that I was a person, not a "thing". We talked for hours. I think he understands. He asked me to forgive him. I don't know if I can. I told him that I'd try. So I will . . . I will try. It might take some time though.' Ruth paused and looked thoughtful, then reached over and took Lydia's hand in hers. 'I'd like you to try too.'

Lydia opened and shut her mouth a few times. This was not something she had been expecting, and she had no idea how to respond. She'd never thought of Caius as someone to forgive. He was the person responsible for driving both her and Ruth from Philippi all those years ago. He was someone from whom she needed to protect Ruth. He was selfish and arrogant. He was thoughtless and careless. He was not someone she had ever thought of as a person worthy of forgiveness.

'Will you try?' Ruth asked.

Lydia nodded reluctantly. It was all she was able to do.

Ruth jumped up and ran next door before Lydia had time to express any of the doubts that were already flooding her mind. She followed her to the street door, her mind a tangle of uncertainty and fear.

Chapter 11

As Lydia stood at the door waiting for Ruth's return, her attention was caught by the man in the shop, who was still talking to Rufus, Marcus and Tertius. She looked over, wondering whether their tale of Hercules and his dog was proving interminable. It was not. In fact, he was regaling them with a story, and on each of their faces was a look of pure delight. It was the look they always had when a story, well told, was unfolded expertly before them.

The man had a rugged, sun-beaten face. Lydia thought he might be around sixty, but he could have been younger. His bearing indicated that he was a veteran of the Roman army. There were so many in Philippi, Lydia had learnt to identify them at a single glance. In her experience, years marching in the sun combined with what they had seen and done as soldiers often meant that they looked considerably older than they were. Not only that, but their years in the army made them tough and argumentative. As a rule, Lydia feared their presence in her shop. All too often, frightened by their aggressive confidence, she would end up selling them what they wanted for less than it was worth.

This veteran seemed different. Rather than driving a hard bargain and leaving swiftly, he was sitting down, apparently enjoying the boys' company, his face alight as he was describing something to them. Their faces mirrored his every expression. Even the naturally reticent Tertius seemed to be joining in. They turned as they became aware of Lydia's presence in the doorway to the shop. The veteran rose politely to his feet and came forward to greet her. His name, he said, was Manius, and he had heard in the city that she might be able to tell him more about a 'Jesus of Nazareth'. Lydia started in alarm. Romans – especially ex-soldiers such as this man – were often hostile to followers of the Way. People like her were labelled 'un-Roman'. It suddenly dawned on her that if it were so widely known in Philippi that she was a follower of the Way then she might be chased out of Philippi for a second time. She felt sick with fear. Ten years on, she had only just come to terms with the devastation of having to leave Philippi the first time. She wasn't sure she had the strength to do it again.

Seeing her troubled face, Manius smiled gently. 'Don't worry, the people I spoke to were talking about your return after all these years, after the visit of a wandering prophet called Paul. They were delighted to have their purveyor of purple back in the city, even more delighted that you had returned with even better purple than before. They couldn't tell me why you left in the first place. I just put two and two together and hoped I was right. Your fine boys here confirmed that I was.'

Lydia glanced over at them. She would have to remind them to be more careful in future. Manius seemed innocent enough, but too little caution could land them all in trouble. She was saved from answering further by the arrival of Caius and Clement from next door. Clement entered the shop with Caius on his heels. Manius turned to them and, recognising fellow Romans, greeted them in sufficiently simple Latin that Lydia could keep up. After a few sentences, however, he reverted to Greek.

Manius shrugged his apology. 'I was an auxiliary not a legionary. I never became fluent in Latin.'

'I was born in Philippi,' said Clement. 'I speak taberna Latin, but no more.'

Caius was noticeably silent. Lydia surmised that he was a Roman citizen from birth – the most Roman of them all – and that his mother tongue probably was Latin.

An awkward silence fell on them. Lydia was aware of the conversation she had promised to have with Caius, but was less and less enthusiastic about the prospect as the seconds marched by; at the same time Manius had asked to know more about Jesus Christ, but she wasn't sure whether this could be talked of in front of Caius. The more she thought about it the less able she became to break the silence.

It was the three boys who had been watching the adults from the far side of the shop who spoke first.

'Manius killed Jesus,' said Rufus.

'Crucified him,' added Marcus, 'till he was dead, quite dead.' Tertius gravely nodded his assent.

They all looked at Manius, assuming that this was just one of the boys' latest tall tales, but Manius raised his hands in a gesture of surrender.

'Well it's not quite how I wanted to tell you, but it is true. I've never forgotten it. It's played on my mind ever since. I crucified so many people back when I was a soldier that I couldn't tell you a thing about most of them. They've all blended into one, a single memory of pain and screams, sweat and agony. But not this man, Jesus. He stood out. There was something about him, even when he was dying, that captured my attention. When I left the army, I received my citizenship, and have wandered ever since. I can't seem to settle anywhere, and everywhere I go I hear of this Paul and that he talks about this Jesus Christ of Nazareth. I keep on wanting to ask who he really was, but have never found the right person. Will you tell me about him? Will you? He's been in my mind for nearly thirty years. I just have to know who he was. The question won't leave me alone.'

Clement, ever big-hearted and responsive, grinned from ear to ear. 'You've come to the right place. We can tell you everything you need to know.' Watching him, Lydia realised how much she had missed his simple, open generosity.

'Clement is quite right. Come into the house . . . all of you,' Lydia added, conscious that Caius had drawn back a touch, suddenly aware that if she was to try to forgive Caius as she had promised Ruth she would, then this was the moment to begin. 'We will tell you everything you want to know. There's quite a lot we'd like to learn too. We can shut the shop,' she said to the boys, whose crestfallen faces indicated that they hated the thought of being left out, even though they had heard something of this story already.

After a short hiatus, in which Artemis, who had emerged from the back of the house at the sound of new arrivals, scurried off to find food, and Ruth was sent running to bring Alexandra from the shop next door, they gathered again in the atrium; the place where so many stories had been told and heard over the past few weeks and months. Lydia reflected, not for the first time, on how sacred it felt to offer and receive each other's stories. It reminded her of the moment when they broke bread together and told the story of Jesus' last supper with his friends. In that moment, the many became one. Moments like this reminded her partially of that event, when in giving and receiving, lives were woven together with unbreakable bonds. Even then, Lydia thought as she looked around the room, they ended up knowing so little about each other.

At first Manius struggled to find the words, but before long, after gentle but expert questioning by Ruth, his story began to take shape. He had grown up in Jerusalem, his father a soldier first in the court of Herod the Great and then of his son Archelaus. They were a family that asked few questions and simply did as they were told, so, although they were aware of some of the excesses of the Herodians, it didn't really trouble them. His father's motto had always been 'don't ask questions if you think you won't like the answers'. It turned out that, when it came to working for Archelaus, it was wiser to ask no questions at all. When the Judeans deposed Archelaus as king and begged the Romans to take over because even Gentile Romans would be better than him, his father had become an auxiliary in the Roman army. Even Manius's supremely pragmatic father had hesitated before joining the enemy force, but, in the end, he shrugged and got on with it. How much worse could it be than working for the Herodians? It had been pretty bad, Manius admitted, but they just lived their lives and got on with things.

When he was fifteen, Manius's father had been killed in one of the many riots that would flare up in Jerusalem as surely as the sun would rise in the morning. In need of money to support his mother and sisters, and after only minimal thought, he too had become an auxiliary. Like his father, he had done what was requested of him without question. Any questions he might have wanted to ask he consigned to the darkest recesses of his mind. It turned out he was good at the job and soon rose to the rank of centurion. When asked what 'the job' was, he squirmed a little. He said over and over again that, at the time, he just did what needed to be done and tried not to think about it too much. He looked around the small group, his face pleading for understanding.

Clement clapped him on the shoulder and nodded his understanding. 'We've all done things we're not proud of.' His face revealed that he too was thinking about what unspeakable things he had done in the past without thought or question.

'Now I think back on it I simply don't know how I did it,' Manius said quietly.

'But what was the "it" that you did?' asked Ruth.

'I was in charge of the crucifixions,' said Manius.

'Surely not all of the time?' asked Alexandra.

'Most of it,' Manius replied. 'There were constant riots and unrest. The Romans felt control slipping away. Public displays of brutality were the only way to impose peace. I was in charge of the prisoners from the moment they knew life would end to the moment it did. Most of the time I just did my job and never questioned it, until one day . . . that day I did, and now I can't stop thinking about it at all.' He tailed off into silence, his brow furrowed.

'What day was that?' asked Ruth, gently prompting him to carry on.

'It had been a difficult week. Festivals usually were. People would cram into the city from north and south, east and west. Tempers would fray and riots break out. But this event started oddly. Most of the time the crowd at a crucifixion would be sullen and resentful, as we intended them to be – they were meant to feel the full weight of Roman peace. The *Pax Romana*: peace won with an iron fist. On this occasion the crowd were thrilled, booing and jeering the prisoner constantly. I didn't understand it. He hadn't robbed or killed anyone. Not like the person we let go instead of him – Barabbas I think his name was – who'd robbed and killed so many people that no one could remember the number. This man – Jesus from Nazareth – was clearly innocent, but he had frightened and annoyed people, and was now suffering the consequences. Even then they couldn't quite agree on exactly what it was that he had said or done that aggravated them so much.

'All around him people were yelling and shouting, pushing and shoving, but he stood in the middle of them, as calm as you like, watching it all unfold around him. Even when we scourged him, he made almost no sound whatsoever, just the odd grunt here or there. We dressed him in a purple cloak, you know.' He said this directly to Lydia, assuming, correctly, a professional interest in the detail. She nodded. She had heard before that Jesus had been dressed in a purple robe and had always wanted to ask where they'd got it from. Full purple robes were rare and expensive. So, although gripped by Manius's story, she took her opportunity.

'Where did you find it – the cloak?'

Manius grinned. 'It's funny you should ask. I can't remember. Maybe we used a soldier's cloak, or maybe we found a bit of purple cloth or a rug hanging about. We were mocking him, dressing him up like he was actually a king, but what we used I just can't remember. What I can remember is thinking how pointless the mocking was. You mock someone to shame them, to bring them down and humiliate them. But with this man nothing we said or did dented his dignity. *I* felt humiliated, but he wasn't. I kept watching him on the way to the crucifixion. He seemed consumed with sorrow, but not frightened or shamed in any way.'

'Did you watch him die?' Clement asked, almost in a whisper.

Manius nodded. 'He died quite quickly in the end. It wasn't surprising really. We had taken our frustration at not being able to shame him out in our flogging. I was astonished he could stand up at all. Shortly after we nailed his crossbeam to the stake, it had gone dark, for no reason that any of us could fathom. It felt as though all the light in the world had been snuffed out. And then he died. When he did, I felt such an overwhelming bleakness that I thought I'd never feel joy ever again. I said the first thing that came into my head.'

'I think we know what you said,' Clement said.

Manius looked astonished. 'How could you possibly know that?'

'You were overheard,' said Clement. 'Some of the women who followed Jesus were there. They heard you say "Truly this man was God's Son!"'

Manius was quiet for a while, the moment clearly playing on his mind. 'Yes,' he said, 'that is exactly what I said.'

'But what we have always wanted to know,' said Alexandra, 'is what you meant.'

Chapter 12

M anius looked at them blankly. 'What do you mean, what did *I* mean? I meant he really was God's Son.'

'But,' Clement leant forward in his enthusiasm, 'did you mean he was a son of a god – a special man – or did you mean that he was the Son of the God – the Son of God? We've discussed it for hours and hours.'

He was right, thought Lydia – they had. The account of what the women had overheard had travelled with the story of Jesus' death to many followers of the Way, and they had in turn wrestled with the question of what the centurion had really meant. Watching Manius's face, Lydia realised that they had, perhaps, missed the point. Manius had responded in the moment with words from his heart, and their earnest attempts to understand what he had meant had given his statement more weight than it deserved. Or maybe not. It was fascinating that thirty years later the moment had stayed with him, had driven him mad with an itch that just would not be satisfied. Perhaps he had made a statement that he was, at last, ready to grow into.

So together, turn and turnabout, they explained to Manius who Jesus was. They explained about his teaching and ministry in Galilee; they explained about his death and his resurrection; they explained about his followers taking the good news to the ends of the earth; they explained about Paul and his imprisonment. All the time, Manius sat listening, taking it all in. After a while tears started pouring down his cheeks. 'What did I do?' he said, over and over again. 'I killed the Saviour of the world. What have I done?'

In the end, and a little to Lydia's surprise, it was Caius who found the words to break through Manius's utter horror. 'We all – every last one of us – get caught up with things that we don't really understand. And when we do, we cause such damage to people, to the world, that it spills outwards all over the place. Sometimes we even know what we're doing is wrong,' here he looked sadly at Ruth, 'but we do it anyway. There's not a single person here who hasn't done something or been part of something that causes harm. You are no worse than the rest of us.' They all nodded their woeful agreement. 'But do you know the most wonderful thing of all? The part of Jesus' teaching that changes everything?'

He really had Manius's attention now. 'Tell me,' he demanded.

'At the heart of everything Jesus said and did was forgiveness. He came to call people to turn around, to live differently and to be forgiven. No one was ever written off. No one.'

Lydia felt a twinge of guilt. She had written Caius off, consigned him in her mind to weeping and wailing and gnashing of teeth, when all along he had been learning the lessons of forgiveness far more powerfully than she ever had.

Manius shook his head sadly. 'Not me. I'm sure it doesn't apply to the person who actually killed him.'

'I think it does.' Lydia was surprised to discover that it was Tertius, the quietest of the three boys, who was speaking. He started to tell the story of Peter, who denied Jesus and was forgiven. Lydia watched him, her heart full. He was so young and so reticent most of the time, but today he spoke with a quiet confidence, his eyes shining.

They talked well into the night. As they talked, Lydia found herself gripped once again by Jesus, the one they all followed. She realised as they talked that, though she had remained faithful all these years, her faith had worn thin. Her unspoken shame at leaving Philippi; the uncertainties of what and what not to believe that she had encountered in the community in Thyatira;

the years of not talking about how she really felt and the pressures of just simply living had worn away her focus and passion until, she now recognised, she would have been hard-pressed to remember why faith in Jesus had so changed her life in the first place. She had become so accustomed to the outward demands of faith that she had forgotten Jesus himself. The Jesus whom Manius had actually met in person – albeit not, given the choice, how he would have chosen to meet him – who gave his life in love, who in his deeds as well as his words showed a different way of being, who turned the world upside down: that was the Jesus she first followed.

As they all parted that night they agreed to meet again first thing the next morning.

They gathered just outside the Neapolis gate; near the stream where Lydia herself had been baptised ten years or so ago. Word had got around and it wasn't just those who had been there the day before. Syntyche was there, and so were others of those who gathered in Lydia's house. There were also people Lydia didn't recognise but assumed met with Clement and Alexandra, about twenty of them in all. Among them was Caius. He told Lydia with no small pride that he had been baptised the month before.

Syntyche baptised Manius in the name of the Father, and of the Son and of the Holy Spirit. As he came back up out of the water, Clement started singing a psalm: 'Blessed are those whose transgression is forgiven, whose sin is covered . . .' And Manius stood there, water dripping off him, sobbing as though his heart would break. A few voices joined in with Clement as he sang, but the psalm was not well known and the sound was reedy and thin. Then suddenly voices from behind them picked up the tune. Lydia turned and there, standing outside the place of meeting, was the man she had seen when she first arrived back in Philippi, with about ten others. Their voices were rich and melodious, the sound hauntingly beautiful as it swirled around them in the early morning air.

Clement, grinning from ear to ear, waved heartily to the newcomer, and he returned the wave in an equally friendly manner but with a greater air of dignity. When the psalm was finished, the gathering began to disperse. Caius and Manius headed back into town together, deep in conversation. Lydia turned to go, but found next to her the man to whom Clement had just waved. He bowed politely, and introduced himself. His name, he said, was Jonathan. He was the leader of the synagogue here – he pointed in the direction of the small place of prayer that Lydia had known so well – and his assistant was Akiva, again he pointed in the direction of the small group of people who had accompanied the psalm so beautifully a few moments before. They were all members of the people of Israel, he told her, a note of pride in his voice, but also followers of Jesus the Messiah.

He apologised for not having come to greet her before. He had travelled to Jerusalem for the Feast of Weeks and had only just returned. Lydia sensed in this a slight evasion, something that didn't quite ring true. It was odd. Jonathan struck her as a man of deep integrity, but this explanation wasn't the whole truth. There was something she couldn't put her finger on that made her wonder what he wasn't saying. She didn't know what it was and she didn't know why she knew it. She just did. Lydia made a deliberate effort to lay down this thought and turned her attention back to what he was saying. He was telling her a story about the fringes on his robe, and an accident, a broken door hinge had ripped some of them as he was passing one day, and he was wondering if he and Akiva might come and buy more dye of just the right colour. Lydia suggested a visit the next day when she could be confident that John could be there. She was sure that in Jonathan's case 'just the right colour' did not mean 'a shade close in colour', and felt the need of John's expert eye to ensure that she could offer what had been requested.

Lydia found herself looking longingly in the direction of the place of prayer, memories crowding around her of the happiest of times spent there, reading and debating the Scripture. Jonathan, catching her glance, enquired if she would like to come and see. Again an air of hesitancy, of something left unsaid, fell over them, but Lydia was so excited to see the place again that, one more time, she laid her suspicions aside. She followed Jonathan and then Akiva into the place. It was, as it always had been, small – no more than a single room. When Lydia, Syntyche, Euodia and their friends had gathered there, it had been sparsely furnished. There was a bench on either side of the room, but little else. The location of the room so near to the river meant that it had a musty smell, not to mention the ever present spiders.

Now, however, the room was transformed. It was cleaner than Lydia thought it possible for it to be. There were cushions and other furnishings, but what really made Lydia's jaw drop in wonder were the paintings. All around the walls were the stories of the people of God. There was Moses receiving the law, and there David anointed by Samuel; there was Ruth and Esther; the prophets, Isaiah and Jeremiah, all captured in vibrant detail. Right in the middle, at the front, was the story of Jesus: his life, his death, his resurrection and ascension.

Lydia became aware that Jonathan and Akiva were watching her, waiting for a reaction. They were not disappointed. Lydia's mouth dropped open in admiration and astonishment. Jonathan nodded in the direction of Akiva.

Akiva shrugged modestly, though his eyes glowed, revealing the delight he was trying hard not to show. 'I think in pictures more than words. The pictures have been in me since I was a small child. One day I was here tidying up and felt the over-whelming desire to paint the walls with what I see when I hear the stories. I started a picture, a small one in the corner, and then found I couldn't stop.'

'They're beautiful. Why has no one else told me about them?'

The heavy awkwardness fell once more. 'I doubt they know they are here. We don't mix much with the other followers of the Way any more.'

Lydia realised she had known that they would say something like this, but was half hoping that she was wrong. 'Did something happen?'

Jonathan spread his hands expressively. 'Nothing specific. Just lots of small things. Jokes made here. Comments made there. Invites not offered, from us as well as them. Epaphroditus was so good at including us. He always would make sure we knew we were welcome. If we didn't come to something he would come straight down here and check if we were all right. Once he went to see Paul, that all stopped. No one invited us to gather all together any more, so we didn't go. And now months have passed and the gap has widened. We only came today because we heard the sound of the psalm and thought we would join in.'

Lydia shook her head sadly. It had never occurred to her before how easily bonds of friendship could become worn and frayed. She reached for words that might provide balm for the pain, a solution for the problem, but all she could come up with was, 'Shall we meet tomorrow, late morning in the shop? I'll make sure John is there.'

All the way back to her shop she chided herself. An appointment to buy purple was hardly the reconciliation that was needed.

Chapter 13

The encounter with Jonathan and Akiva lurked in Lydia's mind all day, troubling her. How had relationships broken down so badly? Surely there was something they could do? She talked first to Clement and Alexandra, then to Syntyche and Artemis, but each, in turn, said how difficult it was to do anything. 'It's more complicated than you think,' was the answer that Lydia received over and over again. She didn't understand, and no one seemed willing to talk about it. In the end it was Ruth, noting her frustration, who tried to help her unpick what was going on. Ruth's natural ability to fall into conversation with almost anyone she met, coupled with her love of weaving stories together into a coherent whole, meant that she had gained a good sense of what had taken place without ever asking anyone directly. As they talked, Lydia marvelled, not for the first time, at her wisdom, remembering the small, unconfident child she had first met all those years ago.

From what she'd picked up from various people, Ruth said, she thought that relationships had begun to sour with the incident that had happened between Epaphroditus and Euodia at Timothy's last visit. Everyone said how much the disagreement had rocked the small tight-knit community. Until then they had lived together harmoniously, even as the numbers of those following the Way had grown and grown. The trust that had existed between the overseers and deacons had smoothed relationships. They reached remarkable agreement on almost everything and where they hadn't, the disagreements were gentle and as harmonious as disagreements could be. It was

Epaphroditus's determination to send help to Paul that had changed everything. The group quickly split into two camps: those who, like Epaphroditus, wanted to care for and support Paul, and those who, like Euodia, were horrified that he was actively attempting to attract the attention of Emperor Nero – the most powerful and unpredictable man in the world. Jonathan and Akiva had naturally taken Euodia's side – Paul's bracing comments about Jewish Christians meant that they regarded him with caution. Syntyche and Clement had agreed with Epaphroditus.

Before they knew it, other chasms had opened up too. Small upsets – like Jonathan and Akiva following Jewish food law, or Syntyche's preference for silence rather than singing – became magnified. And the disintegration began. It wasn't, Ruth thought, that Jonathan and Akiva and their gathering were being excluded. No one met together any more. They just didn't know what to say to each other, and so said nothing. The more they said nothing, the more others worried about what they might have said. Whole edifices had been built around what some people thought other people thought.

'Surely there's something we can do!' Lydia protested. 'We can't just sit around and watch them get further and further apart.'

Ruth tipped her head on one side, deep thought written all over her face. 'Perhaps there is. Perhaps there isn't. Let's pray and keep our eyes open and see what happens.' She got up to go, stopped, then turned slowly. 'You could have that conversation with Caius. The one you were going to have before we all met Manius.'

Lydia felt immediately defensive. 'How would that help? Why would me meeting with someone who arrived after all of this happened make any difference to anything?'

'Well,' Ruth said thoughtfully, reaching carefully for the words she needed, 'every small connection well forged has to contribute to the whole. Don't you think?'

Lydia paused, her emotions raw. She was poised, ready for a protective counter-attack. Why should she be blamed for the breakdown in relationships across the whole of Philippi? Why was it her responsibility to fix things? Why should she be the one to make a first move in any case? These and many other questions charged around and around her mind, while she clenched and unclenched her fists.

Ruth let out a burst of laughter. 'If I didn't know better, I'd think you were going to punch me.' Despite herself, Lydia grinned. Ruth had always had the knack of lifting her out of her worst moods. 'I wonder,' Ruth went on, 'if you've got this around the wrong way? Think of it less as something for which you are blamed and more of a garden for you to tend. It isn't your fault that the garden is full of weeds. Nor is it your fault that the ground is dry from the sun. But if you pull out the weeds and water the plants, they will do better.'

This time she really did go, leaving Lydia deep in thought. After an hour or so, the boys passed through the atrium, and Lydia remembered that she hadn't told John about tomorrow's visit from Jonathan and Akiva. She sent Rufus running to his workshop to let him know of the appointment, but asked Marcus and Tertius to stay behind and mind the shops.

'I have an errand to run,' she told them. She got to her feet wearily. The more she thought about it, the worse the prospect of the conversation became. Putting it off wasn't going to make it any easier. When she got to Clement's shop next door, Caius was in full flow. Buttons, brooches and hair decorations were strewn over the surfaces, while Caius held up item after item in an effort to tempt a particularly picky client. Lydia recognised her right away. She was a much-feared regular in her own shop. Aurelia came from an impeccable aristocratic line. This was something that no one was allowed to forget. Aurelia was the niece of Seneca, Nero's former tutor and current advisor, and the daughter of Gallio, who ten years before had been proconsul of Achaea. Much lower on her oft-recited list of 'significant connections' was her current status as wife of Decimus Licinius Crassus, a descendant of the great general Crassus, made famous for his brutal quashing of the slave revolt led by Spartacus, and one of the current magistrates of Philippi.

Aurelia never missed an opportunity to express her disappointment in their present location. Her father had hated Achaea, and she loathed Philippi. Someone of her status should, she announced regularly, live in Rome and nowhere else. She blamed her husband often, and publicly, for her current sojourn in Philippi, and took out her disdain on anyone unfortunate enough to remind her of her reduced state. She and the unfortunate Crassus would be seen, occasionally, walking in the forum. Invariably Aurelia would be in front, striding out, her husband scurrying to keep up, while struggling to catch and hold onto multiple discarded articles of clothing or decoration that his wife had decided were no longer necessary. Her voice could be heard from one side of the forum to the other as she chided him for his latest perceived misdemeanour. Today's recipient of her contempt was Caius, who was trying, and failing, to interest her in something – anything – that the shop had in stock.

Aurelia sighed dramatically. 'It's all so tawdry. Come.' She clicked her fingers at the four slaves who were pressed against the shelves of the shop lest they be accused of getting in the way. 'We won't waste any more time.' She looked Lydia up and down as she left, no flicker of recognition showing on her face, despite the many hours that Lydia and John together had striven to present her with their best range of purple. Lydia's gaze caught that of Caius as they both rolled their eyes. A current of amusement ran between them. Out in the street they could still hear a steady stream of criticism, turned this time on Aurelia's unfortunate slaves. The sound faded slowly as Aurelia made her way back towards the forum. Her last audible words: 'What is wrong with you, idiot?' floated back to them over the background noise of a summer afternoon.

An awkward silence fell. Lydia had steeled herself to go over and talk to Caius, but foolishly, she realised now, she had not rehearsed what she would say or even how she would begin. After a few moments Caius came to her rescue, his hands nervously pulling at his tunic as he did so. 'I owe you an apology.' Lydia had been schooled from an early age in politeness. Her father had stressed, at every opportunity, the importance of showing honour to those with whom you talked. Instinctively, then, she opened her mouth to insist that no apology was necessary, but for once the words would not come. An apology *was* necessary. Caius's avaricious actions had blighted not only Ruth's life, but her own. She bowed her head in acknowledgement of the truth of what Caius said. Caius's apology when it came was fulsome and heartfelt. He was, he said, mortified now he realised what he had done. He had been so selfish and self-absorbed. It had never even crossed his mind to ask what impact his actions had on those around him. His yearning for wealth had been so all-consuming that he had found it hard to think of anything else. He was appalled by his former self and couldn't bear to think of the damage he had caused. From time to time Lydia glanced at him to ensure that his words, which sounded so polished and rehearsed, were sincere. They seemed to be. Caius's face was creased with what looked like genuine concern. 'I hope that one day you will find it possible to forgive me,' Caius concluded at last, looking at Lydia beseechingly.

Although touched by his apparent concern, Lydia couldn't help remarking on the polished nature of his apology. Caius flushed. 'Clement warned me about that. He told me you'd notice. You see, I practised every night. I wanted to be word perfect. I wanted to make sure I left nothing out. So I learnt it off by heart.'

Lydia looked at him, trying to weigh him up. The problem was that Caius had always been a consummate performer. She remembered him in the days when Ruth still had the pythian spirit. He could hold crowds spellbound by his performance. How could she possibly know, now, where his performing spirit ended and his sincerity began? Did he even know? He struck her as the kind of person who was so good at weaving a story he might genuinely believe his own made-up tale. He might tell it so well that even he could forget that it wasn't true. Then she thought of Ruth. Ruth was the epitome of sincerity, her heart worn constantly on her sleeve, drawing people towards her with her warmth and wit. Lydia also realised that her incessant antipathy towards Caius had brought wounds as well. Ruth had wanted to believe Caius, and Lydia's refusal even to talk to him had bruised her. She took a deep breath.

'Yes,' she said, 'yes, I forgive you.' Even as she said it, she was aware that her words were more of an aspiration than a reality, but they would do for now. Caius certainly thought so. He sagged with relief.

'Thank you,' he said. 'From the bottom of my heart, thank you. I promise you won't regret it.'

Lydia held her tongue and prayed quietly that he was right. And if he was, that she would be able to live up to her promise of forgiveness. She was in no doubt that she had just committed herself to hours of soul-searching and wrestling with her conscience. Forgiveness – especially involving a grudge long-held – didn't happen in the blink of an eye. It took effort and determination. Lydia sincerely hoped it was going to be worth the effort.

Chapter 14

The next day Jonathan and Akiva arrived at a time that was so exactly 'late morning' that Lydia wondered if they had been waiting around the corner until the right moment. John had arrived earlier in the morning with new stocks of purples and linens, and was ready to greet them. Jonathan quickly and efficiently showed him the torn tassels on his gown, and it wasn't long before they had agreed the precise shade necessary, pure Tyrian purple. John asked whether Jonathan would like the tassels dyed by him in his workshop.

Jonathan looked uneasy. 'I don't want to offend you . . . but it is vital that it is done to perfection.'

John, the consummate artisan, looked confused. 'Why would perfection offend me?'

All of a sudden Lydia understood some of the awkwardness that, even now, hung in the air. 'Do people get offended often when you ask that things are done right, according to the law?'

Jonathan nodded sadly. 'I've tried to explain as gently and respectfully as I can that these are our customs, the way *we* worship God. We don't mean to be rude, but there's no getting around the fact that mixing with Gentiles makes us unclean. I think a lot of people just can't understand that. It's why no one invites us to the gathering any more.'

'What gathering?' John asked.

'You know – the one where we all meet to break bread and read Scriptures together. We didn't do it often, and it did get to be a bit of a squash when everyone came, but I used to love it.

Even if we did have to explain every time why we couldn't eat with everyone else.'

John continued to look confused. 'Are we not invited either?' he asked Lydia.

How easy it was, Lydia thought ruefully, for misunderstandings to turn small irritations into vast chasms between people; chasms that very quickly became impossible to cross. 'I don't think they have them any more,' she said, 'not since Epaphroditus went to Rome at least.'

Jonathan looked astonished. 'You mean no one has been invited? It isn't just us?'

'That's exactly what I mean.'

He smiled. Then stopped, a guilty look on his face. 'I feel terrible for feeling so pleased. I'm sad to hear that they no longer meet together, but you have no idea what a relief it is to discover we haven't been excluded. We thought it was personal.'

'No, not personal,' she agreed, 'but it is sad. Maybe one day we can do something about it.'

'One day, perhaps we can.'

'In the meantime,' said John, 'you could come to the workshop and make sure that the dyeing happens to your satisfaction.'

Jonathan relaxed visibly. 'That would be ideal.'

John nodded in his matter-of-fact way. 'With dye so expensive, it would be a shame to get it wrong.'

All the while Akiva stood on one side, a slightly wistful look on his face.

'What about you, Akiva?' said Lydia. 'Do you have need of tassels?'

Akiva looked down at his feet. He mumbled something inaudible.

'Akiva can't afford the Tyrian purple. And I, I'm afraid, have only the money for one set,' Jonathan said.

Lydia glanced down at Akiva's tassels for the first time, and saw that though there was certainly some purple in them, it was only a small amount. They had a somewhat muddy hue.

Lydia was struck with an idea. 'Would you paint me some pictures?'

Jonathan, John and Akiva all looked at her, confusion on their faces. One minute they were talking about tassels and the next she was making a wild request. She grinned and explained.

'Akiva has decorated the inside of the place of prayer with pictures of the story of God. The pictures are beautiful. I thought he could do the same in the atrium and garden here. That way we will be surrounded by our mothers and fathers in the faith as we pray. I'll exchange purple tassels for paintings,' she said to Akiva.

A look of delight crossed Akiva's face. 'Really? Are you sure?'

'Quite sure,' responded Lydia. 'When you dye the tassels for Jonathan, do two sets,' she said to John.

'With pleasure.' The look on John's face indicated that before long Akiva would find himself with an entirely perfect set of tassels.

And so a new rhythm began in their lives. Early in the morning, as Lydia was opening the shops, Akiva would arrive, paintbrushes in hand. Throughout the day the soft sound of psalms, sung gently and prayerfully, could be heard echoing around the house, occasionally boosted in volume and gusto when Clement – who had become a regular visitor once more – joined in. Akiva's gentle, creative presence was a welcome addition to their household. Lydia would often find him deep in conversation with Ruth or one of the boys, with Artemis and to her surprise, also with John. John, who so often preferred his own company and space, was drawn to Akiva's artistry. Akiva in his turn quickly learnt that no one had an eye for colour quite like

John. Passing through the atrium Lydia would often find them holding different pigments up to the light, deep in discussion about how to capture this or that shade.

Best of all, the stories of God's people spread slowly but surely around the bare walls of the atrium. Lydia observed Ruth's influence on Akiva's choice of story. Women filled the pictures alongside the male heroes they represented. One day Ruth dragged Lydia to the wall, and there in pride of place was the story of Ruth. There was Orpah, her back to Ruth and Naomi returning home; there was Ruth, her hand in Naomi's, pointing onwards into the future. Ruth whispered in Lydia's ear, 'Where you go, I will go.' And Lydia found herself quite unable to speak, her heart was so full.

Akiva joined in fully with their life, but would withdraw quietly and with the minimum of fuss to eat alone and to pray at key times of the day. Before long they were so used to it that no one even noticed his comings and goings. To Lydia's great delight, Jonathan and others from the gathering down by the river would drop by to observe Akiva's progress, offering suggestions of stories or characters to include. Sometimes they would stay and talk more about the stories being painted, or of their own faith in the God who had led their ancestors through the desert and to the promised land. Manius and Caius, who knew nothing of the stories of God's people, were particularly voracious, asking question after question of Akiva and the other guests.

One day as he was leaving, Jonathan bowed gravely to Lydia. 'Thank you,' he said. 'You have given us back what we had lost.'

Lydia looked at him, confused. 'What did I do?'

'When we met we were grieving the loss of fellowship; you have returned it to us.'

Lydia opened and shut her mouth a few times, pleasantly surprised, but unsure how to respond. 'I did nothing. All I did was take care of Akiva. I've received back from him so much more than I gave – we all have.'

Jonathan replied, 'Rabbi Shammai used to say, "Make study of Torah a permanent part of your life, say little, do much, and receive everyone with graciousness." What he didn't say was that when you do, you start to build community. I heard Paul say it a few times though, and he was quite right. Small actions can build large change. You might not have known you were doing it, but you were doing it nevertheless. And we – my whole community and I – will be ever grateful to you.'

Lydia found that all she could do was nod her thanks, tears in her eyes.

A few days later, Lydia was in the shop straightening the fabrics when she heard a voice she recognised. Her heart sank. It was the unmistakeable tones of Aurelia, the magistrate's wife, complaining her way down the street in their direction. Reluctantly she went out onto the street, sincerely hoping in, she was aware, a most unfriend-like manner, that Aurelia might be coming back to buy brooches and thereby to torment Clement and Caius in the neighbouring shop and not her. She caught the eye of Clement, Alexandra and Caius, who, likewise, had filed out of their shop at the sound, and grimaced at them. They grimaced back, clearly hoping, in their turn, that Aurelia had come in search of purple, not brooches. She had. Aurelia had decided that their dining room needed to be decked from floor to ceiling in purple as a signal to their guests of their importance. Lydia summoned the boys and sent Rufus running to get John, aware that she would need all the help she could get.

Given Aurelia's importance, she invited her into the atrium rather than into the shop itself so that she could be seated comfortably while she decided on the purples she would buy. She sent Marcus and Tertius into the shop to collect up all the samples of material they could lay their hands on, and Ruth into the back of the house to beg Artemis to rustle up some delicate snacks fit for someone of high status. Almost immediately Lydia sensed her mistake. Rather than sitting down in the chair indicated to her, Aurelia wandered up to the recently painted walls.

Who could blame her? Lydia thought to herself. Their vibrant shades and forms drew the eye from every point in the room. At that moment, Akiva came through the atrium in the direction of the garden, where he was continuing to paint. As he had said to Lydia when requesting permission to continue outwards onto the garden walls, God's story never ends. Lydia wondered whether, before long, her entire house would be covered in paintings. The spatters of paint on his clothing, in his hair and on his face clearly marked him out as the source of the paintings.

'You!' Aurelia's strident voice stopped Akiva in his tracks. 'What are these paintings?'

Akiva, who was nervous at the best of times even among his friends, looked as though he wished he could melt right into the floor.

'Well?'

Lydia stepped in to rescue him. 'My lady, I have asked Akiva to decorate the walls of my atrium, and I think he has done a wonderful job, wouldn't you agree?'

Aurelia flicked a withering glance at Lydia. 'That was not the question I asked. Kindly restrict yourself to answering the questions I do ask, not the ones I don't. I asked what they are. Who do they portray?'

Lydia took a deep breath. She had been fully aware of the intent of Aurelia's question and had sidestepped it on purpose. A dense silence fell for a moment while Lydia gathered together all the shreds of courage she could find. 'They are the stories of God's people. Stories of old.'

'Which god?' snapped Aurelia. 'I don't recognise any of these myths.'

'The most-high God,' Lydia's voice wavered, 'the God of Abraham, Isaac and Jacob, the God who raised Jesus from the dead.'

'I thought we'd stamped them out,' Aurelia snapped, 'when we drove off that other woman – what was her name?' She clicked her fingers at one of her slaves who was standing far back in the vestibule area clearly wishing he wasn't there at all. 'Quickly, fool. The name of the woman. The one we humiliated in the forum.' The slave looked petrified, clearly unable to provide the name, either from ignorance or fear. This made no difference to Aurelia. 'It was a name that made me think of roads. Good journeys.'

'Not Euodia?' Artemis, who had just come into the room with the requested snacks, looked pale.

'Yes, that was it. She said she had no friends, no one else to go to after I'd finished with her, and now I turn over another rock and you all crawl out. I'll deal with you too. Come,' she said clicking her fingers at her slaves as she sailed out of the door and onto the street.

Chapter 15

A stunned silence fell on the room, broken only when Clement, Alexandra and Caius filed in from the street. Their faces made it clear that Aurelia's voice had reached them outside. They were still standing in shocked silence when Rufus returned with John.

'Where is she?' John asked, surprised. He had on his best tunic, the one without any splashes of purple on it. Lydia knew he kept it safely folded away, wrapped in a layer of fabric, as purple got everywhere in his workshop.

'Gone,' was all Lydia could squeeze out.

It was Marcus and Ruth between them who gave a brief, unvarnished account of what had taken place. When they had finished, the stunned silence returned.

Eventually Clement spoke. 'We need to find Euodia, and urgently. I thought she was still cross with us. It never occurred to me she was in trouble.'

Alexandra shook her head sadly. 'How could we not have heard? If Aurelia humiliated her in the forum, why didn't word reach us?'

'Probably because it is such a common occurrence,' said Caius. 'It's her favourite pastime – ruining people. She's the wife of a magistrate too; no one has any power to stop her. Everyone puts their head down and hurries by, lest her gaze fall on them instead.'

'We have to find Euodia,' Clement said again. Despite her horror, Lydia couldn't help noting with admiration the innate generosity of both Clement and Alexandra. They could have

been worrying about what would happen to them now Aurelia
had declared herself their enemy. They could have been worrying about the new threat to their home and livelihood. Instead
their only expressed concern was for Euodia and what might
have happened to her.

Lydia turned to Marcus. 'Go and get Syntyche. She might
know something.'

Marcus sprinted off and returned very shortly with Syntyche,
but she too was horrified by the tale, and knew as little as the
rest of them. They sent all three boys to Euodia's old tenement
building to see if they could find her, but they returned empty-
handed: her apartment had a new family living in it who knew
nothing of its former tenant. They sent them to the forum
where Euodia had a stall, but they came back reporting that in
that spot was now someone selling poorly crafted vases.

Clement and Syntyche called a meeting of the overseers and
deacons to discuss what to do next. Lydia observed wryly, and
not a little sadly, that it took a crisis as great as this to draw
them all together again. The overseers and deacons met in
Lydia's spacious atrium, and Lydia couldn't resist lurking in
the garden, apparently doing some weeding, but really listening
in to their conversation. She lifted her head at one point and
noted that Ruth, John, Marcus, Rufus and Tertius had all
joined her, each weeding away vigorously in their own selected
patch of ground. Crises, she thought to herself, were good for a
weed-free garden if nothing else. Their sudden concern for
weeds in the garden delivered very little in the way of new information. None of the overseers or deacons had heard any more
than Clement or Syntyche had. It seemed that Euodia really
had disappeared overnight; no one knew where she had gone or
why. They emerged from the meeting visibly disturbed and
upset.

Syntyche, seeking refuge in the garden, sank onto one of its
many benches and sobbed. The gardeners all forgetting their

subterfuge of not really being there, rushed to comfort her, though all they could do was to pat her on the back and offer cloths to dry her sodden cheeks. They should have known, Syntyche said over and over again. It didn't matter how deep their disagreement had been, she should not have let their companionship slide away. She had betrayed her dear friend and hadn't even noticed. There was nothing anyone could say to salve her distress. She was right. Someone should have looked for her, and, locked in their sense of self-righteousness and irritation at Euodia's refusal to send help to Paul, no one had.

After a long time of sitting in their guilty grief, Ruth said suddenly, 'What about Euodia's church? They might know where she is.'

Syntyche shook her head. 'We have already looked for them. They have gone too. Not a single person is left.'

Ruth stood up and stretched. An hour or more sitting on the stone bench had cramped even her youthful body. 'We should think about this logically. There are not very many options as to where she might be. Either Euodia has been imprisoned, or she has gone somewhere else, or she is . . .' She tailed off. No one wanted to think about the third option. 'Why don't we send someone to the prison to see if she and the others are there?' In the absence of any better ideas they agreed that this seemed sensible.

They found Clement and Caius in the next-door shop, tidying the stock in a desultory manner. Ruth explained her theory and that the best place to start was the prison. A grim look settled on Clement's face. 'I had been hoping she wasn't there,' he said briefly.

'Shouldn't we find out for sure?' Ruth asked.

Clement nodded gravely. 'I do agree, but I'm not quite sure how to find out. I am not exactly welcome at the prison . . .'

'What about Manius?' Caius asked. 'He still mixes with his veteran friends. He might be able to find out from them. I'll go,' he said hastily and rushed off, evidently relieved to leave the heavy atmosphere of the shop.

'We had better go,' said Lydia. 'We wouldn't want to get in the way of your customers.'

Clement shrugged. 'I haven't had any since Aurelia came. I think it unlikely that you will be in the way.'

As he said this Lydia realised that he wasn't alone. She too had had no customers since Aurelia's visit. She simply hadn't noticed, so caught up had she been in her concern for Euodia. 'You don't think . . .'

Clement nodded. 'I do think. In fact, I am confident that that was exactly what Aurelia meant. She hates us so much that she will drive us out in any way she can – starving us out seems like the easiest option.'

'But why? Why would she do that?'

'Because she can? Because she's bored and cruel and enjoys tormenting people?'

'I think it's more than that,' said Alexandra, who had been sitting quietly listening to the conversation. 'I think she is frightened.'

'Of us?' Lydia was astonished. As far as she could see Aurelia held all the power and they none of it.

'Yes,' said Alexandra, 'of us. Aurelia needs to be at the top of society, lauded and honoured everywhere she goes. To us she is irrelevant. We are gathered together around Jesus Christ. He is our centre.'

Clement tipped his head on one side. 'Does she know that much about us? Would she know that Christ is the centre of everything? I think she just sees us as un-Roman. We don't gather at the temples for sacrifice. We don't jostle for honour at the big feasts. For her, being Roman is the pinnacle of every-thing and she sits near the top of it. We don't.'

'I think you're both right,' said Ruth thoughtfully. 'She is frightened of us because we are different. Though to be honest,

I'd be surprised if she's thought much about it. She's frightened and is reacting. That is all. I can't wait for the day when people don't lash out any more at other people simply because they are different.' Lydia felt old and jaded as she realised how unlikely she thought it was that this moment would come any time soon.

A soft tapping on the street door of Lydia's home next door sent both her and Ruth hurrying into the street. It was Anna, the slave of one of her most regular customers, a shawl wrapped around her head to obscure her identity. She beckoned Lydia to come quickly, looking around her anxiously. Lydia hurried to welcome her into the shop and closed the shutters so no passers-by could see in.

'Are you all right?' Lydia asked, concerned.

Anna nodded and whispered, 'My mistress, Livia, has run out of the dye she needs for her curtains and has been weeping all afternoon.'

Lydia looked at her grimly, recalling Clement's observation about their lack of customers.

'We aren't allowed to shop from you any more. Aurelia has issued the decree that anyone found buying purple from you will be . . .' here her voice sank to a horrified whisper '. . . disinvited.'

Lydia winced. Although, as a trader, she was not nor ever would be accepted into the higher echelons of Philippian society, she had enough clients who were to know precisely what this meant. Being disinvited would mean that you would no longer be invited to any of the great feasts, your friends would quietly slip away, acquaintances would no longer greet you with honour in the street. Shame would follow wherever you went. Aurelia had lost no time in enacting her threat.

'But mistress, Livia is desperate,' Anna continued, a pleading note in her voice. 'Her curtains are only half dyed. She is holding the feast next week and her shame will be complete if the dining room is unfinished. Aurelia would never let her hear the last of it. So we thought . . . we thought it was worth the risk.' The quiver in her voice indicated that Anna was not sure it was worth the risk, but loyalty to her mistress had driven her here anyway.

Lydia rapidly wrapped up the dye of exactly the right shade and let Anna slip quietly into the street. There were, she feared, tough times ahead. A thought wandered through her mind: would they be forced to flee again, just like last time? She shook her head, refusing to entertain the idea even for a moment. This time she would not run. This time she would stay and face whatever came her way. She didn't know how she would find the strength, but she would find it when she needed to. This time she had Ruth and John, Rufus and Marcus and Tertius. She had Clement and Alexandra. She had Syntyche and Artemis, Caius and Manius. She had a whole network of relationships that anchored her here. This time would be different. She wasn't sure how, but it would, definitely, be different.

She turned and started tidying the shelves of the shop. The rhythm of the tidying gave her mind time to still and quieten and as it stilled she prayed. She prayed for Euodia and her small community of believers wherever they might be, for her brothers and sisters in Christ, for her father back in Thyatira.

As she prayed a sense of deep peace fell on her. The future was no more certain than it had been a few moments ago; Aurelia's storm still swirled around her as threatening as ever; she still had no idea what had happened to Euodia or her congregation. Everything was exactly the same, yet felt completely different. She knew that she was held by a great love, and in that love was perfect peace. In that love she could face the future, whatever it held.

Chapter 16

The next few months were quiet for them all. As they left the golden days of autumn behind for the rains and chill of winter, there was, Lydia found, very little to do. Any customers they had came at night under the cover of darkness, and, while they earned enough money to get by, the days dragged interminably with too much time to think and too little to do. Ruth would spend hours at a time roaming around Philippi and would often return from her trips with a thoughtful look on her face. Clement and Alexandra came rarely to the shop next door; there was little point as so few people bought anything from them. Of Euodia there was no word at all. Weeks had turned into months, and still they could find no hint of what had happened to her. After a while they stopped talking about her. The more time passed the more they all feared the worst, but no one wanted to be the person to say it out loud. They remained close as a community, but over them hung a dark cloud of uncertainty.

Lydia couldn't decide whether it was the days full of rain or the hours of time she had in which to imagine the various awful things that might happen to her beloved companions that made the future look so bleak. Whenever the rain allowed she would spend time in the garden, recalling happier times and trying to remember what Philomela's birdsong had sounded like. The more the time dragged on the harder she found it to hang on to that sense of peace that had filled her when she was tidying the shop. Around and around went her thoughts, like the grinding of an ox-cart wheel. What if Euodia was dead? What if Aurelia found a way to bring the full force of Roman might on their small community? They had heard whispers of it happening elsewhere; what if it happened here? What if the pressures on them forced them all apart? What if . . . what if . . .

Lydia's biggest fear, which hung behind everything else, but which she didn't have enough courage to look at, was about her faith. That moment ten or so years ago when Paul explained it to her felt so long ago. She had been swept along by his account of Jesus Christ, Son of God; everything had felt so clear, so certain, so trustworthy. But now time had passed, and all she had to rest her trust on was a remembered conversation with Paul, the community of some dear companions, and a diminishing confidence in it all. The biggest 'what if' of all was what if she had been mistaken and she was gambling the safety of her whole household on a nice idea with nothing behind it? What if she'd been wrong all this time?

One morning, during a lull in the rain, she sat as she so often did in the garden beneath the mulberry tree, when her whirring thoughts were interrupted by a faint knock on the street door. It was a strange sound, as though the person knocking was using every last iota of energy in their knocking. As suddenly as the sound had begun, it stopped. Lydia went to open the door. There was a man there whom she had never seen before. He was horribly thin, his skin stretched over his jutting cheeks and collar bones. His eyes were dark-ringed and sunken. His face had a strange grey hue and he leant against the door post for support. He struggled to speak. 'My name,' he wheezed, 'my name is Epaph—' But he got no further, as he collapsed unconscious in the doorway. A small moan behind them told Lydia that somehow, even in the furthest reaches of the house, Artemis had heard and been drawn by the faint sounds of knocking. She opened her mouth to call for the boys to come and help, but realised that they were already there, clustered in anxious support around a shaking Artemis. Between them they carried

Epaphroditus into a bedroom towards the rear of the house and settled him as best they could.

Over the course of the next few days, Artemis never left his side. Night and day she sat holding his hand, whispering stories of what had happened since he left and, whenever he was awake enough, spooning soup or other liquids into his mouth. What Artemis didn't see during her long vigil was Lydia's house slowly filling up with people. As word spread around Philippi of Epaphroditus's return and serious illness, people trickled in. First Clement and Alexandra, and then Caius and Manius; then members of their own community led by Syntyche; then Jonathan and Akiva and other members from the community down by the stream, as well as a whole range of people Lydia had never met before. At night everyone drifted away, but they would return early in the morning with gifts of food. The hum of prayers and quietly sung songs and hymns filled Lydia's atrium from morning till night.

Then, on the third day of their vigil, another knock drew Lydia to the door. She and Clement had shut their shops in order to be with those waiting and praying, so Lydia assumed it was another incognito customer driven by a need for purple so overwhelming that they were prepared to risk the wrath of Aurelia to get it. She opened the door briskly. Standing there was Euodia. She gazed at her, temporarily lost for words, but as she did so the years fell away and they were back again in the place of prayer relishing their favourite psalms together. Almost before the thought had fully entered her mind, she stepped towards Euodia. 'The Lord is my light and my salvation.'

'Whom shall I fear?' responded Euodia, as she would have done all those years ago. Clement, who had come to the door behind her in case the knock had been one of his customers and who had been eerily quiet for the previous few days, picked up the words: 'The Lord is the stronghold of my life; of whom shall I be afraid?' His melodious voice filled the atrium. One by one the gathered company joined in, their voices blending in the ancient melody. The sound must have filtered to Artemis at the rear of the house because she emerged, bleary-eyed and hazy from lack of sleep, with Syntyche at her side. They looked at Euodia, standing hesitantly by the side of Lydia.

'My sister,' said Syntyche, opening out her arms.

'I'm sorry,' said Euodia, similarly holding out her arms, and instantly the two of them plus Artemis held each other in a long embrace. The people packed into the atrium and garden beyond made a sound together that fell somewhere between relief and approval.

'No,' said Syntyche, 'it is we who are sorry. How could we have let our relationship get so bad? How could we have drifted apart like this? We have been beside ourselves with worry. Where have you been?'

Euodia hung her head. 'I thought you wouldn't notice. It was such a long time since any of us had spoken, and I knew Aurelia would never stop until she had destroyed us all. So I made her think we were alone in our beliefs, me and the few members of my gathering, and then, in dead of night, we left.'

'Where did you go?'

'What did she do to you?'

'Why have you come back?'

'Why didn't you tell us?'

Questions jostled Euodia as she gazed, slightly dazed, at the assembled gathering. 'I . . . I . . .' Her bemused gaze fell on Ruth. A look of vague recognition passed over her face. 'Do I know you?'

'I'm Ruth,' she said. Euodia continued to look bemused. 'Lydia's pythian girl,' Ruth added, no longer so embarrassed by the old definition.

Euodia's face cleared. 'No! Really? But you're so grown up!'

'It happens.' Ruth smiled.

'When did you get back?' Euodia turned to Lydia.

'A few months ago.'

'That makes sense.' Euodia nodded. 'That was around the time we left. There's so much to tell you, but first I must do what I came for. I need to tend to Epaphroditus.'

'How did you know he was back?' Syntyche and Clement spoke over each other in their astonishment.

'I'll tell you everything, I promise, but first I need to see Epaphroditus. I've been so worried about him.' She hustled after Syntyche, already rummaging in her bag and issuing instructions to Artemis, who gladly ran to the kitchen to collect supplies, leaving those gathered in Lydia's house with even more questions than before.

An hour or so later, she emerged, nodding her satisfaction. 'That will do for now. I'm glad I am here, though,' she said to Artemis.

Artemis broke into tears. 'So am I, dear Euodia, so am I. I've wished for your presence more times than I can mention over the last few days.'

Euodia, Lydia remembered, was renowned throughout Philippi and beyond for her skill with herbs and healing. There was no one better to care for Epaphroditus on his road to recovery.

'But how *did* you know he was here?' Syntyche asked again. 'We've been looking for you everywhere and found not the slightest whiff of information about you.'

'Good,' said Euodia, 'just as I planned. We fled to Thessalonica. I thought we'd be safe there even though it's only a five-day journey.'

Clement nodded. 'How clever. Aurelia hates Philippi because it's not Rome, and Philippi is a Roman colony. She'd never stoop so low as to go to a city that might be the capital of the region, but isn't a colony. I can't believe we didn't think of that ourselves.'

Euodia smiled at him. 'I hoped you wouldn't. I thought that hiding just a little out of view was the safest idea, but it was vital you didn't know where I was, that no one knew. I'm sorry that you were so worried, I hoped you might not notice that I'd gone, after, well you know . . .'

The look of shame on Syntyche's face mirrored Euodia's. 'We should never have allowed it to go that far. What happened to us?'

'I don't know,' said Euodia. 'Even now I don't know. The disagreement took on a life of its own and before we knew it, it had consumed everything, our friendship and all.'

Artemis leant forward. 'But how *did* you know Epaphroditus was here?'

Euodia also leant forward and grasped her hand. 'He passed through Thessalonica on his way home. He collapsed, by the grace of God, right by my stall in the forum. So I took him home and nurtured him back to the land of the living again, but he was so anxious to be back, to bring you Paul's letter, that he left before he was fully recovered. I was worried about him and knew he'd relapse, so I waited a few days and followed.'

At that moment Marcus, Rufus and Tertius came, bringing a selection of food for Euodia, clearly at the instigation of Artemis. Euodia looked at them enquiringly. She had an expressive face that could ask questions and make observations without the need ever to open her lips. Lydia remembered ruefully the few occasions when, in the place of prayer, she had realised she had said something very stupid, and her realisation had occurred simply through the look on Euodia's face.

As intended, the boys answered Euodia's unspoken question, with Rufus speaking on behalf of them all. 'We're Lydia's slaves.'

It sounded so harsh when framed like that, so Lydia added, 'Not really slaves, part of the family.'

'But still slaves,' said Rufus solemnly. With a wave of sadness, Lydia had to acknowledge he was right. It was a long time since she had thought of any of the boys as slaves. Even when they were little, back in Thyatira, she had thought them part of her family; not quite sons, but certainly not her property. Now she realised that she had never thought to ask them how they felt. She had the luxury of deciding how to view their relationship and had assumed that, because she treated them well and thought of them as family, they felt the same.

She realised that her face must be revealing her unease because Tertius, gentle, quiet, kind Tertius, patted her hand. 'Family slaves,' he whispered. 'Definitely loved, but not free.'

'Sorry to break in,' said Clement, 'but I really need to know what happened to Euodia. We all do.'

Chapter 17

Slowly, and at first hesitantly, Euodia began telling them what had happened to her. The events had taken place last summer, around the time that Lydia and her household had returned to Philippi. Euodia was in the forum at her usual stall selling herbs and salves of various kinds. She was skilled, and her ointments were sought after by rich and poor alike. No one made ointments and poultices as effective as Euodia's. One day she fell into conversation with a young slave girl, whom she later discovered was a kitchen maid in Aurelia's house. The girl had a black eye and a swollen cheek and was sobbing as she went about her daily tasks. Euodia had beckoned her over and pressed on her a salve and some herbs to help the bruise heal. Over the next few days the swelling subsided and the bruising faded. Euodia kept a close eye on the girl, who came every day to the market to buy bread, and herbs, vegetables and olives from the stalls that were crammed around the edge of the forum.

After that first day, she would pause for a short while at Euodia's stall and exchange a few words of conversation. She was young, Euodia thought, no more than twelve or thirteen, and spoke with an accent that reminded Euodia of someone else she had known from Gaul. She was called Aculia, she told Euodia with a glint of pride, because even as a small child, she had been so quick. Her parents, in their pride at her nimbleness, had named her Aculia. They had died many years before, in a skirmish with the Roman army, and Aculia had been carried off as a slave. She was now learning that being fast is not always a virtue: in Crassus's house, under Aurelia's rule, it was wiser to be silent than it was to be fast. She would talk hesitantly of her life, a life dominated by beatings and cruelty. Aurelia ruled the household with a rod of iron and violent outbreaks of temper. The cruelty cascaded downwards through the whole household. Aurelia would berate the steward, the steward would berate the kitchen slaves, and the kitchen slaves would berate Aculia at the bottom of the pile; berating would often slip into beating. There was no one to stop it and no one to care that it happened.

Aculia would sigh hopelessly as she described the beatings and internally Euodia would rage at the injustice of it all, while on the outside trying to offer wisdom and hope. One day Aculia asked her what gave her so much hope, and Euodia told her about Jesus and his life, his death and his resurrection and how the world was now made new. Day after day Aculia came back for more. Then one day she didn't come back at all. Euodia waited for her, lingering as she packed up her stall at the end of the day, but Aculia didn't come; nor did she come the next day or the next. Just as Euodia had given up hope of ever seeing her again, Aurelia had arrived at her stall at the busiest time of the day with four big slaves. She dragged with her a battered and bruised Aculia. She had caught Aculia a week ago telling the kitchen slaves about Jesus, and had her beaten until she told her where she had heard about him. She pointed at Euodia and accused her loudly of being un-Roman. Euodia did her best to defend herself, but, against Aurelia's strident, confident accusations, she floundered. The slaves flicked herbs and salves off her stall one by one, and then overturned the stall itself. They pushed their faces into hers, and told her never to show her face in the forum again. So began Aurelia's campaign against Euodia.

Euodia did, of course, return to the forum. She was not the kind of person to back down after one frightening incident and, in any case, her livelihood depended on the proceeds from her stall. She went back, but so did Aurelia's slaves. People stopped coming to the stall, terrified of being caught up in the spectacle. Day after day they ruined her goods and her stall; day after day she sold nothing. A week after it had begun, Aurelia herself returned. She wanted to know who else followed this unnatural religion, who else she had to stamp out. Euodia had told her no one did. It was she, and she alone, who believed. She looked around the room, clearly still troubled by her lie. 'I wanted to protect you all,' she said, with desperation in her voice. 'I wanted you to be safe. I thought God was teaching me a lesson. I had been so worried about Paul bringing us to the notice of the Romans that I had refused to help him when he needed us most. Then the Romans had turned on me in my own city. I was going about my own life, in my own way, and they came for me nevertheless. That was my punishment for my heartlessness.'

'Dear one,' said Syntyche, her face crumpled with concern, 'you don't really believe that the God of love, the God who crafted the whole world into being and fills it with life, would be as petty as that?'

Euodia looked at her, light slowly dawning behind her eyes. 'Now you put it like that no, no I don't think I do – but I did. That's why I fled to Thessalonica, me and the members of my church. We thought that if we went at dead of night, we could disappear and no one would notice. I was appalled at what I had done, but also wanted to save you all from the same fate.'

Clement and Alexandra, Syntyche and Artemis and a few others around the room hung their heads in shame at this. The harsh reality was that Euodia had disappeared and they hadn't noticed. They had been so caught up in their own lives. They had distanced themselves from Euodia and her community in their anger at her intransigence, and, when she needed them, had not even noticed her distress. Syntyche threw her arms around Euodia and hugged her for a long time.

'Well that's one job I no longer need to worry about.' Epaphroditus's voice, weak but clearly heard in the silence of the room, made everyone start. He was leaning against the entry to the atrium, propping himself up against it, lest his legs give way. He was holding up a slightly battered scroll, a line drawn around it as a seal. 'A letter from Paul,' he explained. 'He says to make sure Euodia and Syntyche have the same mind in the Lord.'

Euodia and Syntyche ran to Epaphroditus's side. 'I think you will find we are of exactly the same mind right now . . .' said Syntyche.

'. . . that you should be in bed,' Euodia completed her sentence as they used to do for each other in times past when they had been firm friends, just as they had when Lydia had first known them.

'But the letter,' said Epaphroditus again, slight desperation in his voice. 'I brought the letter for you from Paul.' It was obvious that he was at the end of his strength and unable to read it to them, but had used the very last of his energy to deliver it and was determined that his efforts would not go to waste.

Lydia eyed the scroll in his hand anxiously. Was there more bad news in the letter, so important it was worth Epaphroditus risking his life to deliver it? What could it possibly contain that would warrant that?

Jonathan stepped forward. 'Akiva is our cantor; why don't we ask him to read the letter, and Epaphroditus can sit to listen?' Euodia smiled at him gratefully. It was an excellent solution. Epaphroditus handed over the scroll to Akiva, who chose his position carefully for maximum audibility. He took a deep breath and began to read.

'Paul and Timothy, slaves of Christ Jesus to all the holy ones in Christ Jesus who are in Philippi,' people around the room nodded gravely at this and settled in to listen more intently, 'together with the overseers and deacons.' Syntyche, Clement,

Jonathan, Euodia and a couple of others in the atrium caught each other's eyes, clearly pleased that Paul had remembered how their worshipping communities were set up. 'Grace to you and peace from God our Father and the Lord Jesus Christ. I thank my God in every remembrance of you . . .'

Lydia listened on, anxiously waiting for the awful news that she had imagined it contained. The atrium and the garden beyond were silent as the gathered company listened intently while Akiva read on, his lyrical voice adding shading to Paul's own words. The sixty or so people crammed into the space reacted as one as they listened: sorrowing for Paul's dire situation; sympathising and sharing the anxiety of everyone present at the mention of being intimidated by opponents; lifting their heads, inspired as Akiva intoned what sounded like a new song about Christ. They shared significant looks with each other at Paul's urging to act, without murmuring or arguing. Some of them clearly thought they knew who among them should be listening to *that* piece of advice.

When Akiva got to the part of the letter where Paul explained why he had sent Epaphroditus and not Timothy with the letter, a ripple of conversation ran around the room. Of course they'd have liked to see Timothy, especially after refusing him support the last time he was with them, but they couldn't begin to understand why Paul thought they would prefer to see Timothy rather than have their own dear Epaphroditus back with them. They turned to Epaphroditus to ensure he knew their preference and to agree that they had indeed been very upset to hear that he was ill.

Akiva paused to allow the murmuring to die down, and then continued. A little later he faltered again, but not, this time, because of the conversation around the room. The next portion of the letter turned its attention to those Paul called 'dogs, evil workers and people who mutilate the flesh'. He ranted and railed against these people – whoever they were – telling the

Philippians to beware of them. As he went on it became increasingly evident that he was talking about Jews like Akiva and Jonathan. Paul had, he declared, a noble past as a Jew, a member of the tribe of Benjamin and a Pharisee, a past he said he now counted as nothing more than excrement. A gasp ran around the gathered company as Akiva declared this. The gasp was followed by an awkward hush. When Akiva got to 'their end is destruction, their god is the belly and their glory is their shame', Akiva paused in his reading, looking anxiously at Jonathan. 'Do you think he means us?'

Chapter 18

Jonathan seemed to be as flummoxed by the tirade as Akiva was. He lifted his hands and shoulders in a shrug. 'I don't think so?' But his voice rose at the end and made it less of a statement and more of a question. Lydia remembered a conversation she had had with Akiva one day while he was painting the atrium. Neither he nor Jonathan, or indeed anyone else in their gathering, had ever met Paul. When she had first met them, she had assumed that they, like she, had been drawn into the Way of Jesus Christ by Paul, his message and his passion. She soon discovered that this was not the case. The community that met with Jonathan and Akiva had all come to Philippi to trade variously in glass, linen and spices. Philippi's location on the Via Egnatia meant that goods could travel easily eastwards and westwards, making it an ideal spot for anyone seeking to source wares for sale. Akiva himself had come from Capernaum, where he had learnt his skill in trading along the Via Maris. His business in Philippi, he had told Lydia, was still finding its feet. This was why he had been unable to afford new tassels when they first met. The spices he had brought with him from Capernaum were not the ones most Macedonian cooks used, but he was optimistic that soon he would find the right flavours to sell.

He had first heard about the man called Jesus from his father, Solomon. Solomon had been a fisherman in Capernaum working a boat next to someone called Zebedee and his two sons, James and John. One day, during one of the sudden storms that blew up on the Galilee at a moment's notice, Solomon's flat-bottomed boat had been pounded by the waves, and Solomon had been thrown into the sea. The boat, which had been tossed high into the air, landed hard on his back. He had been paralysed that day and, for as long as Akiva could remember, had been in terrible pain and unable to walk, only leaving the house when four friends could be found to pick up his mat to carry him. Once, when Jesus had been at home in Capernaum, his friends had concocted a hare-brained scheme of climbing to the roof by the outside stairs, digging a hole, and letting Solomon down through it with ropes. Jesus had healed him that day, and afterwards Solomon had been spritely and full of energy until his death a few years ago, a little before Akiva had moved to Philippi to try his hand at trading further afield.

As a child, Akiva used to ask Solomon questions about what it had felt like to be healed by Jesus, but his father was strangely reluctant to answer. He kept on saying that for him it wasn't so much about the healing, but the forgiveness of his sins. Akiva used to ask what sins he could have possibly committed lying there on his back on a mat. And his father would laugh and say that he'd have said the same, but then he'd met Jesus. Jesus had looked right into his heart and he, Solomon, had realised how much bitterness there was there. More than that, though, he'd realised in that moment with Jesus looking into his heart that sin wasn't just about what you may or may not have done, or may or may not have thought; it was everything that cut you off from God and those around you. When Jesus told him that his sins were forgiven, he'd felt as light as a feather. So light, he used to tell Akiva with a twinkle in his eye, he thought he would have been able to fly if his legs hadn't begun to move.

Shortly after deciding to move to Philippi, Akiva had met Jonathan and a few others. Jonathan came from a small village called Emmaus, near Jerusalem. His next-door neighbour, Clopas, was quite elderly even when Jonathan had lived there, and he would sit in the sun and tell anyone who passed about the day he'd walked with Jesus from Jerusalem. All the way from Jerusalem to Emmaus they'd walked, he would say, his arms stretched out as though in great surprise, without ever once knowing it was him.

They'd begun reading Torah and praying together, but soon they'd bonded over what they knew about this Jesus. Others had joined them, and now they prayed and read Torah and talked about Jesus whenever they could. But they remained faithful to their heritage, proud members of the house of Israel. The one thing they all had in common was that, although they had all heard of Paul, none of them had ever met him.

All of this Lydia remembered as she looked at their hurt, slightly shocked faces. Although some of the Philippians had been upset by Jonathan and Akiva's insistence on purity regulations and with whom and how they ate, Lydia herself had found them nothing other than kind, courteous and considerate and most definitely not worthy of the description of being 'dogs' or of their god being 'the belly'. She leant forward earnestly, wanting to reassure her friends, but Epaphroditus, weak though he was, got there first.

'Of course he didn't mean you,' he said, his voice thin from fever, but nevertheless carrying to the far side of the garden with a ring of authority. 'What have you ever done to warrant a description like that? How could he mean you? You have never met him. Paul is fighting his own battles, inside and out.'

'So what is he like?' asked Ruth, leaning forward in her enthusiasm.

Epaphroditus smiled at her. 'Passionate,' he said, 'full of energy and vision. But he has suffered over the years from people who have sought to belittle and challenge him, not to mention – and for him this has been far worse – to undermine the good news he has dedicated his life to proclaiming. He's been awaiting an audience before the emperor for so long that I think he's taken the battle inwards. He fights with them in his head day and night. You must know though . . .' here he turned back to Jonathan, 'that there are followers of Christ who think you can only follow properly if you also follow the commands of Torah.'

Jonathan nodded thoughtfully. 'Of course we do, and we also have to admit that what they think does make sense. Jesus himself followed those commands. Peter still does most of the time, so does James back in Jerusalem. *I* don't understand how you can be a child of God and not also a full child of Abraham, Isaac and Jacob. I don't understand it, but now I know you all . . .' he looked around the room with affection in his eyes, 'you follow just as faithfully as I do – sometimes more faithfully.' Here he nodded in the direction of Epaphroditus. 'So I've decided that I don't need to understand. You can follow like you do, and I will follow as I do.'

'Exactly,' Epaphroditus said, struggling a little for breath, but continuing determinedly, 'we all know that, but there are others who try to force their view on everyone else. They are so convinced that they are right that they cannot allow space for anyone else to live differently. Paul has met so many people like this over the years that he lives in constant fear of them. He worries that they will come here and force you to live like they do.' He paused for a moment to catch his breath, looking at Jonathan and Akiva with deep compassion. 'I'm surprised that you are so hurt by someone else's imagined description of you. Even if he had meant you – which we know he can't have done because he's never met you – if you know a description of yourself to be untrue you don't have to accept it. We can't control what other people say about us, much as we might want to. Nor can we force them to think of us as we might want to be thought of . . .' Epaphroditus sagged with exhaustion and tailed off.

Lydia looked at Epaphroditus with admiration. How wise and loyal he was. In a single speech he had defended Paul, and Jonathan and Akiva, and on top of that had inserted wisdom into what could so easily have become a conflict. All of this he did while he was at the very end of his energies. No wonder Artemis and Syntyche saw him as the glue at the heart of their community.

'You make it sound so easy, my friend,' said Jonathan, 'but words like this cut to the soul and are hard to throw off.'

Epaphroditus, however, had used all his energy on his last speech and was beyond words.

'I wonder,' Akiva said thoughtfully, 'whether that's what Father meant. When Father talked about his sins being forgiven, maybe he meant that in that moment Jesus let all the hurts and slights and bitterness that crowded in on him go. Maybe that's what happened, maybe that's what made all the difference to him?'

'It's still easier said than done,' Jonathan grumbled.

'Whatever made you think that following Jesus was easy?' asked Clement.

'I wish he'd forgiven my sins,' said Manius a little gloomily. 'If I hadn't crucified him, he might have been able to.'

'What if he has?' asked Akiva. 'What if all you have to do is accept it? What if it was his dying that made forgiveness possible?'

'That would take some thinking about,' said Manius.

Akiva grinned. 'I wonder if I should read the rest of the letter now?' So he did.

Euodia and Syntyche grimaced and clasped hands when Paul mentioned them by name. Euodia frowned again when Paul thanked the Philippians for their generosity – a generosity that she had fought against so long and hard at the expense of so many of her relationships. And all the while the words rejoice ... rejoice ... rejoice bounced around them in the atrium, then out to the garden and back again.

When he had finished reading, Akiva rolled up the scroll again and went to hand it back to Epaphroditus. Epaphroditus held up his hands and shook his head.

'It is yours now. For you all. I brought it for you.'

Akiva bowed to him. 'I will take it and copy it in my best hand – one for each of our gatherings.'

The assembled group nodded, smiled their agreement to this proposal, and slowly got up to leave. The crisis had passed. Epaphroditus looked a little recovered, even if his lips still showed an alarming hint of blue. They had heard the letter that Epaphroditus had laboured so hard to deliver, and now they would spread out again across Philippi, returning to their homes and families and work.

Euodia rose with the others and started to gather her belongings. Syntyche looked up at her. 'You'll come and stay with me? We have much to catch up on and much to lay to rest.'

Chapter 19

Euodia hesitated, glancing anxiously at Epaphroditus. The immediate crisis was over, but she was reluctant to go too far away in case she was needed again. Lydia intercepted. 'Why don't you both stay here? We can all catch up on old times *and* be close by if Epaphroditus should need you. It also has the virtue of you not risking bumping into one of Aurelia's slaves as you wander the streets.'

'Good idea,' said Euodia, Syntyche and Artemis as one. Clement, who was still nearby with Alexandra, threw back his head and laughed one of his characteristic belly laughs. As he did, Lydia realised, a little sadly, that she hadn't heard him laugh like this for quite some weeks; in fact, not since Aurelia had left their shop. Outwardly, Clement had maintained his usual cheery demeanour, but now, Lydia realised, it had been no more than superficial. The real Clement, whose mirth seemed to bubble up from his toes and through his whole body until it had to burst out of him, had been hidden beneath a weight of worry.

'What are you laughing at?' Alexandra asked.

'Paul's greatest wish was that you would have the same mind, and here you all are thinking the exact same thing, again.'

'I don't think that is quite what he meant,' objected Alexandra.

'I know,' said Clement, unruffled, his eyes still twinkling. 'I take my entertainment where I can find it.'

'Why don't you all stay a while too?' said Lydia. 'I'm sure you have a lot to ask Euodia.'

129

Their conversation that evening was long and restorative. A catching up on the small things of life that gently rewove the web of friendship with Euodia that had frayed, due to time – in the case of Lydia – and conflict – in the case of Syntyche, Artemis and Clement. Epaphroditus was so determined to stay and so exhausted by this determination that they dragged out a straw mattress for him to lie on so that the conversation could flow around him.

At one point, when he looked more alert, Lydia asked him the question that had been troubling her ever since he had insisted that they read the letter. 'What,' she asked, 'was so urgent that you had to risk your life to deliver it?'

'You,' he replied simply, 'you all. While I was away, you all wrote to me – well obviously not you, Lydia, as we didn't know each other – but everyone else did, and as I read your letters I could feel you drifting away from each other. I knew my dear Artemis was wearing herself thin with worry, but I also wanted to get back to you before you drifted too far apart and the chasm between you became so vast that it could never be bridged.'

Lydia nodded, acknowledging the wisdom of what he said. Even she, who had not been present when the rift first began, had settled into accepting it as a reality. Epaphroditus was right: it might not have taken much longer before the grievances between them had set solid and could no longer be mended.

'What we needed was you,' said Artemis.

'No,' said Clement thoughtfully, 'we needed the letter. Much as we love having you with us,' he added hastily, lest he offend Epaphroditus or more likely Artemis. 'What we needed was the reminder of Jesus.'

'Some of us had never forgotten him,' Syntyche bristled. 'We talk about him all the time.'

Clement nodded. 'We do. But I think that we forgot that we don't just need to talk about him, but to think like him, to see the world like he did, to live his story as our story. It may not have been worth Epaphroditus making himself so ill for, but we really did need to hear it. Or at least I did.'

Various people around the room nodded their agreement.

'I'd never heard it said like that,' said Ruth. 'I thought we were just following him along the Way. Living his story as our story is different, I think.'

'It is,' Epaphroditus agreed. 'It is bigger. It's more demanding. It makes more of a difference.'

'Is that why Paul got himself arrested?' asked Euodia. 'So he could live Christ's story right to the end?'

'I think,' said Epaphroditus slowly, choosing his words as he went, 'I think you need to be careful not to mix up what you can see of someone's life with why they do something. You can know *what* they have done, but you can't know *why* they did it. That is their story, and unless they tell you their story you can't know what lies behind.' He turned to Euodia. 'You've created a story about Paul and why he does what he does, but I think that you have misunderstood him. He didn't "get" himself arrested. He was arrested, but once arrested he did want to take the good news of Jesus Christ right to the heart of the empire – and what better way to do that than for a Roman citizen to ask for his case to be heard before the emperor himself?'

'Have you never wondered,' asked Euodia, 'whether Paul is trying to die like Jesus did? Whether he has become so obsessed with living Jesus' story that he wants to die his death too?'

Epaphroditus shook his head. 'I've spent nearly a year with him, and didn't see that in him at all. I don't think he chases suffering, but I do know he isn't afraid of it. I've never met anyone quite like him. He looks suffering right in the face and never flinches, not even for a moment. Christ's story is his story, so much so that he knows death is nothing to fear, because after death comes resurrection and new life.'

He sagged again and Euodia immediately sprang to her feet. 'I think you have done enough for one day, come. Come, let's get you back to bed.'

It was a sign of Epaphroditus's deep exhaustion that this time he did not resist, but allowed himself to be half carried between Euodia and Artemis back to his room, with Syntyche only a few steps behind.

A silence fell among the friends as they sat with their private thoughts. Lydia looked around the atrium, her heart full of love for those gathered there. Her gaze lingered on Ruth. She was growing up and away from Lydia. Lydia, as was only natural, missed the closeness they had had when Ruth was young, but revelled in the person she was becoming. She looked at Clement and Alexandra, such dear friends and so important to her after only a few brief months. Behind them sat Caius and Manius; both men had been gathered in by Clement and Alexandra and had become like family to them all, despite Lydia's initial opposition. In the far corner of the atrium, towards the entrance to the garden, sat John, with Marcus, Rufus and Tertius gathered around him. John had returned to the house while Epaphroditus was so ill and had sat vigil like everyone else over the past few days. He was one of only two people allowed into the boys' inner circle; the other was Ruth. Lydia knew and accepted that this inner circle did not include her. They loved her, she knew that. They would defend her when she needed it, but she was not one of them. The boys had known John since, as small children, they had been brought home by Lydia's father to the house in Thyatira. He had taught them his skills, worked with them to develop their own, and listened to them like no one else – other than Ruth – had. Now they were older they depended on him less than they had, but sometimes they still leant into him, drawing strength from his quiet, steady presence.

They were, Lydia noticed, doing that now. Their faces showing various levels of anxiety. They were whispering quietly to

John, and he, in his turn, was nodding in the direction of the rest of the group who were on the other side of the atrium, nearer to Lydia. They seemed reluctant to speak openly.

Eventually John said, 'Marcus, Rufus and Tertius have a question for you.'

This caused the boys to pull back even more. If they could have melted into the wall behind them they would have done so. It was Manius, who generally preferred to sit and watch than to join in, soaking up what people said without saying much in return, who spoke.

'If I were you,' he said gently, 'after I heard Paul's letter just now and especially after I heard that beautiful poem, I'd be wondering how you take on the form of a slave when you are one already. I'd be thinking that it's all very well giving up your power when, like Paul you have so many reasons to be confident in your Jewish and Roman heritage, but I wonder what it feels like when you have no power at all.'

Rufus, normally the spokesperson for their group, looked down at his feet, suddenly fascinated by the thong on one of his sandals. Marcus gazed out at the garden, as though counting what remained of the leaves on the wintry mulberry tree outside. It was, to Lydia's surprise, Tertius who spoke.

'It feels hopeless,' he mumbled, his face bright red, his words indistinct. 'How do you give up what you don't have?'

'Aren't you happy here?' Even as she asked the question, Lydia realised she had made Tertius's reflection all about her. But at the same time she was aware that she couldn't help it. 'Do you not like Philippi? Would you have rather stayed in Thyatira?'

Tertius looked at her sadly. 'That's not the point. Not the point at all.'

'We love Philippi,' said Marcus and Rufus together. 'We love the city. We love this house. We love you all.'

'I love the forum,' said Rufus.

'I love helping John in his workshop,' said Marcus.

'I love helping Akiva with his painting,' said Tertius. Marcus and Rufus looked as though they were going to go on listing all the things they loved, but Tertius held up his hand. 'I know this is hard, but we do have to tell Lydia how we feel.' John nodded at him approvingly, as though this conversation had been a long time in the making.

Marcus and Rufus squirmed. 'But we don't want to hurt anyone,' said Marcus.

'We're very grateful for all we have,' added Rufus.

'When we talk to the other slaves in the forum we know how lucky we are.'

They had fallen back into their well-worn habit of taking it in turns to speak as though they were really one person. Though this time, it was noticeable that Tertius was not a silent shadow between them nodding his agreement as they spoke; this time he stood off to the side, his arms crossed, his brow furrowed.

Marcus and Rufus stuttered to a halt, clearly sensing the lack of Tertius's support. They turned towards him questioningly.

'I know you think you are being kind,' he said to them, 'but you are not. We have talked for hours about our freedom and how much we yearn for it. But now when, at last, you have the chance to say something, you choose to say nothing. We have just heard Paul tell us to think about whatever is true, whatever is honourable, whatever is just. It's no good just thinking true, honourable and just things, you have to say them too, and what you are saying is none of these things.'

'Tertius,' said Lydia surprised, 'I always thought of you as the quiet one.'

'I was,' said Tertius, 'but being quiet is not the same as having no opinions. All that time I wasn't talking, I was thinking.'

Chapter 20

'Speak,' said Manius, 'we are all listening.'

Tertius hesitated, his bravado wavering for a moment. He looked anxiously at Lydia for permission to continue.

'Manius is right,' she said. 'This is your time to speak. Speak from the heart and hold nothing back. I am deeply sorry that you have not been able to do so until now.'

Tertius smiled at her, his face regaining the gentle, thoughtful look that Lydia was used to. That smile, more than anything else, told Lydia how costly it was for Tertius to be saying any of this.

'I don't think I have been ready until now. I was talking to Manius a few weeks ago and he asked me what it was like to be a slave. I had to say that I didn't know. I can't remember a moment when I was not a slave. One of my earliest memories is of meeting Marcus and Rufus in the slave market. I was terrified and exhausted; hungry and thirsty. Rufus shared his crust of bread with me and Marcus gave me some sips of his water. Then we curled up together at the back of the barn where we were being kept, and we have never been apart since then. I don't know if I had brothers where I came from, but I have them now.'

Marcus and Rufus nodded their agreement.

'Coming to live in your house in Thyatira was wonderful. For the first time that I can remember I was warm, and full of food and safe – most of all safe. Until then I couldn't remember feeling safe – really safe. So safe that you knew you could go to sleep at night and wake up the next day and you would still have food and shelter. Until then my life had been a jumble of fear and hunger and loneliness. Overnight my life changed and, like Marcus and Rufus, I am so grateful for all of that.'

He paused for a moment. His gentle face creased with concern. Ruth went to stand beside him. 'Go on,' she whispered, 'you can do this.' So he did.

'I think we've established that we are lucky slaves – grateful slaves. Not like so many others we meet as we go about our jobs in the market. They meet to show off their bruises and cuts from the beatings they get. Slaves are dispensable – most of them, that is – and anyone can take out their frustrations on them. Last week our friend, Servius, disappeared. We met every day in the forum. We'd chat about all sorts of things and kick stones around for a bit. His master had a terrible temper, he told us, and was violent. He would often come with a black eye or bruises somewhere else. Then last week he stopped coming. We waited for him day after day. He never came back. In the end I saw one of the slaves from his house and asked him about Servius. He backed away, mumbling something about him having been caught stealing bread from the kitchen. He said that we wouldn't see him again and we shouldn't ask about him either. It would bring no good to anyone. He turned and ran away. I could smell his fear. It was a scent I remembered from the slave market. Fear would swirl around us like sewage every single day as one by one we were sold off into an unknown future.

'But do you know, even that isn't really the point? We know we are lucky here. We know that what happened to Servius would never happen to us in this house. What I hate is being someone else's. Can you imagine what it's like to have no say over your life? You – all of you – sit here discussing what you might or might not do tomorrow or the next day. You – Lydia – left Philippi when times got difficult and came back when they were better. You chose. We never have a choice about anything. You don't beat us if we don't do what you ask, but we can't choose to say no. You own our choices. Our lives are mapped out not by *our* decisions and desires, but by yours. We all love being in Philippi, but we didn't choose to come, and no one ever asked any of us whether we wanted to come. You said we were coming. So we did. That is our life.

'You call us family, but we aren't. Ruth chooses what she will do; where she will go and when. We do not. Calling us family rubs salt into the wound. And now this Paul, this Paul whom we've never met, is telling us to give up power and become like slaves. But what do we give up? We're already slaves. We're already the bottom of the heap. How do we go lower? You can only give up power if you have some in the first place. I . . .'

But Tertius had run out of words. His pent-up frustration had carried him on a wave of eloquence that then ran out. He withdrew to the safety of Marcus and Rufus's company, and they turned as one to look a little fearfully towards Lydia. It was clear that this was something they had all spoken of on many occasions, but only Tertius had had the courage to tell Lydia. The guilt that had tugged at the edges of Lydia's mind when they had mentioned it a few hours earlier now landed with full force. She had constructed a world around her own convenience. She had woven a narrative in which she had a happy, contented family, some of whom were slaves, but whom no one regarded as slaves. But it had been a world built on half-truths and fiction. She may not have thought of the boys as slaves, but she had happily treated them that way. Power, she realised with a twinge of shame, meant that you could even shape a story about who thought what about something and then declare it to be the truth.

She stood up quickly. There was only one thing for her to do and she needed to do it now before she thought too much about it. 'Marcus,' she said, 'Rufus, Tertius, in the presence of this assembled company and in front of these witnesses, I hereby free you from slavery. You are no longer bound to me in service. You are free.'

Marcus, Rufus and Tertius looked back at her, stunned. A moment passed, and then Marcus and Rufus turned on Tertius. 'What have you done? We told you not to. What are we going to do now?'

'I don't understand,' stammered Lydia, 'I thought that was what you wanted? Wasn't that what Tertius's speech was all about?'

Manius stepped in again. 'I suspect,' he said, 'that the boys haven't thought about what they do want. They know what they don't want, but not what they do. If something is large and dominating like slavery, like the Roman army was for me, you can know you want freedom, but knowing what you want instead is much harder to work out. It's why I wandered for so long after I left the army. Until I came here, until I met Jesus and you all, I knew I wanted to be free from the brutality and the oppression of the army, but I never worked out what I wanted to be free for. Give them time, they'll get there. You might hire them as servants; that would help.'

'Of course,' she said. 'Did you really think I would throw you into the street? When I told you I consider you to be family, I meant it. John and I will talk, and between us we will work out the best thing to do. You will never be homeless, never hungry, and never unsafe again for as long as you want to stay with us. But when you are ready to go, you may go, and our love will go with you.'

The tension of the conversation was still hanging in the air when they were interrupted by a quiet tapping on the street door. Lydia rose to open it. Standing at the door, with a hood pulled well over her face, was a slave Lydia didn't recognise. The slave whispered that she had been sent by her mistress to buy purple. One of the couches in their dining room had got damaged during a feast and needed repairing. The slave was surprisingly demanding for someone who had come late into the evening, and Lydia was sent running between the dye shop and the material shop back and forth in search of the right shade. In the end the slave left huffily and empty-handed, declaring the purples to be of lower quality than she had been led to believe.

Lydia closed the door after her to find John standing behind her in the vestibule area, an anxious look in his face. He had heard the customer and had come out to offer Lydia assistance.

'She didn't hear me coming,' John said. Lydia could believe this; John's quiet presence would often arrive without any audible signs of his approach. 'She had her arms deep under one of the bales of purple as though she was stashing something there. Then she heard you coming back from the dye shop and pulled back as though she had been standing in the middle of the room all along.'

They went into the material shop and stood before the shelf where John had seen the slave standing. Pulling off the bales of cloth they found hidden right at the back a bracelet made of pure gold, encrusted with jewels bigger than Lydia had ever seen before. It was one of the most beautiful things Lydia had laid eyes on. She looked at John and saw reflected in his face the horror that had begun creeping up her own spine. Something was very wrong.

'We need to get it out of here,' he said urgently.

They rushed back to the atrium and as quickly as possible told their assembled friends what had happened.

'This is not good,' said Caius.

'Really not good,' agreed Manius. 'It is said in the tabernae that this is one of Aurelia's tricks against her enemies, when other methods aren't working. She plants something and sends the lictors to find it. I'd been worried that she might try something like this. I hear from my veteran friends that she is angry that people have been coming to buy purple despite her decree that they should not. One of her friends made the mistake of buying new purple drapes before a fine banquet.'

'I remember those,' said John quietly. 'They were some of my finest work.'

'They were too good, it turns out,' said Manius. 'So good that only you could have dyed them. Aurelia knew right away that they came from you. We need to get this out of here,' he said, brandishing the bracelet.

Caius appeared by his side. They turned as one and moved swiftly to the garden door.

'What will they do with it?' Ruth asked.

'Best not to ask,' said Clement. 'Caius and Manius still know many of their old contacts in the tabernae around Philippi. I'm sure they will make the bracelet disappear, never to be found again.'

'But should we let them?' asked Ruth, her face creased with concern. 'It doesn't feel very Christ-like.'

But there was no time to answer. From the street door there came the sound of such loud, persistent banging that it felt as though the door would crack beneath the assault.

Chapter 21

Lydia went to the door, her heart pounding. The excitement of the past day had driven the worries of the previous months from her mind. The icy dread of wondering what Aurelia would do next had faded happily with Epaphroditus's return, but now it was back in full force. She opened the door to find, as they all knew she would, lictors standing outside. The rest of those present – Ruth, John, Marcus, Rufus and Tertius; Artemis and Syntyche; Clement and Alexandra – all clustered at the entrance to the atrium to watch and offer as much support as they could from that distance. Euodia had been bundled by Syntyche into Epaphroditus's room so that she wouldn't be noticed. The six lictors pushed their way past Lydia and into her cloth shop. They went straight to the spot where the bracelet had been hidden, doing nothing to conceal the fact that they knew exactly where to look. If Lydia had been less anxious she might have found some shred of entertainment in the astonishment that showed on their faces when they found nothing but material, carefully stacked according to each different shade of purple. They began pulling bales of cloth from the shelves into a chaotic mound on the floor.

'What have you done with it?' one of them cried, his voice cracking with fear. It appeared that they too were terrified of Aurelia and what she might do next. They stood for a moment in the middle of the shop, looking at each other as though uncertain about what to do next. Suddenly one of them, the one who had led them into the shop in the first place, came to a decision. He turned to Lydia. 'I summon you to trial for stealing and secreting the property of Aurelia, wife of our magistrate Decimus Licinius Crassus.'

'What proof do you have of this?' Clement had been drawn into the room by the lictors' declaration.

'I need no proof, only accusation, or perhaps you are unfamiliar with the law?'

'I am,' Clement said gloomily, 'far too familiar with how things are done. I know that, while you might be able to accuse someone with no proof, there comes a moment at trial when you do need proof.'

'I would remind you,' the lictor said, 'that in the provinces the magistrates can do whatever they like, and our orders come directly from the magistrate's wife. In any case, she has more status and power than all of you rolled together, and I am far more worried about what will happen to me tonight,' said the lictor, 'than what might or might not happen in the future. Come,' he said to Lydia. Clement instinctively tried to stand in front of her. 'Fair enough,' said the lictor, 'you can come too. Anyone else?' he called to the rest of the group. 'We don't mind how crowded our prisons are.'

Standing behind the lead lictor so he couldn't see her, Lydia shook her head fiercely at the group still clustered around the entrance to the atrium. There was no point in any more of them being taken away. As she looked at them, though, it was clear that her warning was unnecessary. None of them seemed capable of any kind of movement at all.

The six lictors shoved Lydia and Clement out of the door and onto the street. They surrounded them to ensure that they were unable to escape as they walked the short distance through the narrowed streets to the forum and the prison. Their caution was entirely unnecessary. Putting one foot in front of another as they shuffled their way along was all she was capable of, the thought of running anywhere was beyond her. How quickly life can fall apart, Lydia thought, as she walked along in silence.

One minute she had been surrounded by loving, understanding companions revelling in friendship renewed and restored; the next she was being escorted to prison, accused by a capricious and powerful woman. One moment she was comfortable and secure; the next it felt as though she was falling, and that her descent might never stop. She reflected wryly on her months of worrying. She had worried about so much, but it had never occurred to her to worry about this. Maybe that was the problem with worrying, because life catastrophes – the things that come in and shake your world upside down – arrive so quickly and unexpectedly that you could never imagine what they might be. She looked back nostalgically to the things she used to worry about – the spoiling of a batch of dye or a bale of cloth; the inability to get ingredients for Ruth's favourite stew; being snubbed in the street by someone more powerful than her – what she wouldn't give, right now, to have all those things come true rather than this.

Clement, walking next to her, began to hum. She looked at him, outraged. Now was not the time for singing, but Clement was lost in his tune and didn't notice her aggrieved glance. Pretty soon, though, she forgot to be annoyed. The tune was hauntingly beautiful. One that she had never heard before. Faintly, Lydia heard snatches of the words. 'Did not consider equality with God . . . to be clung to . . . Emptied himself . . . form of a slave . . . Obeyed orders . . . to the point of death.' On and on they walked; on and on Clement sang under his breath. As they walked, Lydia felt a sense of deep calm fall upon her. A calm fuelled partially by the melody that Clement sang as they walked and partially by the realisation of what Paul had meant in writing his letter.

It was, she saw with a clarity that could only emerge in disaster, Paul's own imprisonment that had given him the insight to write those words. Epaphroditus had been quite right. Paul wasn't pursuing death like a crazy gladiatorial warrior at the end of his strength. He had learnt to let go of those human instincts that lead to self-preservation and advantage. She remembered her mad dash out of Philippi all those years ago. It probably was the right thing to have done – not least to keep Ruth safe – but she realised now that she hadn't stopped to think about it. Her instinct for flight had kicked in and she had run away. In his letter Paul talked about a different way. Jesus had not taken the safe option. He could have clung to his equality with God and stayed safely in heaven far away from human heartache and betrayal. But he did not cling to it. He poured himself out in love, and became like us. He chose slavery over status; obedience over safety. Living his story, Lydia realised, meant making the same choices. She took a deep breath and started humming along with Clement.

When they got to the prison, they were placed in a cell near the entrance to the jail. Clement, from his years of working here, knew exactly what was going on. They were in an outer cell, and would stay there until their trial. The inner cell – the one Paul and Silas had been in – was kept for those condemned to death or those they wanted to frighten to death. It was late when they arrived and Lydia settled down against the damp, cold wall in the corner, thinking that it would be a long night. Clement sat beside her, still humming the new tune to Paul's hymn of Christ. What felt like moments later, Lydia stirred as daylight streamed into their small cell through a barred window in the wall high above them.

'You slept all night,' said Clement. 'The stress must have worn you out.'

'You didn't?' asked Lydia.

'No.' Clement shook his head. 'Being here reminds me of the person I used to be. I have been confessing my sins all night.' Lydia looked at him. His tired eyes were ringed with purple.

'Don't be too hard on yourself,' Lydia urged. 'You did what you had to at the time.'

Clement sighed, a slightly ragged sound. 'Manius and I have talked about this endlessly. Those of you who have never had to do these things find it hard to imagine what it feels like to have been someone who caused another human being so much suffering. Even Alexandra, who was here with me, finds it hard to understand. Manius knows. You see we can make ourselves feel better by saying that we didn't really know what we were doing back then; that we had no choice, we simply did what we had to. The problem is that we did know what we were doing, and we did it anyway. Manius and I could both have walked away, and we didn't. We told ourselves a story about how we had no choice. It was a good story, and I told it to myself for years. It allowed me to remain the hero in my own story; a good person despite everything I'd done. Last night I realised I needed to take the next step. I needed to tell myself the real story. The one in which I'm not a good person: deep down I knew exactly what I was doing and I did it anyway; I could have walked away, but I didn't. That is something I have to live with. It's been a long night and I've wrestled through most of it. I'm glad you slept,' he added, kind to the last.

Lydia looked at him sadly, grieving for his heartache. The stories we tell about our lives, she pondered, shape not just how other people see us, but how we see ourselves. Some people only ever tell stories that make them look good: stories in which they are the hero of every scenario; in which every misdeed is explained or glossed over. Often they get so caught up in their stories that they believe them, never stopping to wonder whether there might be more to the world than their own care-fully curated narrative. Other people told the 'uncompromising truth', as Clement just had, piling onto themselves blame and reproach. They seemed to present their story with searing honesty, but often ended up with a version as untrue as those who saw themselves as heroes. Could Clement really have recognised what he was doing, and stopped? Lydia pondered whether this, too, was what Paul was referring to in his Christ hymn: that refusing to cling to our versions of ourselves and taking the form of a slave – a form that no one would ever freely choose – was a way of living out Christ's story. Did emptying yourself include giving up what you wanted other people to think about you? The stories you told about yourself? She wondered how to say some of this to Clement, but just couldn't find the words to begin. Clement was such a picture of desolation she couldn't work out what she could say that might reach him.

In the end she was saved from her fruitless effort as the door to their cell banged open.

Chapter 22

There, standing in the doorway, was Tertius.

'What are you doing here?' Lydia and Clement rose to their feet as one.

'I've brought breakfast,' Tertius announced with a grin. He looked down at the pot of food he had brought with him. 'Artemis was worried about you, so it is more like *ientaculum* and *prandium* rolled into one, with leftovers for *cena* too.'

Lydia felt a little queasy with alarm. 'I should have left orders. Made sure everyone knew that you weren't to come. I can't believe Ruth let you. Surely she knew it was dangerous? She must have known that you could be arrested too. You should have stayed away!'

Tertius's grin widened. 'The glorious thing about no longer being a slave is that I can make my own bad decisions . . . all by myself. Those words in Paul's letter have been going around and around my head: "He emptied himself . . . form of a slave . . . to the point of death". When I woke up this morning I knew what they meant for me. Living Christ's story means really living it. It means making the choice to live his story to the full, even if you know that living it will make the future difficult.'

Clement stirred himself from his misery long enough to agree. 'I think you're right. Maybe that is what Paul has been doing all along. He is living the story too, even if it meant going to Rome in a prison ship.'

Tertius grinned. 'And he's found joy in it too.' He turned to Lydia. 'Yesterday you gave me freedom – freedom to choose

– and so I have chosen. I chose to come here. It's probably not very brave. The jailers have let me in and will probably let me out again. But what was important was that I *could* choose. It was the best gift anyone could have given me. You gave freedom to me, and in that freedom I choose to come and bring you food.'

'People looking for freedom don't often find it in prison!'

A voice behind him made Tertius jump, nearly dropping the large clay pot full of food, slightly belying the bravado of his words. Or maybe not, thought Lydia. She felt that she was learning a lot about bravery at the moment. Maybe it wasn't so much about not being afraid as about making the right choices no matter how you feel about them. Maybe it was about not letting fear rule your life.

'Share the food with us and there will be no danger in it for you at all.' The voice at the door came from the jailer who had brusquely, but not unkindly, locked them in the cell the night before. The 'us' turned out to be him and his two companions, who between them guarded the prisoners in the jail. The smell of Artemis' cooking had drawn them from their posts. Artemis' genius in the kitchen rivalled John's genius in the dyeing work-shop. The food was a simple porridge with a few vegetables and meat added, but Artemis had worked her usual magic with herbs and spices, and it transported those in that gloomy cell each to their own place of contentment and safety. In a few moments the only sounds to be heard in the cell were of contented slurping and licking of fingers. When they had finished, Tertius looked into the pot and announced, somewhat despondently, that the food he had brought, thinking it was enough for a whole day, was sadly finished.

'You'll have to take your life in your hands again,' said the jailer, winking at him, 'and bring more.'

And so he did, as did Alexandra and Syntyche, Ruth, Marcus and Rufus. Even Caius and Manius came occasionally with food for them all. Twice a day, Artemis sent them simple, delicious food, and with it came news of the community they had left behind. They were bright spots in otherwise dreary days. Ever since that first night in prison, Clement had changed from someone who saw joy everywhere into someone who showed no sign of seeing anything hopeful anywhere. Admittedly all he had to look at was a small, dank prison cell, but Lydia sensed there was something else going on. He had sunk into himself, barely speaking outside of the two visits a day from their friends. When they arrived, he would rally and play-act his old self, but in between he would sit, his face turned to the wall. Lydia tried time and time again to break through to him, suggesting that he was being too hard on himself, that he should look at things differently, but he merely grunted and turned his face away again. When she got desperate, Lydia even tried singing to him, but she felt self-conscious and her voice wavered and failed.

She looked at him hopelessly, at a loss as to what she could do or say to help. She was trying at all times to hang on to the sense of peace that she had felt on the way to the prison, with increasing levels of determination and desperation. She made a conscious decision to try to hold at bay the ravening horde of worries that snapped at the corners of her mind whenever she let them. What was she going to do about Clement? Would they ever get out of this prison cell? Would Aurelia succeed in destroying them all? What about her business? Was that now over? Had she let Ruth down? What about the followers of the Way? Would they survive this onslaught? Around and around her head these questions flitted. The more she tried to resist them the more they spun around, suggesting an unthinkable and unbearable future.

Then, suddenly, into her mind came a stray phrase from the letter Paul had sent them. It had struck her when she first heard Akiva read it out because it had felt so preposterous: 'Don't fret about anything, but in everything in prayer and entreaty with thanksgiving let your requests be known to God.' Lydia had chuckled to herself when she had first heard it. Telling her not to worry was like commanding the sun not to shine or dogs not to bark. You could try, but worrying had always come to her as naturally as breathing. Her sense of calm of a few days earlier was entirely out of character. She had learnt to live well *because* she worried. Every moment of every day she juggled hundreds of possible bad outcomes and made plans for how she would handle them. Little surprised her because she had worried so much in advance. She frowned in the half-light of the prison cell because in all her years of worrying, she had never even for a moment imagined herself here, facing ruin and who knew what else? Maybe that was why she had felt so serene; it was so far beyond her worst imaginings that all she could do was to take the next step and the next and see what would happen. And now that phrase from Paul came back to her again: 'Don't fret . . . in prayer and entreaty with thanksgiving.' She couldn't for a moment decide what was more difficult – not fretting or offering prayer with thanksgiving – but she had little else to do so decided to give it a go.

To begin with her mind remained blank. She looked around the small cell, at the dark walls, at the small window high up fitted with bars to prevent the escape of prisoners who might imagine scaling the wall to the small gap above them; at the corner where Clement sat unmoving; at the solid door barring her exit. There was nothing here to fuel thanksgiving.

But then she stopped. Her gaze went back to the door. Twice a day that door opened and through it came friends and family who cared enough about her and Clement to risk their own welfare to bring food. There was Clement, who, with Alexandra, had welcomed her back to Philippi with open warm hearts, forgiving her ten years of silence and absence as though it had been nothing at all. There was the barred window, and when she craned her neck she could see blue sky beyond and the hint of the sun shining. There were the walls . . . on second thoughts she could do nothing with the walls. The more she thought, the more other reasons for thankfulness flooded into her mind: Ruth, Marcus, Rufus and Tertius; John, and her father back in Thyatira; dear Euodia and Syntyche now reunited; Artemis and Epaphroditus; Jonathan and Akiva. She realised that she didn't have the strength to form her 'frettings' into words and so she just held them out in her mind, like the shards of pottery you might pick off the floor after a pot has been accidentally smashed.

She wasn't sure what she expected would happen, but when nothing did, she shrugged and went back to looking at the door, at Clement, at the window, and back again, remembering gratefully the happiness she used to know. She wasn't sure quite when it happened, and certainly not how it happened, but little by little Lydia became aware that she felt calmer. The questions that whirled around her mind moved more slowly and her worries felt less all-consuming. She reached for a word to describe how she felt and what came to her was another phrase from Paul's letter: 'and the peace of God which is beyond all our ability to think about will stand guard over your heart and mind in Christ Jesus.'

When she had heard Akiva read that out, it had brought to mind Jacob – her father's friend from Thyatira – who would talk time and time again of *shalom*: a sense of completeness, a wholeness that can only come from God. *Shalom*, he used to say, was more than an absence of conflict and war – though that would be very nice indeed. It was a sense of completeness, of togetherness in community. As she worked out how she felt now in that dark, dreary cell, Lydia realised that Jacob's word *shalom* fitted best. She felt a wholeness that really did defy her ability to think about it. She felt protected from all the 'frettings' that had bombarded her a few hours ago. She smiled, remembering the Paul who had inspired her all those years ago. His lessons might have been hard won through all the years of waiting in prison for a hearing with the emperor, but she was eternally grateful for them right now. She realised she was probably being fanciful after a few days locked away from the outside world, but, just for a moment, she felt as though Paul, from all those miles away, looked at her and nodded his approval. She shook her head and the moment was gone.

She added Paul to her list of thanksgivings and returned to holding Clement before God in prayer. It didn't happen right away – quite the opposite in fact – but a few days later, Lydia suddenly knew what she needed to do.

Chapter 23

Lydia realised that she needed to stop trying to find a solution to Clement's 'problem'. She'd come up with endless elegant ways to get him to see that he was looking at things all wrong. What she hadn't done was to sit with him and listen to him. She'd seen him as a problem to be solved rather than a person to be loved. She went and sat next to Clement. Clement didn't move, neither did Lydia. She sat, praying as she had done for the past few days, but this time making sure he knew she was there. After a long time – she had no idea how long, as time passed so oddly in that cell – Clement turned. 'What?' he asked brusquely.

'Nothing,' said Lydia. 'I just wanted you to know that you are not alone.'

Clement sighed deeply. 'I have never been more alone in my whole life.'

'You may feel alone . . . but you aren't.'

Clement made a small impatient sound and turned his face back to the wall.

Lydia made no comment, but continued to sit there with him.

Eventually Clement turned to her again. 'You can't help me.'

'Probably not,' she agreed, 'but I can make sure you don't imagine you are alone.'

Slowly, almost imperceptibly, Clement got used to her presence by his side, and then little by little began to talk. All those years ago, when he had met Paul and been baptised, he had put his old life behind him. He had turned his back on it all.

Although the new life was not perfect, he and Alexandra had embraced it with joy. Occasionally, often when he was tired at the end of the day, an odd memory would creep back in and haunt him with the recollection of the kinds of things he used to do to those in his care in the prison, but he would banish it with determination and turn back again to his new life. But coming back here – with all the uncertainty about what was going to happen, and then being locked into one of the cells he used to guard – had flooded his mind with too many memories for him to ignore.

Lydia sat and listened as he talked, blanching from time to time as she lived through the memories with him; even at second-hand they were hard to hear. After a long time, Clement stopped. 'I feel so ashamed,' he said. 'In the letter Epaphroditus brought, Paul spoke so boldly about where he came from: circumcised at precisely the right moment; belonging to the people of Israel; from the tribe of Benjamin; a Hebrew born of Hebrews. As a young man, he even *chose* right and became a Pharisee, the most devout of all forms of Judaism. And what did I do? I chose to be the scum of the earth, a jailer in a corrupt and unjust system. I have nothing to boast about at all.'

'I think you missed something,' said Lydia gently. 'I noticed it at the time. Something that just didn't fit in that list.'

'What do you mean?' asked Clement.

'Didn't he go on to say that in regard to zeal he was a persecutor of the church? It struck me as odd. I wonder whether Paul is as haunted by his past as you are. Even when he boasts, he can't stop himself reminding us that he is troubled by what he did.'

'Doesn't it just mean that he was the best Jew imaginable, persecuting Christians to prove his zeal for the faith?'

'Maybe,' said Lydia, 'though I'm not sure Jonathan and Akiva would class zeal quite like that. Their zeal seems to me to lead them to acts of kindness, not persecution. But I can't get over the feeling that being a persecutor of Christians doesn't fit on the list with everything else.'

Clement tipped his head, thinking about what Lydia had just said. 'I wonder how he lives with it?'

'He told us, I think,' said Lydia, casting around in her mind to remember exactly what Paul had written. 'Do you remember the bit where he said that he regarded his past as excrement?'

'Who could forget?' Clement's eyes twinkled for the briefest of moments, reassuring Lydia that the old Clement, who could find entertainment in the most bizarre of details, was still present beneath the layers of his current anguish.

'So that he could gain Christ and be found in him.'

'Yes,' said Clement, 'so that he wouldn't have a righteousness of his own that comes from the law, but one that comes through faith.'

'So . . .' Lydia was trying to work it out as she spoke, 'everything in the past, good or bad, counts for nothing. Who you really are, your relationship with God, comes from faith and nothing more, nothing less.'

Clement sighed. 'He made it sound so easy, but it isn't, is it? I'm sure his faith carries him everywhere he needs to go, but mine? My faith is as flimsy as a spider web. Today I'm not sure I've got any faith at all. If it all relies on how much I believe, I'm in worse trouble than you thought.'

Lydia felt seriously out of her depth, but battled on, aware of how important it all was. 'But did he mean *your* faith?'

'What on earth are you talking about? Who else's faith could he have meant?'

'He said a righteousness that comes through the faith of Christ. What if he meant your faith meeting Christ's own faithfulness? We know how faithful he was.'

'He obeyed orders even to the point of death, death on a cross.'

'So . . .' Lydia felt as though she was flailing around to put something into words she didn't quite understand herself '. . . if you believe, your faith is pulled into his endless faithfulness. We are drawn onwards together in the one who is faithful beyond all our imagining. Isn't the point that it isn't all on you? It isn't reliant on how much *you* believe or how *you* feel about it today or tomorrow. When you believe, you step into the stream of faith and are carried on the current of his faithfulness.'

'You're messing with my head,' said Clement.

'Not just yours,' said Lydia, and they lapsed into silence once more, but it was a different kind of silence. It was a lighter, less gloomy silence; more thoughtful and less brooding. She felt exhausted, but also surprised at herself. She had no idea that she had even thought those thoughts until she had started talking to Clement. A moment or two later Lydia heard the faintest hint of Clement humming, then singing: 'He obeyed orders even to the point of death . . .'

Their conversation must have taken longer than she thought because it wasn't long before the door banged open, revealing, unusually, Caius holding a pot of Artemis' delicious porridge. He had come a few times over the course of their sojourn in the prison, but nothing like as regularly as the others. The jailer and his helpers always followed the visitors in. It now went as read that they would share the food brought twice daily for Lydia and Clement. The small cell was crowded as they crammed into it, but they'd got used to it over the weeks and no longer noticed. They had stayed firmly on safe topics in their conversation as they ate together. Neither Clement nor Lydia had wanted to risk incriminating themselves further with their captors.

Today, however, they had barely begun to eat when the jailer, whose name they had learnt early on was Lucius and who was the one who now held the role that Clement used to have, said, 'What I don't understand is why you bring food every day, without fail. Some families do for their loved ones, though most prefer to stay away lest the shame fall on them too. But you aren't even related, and yet you come, one of you, twice a day. Don't get me wrong, I'm delighted you do. We all are.' His companions grunted their agreement through mouths full of food. 'What I don't understand is *why* you do it. Don't you care about the shame? People might hear that you are friends with a . . .' he flicked an embarrassed glance in the direction of Clement and Lydia, indicating he was aware of how rude he was being '. . . criminal, and your reputation would be in ruins.'

Caius stopped eating, threw his head back and roared with laughter. 'My reputation is already in tatters. I ruined it myself. Clement and Lydia and the whole wonderful community of those who follow Christ helped me to find myself, myself in Jesus Christ. I have gained far more than I ever lost. My reputation matters not a jot. I have something far more important than that.'

'Who is this Jesus Christ that you mention? Is he a new god?' the jailer asked.

And so they told him. They told him about his birth in Bethlehem, his life and teaching, his living and loving, his death and resurrection, his ascension into heaven and the sending of the Spirit.

'He isn't a new god,' Caius ended. 'He is *the* God.'

Clement began singing the hymn from Paul's letter softly at first and then more loudly and confidently. And then they had to begin the explanations all over again about why he had equality with God in the first place; why anyone would sacrifice status and power; why lowering himself – the most horrifyingly un-Roman thing you could imagine – was at the heart of it all. And most of all, why they all now sought to live Christ's story themselves.

It took a long time; the jailer kept on asking them to go back to the beginning again. In the end he shook his head in wonder. 'I can't understand why anyone would give up their honour and reputation for any reason. It's all you have to stand on in life. I don't see why this Jesus Christ gave it up, and I don't see why you would do the same. Look what happened to him!'

'Isn't that a rather shaky foundation, what others think about you?' Clement asked. 'Look at Lydia and me: our reputations are ruined not from anything we did, but because Aurelia took against us.'

'Aurelia takes against lots of people,' Lucius said. 'The prison would stand empty if it weren't for her.'

'Exactly,' said Clement. 'None of us has any control over what others think about us. Our reputations are here today and gone tomorrow. Caius ruined his himself; I lost mine when I met Paul right here in the prison; Lydia did nothing other than believe in Jesus Christ quietly in her home, but we've all of us lost our standing in the city. What I do have, however, I will never lose: I have status with God – a righteous status – not built on anything I have or haven't done, but built on faith.'

Lucius shook his head. The ideas were too big and too new for him. So they began again from the beginning. In the end he stood up and shook his shoulders.

'I don't know what to think. I can't decide if you are all mad or not.'

'We can talk again any time you like,' said Clement.

'I'm not sure we can,' said Lucius, looking at both Lydia and Clement with regret. 'I wish I'd asked you earlier now, but I didn't think to until I heard.'

'Heard what?' asked Lydia.

'You'll see,' said Lucius. 'Come on you, or you'll be locked in too.' He ushered Caius out of the small cell and the door banged shut behind them.

Chapter 24

Early the next morning, the heavy door to their cell banged open unceremoniously. Standing there were six lictors that towered over Lydia and Clement.

'Up you get,' their apparent leader said brusquely.

'Why?' asked Clement, still befuddled from sleep.

'Your trial. Today.'

Lydia thought that this lictor made John appear positively garrulous.

'But we've had no notice,' objected Clement.

In fact, Lydia thought, they had received a bit of notice, the jailer had hinted as much last night, but their tired brains had refused to let the information sink in and, in any case, now was not the moment to mention it.

'Our arguments are not ready. It's all wrong. It isn't fair,' Clement continued, a note of desperation in his voice.

The lictor shrugged his indifference. 'Keeping the magistrate waiting won't help your case. You can come or we can drag you, your choice.'

At this, Clement's defiance crumbled, and he and Lydia scrambled up quickly to follow the lictors from the cell. The cell, though not completely dark, had been lit by only one window high up in the wall, giving a constant twilight effect. As they walked into the bright Philippi morning, they blinked and shaded their eyes against the glare, struggling to focus on the familiar route. The lictors marched them briskly through the streets to the house of Decimus Licinius Crassus.

'That's strange,' whispered Clement. 'Why isn't the trial in the public buildings?'

Lydia knew so little about what was going on, she had no idea what counted as strange and what didn't. Once in the house, they were ushered through the vestibule and into the spacious atrium beyond. Similar in design to Lydia's house, this house took elegance to a new level. It was more than twice as large as Lydia's beloved atrium; its ceiling was lofty, lending a spacious airy feel, and its floors were covered in intricate mosaics featuring animals of all kinds. It was stylishly furnished with, Lydia observed, some of John's best work in shades of purple. On the other side of the pool that collected rainwater from the roof was an elaborate seat, also draped in purple from Lydia's shop, but, besides them and the lictors, the room was completely empty.

The lictors flexed their shoulders, folded their arms and stood, two behind them and two on either side, clearly settling in for a wait.

'Why were we brought so early? They aren't even here!' Clement reverted to his outrage of earlier.

The chief lictor shrugged, saying nothing. His face communicated that he couldn't be less interested if he tried.

Lydia laid her hand on Clement's arm. 'Hush,' she whispered, 'we'll gain nothing by antagonising them.'

'Why aren't you anxious?' Clement turned on her instead. 'What's wrong with you?'

Lydia paused for a moment to check that she wasn't fooling herself, covering up her anxiety with a layer of fabricated calm. She concluded that she might be – she'd find out later. For now, she felt as calm as she appeared.

'I don't see the point,' she said. 'We still don't know what will happen. I'll be anxious – I promise – when I know what I've got to be anxious about.' She thought for a moment, then added, 'Last time, I fled in terror before a baying mob. I ran all the way home and stayed there for ten years. I missed so much, and am determined never to do that again. This time I'm turning to face it. Whatever the future holds I can face with the peace of God surrounding me.' She paused again, feeling the need to be absolutely truthful. 'At least today I can. Ask me again tomorrow, I may have changed my mind then.'

'Today will do,' said Clement, smiling at her, 'and I'll stand with you.'

'I know you will,' said Lydia. 'That's what I missed by running away.'

Just then they heard the sound of raised voices coming from the back of the house. There was shouting, something smashed, a bit more shouting, and then there emerged into the garden a man. He didn't appear to have been the one shouting, or at least if he had, he had composed himself again right away. He was dressed as a magistrate, but he did not look as Lydia had expected Crassus to look. She had thought him to be a diminutive, nervous man; he had certainly appeared that way when seen at a distance across the marketplace. This man, however, did not appear to be either of those things. He was well built and clearly at ease with himself. He strode into the atrium with a confidence suggesting that nothing and no one could intimidate him. He nodded his greeting and introduced himself.

'My name,' he said, 'is Appius Horatius Valens, magistrate of this city. I've just been talking to my fellow magistrate, Decimus Licinius Crassus. He tells me that his wife has had two miscreants arrested for stealing a valuable bracelet. He is, he tells me, concerned that this whole case will tarnish his reputation. There are tales already of Aurelia taking his power for herself and of Crassus bending to her will.' The look on Valens's face suggested that he himself might be the source of a number of these stories. 'He is worried that this case will add to them. His honour, he thinks, is in jeopardy, and he hopes

LYDIA

that I will provide a way out. You may have heard our . . .' he paused and raised his eyebrows '. . . conversation?' Watching him, Lydia thought that he was enjoying the whole scenario far too much. 'I pointed out,' Valens continued, 'that since neither of you is a Roman citizen, it's unlikely that anyone would care what happened to you. But he pointed out that you and your servant, John I believe his name is, are the source of the finest purple in the whole of Macedonia, and that while those in Rome may not care, there are many in Philippi who would. Tell me,' he said, moving over to a couch to his left, 'did you produce this purple?'

'May I?' asked Lydia.

'By all means.' Valens beckoned her closer.

As she got closer, Lydia recognised the purple immediately. John had been experimenting and had produced a shade that even he had never managed before. A perfect blend of Tyrian purple and Turkey red, both vibrant and rich. 'Yes,' she said. 'It was an experiment, but a happy one I think.'

'My wife has been wanting this shade ever since Aurelia paraded it before her at a dinner party. If I let you go, will you make some for me?'

'I . . . I . . .' Lydia stammered and began shaking. She had thought she was ready for anything, but had not imagined this. She saw a trap closing around her. She didn't imagine for a moment that one bolt of cloth would be sufficient. If she agreed, she would be giving free goods to Valens for the rest of her life, but if she said no she would be committing both herself and Clement to a grim future. What should she do?

'Well?' said Valens. A flinty look on his handsome face indicated that he was accustomed to getting what he wanted immediately.

She cast about desperately for the right thing to say. She turned slightly and saw that Clement had followed her to the couch.

'I told you I'd stand with you,' he whispered in her ear. 'Or,' he said loudly, 'you could try us fairly for whatever crime we have been charged with.'

'Whatever gave you the idea that you have the right to be tried fairly for anything? After all, you aren't Roman citizens. I could have you flogged and thrown in prison before running you out of town – like your great hero Paul. Yes I know all about him – and, unlike him, you would have no one to appeal to . . . no one at all. You should look around you and grasp who has power and who does not.'

Again Lydia thought back to the hymn that Paul had sent in his letter. Here again the words of his hymn came back to her. Here again she understood what he had meant about emptying yourself and being obedient to the point of death. Everything in her screamed out that she should save herself, make any promise, accept any arrangement that would free her. But in her head Paul's phrases swirled around, suggesting that she should stand still and face the trouble before her; to do what she'd claimed to Clement a moment ago that she intended to do, to turn and look into the crisis rather than to run from it; to hold her head high and insist on justice even when there was little hope of it. She felt Clement straighten beside her and knew that he was thinking the same thing.

So she pulled her shoulders back, lifted her head, and said with as much dignity and formality as she could muster, 'We would prefer to be tried – fairly or not – for the accusation made against us. We will not beg or make a deal. Whatever decision you come to we will accept.'

Valens was dumbfounded. He was not used to encounters ending like this. What usually happened was that he made a few veiled threats. The people before him, knowing how much power he had, would beg and plead with him. He would then 'generously' offer them a deal that involved them giving him gifts or paying him money, and the case would be dismissed. He rarely ever actually tried a case. This was the deal he had struck with Crassus. He would bribe Lydia and Clement. The case would not be tried, and all would be well. The sound of shouting, which had drifted towards the atrium where Lydia and Clement were standing, had come from Aurelia, who had felt her influence over Crassus – and indeed the rest of wealthy Philippi – slipping away. She wanted what she saw as a vindication of her honour. She was not happy at the thought of Valens quietly and adeptly allowing her case to fold. If he did this, every time she found someone to pick on, who would fear her might in the future?

The problem was that the elite citizens of Philippi had suddenly discovered, somewhat to their surprise, that they did care what happened to this pair of lowly non-citizens. Or more accurately, they cared about what happened to one of them. They cared nothing for Lydia or Clement personally. They were supremely uninterested in their strange devotional practices – outside Rome there were endless odd cults – why should it trouble them? It would have been different if they were Roman citizens, but they weren't. Most of the nobles assumed that all non-citizens were contemptible, and nothing would surprise them about what they got up to. What they did care about, however, was the quality of Lydia's – and to a lesser extent Clement's – wares. Lydia might only have been back in Philippi for a few months, but already her reputation had spread far and wide. The nobles were already missing their purple cloth due to Aurelia's ban on them visiting Lydia's shop, and were concerned that Aurelia's antics were going to deprive them permanently of the finest purple to be bought outside Rome. Feared though Aurelia was, they all thought she had gone too far. So they had pressured Crassus to drop the charges. Crassus, caught between the outrage of his fellow nobles and the fury of his wife, had done what he did best: he had ducked, and handed the issue to Valens, whose corruption and love of bribery he trusted above all else.

What no one had accounted for was the integrity of Lydia and Clement. Their refusal to play the system put Valens in an impossible position. He would have to try the case. If he found them guilty, he risked the wrath of the nobles, not just in Philippi, but across Macedonia; if he found them innocent, Aurelia would never forgive him, and both Crassus and Aurelia would make his life a misery. Used as he was to a comfortable, pampered life in which everyone bowed to his command and gave him exactly what he wanted, he was ill-prepared to face two people who were willing to take a stand.

He frowned. 'I think I need to talk to Crassus,' he said.

Chapter 25

Before long the sound of raised voices could be heard once more, echoing through the house and bouncing off the high ceilings of the atrium. Lydia glanced at the ceilings speculatively, wondering how much of what went on in the 'private' parts of her house could be heard in the more public atrium. If she ever got out of here, she thought, she would make sure to find out. The lictors stood, feigning either a disinterest or an inability to hear, though Lydia suspected that they were listening as intently as they could to the argument in the rooms beyond.

After a considerable amount of time, three figures emerged from the back of the house. Valens, Crassus and Aurelia looked anxious, distraught and furious respectively. Crassus sank into the chair that was placed facing the entrance across from the rainwater pool and signalled to his servants to bring a second chair for Valens to sit in. It was noticeably less grand and, not located on a platform as Crassus's was, it was much lower too. Nevertheless, Valens sat straight, with his soldier's bearing, and Crassus – who was every bit as diminutive and nervous as Lydia had expected him to be – slumped as though already defeated in his chair. As a result, Valens's head was at a level with Crassus's, despite the difference in the height of the chairs.

'I accuse these two barbarians,' said Aurelia, her voice pulsating with wrath.

Valens raised his hand in a gesture intended to cause her to stop.

She took no notice, but raised her voice in tone and volume: '. . . of treason and of theft.'

Valens, seeing that he would need to interject, raised his voice to speak over hers. 'To my knowledge, they are not barbarians. Admittedly, they are not citizens.' His elegant aquiline features conveyed the disdain that this acknowledgement deserved. 'But,' he continued, 'because they are not citizens they cannot be accused of treason. They are by their nature un-Roman, so we cannot expect from them the standards we expect of Roman citizens. As I have already told you, we are here to try the accusation of theft and nothing more.' The tension between the two of them crackled, and Crassus sank deeper into his chair, despair written all over his face. He spent much of his time attempting to avoid conflict with ... well anyone ... but especially with his wife. This morning he seemed doomed to be dragged into a conflict that he could neither prevent nor control.

'Proceed with the allegation of theft,' said Valens. And so the subject of the argument they had just heard in the distance became clear to Lydia and Clement. Aurelia had wanted the trial to be about their Christian faith, and Valens had overruled. His decision to downgrade the trial from treason to theft meant that the focus would be on the bracelet and nothing more.

'They stole my bracelet,' Aurelia began.

'Describe it.' Valens was determined not to allow Aurelia to get into her stride and dominate the proceedings.

'Solid gold, fitted with rubies all around.'

Crassus raised his head. 'My mother's bracelet?'

Aurelia nodded. Crassus's face wrinkled with thought. 'But ...'

Aurelia glared at him, but Valens, sensing a source of potentially valuable information, said, 'Go on.'

Crassus sensed danger and shook his head. 'Nothing, I must be mistaken.'

But Valens was unyielding. 'Fellow magistrate, if you have information pertinent to this case, it is your duty to Rome, to the emperor and to your fellow citizens to declare it and to do so now.'

Crassus paled. He mumbled, 'I thought you were wearing it last night at dinner. I always notice when you wear it. It reminds me of her. When you said they had stolen your beloved bracelet, it didn't occur to me to think that you meant that one.'

Silence fell over the atrium. Lydia had never imagined that she would see Aurelia lost for words, but now she was. A range of emotions – embarrassment, horror, anger and, finally, resignation – passed over her face one after the other. 'I have two that look very similar,' she blustered.

But Crassus was unaccountably and suddenly unmovable. 'No, no you don't. You have only one. Did you think I wouldn't notice?'

'In any case,' Aurelia attempted to plough on regardless, 'I thought we would be discussing the real issue – their treason – not the minor matter of the theft.' It was becoming clear that Aurelia had used the supposed theft of the bracelet as a ploy to trigger Lydia's arrest, but had never really planned to try her for the crime. She had banked on trying Lydia for, what was in her mind, the greater crime of being un-Roman. She had known she could manipulate Crassus into making whatever judgement she wanted, and had never thought through the lesser accusation. Now, in front of Valens, who had no desire whatsoever to alienate his noble friends by banishing their beloved purveyor of purple, her flimsy case began to unravel.

Valens raised his hand and this time succeeded in cutting her off. Discomfited as Aurelia was, his commanding gesture was more than enough to stop her flow of words. He rose even higher in his seat. He had suddenly seen a way out of this impossible scenario with his dignity intact. It was a gift that he had no intention of letting slip through his grasp. He turned to Lydia and Clement.

'How long have you been in prison?'

Lydia was unsure – all the days in the dim, dreary cell had blended into one. 'A couple of weeks, maybe more?'

Clement agreed, 'A little more I think.'

'So,' and here Valens failed to conceal his enjoyment as a smile played around his lips, 'your accusation is that last night after your dinner, which I hear went on into the early hours, these two broke out of their prison cell, stole your bracelet and then locked themselves back in, without anyone noticing?'

'Of course not! They stole it on the day they were arrested.'

'I remember that day,' said Crassus, suddenly emboldened. 'I was here in the atrium the whole day. I had a number of clients to send on errands when they came for *salutatio*, and then I needed to talk to my steward from Rome who had come to discuss alterations to our Roman villa for when we return. I remember it because you came in at the end of the meeting and announced that you'd thought of a way to "get rid" of that pesky purple seller at last. But they didn't come to the house; I would have noticed.'

'Will you shut up,' Aurelia snapped. Things were going from bad to worse. Her tale was crumbling, not only with the gleeful help of Valens, but, now it appeared, with the assistance of her own husband too. Having, reluctantly, told the truth a moment ago, he now appeared unable to stop.

'So how did they steal it from you?' asked Valens, attempting to look innocent as he sprung what he knew was a fatal trap.

'My maid took it with her when she went to buy purple from their shop. They stole it from her then.'

This caused Crassus to sit bolt upright in his seat. 'What was your maid doing with my mother's precious bracelet?'

'She . . . I . . . she . . .' Aurelia stammered, backed into a corner with no apparent way out.

In the many idle moments available to her over the past weeks, Lydia had always wondered how Aurelia would explain

LYDIA

the arrival of the bracelet in her shop. It was so clearly a set-up.
Everyone involved had known it was. Even the lictors who had
come to arrest her had done nothing to conceal that they knew
what the plan was. In less sanguine moments, she had assumed
that everyone would know that it was a fiction, but wouldn't
care. Now she allowed herself a glimmer of hope. Perhaps they
would care. Perhaps the deceit would be revealed for what it
was.

Valens clicked his fingers at the lead lictor. 'You! Where was
the bracelet when you found it?' he asked.

The lictor looked scared and muttered something inaudible.

'Speak up!' By now, Valens was enjoying himself too much to
allow any element of this unfolding drama to pass unnoticed.

'We . . . didn't . . . find it.' Looking between Aurelia and
Valens, he was barely able to squeeze the words out. His expression indicated that he was unsure which of these two personali-
ties battling it out before his eyes frightened him more.

'It wasn't there?'

'It might have been, but we couldn't find it.'

'So to recap, you arrested a woman – and her friend – for
stealing a bracelet you didn't find, when she had not been to the
accuser's house, nor the accuser to hers. The only connection
was a maid who should not have had possession of the bracelet
at all. Am I right?'

The lictor mumbled again.

'AM I RIGHT?' Valens rose to his feet and bellowed his
question.

'Yes, yes you are right.'

'I have to ask . . .' Valens's tone altered again – from razor
sharp questioning to righteous anger, to light but curious
conversation. 'How did the bracelet come to be back in your
possession?' he asked Aurelia.

'It just reappeared,' said Aurelia. 'One day it wasn't there
and the next it was.'

'And you didn't think that this might affect your accusation? That we might struggle to believe a story that two people stole a bracelet from your maid, who should not have had it in her possession, only to return it to you the next morning, from their prison cell, so that you could wear it whenever you chose?'

'I . . .' said Aurelia. She looked to Crassus for help, but he shrugged and turned his face away. Crassus's desire was for life to be as smooth and untaxing as possible. The way he had learnt to achieve this was to line up behind the strongest power in the room. Until now that power had always been Aurelia, but the events of the past ten minutes had changed that. There was a new power in the room, and Crassus was not going to challenge it, not even for his wife.

Valens, consummate performer that he was, let the silence hang for a moment, and then another moment. In that silence, the strength of Valens's newfound power was established and then reinforced.

Crassus turned away from his wife.

Aurelia was flushed, her defeat showing in her cheeks.

The lictors looked anxiously at Valens lest his wrath turn back on them. But Lydia and Clement stood a little taller, a glimmer of hope beginning to grow and take shape. Lydia glanced at Clement and saw her own emotions mirrored in his face. Her gaze turned back to Valens and her heart lurched with fear. As a child she had watched a boy play with a mouse he had caught in a trap. He let it out and allowed it to scurry away from him, but then, quick as a flash, he grabbed its tail and dangled it in the air before dropping it and allowing it to scramble away again. This had gone on for nearly an hour before he finally killed it. Lydia had never forgotten the look on his face while he did this. It was a look of pure, gleeful power. When she had turned back to Valens she had seen that same look – the look of someone who knew how much power he had, but who gained enjoyment from allowing his victim to imagine they might escape before crushing their hopes time and time again.

He held her gaze for a few moments. 'You should just have given me the purple.' He paused as though deciding what he might do, watching both Lydia and Clement lazily through half shut eyes. He seemed to be waiting for something. Lydia wasn't quite sure what it was, but knew that whatever it was she mustn't give in to him. She lifted her head, threw back her shoulders and held his gaze.

'You could beg,' he said at last.

'No, we couldn't,' replied Lydia.

'I don't think so,' said Clement at exactly the same moment.

'Suit yourself.' He shook his head in mock bemusement and clicked his fingers at the lictors. 'Flog them, then let them go.'

Chapter 26

'That's not fair!' shouted Clement.

Valens's lips twitched with triumph. 'He who has the power decides what is fair.' He looked around the room. 'I think we can agree that in this situation I am the one with the power?' The lictors nodded their agreement eagerly.

'But we have done nothing!' Clement protested.

'I think that you did do something,' Valens responded, enunciating his words carefully and with emphasis, his sharp eyes searching their faces for clues. 'You know something about that bracelet that you haven't yet said. You could tell me if you like.' He folded his hands over his stomach and tapped his two index fingers together.

Clement and Lydia exchanged a swift look. He was, of course, right. They *had* seen the bracelet. They *had* handled it and *had* sent it away with Caius and Manius. But Caius and Manius were Roman citizens. If they were brought into this, the charge of 'un-Roman-ness' that they had escaped by being so unimportant could stick to Caius and Manius instead. Valens raised his eyebrows in challenge. Lydia realised that he had been setting a trap, not just for Aurelia, but for them too. He had known that there was more going on than was being reported, and now he had them in his grip. Either they accepted their fate or they incriminated their friends. Like the mouse-torturing boy from Lydia's childhood, he was holding them high in the air by the tail as they scrabbled for freedom.

'Well?' he asked.

'We will accept the punishment.' Clement bowed his head in defeat.

'Of course you will,' Valens agreed, 'and if I find out how you did it, you – and your friends – will suffer my retribution.' He cracked his knuckles gleefully, leaving no one in any doubt as to which outcome he hoped for. 'Take them,' he said.

'How's that feeling of peace now?' Clement asked her, as they were hustled from Crassus's house to the middle of the forum.

'Strangely, well intact.' Lydia was surprised at herself. She looked back on those long months when she had worried so much about the many things that could go wrong in her life. Now the worst was upon her, she felt remarkably calm. Thinking about what might happen was far more stressful than facing it when it did happen. 'Take courage, dear friend,' she said. 'Stand firm in faith.'

'You too,' whispered Clement, his voice full of fear. He, unlike her, had seen many floggings and their aftermath. There was, she thought, a certain blessing that came with ignorance.

Later, when she tried to recall what happened next, she found that the events had joined together into one long, painful blur. There were the heckles of the crowd; the familiar smells of the market stalls overlaid with the metallic tang of her own fresh blood. There were the grunts of the lictors as they brought down their rods time and time again. There was screaming – hers or Clement's she couldn't tell – and there was pain, a pain so bitter and sharp her mind would skitter away from it every time she tried to recall it. And then, after what seemed like an eternity, there was silence.

She was untied and dropped unceremoniously to the ground. A moment later she was lifted gently and lovingly, soothing words and whispers of reassurance sounding in her ears as she was carried swiftly through the streets. Then there was pain again as something was spread gently but firmly on her back.

She was held up briefly to drink a bitter-tasting liquid, and then sleep took her. Her sleep was fitful and her dreams populated with Valens's malevolently triumphant smile and Aurelia's screeching accusations. The phrase 'you should have just given me the purple' swirled around and around, but, in her dream, every time she went to get the purple, the shelves of the shop were bare save for hundreds of golden bracelets that rattled at her provocatively. From time to time she was held up again as she was given another bitter-tasting drink, and then there was the searing pain on her back once more as someone spread a strong but not unpleasant smelling ointment on her flayed skin. Then sleep would come again.

Eventually, she woke, clear-headed but stiff. She raised her head from the bed on which she had been lying face down, feeling the muscles in her neck cramp from lack of use, and saw that she was in her own bedroom.

'She's awake. Euodia, she's awake,' Ruth's voice cried in her ear, causing her to start with its nearness.

All at once the room was filled with people, their voices talking above her, expressing their worry for her condition and their relief that she was now awake. She found she was unable to lift her head far enough to see them, but recognised the voices of Ruth and Euodia, Syntyche and Artemis, Marcus, Rufus and Tertius. Outside the door she heard more voices, but all of a sudden she felt overwhelmed, unable to take it all in, so she put her head down again and closed her eyes and drifted back into sleep. This time, however, her sleep was more peaceful and her dreams less disturbed. The next time she woke, the room was quiet. She lifted her head and saw Ruth, sitting next to her on a straw pallet, her head lolling in sleep.

As she moved, Ruth's eyes snapped open. 'You're awake again.' She smiled. 'We were worried about you for a while. You've been asleep for days.'

'Clement?' Lydia's parched lips would barely move.

'Clement is fine. He woke up yesterday and has started singing again. If you listen carefully you might just hear him.'

Lydia strained her ears and then smiled. Very faintly she could hear Clement's voice in the distance: 'form of God . . . a thing to be clung to . . . form of a slave . . . death on a cross . . .'

'He's here? Can I see him?'

Ruth smiled. 'Yes, Euodia decided it was easier to care for you both under the same roof. She has been working so hard, what with you both, and Epaphroditus. She's been teaching me some of her skills so I can help, but no, you can't see him. She's anxious not to disturb the cuts on your backs. You need to stay still for another few days at least until they heal a bit better. Clement is already protesting about the inactivity. Poor Alexandra is going to have a tough time ahead keeping him still. At least my patient is more biddable.' She looked at Lydia fiercely. Lydia subsided right away, cherishing the awareness that, for now at least, their roles had reversed and there was nothing for her to do but receive the care Ruth was offering.

'I'll be good,' she said faintly.

'You will indeed,' agreed Ruth.

'So what happened?' she asked Ruth, aware that there was little else she could do.

'I would say make yourself comfortable, but I imagine that will be difficult,' said Ruth. 'So I'll begin anyway.'

'I'm going nowhere,' said Lydia.

'Too right you aren't. Now put your head down; you'll get a crick in your neck.'

Lydia meekly obeyed.

'We all gathered together on the day you were arrested and prayed and prayed. We were desperate to help, but knew there was nothing we could do. I was jealous of the others who were able to bring you food. I wanted to go so much, but they wouldn't let me.'

'I should think not!' said Lydia with as much vehemence as her battered body would allow. 'It would have been far too dangerous for you.'

Ruth looked as though she wanted to argue, but then thought better of it and carried on. 'In the end there was something I could do. Once you had been arrested, people started coming back to the shop. It was as though Aurelia had lost her power. Everyone who had been staying away suddenly came back. They came in droves, all through the day. John and Marcus spent nearly all their time in the workshop creating new dyes and dying endless bolts of cloth. Akiva gave up painting and worked with Tertius selling the dyes, while Rufus and I sold cloth. The one thing you don't have to worry about is money. We have made so much in the past week you could shut up shop for months without a care in the world.'

Lydia reflected ruefully that money had been – and continued to be – the least of her troubles, but she decided not to share this thought with Ruth.

'Next door, Alexandra and Caius also worked hard selling trinkets and other items. Our businesses were thriving. Then a few nights ago Caius came running back from the prison saying that your trial would be the next day.'

'How did he know?' Lydia asked.

'Apparently the jailer said something,' Ruth replied. 'Caius thought you hadn't realised what he'd said, but he did and rushed home to tell us. We went back early the next morning and watched as you were marched from the prison to Crassus's house. You didn't notice us. We thought you looked as though you were in a daze.'

Lydia chuckled, but stopped suddenly as pain shot through her back. 'I felt so peaceful that day – as though I could face anything at all.'

'And you did,' said Ruth.

'Yes I did. After all those months and years of terror, worrying about all the terrible things that might happen to us, something awful did happen, and I faced it. I feel as though I wasted a lot of time with all that worry. When at last something truly bad happened, I discovered I had the strength to endure it after all.'

Ruth went quiet for a bit. 'I should have come with you,' at last she burst out. 'I'm meant to be the one who goes wherever you go. I promised you I would. We named me Ruth because of it, but when the moment came I froze. I couldn't move. Clement stepped in, but I let you down.' Her voice wavered as she allowed the tears to flow.

'No!' Lydia was horrified by what Ruth had said. 'No one, least of all me, expected you to get yourself arrested too. What a terrible thought. We ran away last time to keep you safe. Whatever gives you the idea that I would, for a moment, have wanted you to come to prison with me?'

'I always imagined myself to be brave.' Ruth's voice still wobbled. 'But when it came to it, I wasn't.'

Lydia wished heartily that she was able to lift her head and look properly at Ruth, but her back hurt so badly she was simply unable to. She reached out her hand instead and blindly found Ruth's. 'Dear one,' she said, 'I think you are mistaking bravery for foolhardiness. Bravery isn't seeking out danger. It isn't putting yourself in the way of danger simply to prove you are brave. That is foolhardy. Bravery is facing what you need to face and doing it with courage. This trial was mine to face, and, it turned out, Clement's as well. It was not yours. One day you will have to face your own crisis. When you do, I think we will find you are every bit as brave as you imagined yourself to be.'

Ruth grasped Lydia's hand tightly – it was the only part of Lydia she could hold without fear of hurting her – and sobbed out her anxiety and heartache; her guilt and her fear. Lydia held on to her, wishing she could wrap her up in an embrace as she used to when Ruth was smaller. After a while, Ruth's sobs subsided a little, the occasional hiccup indicating that the worst of the storm had passed. So Lydia felt able to ask, 'The thing I've been wanting to know ever since the trial is how did Aurelia get her bracelet back?'

'What do you mean?'

'It was what made Aurelia's case fall apart. It turns out it was Crassus's mother's bracelet, and Aurelia had worn it to a dinner the night before, and Crassus had recognised it. It all came out in the trial. I wondered at the time how Caius and Manius managed it.'

'I've no idea,' said Ruth. 'Caius and Manius wouldn't say. They said it was better if we didn't know. But wait . . . they found you innocent? They flogged you, even though they knew you were innocent?'

Chapter 27

'I can't believe they still flogged you.'

Lydia's heart lifted as she listened to the outrage in Ruth's voice. She might be blossoming into a mature and thoughtful adult, but her sense of right and of justice remained as fully intact as it had been when she was a child. For Ruth, things were simple – either they were right and just or they were wrong and unjust. Nothing lay between the two. One day, Lydia thought, she would learn that life has more contrasts and shading than that, but for now her heart rejoiced in Ruth's unwavering indignation.

'They did it because they could . . . and to teach us a lesson about the power of Rome, or rather the power of Valens, who is Rome here as far as we're concerned. I think he wanted to send a message to Philippi, and we were it.'

'So Aurelia won in the end after all,' Ruth said.

'Oh, I don't think she won, whatever winning looks like here. Flogging isn't what she had in mind for us. I think she was hoping to get us driven out of town. I saw her face when Valens sent us to be flogged; she was disgusted. I think we'll find that she lost more than we did.'

'More than the skin off your back?'

'It will heal.' Lydia surprised herself again at how phlegmatic she could feel about the whole episode. 'But Aurelia has lost something far more important – to her at least. She used to rule this city. Crassus and Valens may have been the magistrates, but she was the one everyone feared. The fear of being shamed by Aurelia kept everyone in check, but now she has been shamed.

She clung to her status with every last ounce of her strength, and now it is gone. The story of our trial won't stay secret for long. I imagine it is spreading through the forum and around the tabernae as we speak. It won't be long before we hear news of her departure.'

'So we have nothing to worry about any more.' Ruth breathed a sigh of relief.

'Well, I wouldn't say that,' said Lydia.

'You're wearing her out.' Euodia bustled into the room with a pot of the strong-smelling ointment that Lydia remembered from her fitful dreams.

'She was about to tell me something really important,' exclaimed Ruth, revealing the briefest glimpse of her younger self in the vehemence of her frustration.

'Tomorrow will do. Now Lydia must sleep. Come help me.'

Together they began spreading the ointment on her back. It was agony at first, but very soon its soothing power began to work and Lydia felt her eyelids get heavy. She slept soundly and only woke the next morning when Euodia came in to apply the ointment once more.

Euodia expressed her satisfaction with her handiwork – speaking largely to Lydia's back – and then declared Lydia well enough to get up. She expertly applied bandaging to Lydia's wounds, all the while adding caveats to her permission to rise: she should not tire herself out; should not make any sudden movements; should not lean on her back (Lydia thought this an unnecessary instruction, but nodded her assent anyway); should make sure her linen tunic didn't stick to the bandages. On and on the instructions went, and soon Lydia stopped listening. The torrent of instruction was strangely comforting as it swirled around her. Eventually, Euodia was finished, both with the bandages and with the caveats, and helped Lydia carefully to her feet. Though unsteady at first, with Euodia's help she shuffled out to the garden, where she found Ruth, John,

Marcus, Rufus, Tertius, Artemis and Epaphroditus, Syntyche, Clement and Alexandra, Caius and Manius, and even Jonathan and Akiva, all waiting for her.

'I said you couldn't all be here,' Euodia scolded them. 'You'll wear her out.'

Their smiling faces beamed back at her without a hint of repentance.

'We know what you said,' said Caius, 'but we didn't expect you to think that we would listen. Our beloved Lydia has suffered and come back to us, and we couldn't let that happen without celebrating her return.'

They moved apart to reveal a chair well stacked with cushions between two similar chairs, one already containing Clement and the other Epaphroditus.

'We got a chair ready for you,' Ruth said somewhat redundantly as she helped Lydia to sit down and settled her carefully with cushions so that she could sit upright with her back away from anything that might touch it.

For a while there was a hubbub of greetings and care expressed. The phrases 'we were so worried'; 'we prayed every day'; 'I'm so glad you're all right; 'we missed you' hung in the air as each person tried to express what they felt, but all at once.

It wasn't long before Euodia signalled that it was enough. 'I will not have you tiring my patients,' she said sternly. 'Go back to your work.' And so in ones and twos they drifted away.

'We're going to make dye to replace all that we sold while you were in prison,' said Marcus, his eyes shining with excitement as he went with John off to the workshop.

'Artemis is teaching me to cook,' whispered Rufus as he followed in Artemis' footsteps to the kitchen. Syntyche followed to offer any assistance they might need.

Akiva and Tertius stood awkwardly in front of Lydia. 'We will take care of your shops until you are well again, but I have been learning how to make mosaics and would like to take

Tertius as my apprentice, with your permission. He has a remarkable skill.'

Lydia looked enquiringly at Tertius. His pleading eyes told her all she needed to know.

'You don't need to ask my permission,' she said. 'Tertius is free.'

'We know,' said Akiva, slipping into Marcus and Rufus's old habit of speaking for Tertius, 'but we would like your blessing.'

'You have it,' smiled Lydia.

'One more thing.' Akiva looked anxious. 'May we begin by building you a mosaic into the floor of the atrium? I thought maybe a shepherd with his sheep?'

'That's a wonderful idea. Yes, yes you may.'

Ruth leant over and grasped Lydia's hands. 'The boys are growing up.'

Lydia looked at her, temporarily lost for words. This was her little Ruth, only five years their senior, now so grown up herself.

Alexandra signalled to Clement she was going to the shop next door. Clement began to struggle to his feet.

'Oh no you don't,' said Euodia. 'You have to rest a few more days first.'

Clement's face creased with frustration and concern.

'We'll go and help in a minute or two,' Caius said, indicating Manius who was beside him, 'after we've had a moment to catch up.'

'This resting is getting tedious,' grumbled Clement.

'How long have you been up and about?' Lydia asked Clement, surprised.

'Since yesterday. It seems that my back is tougher than yours. Either that or I was driving people mad with my singing. I think Euodia thought that if I was out here talking to the infinitely wise Epaphroditus, I couldn't be singing or grumbling.'

'The thought did cross my mind,' said Euodia with a hint of

the twinkle that Lydia remembered from when she had first known her. 'Though,' she added tartly, 'even I prefer the singing to the grumbling.'

Clement grinned, accepting her rebuke with good grace. Lydia was relieved to observe signs of the old, light-hearted Clement she now knew so well, rather than the gloomy, self-critical Clement of their prison cell.

'What did you talk about without me?' asked Lydia, attempting to distract Clement from his need for activity.

'I asked Caius and Manius how they got Aurelia's bracelet back to her,' Clement said, 'but they wouldn't tell me without you being here.'

'Perhaps it would be better if you don't tell us at all.' Lydia's sense of ease disappeared in an instant as she remembered with foreboding the look on Valens's face as he sent them off to be flogged.

'Whatever do you mean?' asked Alexandra.

'I think Caius and Manius are in danger,' said Lydia. 'Valens told us. Maybe it would be better if we just don't know.'

'This was what you were about to tell me last night, isn't it?' asked Ruth.

'Yes.' Lydia took a slightly ragged breath. It appeared that her newfound peace only stretched to what might happen to her – threats to her friends were as terrifying as ever. 'Valens has said that if he ever finds out how Aurelia got her bracelet back he will bring down retribution on the perpetrators. You both are Roman citizens; your punishment would be much greater than ours. You could be banished.'

'Don't worry,' Caius said, 'he won't find out.'

'We were very careful,' added Manius. 'But even if he does find out and banish us, we're both seasoned travellers, so we'll be fine. Just you see.'

'Why don't we tell them what happened?' said Caius to Manius. 'It might ease Lydia's concern.'

'What about my concern?' said Clement, in mock outrage.

Caius said, 'You are covering it well, old friend.' They all laughed. An easy camaraderie re-established between them after the trauma of the previous days.

'You see, Aurelia's steward is an old friend of mine,' said Caius. 'I used to sell him stuff back in the day.' Here he nodded at Ruth, indicating he meant back in the day when he owned her as a slave.

Ruth winked at him. 'Best not to think too much about that.'

'I try not to, but very occasionally I have to. Aurelia's steward recognised me after I came back, and we would spend evenings in the taberna, on the occasions when Aurelia had gone out to disparage someone else's banquet rather than throw one herself. His life in Aurelia's villa has been miserable for years. He is charged with maintaining the most extravagant lifestyle imaginable. He thought it would be fun, but it is not. Money and cruelty rule his life. He is expected to hand down punishments for the smallest offence, and often receives them himself. We talk about how hopeless it feels for him every time we meet. He loathes Aurelia and was delighted to help us. We took the bracelet to him and he slipped it back inside Aurelia's jewellery casket. No one will ever find out.'

'But what if they do? What then?' asked Lydia

'Then we'll face the consequences with, I expect, approximately half the courage that you did,' said Manius.

'I might manage a quarter of it,' said Caius.

Manius reached out and touched Lydia very lightly on the shoulder. 'Don't let Valens knock you off course,' he said gently. 'You don't live in his world like we do. You just serve Roman citizens in your shop; we are citizens. We, Romans, have been watching Valens for months. Everyone knows that he has been looking for ways to gain power over Crassus. This whole incident has given him an unforeseen advantage, and he will use it. We are pawns in his deadly game. He may forget about us, or he may not, but we can't be held hostage by his ambition. What he was trying to do was to sow seeds of doubt and fear in your mind. Don't let him.'

'Clement tells us you wouldn't do a deal with him to drop the charges,' Caius chipped in. 'I wish I could have been there to see his face. He would have hated that so much. Aurelia exercised power by shaming people whenever she could; he does it by holding something over them and making them pay somehow to forget it. I was talking to someone only the other day who is being bled dry by Valens in return for keeping his secret safe. You did the right thing, you really did.'

'My advice,' said Manius, 'is to put him out of your mind. Don't fret, and let the peace of God guard your heart.'

Lydia looked at him, surprised. 'That's what Paul said.'

Chapter 28

M anius grinned. 'Guilty as charged. I've been reading and rereading Paul's letter ever since you both were taken to the prison. It kept coming back into my mind. After you were taken away, the phrase wouldn't leave me. So I went back to the letter to look again. In the end I went back to Akiva so often, he copied one for me. What struck me when I heard Akiva reading the letter out loud to us was that Paul's advice came directly from his own experience, of how to cope when the world around us looks uncertain and frightening – like it does now. He's learnt so much, inside his prison cell, about how to live when the world spins out of control, and it seemed to me that he was trying to pass his experience on to us. I didn't understand it at first, but when you were both in prison it suddenly made sense. There's a passage that I think is important just before the poem – you know, the one Clement's been singing so much that none of us can get it out of our minds.'

'We know.' Ruth grinned. 'I woke up singing it this morning!'

Manius reached into the folds of his tunic and pulled out an already dog-eared scroll. He spent a moment rolling and unrolling the scroll until he found the right spot. 'Here it is,' he said, and began to read. ' "If there is any reassurance in Christ; if there is any comfort in love; if there is any companionship in the Spirit; if there is any compassion and kindness, top up my joy by thinking the same thing, by having the same love, being united, thinking a single thing." '

'That is all very well,' said Syntyche, 'but I don't understand what it means. Surely Paul knows that we don't think the same thing. We never have. Why would he tell us to do something that's impossible? We couldn't even think the same thing about whether to send him money or not. Only a few weeks ago, before Euodia came back to us, we had drifted so far apart we didn't even notice that Euodia had moved to a new city.'

'And anyway,' said Ruth, picking up Syntyche's theme, 'how would we decide the one thing we're allowed to think? Who gets to decide who is right and who is wrong? It seems crazy to me.' Ruth became more and more agitated as she spoke. Lydia thought fondly that she had always had an independent mind. Telling Ruth to think what someone else wanted would be like telling her to change the colour of her eyes at will. It simply couldn't be done.

She laughed. 'The day you agree with anyone just because you feel you should will be an unusual day indeed.'

Ruth grinned back at her. 'I didn't say I was planning on doing it any time soon. But I wish I could understand what Paul was talking about.'

Manius nodded. 'I know what you mean. I puzzled over that myself for ages, and then it came to me. I think Paul does go on to say what he means. Listen . . .'

They waited expectantly.

'Sorry,' Manius said, 'I lost my place. Ah, here we are. "Don't act from selfish intrigue or vanity, but in humility regard others as better than yourself. Don't look out for your own concerns, but let each person look out for the concerns of others." See?'

'No not really,' said Ruth.

'I think I do,' said Caius slowly. 'Aurelia and Valens are locked in a dangerous battle over who has the most power. They will do anything to defeat the other one. Anyone and anything will be used as ammunition if it gives them an advantage. Valens has won for now, but he will be watching his back waiting for Aurelia – or someone else – to take him down.' He paused, his head on one side, a thoughtful look on his face. 'I realise now that this is who I used to be. It consumed me. I'd have done anything to end up on the top of the pile. The problem is that there's always another pile, always someone above you. It never ends. What Paul is talking about here is another way of being. If we genuinely do believe that Jesus Christ has changed the world, if we know what love is, if we understand companionship in the Spirit, if we want to stand up for compassion and kindness, there is only one thing for us to do. We stand together. We don't celebrate ourselves and our own worth, we celebrate each other. Paul isn't talking about us agreeing with each other all the time. He is talking about standing shoulder to shoulder, side by side, supporting each other when we need it, rejoicing in each other's strengths, not in our own.'

'I've never heard you so passionate!' smiled Manius.

Caius grinned back at him. 'It's nice to have something important to be passionate about. I used to be passionate about making money and obsessed about what other people thought of me. Then Julius stole all my money and I squandered my reputation. I was left with nothing. It took me a while to work it out, but I know now that I've wasted so much of my life on things that don't last.'

Euodia cleared her throat, pointedly.

Caius took the hint. 'I think it is time for us to go.'

'And me,' said Ruth. 'Will you be all right?'

'I'll look after them, all three of them,' said Euodia sternly.

Clement, who struggled to keep still for very long, rose with them and started pacing around the garden humming under his breath.

'Good luck,' winked Ruth to Lydia as she left.

It didn't take Lydia long to realise, however, that she was not the focus of Euodia's concern, nor indeed was Clement. It was Epaphroditus whom she kept on popping into the garden to check on, a look of concentration on her face as though she was listening attentively for something. Lydia, alert to her concern, began listening too. Although Epaphroditus appeared cheerful and at ease, there was a slight rattling noise that happened every time he breathed.

After a while she said, 'Are you quite recovered from your illness?'

Epaphroditus turned to her, a thoughtful look on his gentle face. 'No,' he said, looking at her keenly. 'I think you have noticed that I am not?'

Lydia inclined her head to him, accepting the truth of his statement. He flicked his eyes to Euodia and back to Lydia again. 'Euodia knows, but the others don't yet. I think this is my last spring. The illness I caught in Rome has a firm grip on me. I feel my heart fluttering inside me. I struggle more every day to breathe. Before long, I will go to be with Christ.' He took what sounded like a long, painful breath. Lydia glanced at him, but his face did not seem to match his words. On his face was a look of profound joy.

'I don't understand,' she said. 'Aren't you sad?'

He smiled at her, a look of gentle contentment in his eyes. 'Of course I am, but I'm also joyful. I'm sad to leave my beloved friends. I worry about Artemis; she will miss me more than anyone – you will look after her, won't you?' He leant forward in his concern, and Lydia noticed how hard this simple movement was for him.

'Of course,' Lydia agreed. 'I can't imagine life without her now.'

'Nor she without you,' Epaphroditus said. 'I can't thank you enough for caring for her. I worried about her all the time when I was in Rome. When I heard that Alexander had died, I worried even more. Then I heard that you had returned and she had come to live here. I hoped, then, that she had found a family to love.'

'She has,' Lydia said, 'but she'd rather have you, I think.'

Epaphroditus nodded. 'I think she would. Actually I think she'd like to have both of us. And I would love to stay for her, but my ailing body has other ideas.' A look of contentment settled back on his face.

'Aren't you afraid?' Lydia asked bemused.

'A little, but only with the kind of fear I felt when I set off to Rome to take the gift to Paul. The unknown is always a little frightening.'

'But death is surely so much more than a bit unknown?'

Epaphroditus tipped his head on one side and thought for a moment. 'Maybe, but I'm not sure it's that unknown. I might be wrong, but it'll be too late by then for me to let you know!' He turned to Lydia, a twinkle in his eye. 'I feel as though I'm facing a grand new adventure, like I did when I went to see Paul.'

Lydia smiled back at him, but shook her head slightly; seeing death as an adventure was a little beyond her grasp. 'I don't understand,' she said. 'You knew who Paul was when you went.'

'Only a little. I hadn't met him in person like you had. I only knew him in other ways – in his letters, through his friends, in stories people told me about him. I knew the key features of my visit – where I was going and why – but I didn't know the details. Strangely, this feels very similar. This time, I'm departing to be with Christ. I've never met him in person, but I know him in other ways.'

Lydia nodded. It still seemed strange, but it did make sense to her. 'Did Paul talk about dying?'

Epaphroditus nodded. 'He knows that the moment of his death is never that far away: his health is fragile; his enemies are circling; if his trial before the emperor goes wrong he might be executed. But he is at ease whatever happens.'

'I got the impression in his letter,' mused Lydia, 'that he might prefer to die?'

Epaphroditus wrinkled his forehead in thought. 'I think it is a bit more complex than that. He is tired, that is for certain. His imprisonment has been long; his strength – even Paul's great strength – is waning. His enemies loom large in his mind – you saw that in his letter?'

'We all did.'

Epaphroditus pulled a sympathetic face. 'Poor Jonathan and Akiva, it was hard for them to hear.'

'They'll recover. I can see how easy it would be for Paul to imagine that those who hold fast to their Jewish heritage might all react to his message in the same way.'

'It is certainly understandable, but not, perhaps, kind.'

'No, indeed,' Lydia was forced to agree. 'He could certainly have been more kind.'

'I think,' said Epaphroditus, 'that Paul feels profoundly responsible for the Gospel. So he is tired, bone tired, but he doesn't feel as though he is quite finished yet.'

'Do you?' asked Lydia, conscious of what Epaphroditus had told her a few moments before. 'Do you feel finished?'

Epaphroditus started a little. 'That is a rather harshly phrased question.'

'Sorry. I didn't mean it to come out quite like that. It was the way you phrased what you said about Paul that made me wonder.'

'No, you are right. I hadn't made the connection. I think . . . I think perhaps I do feel finished. I have always seen myself as the go-between. I went between the overseers and the deacons here in Philippi, backwards and forwards until I felt their fellowship in the Gospel was secure. Of course I nearly wrecked everything by my insistence on being a go-between with Paul, but I think perhaps I do feel as though my work is complete. It causes me such joy to see you all working together, supporting each other, and even standing with Paul.'

'Well, most of us anyway,' said Lydia.

Epaphroditus chuckled. 'I think Paul would consider most of you standing with him to be a triumph.' His chuckle ended in a coughing fit. When he could speak again he said, 'I could certainly use a body like Christ's glorious body rather than my own humble one.'

Just then, their attention was caught by the most beautiful birdsong fluting in the branches above their heads. Lydia lifted her head cautiously, as her back still hurt with any sudden movement. She saw a small brown bird among the green of the newly sprouting leaves.

'Philomela!' she exclaimed. 'Philomela's back!'

Chapter 29

No one could have been more astonished than Lydia when her expression of joy at the return of the small brown bird turned into a single tear sliding down her cheek, or when that single tear was followed by another and another until she was sitting on the chair under the mulberry tree weeping as though she would never stop.

Hearing her, Euodia bustled in indignantly. 'I knew you would wear yourself out. It was too much, too soon. People should listen to me.' She carried on, huffing her care for Lydia in staccato sentences laden with irritation. The tender-hearted Clement stopped his pacing around the garden and rushed over to Lydia, clumsily patting her hand in his anxiety at her distress.

'Shall I get Ruth?' he asked the air around him, as Lydia was unable to respond to anyone or anything at this point.

'No,' Epaphroditus spoke from her other side. 'Give her a moment. When her breath returns, she will be able to tell us what she needs.' He sat there peacefully waiting as Lydia recovered herself and was able to take a breath and speak again.

After a while her ragged sobs subsided and she took a couple of experimental breaths. She was certainly able to speak, but now found herself too embarrassed to do so. Clement was gazing at her in an apoplexy of anxiety; Euodia was standing with a herbal draught, ready to send her back to bed. Their concern overwhelmed her. She turned to Epaphroditus. He was sitting on his chair next to her, calmly gazing up at Philomela in the branches of the mulberry tree above him, waiting for her to be ready.

'I thought she had died,' she hiccupped.

'She's a nightingale,' he responded. 'Nightingales fly off for the winter, but they normally come back. Look, she's coming down to say hello.'

He was right. Philomela had stopped singing and hopped down, branch by branch, until she perched on a low branch right by Lydia's head. The small bird tipped her head and looked enquiringly at Lydia.

'She wants some crumbs,' said Euodia, distracted temporarily from her protective fury. She bustled off to Artemis in the kitchen to see what she could find. The crisis having passed, Clement went back to his pacing around the garden.

'I embarrassed myself,' said Lydia. 'I was so proud of myself and how well I had coped, and now a small brown bird appears, and I dissolve.'

Epaphroditus tipped his head in a movement that mimicked Philomela's enquiry of a few moments ago. 'Why would you think that caring is embarrassing?'

'I need to be strong,' said Lydia. 'Strong like Paul and . . . well you.'

'Why?' asked Epaphroditus.

'If I'm not strong,' said Lydia, 'I might fall apart entirely.'

'Perhaps there is a midpoint between never flinching at anything and falling apart? That's where I exist. I face what needs to be faced, but when I need to weep, I do that too. So does Paul.'

'Paul cries?' Lydia couldn't hide her astonishment. 'The apostle Paul? The person I met?'

'Not all the time, obviously, but when he needs to, yes. I saw him crying many times in prison. He weeps in frustration at being in prison so long; he weeps in anger at those who set out to destroy his message; he wept for the community here when he thought you were at odds with each other. There's nothing wrong with weeping, dear Lydia. I think even Jesus wept.

Weeping can be a sign of strength – of the strength of your love for the world and of the passion you feel. Even if we are weeping because we are overwhelmed, that's all right too. We all are from time to time. True strength lies in acknowledging it, in taking time to heal, and then turning to face the next challenge.'

Lydia looked at him, astonished.

It seemed that Euodia had been watching her from a distance because she now swooped in and insisted Lydia go and rest. After an initial reluctance, Lydia had to admit that she was exhausted and allowed herself to be chivvied back to her room.

She slept dreamlessly for a few hours and woke with a strange sense of clarity. She knew exactly what she needed to do next, though she had no idea why. She got up by herself and made her way out to the garden. She was delighted to see that John was there. He had come with Marcus to replenish the dye and cloth supplies, and was now sitting with Epaphroditus in the sunshine. Lydia couldn't help but notice that they were sitting in perfect, companionable silence.

John got up when he saw Lydia approaching, and prepared the cushions for her to sit down. The other chair, the one that should have been occupied by Clement, was empty. John observed her questioning glance. 'I sent him back to the shop. He was finding the inactivity tiresome and I feared that even the saintly Epaphroditus would find his restless humming tiresome.'

The saintly Epaphroditus pulled a face that suggested John might have been right. 'You look as though your rest has given you a sense of purpose?'

'It has,' said Lydia. 'I think I know what I should do about Valens.'

John and Epaphroditus looked at her questioningly, so she leant forward and told them her plan. They talked about it for a long time, looking at the idea from all angles. In the end, John nodded. 'I agree, and he won't be expecting it.'

At that moment, Marcus came out into the garden. He'd finished filling the shelves in the shop, and was coming in search of John. Lydia was pleased to notice that, though as close in terms of friendship as ever, the boys were growing into their own skills and passions: Marcus as a dyer under the expert eye of John; Rufus as a cook with the help of Artemis, and Tertius as an increasingly talented artist and mosaic maker, under the tutelage of Akiva. Marcus had heard the tail end of John's sentence.

'Who won't be expecting what?'

John nodded his head in Marcus's direction, indicating that he thought Lydia should tell him the plan. Lydia tried to signal with her eyes that she thought they shouldn't drag the boys into this. But John nodded again firmly.

Marcus watched them, his eyes sparkling. 'The more you try not to tell me, the more agog I shall be. Best just tell me right away; it will save me hours of hanging around listening in to your conversations.'

Lydia was a little shocked. 'Surely you don't do that?'

'Of course. How else will we find out what is going on? When we were slaves, what you decided affected our wholes lives, but you never talked to us about it. So we learnt how to listen so that we would know what was coming our way. I've only been free a short while, I'm not out of practice yet.'

Lydia sighed. Every day, at the moment, it felt as though she was learning things about her life that were a complete surprise. She told Marcus her plan. He listened intently. 'I love it. He really won't be expecting that. I'll do it.'

'No,' objected Lydia. 'I can't put you in harm's way. I'll do it myself.'

'You can't even walk to the end of the street and back at the moment,' said Marcus, 'and in any case, what if I choose to put myself in harm's way?'

'He's right,' said John. 'In Valens's eyes he is the least important person. There would be no point in making a spectacle out of him. He's not a citizen nor is he a slave of a citizen. He is the right person to do it.'

Reluctantly Lydia was forced to agree. Marcus slipped away and returned a few moments later with Rufus from the kitchen and Tertius from the atrium.

'We'll all do it,' he said. Rufus and Tertius, standing behind him like they used to do when they were slaves, nodded their assent. John winked at them across the garden.

Lydia turned on him accusingly. 'Did you mean this to happen?' He shrugged and smiled and said nothing.

Ruth, when she heard about the plan, was keen to join them, but it was the boys themselves who dissuaded her. 'This is for us to do,' they said. And Ruth, unusually, backed down.

John and Marcus disappeared back to the workshop. They were gone a few days, and while they were gone Lydia's strength returned to her bit by bit. When they returned, there was a satisfied look on their faces and a large packet tucked under Marcus's arm.

'That should do it,' John said.

The boys set off on their errand, buzzing with excitement. Lydia stood with Ruth at the doorway, waving them off. Ruth squeezed her hand. 'It is the right thing to do. This *is* living our lives in a manner worthy of the Gospel.'

'I know,' said Lydia. 'I just think I should do it myself.'

'Sometimes . . .' said Ruth, 'sometimes you have to allow people to help you. Like Paul said, we have to stand firm together.' They walked back into the garden. Euodia was fussing around Epaphroditus, making sure his cushions propped him up in just the right way. Artemis had popped out of the kitchen and was standing in the doorway between the atrium and the garden watching. Ever since her conversation with Epaphroditus, Lydia had wondered whether Artemis knew what Epaphroditus suspected about his impending death. One look at Artemis' face told her all she needed to know. Ruth, Lydia suspected, did not know, but was so empathetic that she knew when someone was in need of care. They went to stand on either side of her. Ruth flung her arms around her in a full embrace, but Lydia, still in some pain, had to content herself with holding onto her hand.

'What will I do without him?' Artemis whispered, as much to herself as to anyone else.

Lydia opened her mouth to utter the accustomed platitudes – 'you'll be fine'; 'everything will work out all right'; 'there's no need to worry' – but even in her head they sounded hollow. 'I don't know,' she said. 'I really don't know, but I do know that whatever we do we'll do it together.'

Epaphroditus looked over at the three of them and indicated that they should come and sit near him. The sun of an early spring day shone down on them. They sat there for an hour or so, saying little of any consequence. They discussed the buds on the mulberry tree; the green shoots poking through the soil. Ruth regaled them with tales of picky customers, impersonating the tone of their voices and even their facial expressions with uncanny brilliance. From time to time Philomela would flutter down and look enquiringly for crumbs, which one or other of them would obediently provide. It was a gentle, easy time. A time, Lydia thought, to store away in the memory and bring out again when days were dark and troubled. Despite that, she couldn't help glancing anxiously towards the door, waiting for the boys to return from their errand.

Eventually, she could bear it no longer and went out onto the street. She had no idea why; the streets were so narrow in that part of Philippi that it was impossible to see people coming even if you were looking out for them. She met Clement, Alexandra and Caius standing outside their shop, talking through the windows to Akiva and Manius in her own shops.

'The boys said they were going on an important errand,' Caius said.

'But they wouldn't tell us what it was,' Alexandra added.

'So we've been waiting for them to return,' completed Clement.

Despite her growing anxiety, Lydia couldn't control a giggle. 'Do you know, you've started talking like them?'

'It appears we have,' said Clement. 'I understand now why they do it. It brings a strange comfort.'

'Look!' Alexandra's voice sounded a little on edge. 'Is that them?'

'Maybe,' said Caius. 'Yes I think it is.'

Lydia craned her neck. He was right, they had just turned a corner a little further down. Were they on their own? Yes, yes they seemed to be. Were they all right? Again yes. In fact, they looked exultant. Their eyes were sparkling and they were jumping on each other as they walked, like they used to as children.

'How did it go?' she asked when they at last arrived.

'It was brilliant,' said Marcus.

'He wasn't expecting it at all,' said Rufus.

'Totally speechless,' added Tertius.

'But what did you do?' came a chorus of voices.

'Come inside and we'll tell you,' said Lydia.

Chapter 30

They gathered in the garden, with Epaphroditus still sitting on one chair, Lydia again taking her place on another, but with the third vacant because Clement refused to sit while others were standing, and no one else wanted to take the chair. Marcus, Rufus and Tertius stood at the entrance to the garden, facing the chairs and the expectant crowd.

The questions came thick and fast.

'Where did you go?'

'What did you do?'

'Who was surprised?'

'What happened?'

The noise was so great that Lydia struggled to be heard over the clamour. Marcus put two fingers between his lips and whistled loudly. The hubbub ceased immediately.

'If you have questions,' he observed, 'it is wise to allow those who can supply the answers to speak.' He grinned over at Lydia. He was enjoying this. 'Lydia can tell you the beginning of the story, and then we will continue.'

All eyes turned to Lydia. Philomela hopped onto a low branch as though to listen in as well.

'When we were on trial,' Lydia said, 'Valens asked me to give him a bolt of cloth like the one I had sold to Aurelia. Apparently his wife had admired the shade that John had produced and wanted some to rival Aurelia's own display. He implied that if I gave him the cloth he would ensure the charges against me were dropped. Clement and I knew it was the wrong thing to do, and refused. But his question wouldn't leave me. It kept returning to me as though it was unfinished business. Then, something Epaphroditus said made me think about it all over again. It was about strength – acknowledging how overwhelmed you feel and then turning to face the next challenge. Suddenly I knew that rather than cowering here hoping Valens would forget me, I needed to do something bold, something unexpected, something ridiculously generous.'

'So,' Marcus continued, 'John and I spent the rest of the day creating a new batch of dye. If anything, it was better than the one that we made for Aurelia.' He looked over at John, who nodded his acceptance of this claim. 'We then dyed a few bolts of cloth, fixed them, and brought them here. Tertius, Rufus and I carried them to Valens's house ourselves. We waited in line with the other clients for the morning *salutatio*, and were eventually welcomed into the atrium. There were a few clients in front of us, but we could tell that Valens had noticed us – and our bundle – he kept on glancing our way and waved the clients away quickly until it was our turn.'

'I opened the bundle in front of him,' said Rufus, picking up the tale. 'I was more dramatic than I had intended to be. It slipped as I was unwrapping the last layer, and swathes of deep purple cloth billowed around the atrium. Valens was flabbergasted. He wanted to know what kind of joke this was and why we were doing it.'

'I told him exactly what you asked me to say to him,' Marcus said to Lydia. 'I told him that it was a gift to his wife from Lydia the purple dealer, given freely without the expectation of anything in return. We turned to go like you said we should, but Tertius turned back.'

'What did you say?' asked Lydia.

'I really wanted him to understand,' Tertius said. 'I wanted him to know that we work to different rules, that we have a different vision of the world, not like his at all. So I said, "*This* is what it means to be true, honourable and just."'

'Were you quoting from Paul's letter?' Manius asked, pulling the now very dog-eared scroll from his tunic. 'Those words sound familiar.'

'I was trying to, but I couldn't remember it all. I just did the best I could.'

Manius nodded absently as he rolled and unrolled the scroll, searching for the passage he had in mind. He tutted, frustrated when he couldn't find it.

Epaphroditus said, 'I think you might be thinking of "whatever is true, whatever is honourable, whatever is just, whatever is pure, whatever is agreeable, whatever is praiseworthy, if there is any goodness, if there is anything worthy of approval, think about these things"?'

'Yes,' said Tertius. 'As I looked at him, all I could see was the opposite of this. He is driven by greed and self-promotion; by lying and deceit. I wanted to show him that there is a better way to be, that he could choose to be different. I had so much I wanted to say to him, so many words built up inside me, but in that moment all I could manage was "this is what it means to be true, honourable and just". I ran out of words, so all I could do was look at him. For a moment or two I stood there just looking at him, and he looked back at me. In his eyes I saw such fear. I think he only knows how to live if he is controlling someone else. He has no capacity to imagine an act of ridiculous generosity that asks for nothing in return. The look lasted for only a moment, but then he turned and waved his hand in dismissal.'

'Do you think it will make a difference?' asked Alexandra.

'We can't know,' said Lydia. 'We could pray for him though, that the seed Tertius tried to plant today will take root and grow.'

'I didn't mean that,' said Alexandra. 'I was wondering if he'd leave us alone now.'

'We can't know that either,' said Lydia. 'I think that was what came to me suddenly yesterday. We need to live what is true and honourable and just and pure and all those other things, and not just live in reaction to people like Valens the whole time.'

'Who are you and what have you done with Lydia?' asked Ruth, chuckling. 'That doesn't sound like you at all.'

'No,' said Lydia, 'it doesn't, does it? I must say I'm surprising myself.'

'So what do we do while we wait to find out if Valens is coming after us?' Alexandra was still shaken by the events of the previous days. 'How are we meant to live like this, looking over our shoulders the whole time?'

'Would you like to know what I think Paul would say?' Epaphroditus's voice was, Lydia thought, a little fainter than the last time he had spoken. Faint though the sound was that he made, people turned to him expectantly, but he was overtaken by a coughing fit that rendered him incapable of speaking for a while.

'I think I know,' said Manius. 'I think he'd tell us to rejoice.'

Epaphroditus nodded, still trying to catch his breath.

'But that's insane,' Alexandra said, clearly on edge. 'How on earth are you meant to rejoice when the world is closing in on you?'

They looked at Epaphroditus, but he shook his head, still unable to speak. Lydia looked at him anxiously; she'd noticed his breathing deteriorating even further over the past few days. She flicked a glance at Euodia and noticed a matching look of concern on her face.

Manius said thoughtfully, 'I think, perhaps, that it is about perspective. I don't think Paul is suggesting we skip around humming merrily all day every day no matter what befalls us.'

Clement's eyes twinkled. 'Like me, you mean? Mind you, even I lost my sparkle for a while in jail.'

Manius grinned and judiciously avoided answering. 'Paul tells us to rejoice in the Lord, to delight in him. He of all people surely wouldn't be saying that we should rejoice about being imprisoned, or about facing death, or about having the skin flayed off our backs. It's in the Lord that we are meant to rejoice. Rejoice in – take delight in – what is steadfast and certain and sure. Rejoice in that and let the rest take care of itself.'

'But how?' Alexandra's pent-up anxiety of the past week spilled out in a belly roar. 'How are you meant to rejoice when the world is falling apart around your ears?'

Lydia suddenly remembered her experience in the prison cell. So she tried to explain about giving thanks morning, noon and night, about holding the fragments of her fretting before God, about focussing on Jesus and his love. She told them about how hard it was at first, but how, after a while, it began to make more sense, and how it felt that, while the worries that had taken up so much of her waking – and indeed sleeping – existence didn't disappear, they felt so much more manageable. She told them that taking delight in the things that were good and nourishing had steadied her.

'I get that,' said Caius. 'I used to delight in all the wrong things. Money made me rejoice more than anything else, but then my ship went down and Paul healed my slave girl, and Julius ran off with everything I had, and I had nothing left to rejoice in. I used to rejoice in my status, but then I lost that too. I've learnt to rejoice in the one thing that will never change. Life is no less troubling, but I have an anchor now.'

Alexandra sighed. 'I understand what you mean, but I'm not sure it would work for me. I'm finding it hard to concentrate, let alone rejoice.'

Artemis nodded empathically. 'I know what you mean.' Her gaze was fixed firmly on Epaphroditus. They carried on talking about delight and joy and rejoicing, but Lydia was no longer listening to them. For a while she had been listening instead to the sound of Epaphroditus's breathing. It had become ragged and uneven, with an increased rattle as he breathed in and out.

She moved towards him, and with her moved Artemis and Ruth. Euodia was already there, kneeling by his side. After a while the others noticed too. Their conversation faltered as they gathered around his chair. As if part of their group, Philomela hopped down onto the branch just above Epaphroditus's head, her head tipped to one side. Epaphroditus opened his eyes, a look of pure radiance on his face. His breath rattled again, but his lips moved to form a word: 'Joy,' he whispered, 'joy in the Lord.' He breathed again. 'Be with Christ, joy.' Then there was silence. They waited for another breath, but it didn't come. Stillness settled around them in the garden, a stillness so great it was palpable. Then into the stillness broke the most beautiful birdsong.

Philomela had flown back up to the top of the mulberry tree and sang and sang and sang. Until that moment Lydia had always puzzled over the legend that the nightingale's song was a song of mourning. Until now she had only heard its beauty. In the stillness of the garden she heard the deep sorrow too. Joy intertwined with grief; grief with joy.

Epilogue

Lydia was in the fabric shop, straightening the bales of cloth. A few months had passed since Epaphroditus's death. They still grieved for him. He might have considered his task finished among them, but they missed him. His absence was a gaping hole at the heart of their community; a hole that some days felt intolerable.

Following Epaphroditus's death, Euodia had gathered together her belongings and declared her intention to return to Thessalonica. They made a half-hearted attempt to stop her, but, as she said, her business and her small church community were there, and she needed to go back. What surprised them all was Syntyche declaring her intention to go too.

'But we need you here,' Lydia had stuttered, conscious of her selfishness, but unable to hold it in.

'You'll cope,' said Syntyche, unmoved. 'I lost my dear sister in the Lord, and now I have found her again and I will not let her go.'

They waved them off a few days later. Lydia felt the insincerity of her smile as they called and waved and wished them well on their journey.

'You're wondering who's going to lead your gathering now,' Clement had whispered in her ear. 'Don't worry, we'll think of something.'

And they had. The overseers had gathered together in Lydia's atrium and talked for hours. Lydia didn't even think of pretending to garden so she could listen in; she was too anxious for that. The gathering of followers of the Way was so important to her, but she simply did not feel that she had the skills to lead them, and who else would they ask? She went for a long restless walk. When she returned, she found the overseers about to leave, and Caius in deep conversation with Clement and Jonathan. Manius saw her approach and beckoned her over.

'The overseers think I should lead our gathering, but I'm worried that you will mind.'

Lydia had blinked at them and blinked again. She had never thought of Manius like this. But then she remembered his help and thoughtfulness, of how he and Caius had solved the problem of Aurelia's bracelet; how he had pored over the letter from Paul, committing it to memory. Suddenly she realised that she could, very easily, imagine him as their overseer.

'I think it's a wonderful idea.'

'We think so too,' Clement said.

And it had been brilliant. Manius took to leading their small community like a duck to water. With Artemis' help as deacon, it felt as though he had been doing it for ever.

She smiled as she thought about it. Who would have imagined, when they arrived back here a year ago, that things would work out like this?

At that moment a stranger walked into her shop. He was tall, with a gentle, kind face. The tassels on the bottom of his clothing announced that he was Jewish. Lydia glanced at him and looked again. Wait . . . perhaps he wasn't a stranger after all. He looked a little familiar. Her thought processes must have shown on her face because he smiled and helped her out.

'I'm Timothy, a companion of Paul. You may remember me?'

Lydia felt flustered. How could she have forgotten him?

It seemed though that Timothy could read her mind. 'Paul is such a big personality that it is easier to remember him and not the others around him.' He seemed completely comfortable with this state of affairs. Lydia remembered that this was how he had been all those years ago in Philippi: gentle, at ease with himself, and not often ruffled by what was going on around him.

'Come in . . . come in!' she said.

Timothy turned at the sound of loud singing in the shop next door. 'Is that Clement?' he asked. 'I'd recognise that voice anywhere.'

'I'll get someone to bring him and Alexandra,' Lydia assured him. 'Come through to the atrium.'

Hearing voices, Artemis and Rufus emerged from the kitchen area as they so often did to find out what refreshments might need to be provided. Lydia sent Rufus running for their neighbours, while Timothy greeted Artemis with joy.

'How are you enjoying the return of your dear brother?' he asked solicitously. 'He was so concerned for you. For you all, but especially for you, Artemis. At first we planned that I would come. I had various places to visit along the way, and my last visit went so badly I was keen to put things right. But in the end Paul felt it better if Epaphroditus came.'

Artemis had turned the colour of marble and seemed incapable of speech.

'Perhaps you had better sit down,' said Lydia, as much to Artemis as Timothy. 'You seem not to have received our letter. Epaphroditus became ill again on his way back and died a few months ago. We wrote to Paul, but the letter seems not to have arrived.'

Timothy sat in silence for a few minutes. When he finally looked up, there were tears in his eyes. 'I will miss him.'

Artemis nodded at him, still incapable of speaking of her loss, so it was left to Lydia to say, 'We all do. His absence leaves a gaping hole in us all.'

They sat together in silence. Out in the garden Philomela started singing, as though she knew her song was needed as a balm to their hearts.

A few minutes later people started arriving. Messages seemed to have been sent out across the whole city, because it wasn't just Clement, Alexandra and Caius from next door, but Jonathan, Akiva and a few members of their community, plus others from around the city.

'I'm sorry you missed Euodia and Syntyche. They would, I know, have loved to see you . . . despite everything.' Clement tailed off as he remembered just how difficult Euodia's last meeting had been with Timothy. Perhaps Timothy would not have wanted to see her.

But Timothy smiled. 'I saw her on the way. It's probably why I missed your letter. Even though it is summer, I thought I'd travel the long way and drop in on all the people I wanted to see along the Via Egnatia. I was in Thessalonica before I came here. She and Syntyche send you greetings. I thought there was something they weren't telling me. It all makes sense now. She wanted me to hear about Epaphroditus's death in his home. In this place where he was known and deeply loved.' He gazed around, a wistful look on his face.

Lydia felt a lurch of sympathy for him. He spent so much of his life travelling, taking messages here and there, but never spending long enough to be at home in the way Epaphroditus had been here.

'I'll travel south after this,' he said. 'Paul was anxious that I find out how the Corinthians are getting on. He does worry about them.'

Lydia smiled. 'So I hear, and with good reason?'

Timothy grimaced. 'Maybe. I've always wondered whether they annoyed Paul on purpose, for the fun of it.' He paused. 'After that I thought I might go on to Ephesus; it's not Lystra, but it does feel like home.'

They spent the next few hours in easy conversation, talking about Paul's letters, the other communities Timothy would visit on his journey, his hopes for going to Ephesus, and what he might find there. After a while, he stretched and stood up.

'Won't you stay with us?' asked Lydia. 'You will remember, I have lots of space.'

Timothy bowed politely. 'I do remember, and I thank you for your hospitality both then and now, but Paul gave me clear instructions that I was only to stay where the followers of the Way were in trouble, where they needed help or support of some kind.' He gestured around the room. 'There is no doubt in my mind that you don't. I can write to Paul that his prayers of joy as he remembers you can continue unabated.'

Lydia accompanied him to the street door. 'I wish I knew what was going to happen to Paul,' she said. She had wanted to ask earlier, but something had held her back. 'I wonder if he will ever be released from prison?'

Timothy turned back to her, a look of sadness in his eyes. 'So do I,' he said. 'So do I.'

And with that he turned and walked south towards the Neapolis gate. Behind her Lydia could hear the sound of Clement singing:

> Think this among you, which was also in Christ Jesus, who though he existed in the form of God did not regard equality with God as something to cling to but he poured himself out taking the form of a slave, becoming just like humans and, being found in human form, he lowered himself and became someone who obeyed orders even to the point of death, the death of a cross.
>
> Therefore, God exalted him extraordinarily and graced him with the name that is above every name, so that at the name of Jesus every knee, whether in heaven, on earth or under the earth, would bend and every tongue acknowledge that Jesus Christ is Lord to the glory of God the Father.

As she watched Timothy's retreating back, Lydia whispered quietly, 'Amen and Amen.'

PART TWO

Notes

Introduction

Lydia: A Story is a companion volume to my previous book *Phoebe: A Story* (Hodder, 2018), though it stands alone and you don't need to have read *Phoebe* in order to read *Lydia*. In *Phoebe* I set out a vision for what I was hoping to do in writing in the way that I did. My vision remains the same in this book. My intent is not to write a novel. Novels are stories that exist for their own sake and which are constrained only by the imagination of their author. This book, like *Phoebe: A Story*, is constrained not just by what can be found in Acts 16 and the epistle to the Philippians, but also by the scholarship and writing surrounding both texts. What I am trying to do is to bring the context and the scholarship to life and to give a sense of what it might have felt like to live in Philippi at the time Paul sent his letter. There are also key elements of theology and exegesis that I am trying to convey, and from time to time these need to overtake the story. The story I have written is very clearly in my mind a vehicle for presenting the theology, not a story in its own right. I have tried to make the theology as dynamic and engaging as I can, but this is not always possible, given the history and complexity of the scholarship that lies behind some of the issues raised.

You will notice as you get into the story that I have talked about one passage more than any other. If you know Philippians as a letter, it will not surprise you to know that this is Philippians 2:5–11. My focus on this passage is deliberate and reflects my understanding of the letter. In the notes below I present something of the scholarship on Philippians 2:5–11, also known as the Christ Hymn, and the varying beliefs among scholars about when it might have been written. The more I've studied Philippians, however, the more convinced I have become that its theology emerges from and is woven around this passage. That is why it plays such a central part in this story.

This book is an act of historical imagination. In other words, I am imagining a set of characters who might have been the kind of people who first received Paul's letter to the Philippians. My imagination is informed by historical research and scholarly discussion, and seeks to bring to life the issues and debates surrounding both Acts 16 and the epistle to the Philippians. In some ways I see the exercise as a 'theological pop-up book', lifting events and characters off the page to give them an additional dimension as you read. As a result, and above all else, I am trying to remind you that, just like today, people come to Paul's letters with different lived experiences, different values and dreams and, as a result, they react to his theology differently. The ancient context was as varied and vibrant as our own is today, and we can't really understand how Paul was received by his first audience unless we hold this firmly in our minds. People who were Roman citizens would have experienced his message quite differently from those who were not; those who were Jewish would have felt differently from Gentiles; slaves differently from those who were free, and so on. This all affects the shaping and impact of Paul's message, and this is what I am trying to communicate in the way I have presented the story. One of the major themes of *Lydia: A Story* is that each of the characters we meet has a story, a story that has shaped who they are as people. That story affects how they receive The Story, the story of Jesus Christ, Son of God.

The more I have engaged with stories as a vehicle for New Testament theology, the more convinced I am that they convey something that the usual style of New Testament writing alone cannot. There is something about personal experience and the emotion that emerges when we imagine the impact of certain ideas on actual people's lives that can only be captured and expressed through storytelling. For example, when we imagine what it might have felt like for someone who was a slave to listen to Paul's Christ Hymn lauding 'taking the form of a slave', the theology takes on a new and challenging dimension. A story cannot, even for a moment, be thought to be able to convey the whole of New Testament theology, but I do think that it provides a helpful additional lens through which certain, otherwise unobserved, features can be brought to the fore.

One of the interesting features about writing a story is that you have to come down on one side or another in scholarly debates. Often debates become so entangled and complex that it is tempting not to decide who you think is right and who wrong, but to acknowledge the complexity and move on. In a story, this is not possible: a decision has to be made in order to represent something in the text. For someone like myself, who likes to leave multiple options in play, this presents quite a challenge! I am conscious that this story could have taken a number of different paths had I chosen another option in the scholarly debate.

I cannot stress enough that this story does not present what did happen, but what might have happened. Even then, I am acutely aware that from a twenty-first-century perspective we cannot have full access to life in the first century: our experiences, our world view and our psychology are so different that we can at best, to quote from another of Paul's letters, 'see in a mirror dimly' (1 Cor. 12:12). Nevertheless, dimly is better than not at all, and it is still worth doing even if we know how limited the enterprise is. I hope that this story will encourage you into your own act of imagination as you read Scripture, and that this will bring it to life in a new way. The notes that follow are another way of bringing the text to life. I hope to introduce you to some of the debates and issues that lie behind the text and, as with the story, I hope they give you a fresh insight into Philippians and its importance as a letter.

I deliberately focussed the story around four women, two known from Acts – Lydia and the slave girl healed by Paul – and two known from Philippians – Euodia and Syntyche. Other characters are woven around them, but the story circles around these four, with its main focus, as the title of the book suggests, on Lydia. The intention here is to try to give a greater voice to four characters who, though known to readers of the New Testament, are often overlooked or underestimated.

In the notes where there are quotations from the Bible they are my own translations unless otherwise indicated.

Setting the scene

ACTS AND PHILIPPIANS

The first part of this story draws on an exploration of Acts 16, and the rest of the story on the epistle to the Philippians. If you would like to study Philippians in more depth, a good quality commentary will help you. One of my favourite commentaries on Philippians – because it avoids being too technical while presenting some of the most important of modern scholarship on the epistle – is M. F. Bird and N. K. Gupta, *Philippians* (Cambridge University Press, 2020).

Also good are M. Bockmuehl, *The Epistle to the Philippians* (Continuum, 2006); G. D. Fee, *Paul's Letter to the Philippians: The New International Commentary on the New Testament* (William B. Eerdmans Publishing Co., 1995), and M. Silva, *Philippians* (Baker Academic, 2005).

On Acts, my favourite commentary is J. Fitzmyer, *The Acts of the Apostles* (Yale University Press, 2007). Also very helpful (though possibly too detailed for most) is C. S. Keener, *Acts:*

Notes

An Exegetical Commentary: Volume 3: 15:1–23:35 (Baker
Academic, 2014).

PHILIPPI

The very centre of our story focusses on Philippi and therefore
it is important to understand what Philippi was like in this
period. The Roman historian Strabo stated that Philippi was
first called Krenides when it was founded by Callistratus, an
exile from Athens, who brought with him settlers from the
island of Thasos in the fourth century BC (see Strabo, *Geography*,
VII, frags 41, 42). It gained the name Philippi when the father
of Alexander the Great – Philip of Macedon – captured the city,
attracted by the gold and silver mines in the nearby Mount
Pangaeus in 356 BC.

In the second century BC, Macedonia, the name for the whole
region surrounding Philippi, was incorporated into the Roman
empire, and was initially split into four districts or divisions,
each with a capital. The first district in the east included
Philippi, though Philippi was not the region's capital. One of
the problems of Acts 16:12 is that it appears to say that Philippi
was 'a leading city of the district of Macedonia'. But it wasn't.
Other cities like Thessalonica were much larger and much more
important. Verhoef argues that a better translation of the
phrase is that 'it was a city of the first division', remembering
the four divisions of the previous century (E. Verhoef, *Philippi:
How Christianity Began in Europe: The Epistle to the
Philippians and the Excavations at Philippi* (T&T Clark, 2013),
4). This certainly makes more sense.

Around the time of the mid-second century BC, the Romans
began work on the road – the Via Egnatia – that would have such
a major impact on the life of Philippi at the time of Paul. When it
was finally completed, the road ran from Dyrrhachium in the west,
in modern day Albania on the Adriatic Sea, all the way through to
Byzantium in the east, passing through Philippi and Neapolis on

the way. This formed an overland trade route from Rome east-wards. Scholars calculate that it would have taken around twenty-four days to travel from Rome to Byzantium on the Via Egnatia and, although travel by sea would have been faster, the overland route could be taken at any time of year, in contrast to travel by sea, which was dangerous during the winter months.

Around 42 BC, Philippi became a full Roman colony, as Acts 16:12 notes, using the Roman word *kolonia* simply transliter-ated into Greek. Roman colonies were particularly important in the Roman empire. They began life as outposts of the Roman empire into which Roman citizens were relocated in order to subjugate the local population. Before long, however, colonies had more to do with status than peace, as they were seen as being a small bit of Rome itself planted around the empire. Philippi became a colony after a major battle between Brutus and Cassius on the one hand, and Octavian (later known as Emperor Augustus) and Mark Anthony on the other. Octavian and Mark Anthony were victorious and Mark Anthony settled a large number of military veterans in Philippi, making it a colony and changing its name to the less than snappy *Antonii Iussu Colonia Victrix Philippensium* (by the order of Anthony, the victorious colony of the Philippians).

Approximately eleven years later, Octavian defeated Mark Anthony and later renamed Philippi *Colonia Iulia Augusta Philippensium* (the colony of the Philippians of Julius Augustus), granting it the status of *Ius Italicum*, which meant that Philippi had the same legal status as a city in Italy. Significantly at this point, Augustus settled a cohort (around a thousand soldiers) of the praetorian guard in Philippi. Around this time the official language of Philippi became Latin rather than Greek, as is reflected in the various inscriptions that can be found in the city. The official and public face of Philippi at the time of Paul, then, would have been Roman, but the city's population was still largely Greek. Peter Oakes estimates that at the time of Paul the population of Philippi would have been around fifteen thousand, with roughly 30 per cent of these being Roman citizens, 50 per cent being free Greek, and around 20 per cent slaves. As a result, the official face of Philippi was Roman, even though the majority of its inhabitants were Greek.

For more detail on Philippi in the first century see R. Ascough, *Lydia: Paul's Cosmopolitan Hostess* (Liturgical Press, 2009), 19–27; P. Oakes, *Philippians: From People to Letter* (Cambridge University Press, 2000), and – especially good – E. Verhoef, *Philippi* (T&T Clark, 2013).

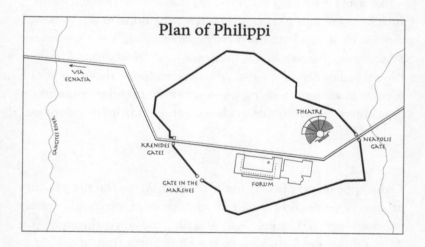

Plan of Philippi

A note on inscriptions: Inscriptions will be mentioned from time to time in these notes, and it is worth noting their importance. One of the challenges for studying the ancient world is attempting to identify what life was like. Although we can glean a certain amount from things that were written, these accounts can be biased, reflecting the authors' own views, and even more importantly often omit information because it is not relevant to what they were writing. The practice of dyeing is an important case in point. There is, unsurprisingly, very little evidence for the practice in literature; few books were written about it or referred to it. This is where other forms of writing become important. The study of epigraphy explores written evidence from a range of sources, but particularly inscriptions on buildings, which were often given in memory of people who were important at the time. In places like Philippi it is possible to build up a picture of who was there and what they did from a detailed study of inscriptions.

This provides a fascinating insight into life as it actually was, in contrast to life as key authors wanted to depict it. It sheds light on those who wouldn't naturally feature in literary texts – like dyers – or who might be overlooked for other reasons – such as women. A particularly interesting book in this area was written by Bernadette Brooten (*Women Leaders in the Ancient Synagogue: Inscriptional Evidence and Background Issues*, Brown Judaic Studies, 1982) who demonstrated the influence of women in ancient synagogues, contrary to popular opinions on the subject, as a result of evidence gathered from inscriptions.

Lydia

Lydia appears very briefly in the Bible, in Acts. The story occurs at a very important point in the account of Paul's travels proclaiming the Gospel. Paul and Silas travelled through Asia Minor, but were forbidden by the Holy Spirit from speaking in Phrygia, Galatia or Bithynia and went instead to Troas (otherwise known as Troy). During the night Paul had a vision in which a man from Macedonia (the region in which Philippi was located) begged him to come and help. In response to the dream Paul and Silas sailed from Troas via Samothrace to Neapolis, which was the nearest harbour to Philippi.

It was there that they met Lydia, who not only listened eagerly to what Paul said, but was baptised by him. Lydia, therefore, was the first person to become Christian in what we would now call the West (though ironically she, herself, was from Thyatira in the East, see below for more on this). What we know of Lydia is limited to a few phrases in Acts 16:13–15:

> [13] *On the Sabbath day, we went out of the gate beside the river, where we believed there was a place of prayer, and sitting down we spoke to the women who were gathered there.* [14] *And a certain woman by the name of Lydia, a dealer in purple from the city of Thyatira, a worshiper of God, listened. The Lord opened her heart to pay attention to the words spoken by Paul.* [15] *After she and her household were baptised, she urged us, saying 'If you have judged me to be faithful to the Lord, come and stay at my house.' And she persuaded us.*

From this, a few phrases give us some key details about Lydia: she dealt in purple; she was from Thyatira; she was a worshipper of God; she could be found in a place of prayer on the Sabbath, and had a house into which she could welcome Paul and Silas. There is only one more mention of Lydia in Acts, or more accurately of her home, since Paul and Silas returned there after their imprisonment, before travelling onwards to Thessalonica. The only other detail worth noting is one of absence. Despite her central role in Paul's visit to Philippi recorded in Acts 16:13–15, Lydia is entirely absent from Paul's letter to the Philippians. We are left to guess whether this means she has simply moved from Philippi, or has lost her faith or indeed her life. I chose to imagine that she moved away (for reasons laid out as the story unfolds), but later found the need to return. It allowed me to re-include her in Philippi's story even though she is not mentioned in Paul's epistle.

These five key details from Acts 16 are so central to our story that they will be explored in detail here by way of setting the scene.

Dealer in Purple

Lydia is most famous, popularly, for being a dealer in purple, though even this small detail is not as straightforward as it might first appear. There are three key strands to this fact that intertwine and affect how we view Lydia as a whole: what kind of purple she traded in; whether she was just a dealer or a dyer as well, and, connected to this last point, how wealthy this meant she was.

We need to begin with purple itself. Purple was highly sought after in the ancient world – it was the colour of kings and hence of high status. In the Roman empire, purple trimming – or in some instances the entire garment dyed in purple – was a sign of status and was worn by magistrates, military commanders and other aristocrats. Purple was such a symbol of wealth and power that, although it could only be worn by certain distinguished Romans on their togas, it could be – and was – used by others in other ways, such as house furnishings. Purple items were, therefore, expensive and much prized. In the early fourth century BC a pound of purple silk was worth three times the equivalent amount of gold.

There were, however, different kinds of purple. The most famous is 'Tyrian purple', derived from murex shellfish found on the coast near Tyre (modern Lebanon), but also all along the eastern Mediterranean coast. The reddish purple dye the snails made was produced by boiling and grinding thousands of snails (research indicates that 12,000 snails produced around 1.4 g of dye). Although Tyrian (murex) purple was particularly sought after, archaeological evidence indicates that purple was made in other ways too. One of those is by using the root of the madder plant. Indeed, Thyatira (see below), which is said to be where Lydia came from, was known for its growth and production of dye from the madder root. The shade produced is known today as 'Turkey red', but madder root has been found in many purple materials from the Roman world. D. E. Graves argues persuasively that a trader like Lydia would probably have sold a variety of different purples: murex purple, madder purple, and probably others too, maybe even made by mixing different dyes together.

This brings us to the question of whether Lydia produced the dye, or just sold it. Some scholars, notably Ivoni Richter Reimer and Luise Schottroff, argue that Lydia was involved in the production of dye, not just in selling it, and therefore should not be viewed as wealthy, but as someone who worked hard to make a living. It is very difficult to tell from the scant evidence available whether Lydia was an importer and retailer (and therefore probably more wealthy) or a producer and labourer (and therefore probably poorer). One of the interesting features to observe is that the dyeing process was a messy and smelly business (murex dye was especially smelly, and there is evidence that producers struggled to disguise the smell of the dye on the finished product). Graves therefore supposes that she would have bought materials to sell from a dyeing plant located well away from any residential areas. As a result, I have hypothesised that Lydia sold a variety of purples in Philippi, but had brought John to Philippi with her to oversee a dyeing workshop located outside the city.

This brings us to the final point of Lydia's wealth – or otherwise. Arguments about this, in my opinion, stray too close to absolute categories: either she was rich or she was poor. As a trader, Lydia would have, in modern terms, been middle-class, neither very rich nor very poor. She appears to have been wealthy enough to have had a 'house' (Acts 16:15), but not so rich that she could give up trading. While it is possible, as Reimer and Schottroff argue, that Lydia was much poorer and working directly in production as well as retail, this would not explain why Lydia was able to offer hospitality to two people with apparent ease.

For more on the discussion about dealing purple, see Ascough, *Lydia: Paul's Cosmopolitan Hostess* (Liturgical Press, 2009, 76–81) for a clear and helpful summary. For much more detailed argument see in particular I. R. Reimer, *Women in the Acts of the Apostles: A Feminist Liberation Perspective* (Augsburg Fortress, 1995), and D. E. Graves, 'What Is the Madder with Lydia's Purple? A Re-examination of the Purpurarii in Thyatira and Philippi' (*Near East Archaeological Society Bulletin*, 2017), 3–29. (This article available online is utterly fascinating and contains more information on purple at the time of Lydia than you might have thought possible.)

It is worth noting that a few scholars consider Lydia to be unhistorical or at the least to be more important as a 'type' within the text than as an actual character. These approaches are very thought-provoking, as they raise questions about what Luke was trying to achieve as he wrote Acts. Ultimately I was not persuaded by them, but to anyone who is interested in the question I would recommend reading A. Gruca-Macaulay, *Lydia as a Rhetorical Construct in Acts* (SBL Press, 2016), and S. Matthews, *First Converts: Rich Pagan Women and the Rhetoric of Mission in Early Judaism and Christianity* (Stanford University Press, 2002).

THYATIRA

Thyatira, Lydia's home town according to Acts, is in a region in Asia Minor called 'Lydia'. This raises the question of whether Lydia was more of a nickname derived from her home town. There has been extensive discussion about whether Lydia was a freed slave who was called by the name of her region. There are a number of inscriptions from the ancient world that connect people who freed slaves with the purple trade. There are, however, also a number of inscriptions to women with the name Lydia who had wealth and status in the ancient world.

There is too little evidence to be confident about whether Lydia was a former slave or not, and in this book, since in my previous volume I chose to make Phoebe a former slave, I chose not to make Lydia a former slave too. (See the discussion on this in Ascough, *Lydia*, 6–7.)

Thyatira was an ancient city, even in the first century, and had been inhabited since 3,000 BC. As with many ancient cities, it had been occupied by numerous different empires, most recently before the Roman period by the Greeks who settled it with soldiers from Macedonia (which could potentially mean that much, much later someone like Lydia from Thyatira could find familiarity in a city like Philippi). Later, in the mid second century BC it became part of the Roman empire. Thyatira was an important trading centre, and there have been extensive inscriptions found in the city to indicate that not only were there many different guilds in the city, but the dyeing guild was crucial to its economy. As we noted above, Thyatira was well known as a producer of purple dye, though more likely a dye that came from the madder root than the better known and expensive murex shellfish.

It is also interesting to notice that there is an inscription in Thessalonica (a city also in Macedonia, around a hundred miles from Philippi) to Menippus, a purple dyer from Thyatira.

WORSHIPPER OF GOD
One of the more curious facts that Acts reports about Lydia is that she was a 'worshipper of God'. The phrase is frustratingly vague and uninformative and could mean a range of different things. The word translated as 'worshipper' comes from the verb *sebō* and means to show reverence or devotion. It occurs eight times in Acts, and is used for those who have a connection to Judaism (Acts 13:43, and notice especially the reference in Acts 18:4 to Titius Justus who was a worshipper of God), but also for those who worship other gods like

Artemis in Ephesus (Acts 19:27). In this instance, however, it is unlikely that it means Lydia has a propensity for religious worship (not least as this would describe everyone in the ancient world) because the Greek says that Lydia was a worshipper of THE God. This suggests that the reference is to Lydia's relationship to Judaism. The question is what that relationship was. Many scholars conclude that the phrase refers to Lydia being a 'God-fearer', the term used to describe those who have been attracted to Judaism, but have not converted. The problem is that we know frustratingly little about what this might mean. The most common description of this kind of person comes from Acts, and there is a lively debate about exactly what it refers to and, indeed, whether 'God-fearers' is really a category at all. (See discussion in A. T. Kraabel, 'The Disappearance of the "God-Fearers"' (*Numen* 28, no. 2, 1981), 113–26.) At the very least, the phrase 'worshipper of God' appears to suggest someone who is attracted by the tenets of Judaism and who gathers with others to reflect on them.

PLACE OF PRAYER

This 'gathering' with others is suggested by the next word we need to explore – *proseuchē*. The word is used twice in the story about Philippi, once in verse 13 and once in verse 16. The second usage: 'One day, as we were going to the place of prayer' cements the impression from the first usage that this is not an impromptu meeting place, but a place that was regularly used for meeting and prayer. The reason why this is so important is that the usual name for a Jewish place of meeting and prayer – synagogue – isn't used here. This raises the question of why not. Many proposals have been put forward: that it was an outdoor meeting place; that it was the usual word for a Jewish meeting place outside of Israel (though this doesn't explain why Luke uses the word synagogue elsewhere); that it refers to non-observant Israelites, and so on.

It seems to me, however, that there is a very simple explanation of why the place where Lydia and the other women were praying was not called a synagogue – because there were no men present. Later Judaism makes very clear that a synagogue is only a synagogue when there are ten men present. While, in the earlier period, this expectation may have been less fully enforced (see in particular the study by B. J. Brooten, *Women Leaders in the Ancient Synagogue* (Brown Judaic Studies, 1982)), there is no evidence at all that a gathering entirely made up of women could have counted as a synagogue (see Ascough, *Lydia*, 113). Contrary to the argument of some, that men were present, just not mentioned, it is worth noting that the rare feminine plural is used to describe the gathering. The feminine plural can only be used when there are no men present; if even one man is present the masculine plural would be employed. This, therefore, strongly suggests that we are to imagine a female-only gathering.

HOUSE
Although the word *oikos* can be a little vague and could refer to a tenement building as well as a privately owned house, the way Luke describes Lydia's easy and welcoming hospitality suggests that she had both the space and the means to welcome two or more strangers into her house. She is likely to have had at least moderate means, and therefore lived in a house not an apartment. I have imagined that this house was similar to many Roman houses of the period (see page 244).

Dating

The dating of the epistle to the Philippians, and hence of this story, is dependent upon where we imagine Paul to have been imprisoned while he was writing it.

Paul mentions his imprisonment in Philippians 1:7, 13–14, 17. Alongside this he also mentions that during his imprisonment, the Gospel has been known among all of the 'praetorium', translated in the NRSV as the Imperial Guard and in the NIV as the palace guard. The praetorium normally referred to the emperor's elite guard, which was stationed in Rome, but it was also used to describe a provincial governor's headquarters and the troops stationed there (notice that the place Jesus was led away to in the Gospels just before his crucifixion was called the praetorium in Mark 15:16 and John 18:28, 33; 19:9).

Traditionally, Paul was thought to have written Philippians and Philemon (and for some, though not all, also Colossians and possibly Ephesians) from prison in Rome while he was awaiting trial before the emperor. This makes sense of Paul's evident fear about the future and the reference to the praetorium. In more recent scholarship, however, a strong case has been made for the letters to have been written in either Ephesus or Caesarea Maritima. The evidence, in particular for Ephesus, is that it would be much quicker and easier for Epaphroditus and Timothy to travel between Paul and the Philippians to Ephesus, which was much closer than Rome (466 miles, not the 4,608 miles to Rome).

The problem with Ephesus as a location is that there is no evidence for a praetorium there nor, indeed, that Paul was imprisoned there. The key discussion about the praetorium relates as much to the governor's palace as to the elite guard themselves. Those who favour Ephesus as a location argue that the praetorium refers to the soldiers who were attached to the governor's palace (as it does in Mark 15:16) not to the emperor's guard. The issue is that the governor's residence was only called a praetorium in an imperial province (as Syria was) not in a senatorial province (which is what Ephesus was). See discussion in E. Verhoef, *Philippi*, 27.

The debate rages on about the most likely location for Paul's imprisonment while he wrote these letters, with opinions split largely between Rome and Ephesus. For me the arguments about the praetorium, and the importance of the Via Egnatia for travel in the region, which made travel to Rome far easier than it would be otherwise (see page 220), tip me towards Rome as the most likely location. Those who have read my previous book, *Phoebe*, will also recognise that this means *Lydia* fits alongside that book, as a companion.

If we do accept that Paul wrote Philippians from prison in Rome, then this would date our story to the early 60s AD, a little over ten years after Paul's visit to Philippi, which is recorded in Acts 16. This visit can be dated relatively accurately because, after leaving Philippi, Paul travelled onwards to Corinth (Acts 18) where Gallio was said to be proconsul. Gallio was only proconsul for a year: AD 51–52. This means Paul was probably in Philippi in AD 50–51. If Paul was imprisoned in Ephesus, not Rome, while writing Philippians, it doesn't make much of a difference to the overall context; all it does is bring the date forward by about five years.

For more on the location of Paul's imprisonment see the discussion in the introduction to M. Bockmuehl, *The Epistle to the Philippians* (Continuum, 2006), 25–32, which opts for Rome, and the counter view in M. Bird and N. Gupta, *Philippians*, 20–24, which argues for Ephesus.

Paul's letters

One of the primary ways we meet Paul is through the letters he wrote to various groups and individuals. Some letters, like the epistle to the Philippians, were written to places where he proclaimed the good news of Jesus Christ for the first time, and where, following his visit, a church was founded; other letters, like the epistle to the Romans, were written to groups of Christians most of whom Paul had not met; others still, like the epistle to Philemon, were written to individuals. There is no doubt that Paul wrote more letters than have survived. 1 and 2 Corinthians, for example, make mention of another two letters Paul wrote that we no longer have. Paul's epistles were written for a variety of reasons: some were written to explain the Christian faith; some were written in response to a particular situation; some were written to offer encouragement and thanks.

One of the key features of Paul's letters is that they provided a way for him to begin or maintain contact with groups of Christians around the Roman empire. It is worth noting, though, that this was not the only way in which he made or maintained contact. Paul himself travelled widely, but also sent envoys like Timothy, to visit on his behalf. The significance of Paul's letters for the church today is that we still have some of them millennia after Paul and his companions died. The letters continue to give us insights into what it was like to be a Christian in the first decades after the death and resurrection of Jesus, and what major issues and concerns arose within these earliest communities. Letters like Paul's epistle to the Philippians are particularly interesting as, reading between the lines, they show us the challenges these Christians faced as well as the faith that sustained them through these challenges.

For more on Paul's letters and on the process of letter writing see E. R. Richards Jr, *Paul and First-Century Letter Writing: Secretaries, Composition and Collection* (Apollos, 2005).

The historical reliability of Acts

Another factor that needs exploring is whether we can rely on Acts as an historical source. At the end of the nineteenth century and beginning of the twentieth century, certain key scholars such as F. C. Baur and A. von Harnack raised questions about the reliability of Acts on the grounds that it had a clear theological agenda (i.e. telling the story of how the good news of Jesus Christ reached to the ends of the earth, and most particularly to Rome). Although this view was widely held for many years, scholars have now questioned this position, recognising that many ancient histories were written with the clear intention of arguing a particular point and that this should not lead us to jettison the historicity of their narrative entirely.

As a result, and given the importance of the episode recorded in Acts 16:11–40 for setting the scene of Christian community in Philippi, I have taken the events recorded there at face value. This is also one of those occasions, mentioned in the introduction, where a decision needs to be made because this is a story and not a more general piece of New Testament theology.

For more on this discussion see M. Hengel, *Acts and the History of Earliest Christianity* (Fortress Press, 1979), and C. J. Hemer, *The Book of Acts in the Setting of Hellenistic History* (Mohr Siebeck, 1989).

Notes

Chapter 1

For notes on Lydia herself, on dyeing and dealing in purple and on Philippi see 'Setting the scene', p. 222.

NEAPOLIS (THRACE)

The city of Neapolis (today known as Kavala and not to be confused with the Neapolis that can be found in Italy in this period) was founded around the seventh century BC by inhabitants from the island of Thasos which is about thirty miles off the coast. When Philip of Macedon took over the city of Philippi, he also captured the nearby Neapolis (10 miles away) and made it Philippi's harbour. The city remained important, though small, as it was on Via Egnatia and was also a sea port. It was dwarfed in this period, however, both by the Roman colony of Philippi and by Thessalonica, which lay around two hundred and sixty-five miles to the west along the Via Egnatia.

DYEING GUILD IN THYATIRA

For thousands of years, guilds, associations of craftspeople and traders, were vital for business. Those who engaged in the same business, such as dyeing, would form a professional association to regulate price and production. Guilds could often be highly influential in the day-to-day life of cities and towns. Thyatira's connection with dyeing is well attested from many inscriptions, and it is clear from them that the dyeing guild was very important within the city and surrounding region. It is also interesting to notice that, within the dyeing guild, purple dyers were of particular importance (out of twenty-eight inscriptions found in Thyatira, fifteen are to purple dyers).

Chapter 2

BAND OF WOMEN

As noted on page 229, the key feature of the gathering that Paul found outside the city gates was that it consisted exclusively of women. As a result, it would have had no official or recognised status. Nevertheless, Luke suggests that when Paul was searching for his accustomed Jewish gathering place as the first place he visited in a location (something that he did in every new place he visited) he found instead a band of women in a place of prayer. There is nothing in the narrative to suggest that Paul was disappointed or found it lacking in any way in contrast to his usual visit to a synagogue.

Evidence from early synagogues indicates that a gathering of this kind, even though not a formal synagogue here, would have taken the form of a discussion of Scripture. It would be normal custom that whenever a more qualified person arrived – such as Paul was, having studied we are told in Acts 22:3 with the renowned Rabbi Gamaliel in Jerusalem – then whoever was gathered, male or female, would defer to them. It should be noted, however, that in the ancient world men were always preferred as teachers (see discussion in Keener, *Acts,* vol. 3, 450–1).

A PLACE OF PRAYER

For more on why this is called a place of prayer and not a synagogue see Introduction, page 228.

The account in Acts that records Paul's visit to the 'place of prayer' is significant and worth pausing with for a moment. It was Paul's custom, when arriving in a new place, first to go into the synagogue and from there to proclaim the Gospel to others in the place. As we noted in the introduction, it is likely that the 'place of prayer' was not a synagogue because there were insufficient men for it to be one. Nevertheless, although not a full synagogue, it was where Jewish devotion was taking place and therefore the logical place for Paul to go at the start of his visit.

What is impossible to know, either from Acts itself or from external evidence, is whether the place of prayer was an actual building or simply a place where people gathered out of doors. Views on this subject are reached by guesswork and little more. Some argue strongly for an open-air meeting; others equally strongly for a building. Reimer assumes that the place of prayer was also Lydia's home, which itself was also a dyeing work-shop, located outside the city because of its abhorrent smell. In my view, this takes the guesswork a little too far and connects up too many strands in one (see Reimer's argument in *Women in the Acts of the Apostles*).

The next question posed is where it was sited. Historically scholars have assumed that the river by the house of prayer was the Gangites which lay one and a half miles to the west of the city out of the Krenides gate. The problem is that one and a half miles is further than the permitted Sabbath day's journey (a permitted Sabbath day's journey is laid down in Exodus 16:29 and Numbers 35:5 as 2,000 cubits or around three quarters of a mile). As a result, I have opted to locate the place of prayer in the other most likely location, by the Neapolis gate, where a stream flows just outside the gate and well within a Sabbath day's journey from any point within the city. It is also interesting to note that there are two fourth-century churches here, one just inside the gate and one just outside. It is possible that they reflect a popular memory of Paul's visit here. (For more on this see Keener, *Acts vol 3*, 446–48.)

There is extensive discussion about the gathering place being near a river. It is worth noting that purification rites were much easier to undertake near a river, and that a good number of synagogues outside of Jerusalem were located near rivers. It might be that, upon learning that there was no synagogue in Philippi itself, Paul's natural instinct was to look near a river that was less than a Sabbath day's journey from the city.

SYNAGOGUES IN PHILIPPI

The first reference to a synagogue in Philippi can be found in an inscription from, probably, the third century AD. The inscription says that anyone who lays a body (i.e. buries) on the tomb of Flavius Nicostratos Aurelius Oxycholios must pay a fine to the synagogue. This makes it clear that two centuries after Paul's visit, there was something easily definable as a 'synagogue' in Philippi. I have imagined a synagogue (which took over from the place of prayer) much earlier than that. It is very difficult to prove when the first synagogue, which would have been recognised as such, was found in Philippi. If the theory put forward above, that the 'place of prayer' was so named because only women worshipped there, the building would have become a synagogue when enough Jewish men began worshipping in it. In later Jewish tradition enough men for an assembly or *minyan* (a Hebrew word that means count or number) is ten. This tradition can be traced back to Numbers 14:27 which calls the ten spies who came back from Canaan 'an assembly', implying that you need ten to make up an assembly. Crucially women were not counted in this ten.

PAUL'S APPEARANCE

The earliest description of Paul can be found in the Acts of Paul and Thecla II:3, an apocryphal story about Paul that was written in the mid second century AD. The New Testament apocrypha is a loose collection of writings about Jesus and his followers that were written by early Christians, but were not considered to be authoritative enough to be included in the canon of the New Testament. In the Acts of Paul and Thecla, Onesiphorus describes Paul as:

> a man little of stature, thin-haired upon the head, crooked in the legs, of good state of body, with eyebrows joining, and nose somewhat hooked, full of grace: for sometimes he appeared like a man, and sometimes he had the face of an angel.

The text dates to the mid second century AD, and though it cannot be demonstrated to be accurate, it is the fullest description of Paul that exists. It also rings true with some of the statements that Paul makes about himself, such as 2 Corinthians 10:10, in which Paul acknowledged that his opponents said, 'His letters were severe and powerful, but his physical presence was weak and his word contemptible.'

CLOTHING IN THE FIRST CENTURY

Jewish men would have looked immediately and recognisably different from Roman men due to their clothing. Men who were Roman citizens wore a short-sleeved (or sleeveless) knee-length tunic over which would be draped a woollen toga (a half oval piece of cloth approximately six feet by twelve feet, draped over the shoulders and around the body). The toga and sometimes also the tunic was normally white, but could have purple borders depending on the rank of the person wearing it. Togas were a strict sign of status, and the purple border indicated a person's standing in society. There is, however, evidence that sometimes people would wear purple even if they were not eligible to do so. Freedmen and slaves were forbidden from wearing a toga, but could wear almost anything else of their choosing.

Jewish men also wore an under tunic, but this would often have been longer, sometimes even ankle length. The outer garment or cloak was a heavy woollen rectangle open at the front and with holes for the arms. Numbers 15:38–39 and Deuteronomy 22:12 dictate that fringes or tassels (*ṣitṣit*) were to be attached to the corners of a garment and served as a reminder to keep God's commandments. *Tefillin*, or phylacteries (i.e. black leather boxes worn on the head and arm), would have been worn normally only for midweek morning prayers. Notice also that the fringe would have had at least one purple/ blue strand:

> [37] *The Lord spoke to Moses, saying:* [38] *Speak to the children of Israel, and tell them to make tassels on the corners of their garments throughout their generations and to put a blue cord on the tassel at each corner.* [39] *You have the tassel so that, when you see it, you will remember all the commandments of the Lord and do them.* (Numbers 15:38–39a)

As a result, someone familiar with Judaism would easily be able to identify a Jew from their clothing. For a fascinating article on fringes see J. Milgrom, 'Of Hems and Tassels', *Biblical Archaeology Review* 9, no. 3 (1983), 61–65.

It is never mentioned anywhere in Acts, or in his epistles, whether Paul dressed more like a Jew or more like a Roman. The one hint we have is the surprise expressed by Roman officials in Acts when Paul reveals his Roman citizenship. This implies that he didn't look like a Roman. For this reason, and because Paul remained proud of his Jewish identity (see Philippians 3:4–6), I have assumed here that he dressed according to Jewish custom, with fringes, and that Silas (who came from Jerusalem) and Timothy did the same. I have assumed that Luke, because he was either a Gentile or a god-fearer, was dressed in Greek clothing, unlike the other three.

SILAS AND TIMOTHY

Silas (probably also known as Silvanus and therefore also mentioned in Paul's epistles) was first mentioned in Acts 15:22 as one of the leaders who had been selected by the Jerusalem church to accompany Paul and Barnabas to Antioch. After Barnabas left Paul in Acts 15:39, Silas – and later also Timothy – became Paul's companion on the next stage of his journey. Silas was imprisoned with Paul in Philippi (Acts 16:16–40), but there is no mention of Timothy being imprisoned with them.

There is a little confusion over Silas's name. Silvanus was a Roman deity, and some scholars think that Silas is the Greek version of the Latin name, Silvanus. Fitzmyer in his commentary on Acts suggests that Silas might be the Greek version of the Aramaic Seila, which in turn is a version of the Hebrew Saul. Thus Saul would have been his Hebrew name, Silas his Greek, and Silvanus his Latin name, but he was called Silas by Luke to avoid confusion with Paul, who was also known by the Hebrew name of Saul until he travelled more widely in the Roman empire, where he was known by his Latin name, Paul. For more on this, see J. Fitzmyer, *The Acts of the Apostles* (Yale University Press, 2007), 564.

Timothy was from Lystra, in central Asia Minor/modern Turkey. He was one of Paul's most significant companions. He is regularly cited as writing letters with Paul (especially 2 Corinthians, Philippians, Colossians, 1 and 2 Thessalonians, and Philemon) or as sending greetings (Romans). He was a trusted envoy of Paul to congregations (see 1 Corinthians 4:17; 16:10; Philippians 2:19), and was clearly valued by him. Acts 16:1 recounts that although Timothy was Jewish because his mother was Jewish, his father was a Greek, which means that he had not been circumcised. Slightly surprisingly, Paul ensured that he was circumcised before accompanying him. The reason for this seems to be that, although Paul did not encourage

Gentile followers of Christ to convert to Judaism, Timothy was already Jewish, and it would have reassured the many Jews whom they met as they travelled to know that he was circumcised. It is worth noting that this is one occasion when Paul's apparent hard line stance was moderated due to practical considerations.

Slightly oddly, although Timothy is mentioned in Acts 16:4 as accompanying Paul and Silas, and mentioned again in Acts 17:14 as staying behind with Silas in Beroea, he is not mentioned in the intervening verses – only Paul and Silas are imprisoned, only Paul and Silas are said to go to Thessalonica. It is also worth noting that the author of Acts – assumed to be Luke – describes Paul's travels in the first person plural – we – throughout. This implies that he is there too. I therefore assume a travelling group of four in Philippi (Paul, Silas, Timothy and Luke, though there may have been more or indeed fewer).

For more on Timothy see B. J. Malina, *Timothy: Paul's Closest Associate* (Liturgical Press, 2008).

JUDAISM IN THYATIRA
Many scholars are agreed that Lydia is likely to have first learnt about Judaism from her home city of Thyatira, since there does not appear to have been a sizeable enough Jewish community in Philippi itself to have attracted her interest. We know from inscriptions that Thyatira – and indeed the whole of the region of Lydia – contained a large Jewish community, and it makes sense that Lydia had learnt about it there. See discussion in A. T. Kraabel, *Judaism in Western Asia Minor Under the Roman Empire: With a Preliminary Study of the Jewish Community at Sardis, Lydia* (Harvard University, 1968), 155–97.

Notes: Chapter 2

A ROMAN DOMUS OR HOUSE
When we imagine Roman houses, we often imagine something
similar to what I am describing in these opening chapters:
spacious single-storey dwellings built on a floor plan like the
one below. In Rome itself, only the wealthiest of citizens could
afford to live in such dwellings, while the majority of people
lived in tenement or apartment blocks. Archaeological evidence
indicates that the ground floors of tenement buildings contained
workshops or other shops. Above these, though still on the
lower floors, were opulent apartments occupied by wealthier
citizens who could not afford a domus. The higher up you lived
in the tenement blocks the poorer you were likely to be, as fires
often broke out on the highest floors, and it was very difficult to
escape.

Outside Rome, more people could afford to live in a domus,
so it is not unlikely that a successful business person like Lydia
(assuming that she was successful) – who is said by Acts to
dwell in a house – would dwell in a more spacious domus. There
is extensive discussion among scholars about the kinds of
buildings in which the earliest Christians might have met. The
answer seems to be a wide range of buildings, but most
commonly in workshops or tenement buildings. I have set this
story largely in Lydia's domus solely because Acts appears to
point us in this direction.

For more on housing in the Roman world see the helpful
descriptions in P. Oakes, *Reading Romans in Pompeii: Paul's
Letter at Ground Level* (SPCK Publishing, 2009), 89–97. See
also E. Adams, *The Earliest Christian Meeting Places* (T&T
Clark, 2015) for a full discussion of the kinds of places in which
the earliest Christians would have met to worship.

It is also worth noting that Roman houses often had shops or
workshops facing the street, with the family rooms at the rear
of the property. A trader like Lydia would probably have sold
her wares from the front of the house and lived in the rooms

further back. Here is a plan of a classic Roman house such as would have been found throughout the empire:

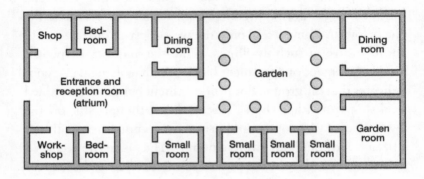

Chapter 3

CLEMENT

Clement is mentioned in Philippians 4:3, shortly after Euodia and Syntyche. His identity is unknown beyond that he is cited by Paul as a co-worker and that his name is written in the book of life. Clement is a Latin-based name, so indicates a Roman connection. Acts 16 mentions an unnamed Roman jailer who later became Christian. I thought it would be fun to connect the two and have him influential in the Philippian Christian community when Lydia returned. It is a flight of fancy, nothing more. The one element that has more support is the supposition that Clement was an *episkopos* or overseer, as mentioned by Paul in Philippians 1:1 (for more discussion on Paul's use of *episkopoi* and *diakonoi* see page 266). Various scholars argue that this was also the role of Euodia and Syntyche, so it would make sense if Clement were too, since they are mentioned together in the same verse.

A ROMAN ATRIUM

During the Roman empire, and in the houses of the wealthy, the atrium was the reception room of the house (see plan above).

They were light, airy spaces, lit by the *compluvium*: a hole in the roof that was designed to let rainwater into the *impluvium*, a marble lined pool below. The householder would often sit on the opposite side of the *impluvium,* facing the *vestibule* or hallway, and hence the guests who entered the house. Although in the period of the Roman republic the atrium was often a family room, by the time of the empire it was a much more formal reception area, with family rooms located towards the back of the house. Even non-citizens like Lydia would have been accustomed to treating the space in this way.

Roman dining rooms
In the Roman world a dining room, known as a *triclinium*, was a place of strict hierarchy. A normal-sized house, such as Lydia's, would probably have had a dining room containing three couches, each of which could fit three people. Larger houses would have been able to accommodate more guests. Guests would be seated in a strict hierarchy, with the most important closest to the host, on their right and left. If more than nine people were invited to a feast then they would be seated outside the dining room, in other rooms, again in order of importance. This hierarchy was a vital part of all dining experiences – even in the Galilee and Judea of Jesus' day – and makes sense of numerous passages such as Luke 14:10, in which Jesus encourages his followers to sit in the 'lowest place', i.e. the least honoured place.

In such settings slaves and servants would bring the food to the guests; they would never expect to sit and eat with them. It is clear from passages like 1 Corinthians 11:17–22 that this custom of hierarchical dining caused division in early Christian communities, especially when they commemorated Jesus' last meal with his followers. It is one of many practical issues that the earliest followers of Jesus had to wrestle with, an issue that ran counter to everything they knew about honour and status.

For a more detailed discussion of the social issues hinted at in 1 Corinthians 11:17–22 see J. Murphy-O'Connor, *St. Paul's Corinth: Texts and Archaeology* (Michael Glazier, 2002), 153–61, and B. Witherington, *Conflict and Community in Corinth: A Socio-Rhetorical Commentary on 1 and 2 Corinthians* (William B. Eerdmans Publishing Co., 1996), 247–52.

PYTHONESS OR PYTHIAN SPIRITS AND
THE TEMPLE AT DELPHI
The description of the slave girl in Acts 16:16 was that she had a *pneuma pythona* (a pythoness or pythian spirit). Later in the Roman empire, the phrase was used quite generally to describe an 'oracular spirit' (in other words someone who spoke with the authority of an oracle), but most scholars believe that in the earlier period this phrase referred specifically to 'the Pythia'. The Pythia was the name of the high priestess, who pronounced oracles in the temple of Apollo at Delphi – anyone with a pythian spirit was thought to pronounce oracles with the same authority as the Delphic oracle.

The Pythian oracle can be dated to at least the eighth century BC and possibly earlier, and continued to be an important phenomenon until the fourth century AD. Originally the Pythia was a young girl, but, in the third century BC after the Pythia had been kidnapped and raped, an older woman, often a peasant, was chosen instead. People who sought the advice of the Pythia would journey to Delphi, be prepared in advance by the priests who served the temple, and then would put their question to the Pythia, who would offer counsel as to how they should act in the future.

For an extensive discussion of the Pythian oracle see Keener, *Acts*, 492–504.

DELPHI
The temple at Delphi, dedicated to Apollo, the god of archery, music, dance, truth and prophecy, was the most important in all of the Greek world. The Greeks thought Delphi to be the centre of the world, since according to legend Zeus released two eagles, one in the east and one in the west, and they met in Delphi. Legend also declared that the temple originally belonged to Gaia, the goddess of the earth, whose child – Python – guarded it. Python was slain by Apollo and its body fell into a crevice and rotted. Anyone who stood over the crevice would be overtaken by the fumes and fall into a trance and thereby be filled with the presence of Apollo.

It is important to remember that, for Greeks, Delphi was a holy place, and its influence was at its height during the Greek republic. The oracle was consulted for matters of state as well as for personal concerns and so sat right at the heart of Greek identity and politics. The Romans conquered Delphi in 191 BC, and in 86 BC it was stripped of many of its treasures by General Sylla. Many Romans still visited the oracle, but the temple never again achieved the prominence that it had had during the height of the Greek republic.

Romans who lived in a colony such as Philippi, therefore, would have known and respected the tradition of the pythian oracle, but, as is seen in Acts 16, would not necessarily treat it with the reverence that a native Greek might have done.

Chapter 4

DEMON POSSESSION, THE PYTHIAN SPIRIT AND THE BIBLE
You can't read far in the Gospels and Acts before encountering 'demon possession'. A belief that demons possessed some people and forced them to act in certain ways was commonplace in the ancient world (and indeed for many centuries after that). What is hard for us to do is to work out how that relates

to any experience that we might have today. The difference between the world view in the first and twenty-first centuries is so vast that it is probably unwise to try to map one onto the other; to do so risks a simplistic and inaccurate equation between demons and, for example, psychosis which is profoundly unhelpful. Not only that, it also contributes to – even fuels – popular misconceptions of mental illness being connected with evil. What we do know, however, is that Jews, Greeks and Romans all believed that it was possible for human beings to be possessed by demons in such a way that it affected their behaviour and their ability to fit into wider society. We also know that many cultures both throughout human history and today similarly believed and continue to believe in demon possession. As Keener notes, 'Anthropologists today generally try to study the phenomenon from the perspective of societies that claim it, instead of imposing a Western interpretive grid on it' (Keener, *Acts*, 516).

What is interesting about the account of the slave girl in Acts 16:16 is that she does not appear to have been detrimentally affected by the pythian spirit, quite the opposite in fact. People sought her out and paid money to receive her insights. It is also worth noting that Luke doesn't say that she had a 'demon' (*daimonion*), just the pythian spirit (*pneuma pythona*). What connects demon possession and the slave girl, however, is that both recognised the 'truth'. In the Gospels, the demons recognised who Jesus was, and in Acts 16 the slave girl recognised who Paul was. What is unclear in Acts is why this upset Paul so much. She proclaimed nothing other than the truth. You might have thought that Paul would have been pleased to have someone recognise and acknowledge who he was. The issue may have been that the recognition came from the pythian spirit not from the girl herself, but the whole episode is less clear than it at first appears.

For more on demon possession see E. Ferguson, *Demonology of the Early Christian World* (Edwin Mellen Press, 1984).

Notes: Chapter 4

JOINT OWNERSHIP OF SLAVES

Acts 16:16 refers, slightly unusually, to the slave girl having more than one owner. While this could refer to a husband and wife partnership, it would be unusual, as normally any reference to a man was taken to include his wife as well. There would therefore be no need to mention a 'wife' alongside her husband as co-owner. More likely is that the girl's worth as a giver of oracles was so great that she was owned by a consortium of masters who all profited from her prophetic skill. I have imagined here a partnership of two, though the Greek plural could refer to more than this.

ORACLES AND FORTUNE-TELLING

The NRSV intriguingly translates the Greek verb *manteuomai* as 'fortune-telling'. While this is a possible translation, it feels as though it trivialises what the people of the ancient world thought was going on. This is the verb used for prophesying and for 'giving an oracle', as at Delphi with the Pythia. The idea was that Apollo – the god of prophecy – would speak to the person seeking counsel through the mouth of the person with the pythian spirit, in this case the slave girl. Whatever the girl actually said, it is clear that her owners, as well as those seeking counsel, thought that she was prophesying. As a result, it would make more sense to translate verse 16 as '(she) brought great profit to her owners by prophesying'.

THE FORUM

In Roman cities the forum was not just a marketplace, but a place where debates were held. It was the public square of any Roman colony. The forum was often surrounded by Roman baths, temples, and other places of business. It was particularly important in Roman cities, but most ancient cities had similar areas. In order to maximise the number of dwellings that could be crammed within the safety of the walls, most streets in cities were very narrow. Only the marketplace/forum and spaces by the city gates were more spacious – whenever references are made to wide space or roads in biblical texts, they are referring to these particular locations within a city.

The forum was the place where everything important happened. It contained market stalls, but was also the place where public debate and teaching occurred. It would therefore have been a natural place for Paul to proclaim the good news of Jesus, and also the natural place for someone with a pythian spirit to ply their trade.

As a Roman colony, Philippi's forum was built following the Roman model rather than the Greek model (called in Greek an *agora*). A Greek agora was square, in contrast to a Roman forum, which was rectangular (Philippi's forum was 230 by 485 feet). The street plan of the city also followed a Roman design, which meant that a north–south street intersected the east–west street through the middle of the forum (in contrast to Greek cities, which had parallel streets).

For more on this see Keener, *Acts*, 549. See plan of Philippi above on page 221.

Chapter 5

WHAT HAPPENED TO THE SLAVE GIRL?
There is no evidence in Acts about what happened to the slave girl after the exorcism, beyond the details that her owners were furious due to the removal of their revenue stream. There is no doubt that the girl would have experienced a drop in prestige in the household and might even have been sold on to someone else. Indeed, Keener wonders whether the potential impact on the slave girl was why it took Paul a few days to cast out the spirit (Keener, *Acts*, 547–48). What Acts does not tell us is what happened to her next. Reimer hypothesises that the Christian community bought her freedom (Reimer, *Women in the Acts*,

180–84). It is a hypothesis that I have chosen to adopt here. There is no evidence for it, nor is there evidence against it, and from a narrative perspective it allowed me to keep the slave girl, whom I've named Ruth, in the narrative easily.

MAGISTRATES AND LICTORS

The word that translates as magistrates is *stratēgoi*, but probably refers to the Roman title *duumvirs* (or *duovirs*). In a Roman colony like Philippi the magistrates might have had the title 'Praetor'. In all aspects of Roman public life, two men were appointed to oversee justice whether in Rome itself or in one of its colonies. The magistrates were elected normally for a period of a year. The Roman justice system rested on accusation, such as we see here, and normally consisted of someone of a higher status accusing someone of a lower status. The assumption of the accusers here is that as Roman citizens (which they are assuming Paul and Silas are not) they could declare that these foreigners were disrupting the city and could call for them to be punished accordingly. By law, each magistrate would have had six lictors who acted as bodyguards/enforcers. Although the lictors are not mentioned by name here, it is likely that it was they who beat Paul and Silas with rods (lictors carried the magistrates' rods of office) and then delivered them to jail. Scourging was common in the Roman world either as a prelude to execution (as for Jesus) or as a warning to the culprit and others not to repeat the action.

One odd feature of this account is that Roman law did not allow Roman citizens to be beaten, yet Paul did not claim citizenship here, before the beating, as he did in Acts 22:25–29. Scholars have varying views about why Paul did not claim to be Roman at this point in the story, but there are no conclusive answers given in the debate.

Notes: Chapter 5

ROMAN PRISONS

Roman prisons were not used as they are widely used in the modern world. By and large they were not used as a punishment, or at least they were not meant to be used like that. Indeed, there were various laws in place at the time which were intended to discourage such a practice. Prisons were most commonly used to hold people until trial or, after trial, until execution. It is clear from Acts 16, however, that Paul and Silas were jailed for neither of these reasons – they had been tried already by the magistrates, and had not received a sentence of death. Therefore, their imprisonment was meant as a punishment. How long the magistrates intended to keep them is unclear, possibly only until the morning, when they could be evicted from the city.

It is also unclear where the prison was in Philippi. Most Roman cities would have had a prison near the public buildings. The site traditionally believed to have been the prison, just north of the forum, is today thought to be too small, but the location would have been somewhere near the middle of the city and not far from the forum. The description in Acts 16 suggests that the jailer lived at least nearby if not in the prison itself.

For more on prisons and Paul's imprisonment see B. Rapske, *The Book of Acts and Paul in Roman Custody* (William B. Eerdmans Publishing Co., 1994).

STOCKS

The practice of putting prisoners in stocks was partially for security, but also partially for torture. A large piece of wood, split down the middle, had holes in it and was anchored to the ground. Prisoners' feet were inserted through the holes, and the piece of wood closed around their ankles. In order to increase their pain, their feet were often inserted through non-adjacent holes, far apart, which would force them to lie down on the prison floor. Once in the stocks, they would be unable to change position.

See discussion in Rapske, *Custody*, 126–127.

HYMNS OF THE EARLY CHURCH

The most common hymns or songs sung in the early church appear to have been psalms. They were certainly sung by Jesus and his disciples and, as many of the earliest Christians were Jewish, they would have known them and passed them on. Various Pauline passages (1 Cor. 14:26; Eph. 5:19; Col. 3:16) also suggest that songs focused on Christ were sung too. One of the big discussions is whether passages like the Philippians Christ Hymn were, in fact, sung as songs (and indeed whether the hymn pre-dates Philippians). Although much scholarship from the twentieth century established as 'fact' that Philippians 2:5–11 was a pre-existing hymn that was incorporated into the epistle by Paul, scholars today are less convinced by the theory, largely because the passage fits so well theologically with the rest of the epistle (for more on this see page 294).

For a careful exploration of the issues see R. P. Martin, *A Hymn of Christ: Philippians 2:5–11 in Recent Interpretation in the Setting of Early Christian Worship* (IVP US, 1997).

EARTHQUAKES

Earthquakes are common in the region around Philippi and were understood in the ancient world to be miraculous signs from God. There are extensive stories told in both Jewish and Greek literature in which heroes (in Greek literature these were often gods) were vindicated while held prisoner by an earthquake that freed them. It seems likely that Luke's audience would have made connections in their minds with this widespread tradition, and seen the story as a sign of Paul and Silas's vindication in a similar kind of way.

See the discussion in Keener, *Acts*, 587–591 for a full list of parallels.

Chapter 6

PAUL'S ROMAN CITIZENSHIP

There are only two references to Paul's Roman citizenship in the New Testament, both of them in Acts. One in Acts 16:37–38 and one in Acts 22:25–27. The sparsity of reference to Paul's citizenship and the fact that both references are found in Acts (and not in Paul's own letters) have led many scholars to question whether it was true, suggesting instead that Luke included it to appeal to such readers as would only have been interested in Christianity if it were properly respectable to a Roman audience. For such an argument see J. C. Lentz Jr, *Luke's Portrait of Paul* (Cambridge University Press, 1993).

Other objections to Paul's Roman citizenship include a scepticism that a Jew, born that far east in Tarsus, could realistically have had such a high honour within Roman culture, and that Paul never uses the full three names of Roman society (known as the *tria nomina* – all Roman citizens had three names: the praenomen, the nomen, and the cognomen). He is only ever known by one name. Scholars who accept and support Paul's Roman citizenship point to evidence of Roman citizens – even Jewish Roman citizens – as far east as Ephesus (which is further east than Tarsus) and also note that many Romans were known only by one or two names, not the full three. For a characteristically full and carefully argued view see Keener, *Acts*, 619–33.

It is very difficult to prove that Paul was, in fact, a Roman citizen, but it is also very difficult to prove that he was not. It is possible that Luke intended it to improve Paul's status in the eyes of others, but on the other hand a deep embedding in Roman culture would explain why Paul had a Roman name

(Paul) as well as a Jewish name (Saul), and why he was so comfortable travelling around the Roman empire.

It is interesting to note that Silas is included by Paul as a Roman citizen here. We know even less about Silas's citizenship than we do of Paul's, but it is worth noting that many scholars think Silas is the Silvanus mentioned in 2 Corinthians 1:19; 1 Thessalonians 1:1 and 2 Thessalonians 1:1. Silvanus is clearly a Latin name, and may support this assumption here.

HONOUR AND SHAME CULTURES

Like many ancient cultures, Rome was driven by the principles of honour and shame. In such cultures every decision made and every action undertaken was driven by the consideration of whether it would contribute to or detract from the esteem in which a person or family was held. Self-esteem was almost unheard of in the ancient world – it certainly didn't matter very much. Far more important was the esteem in which others held you. Honour and shame were also a fundamental part of the power dynamic – you showed honour to those you thought to be more important than yourself, and shamed those less important. For a helpful discussion of this and how it affects the way we read the New Testament, see this podcast from the Bible Project: https://bibleproject.com/podcast/honor-shame-culture-and-gospel/.

The exchange between Paul and the magistrates in Acts 16 is packed with the honour/shame dynamic. The magistrates clearly believed that they could shame Paul and Silas by flogging them without a trial, jailing them overnight, and then sending them away secretly because as magistrates and Roman citizens they had more power than these travelling Jewish prophets. It is interesting to note that Paul accepted the first two elements (flogging and being put in jail), but baulked at the third, probably because being dismissed quietly was the worst shaming. They were deemed so unimportant that dismissing them and not allowing them to see anyone else in the city was thought to be acceptable. It was at this point that Paul drew the magistrates' attention to his citizenship. In doing this he turned the tables on the honour/shame dynamic, revealing that he was not as powerless as they had thought he was, and that by treating him as badly as they had, they had shamed someone who was maybe not an equal, but was not as far below them as they had believed. By doing this, the magistrates had, in fact, shamed themselves publicly.

THE KRENIDES GATE
The Krenides gate was in the north-west corner of the city wall of Philippi. The Via Egnatia entered (or exited depending on what direction you were going) at the Neapolis gate near a stream, and continued north-west through the centre of the city, past the forum, and exited at the Krenides gate, from where it continued west in the direction of Thessalonica.

See page 221 for a map of Philippi.

Chapter 7

ROMAN GARDENS
As the floor plan on page 244 illustrates, it was common for Roman houses to contain a courtyard or outdoor room beyond the atrium. As with modern gardens, what would be grown in such spaces would differ from house to house, but flowers and vegetables, herbs, fruit bushes and vines were often grown in these spaces, around a patio where people could sit and relax. A particular favourite in many Roman gardens were mulberry bushes, indeed some think that the mulberry was introduced into the UK by the Romans, who were so attached to them and their fruit that they brought them with them.

NIGHTINGALES

Nightingales are an important feature in both Greek and Roman writing. The most famous tale, as retold by Ruth in this story, features Philomela, who was raped and mutilated by her sister's husband, Tereus. The story was told widely in Greek circles, but its most famous telling can be found in Ovid's *Metamorphosis* 6.438–674, and it is also referred to in Shakespeare's Sonnet 102. It is worth noting that Greek and Roman tradition, inaccurately, assumed it was the female birds that sang, hence the association with Philomela. In reality it is the male nightingale that sings. Given the widespread tradition in Greek mythology, however, that it was the female birds that sang, I have kept this in the narrative.

Nightingales are common across south-eastern Europe and are migratory, spending their summers (March to August) in Europe, and their winters in Africa. They are small (15–16 cm in length) brown birds, and are renowned for having a striking and beautiful song. While Ovid's account suggests that the nightingale's song is melancholic, others portray it as joyful.

ROMAN MEALS

The Romans ate three meals a day: *ientaculum* (breakfast), which often included bread, dates and honey and sometimes also cheese and olives; a light meal in the middle of the day (*prandium*) which consisted of cold meats and fish, often leftovers from the meal the previous evening, and the *cena*, which was a larger meal, and for those with money would have consisted of many different courses and types of food.

OVERSEERS AND DEACONS

One of the most unusual features of the letter to the Philippians is that Paul addresses it to 'all the saints in Christ Jesus who are in Philippi, along with *episkopoi* and *diakonoi*'. The challenge is to decide how to translate these two words. The second is easier than the first. The word *diakonos* is the usual word for servant, but a few times in the New Testament (particularly here and in Romans 16:1–2 when Paul introduced Phoebe) it is used in a way that suggests it had a particular meaning within Christian communities that communicated more than simply 'servant'.

Acts 6:1–7 records the appointment of the first seven deacons whose task it was to ensure that the widows from the different communities in the earliest churches – Hellenistic (i.e. Greek-speaking) and Hebrew (i.e. Aramaic-speaking) – received a fair distribution of food. As a result, many through the centuries have assumed that the role of a deacon is that of humble service. The painstaking work of J. J. Collins, however, has shown that this is not all the deacons did. For example, Stephen and Philip, who were among the first seven deacons selected, also proclaimed the Word (see Acts 6:8–15 and 8:5). As a result, it is more likely that while deacons did oversee daily distribution of food to widows, this was not the sole extent of their 'service'. They were commissioned agents asked to undertake a range of tasks. In this instance it is interesting to note that they are referred to alongside *episkopoi*.

Churches that have a threefold order of ministry often trace these three roles – bishop, priest or presbyter, and deacon – back to the New Testament. It is certainly true that all three are mentioned in the New Testament and that, in the post New Testament world, these three grew into the threefold order of ordained ministry that is recognisable today. It is harder to argue that bishop, priest and deacon were three identifiable roles, related to each other and fully formed in their definition in the New Testament period. One of the problems is that bishops, priests or presbyters, and deacons never occur together in the same text. The closest we have is this text, Philippians 1:1, which has bishops and deacons together. As a result, some think that in the earliest period bishops and presbyters were the same thing. This is certainly implied by 1 Clement 44:1–5 which seems to use the terms interchangeably:

> Our Apostles, too, by the instruction of our Lord Jesus Christ, knew that strife would arise concerning the dignity of a bishop; and on this account, having received perfect foreknowledge, they appointed the above-mentioned as bishops and deacons . . . Happy are the presbyters who finished their course before, and died in mature age after they had borne fruit; for they do not fear lest anyone should remove them from the place appointed for them.

Alistair Stewart particularly interestingly suggests that each assembly in Philippi had its own overseer, or bishop, and that when these overseers came together they were known as elders (*presbuteroi*).

Stewart's argument sheds some light on Philippians 1:1. The threefold order of ministry as people understand it today functions with an understanding of 'monepiscopacy', in other words, a single bishop to oversee an area – whether it be a city like Philippi, or a wider geographical area. It is clear from Paul's address, however, that there was more than one bishop in Philippi. This suggests that Stewart is right – at least in part – and that each gathering had an overseer and probably a deacon as well. Philippians does not mention elders, however, and when Paul addresses the *episkopoi* together he does not use *presbuteroi*. That part of Stewart's argument could be right, but can't be demonstrated from Philippians.

For this reason, I call this role 'overseer' rather than 'bishop' to avoid a confusion with the later period. It is unclear when the practice of 'ordination' such as we know it today began, but as the first 'deacons' in Acts 6:6 were commissioned by the laying on of hands, it is not too much of a stretch to imagine overseers might have been too.

For a very interesting exploration of these issues see
A. C. Stewart, *The Original Bishops: Office and Order in the
First Christian Communities* (Baker Academic, 2014). See also
J. N. Collins, *Diakonia: The Sources and Their Interpretation*
(Oxford University Press, 1990), and P. Gooder, 'Diakonia in
the New Testament: A Dialogue with John N. Collins',
Ecclesiology 3, no. 1 (2006), 33–56.

THE CHURCH IN THYATIRA

It is fascinating to note that there is a reference to a church in
Thyatira in the New Testament itself, albeit not a very flattering one. The letters to the seven churches in Revelation include
a letter to the church in Thyatira, commending their works of
love, faith, service and patient endurance, but condemning
them for tolerating 'that woman Jezebel, who calls herself a
prophet and is teaching and beguiling my servants to practise
fornication and to eat food offered to idols' (Rev. 2:18–28).

A later Christian sect from the third century AD argued that
this reference to the existence of a Christian community in
Thyatira was not only untrue, but also demonstrated that the
book of Revelation was untrustworthy. The sect were called
'the Alogi' by one of their greatest opponents, Epiphanius of
Salamis, who wrote in the fourth century AD. Alogi is a play on
words to hint that not only were they illogical, but they denied
'logos theology' which is laid out so poetically in John 1:1–18.
Few scholars are persuaded by any of this evidence, on the
grounds that Epiphanius was writing so long after the first
century, and also that the Alogi were vehemently opposed to
another group from this period, the Montanists, for whom the
book of Revelation was a key text.

The accusation in Revelation against 'Jezebel' is interesting.
It reveals that there was a woman in leadership of this community when Revelation was written, but that she had encouraged
the community to act in what the author of Revelation thought

was a less than orthodox way. Reading between the lines of the accusation it appears as though 'Jezebel', who in 1 Kings 16 to 2 Kings 9 is presented as the person who led God's people astray in worshipping other gods, has been allowing Christians in Thyatira to continue with other forms of worship. This would have been a strong temptation for anyone in this period since the entirety of life throughout the Roman empire focussed around the worship of a wide variety of gods. Refusing to take part meant cutting oneself off from normal life and participation in society.

In this period, the eating of meat at all would almost certainly have involved eating 'food offered to idols', since the vast majority of all meat consumed in the Roman world came from sacrifices. The question of whether you should eat food offered to idols was also a matter of concern in the Pauline churches as well as here. We find reference to it especially in 1 Corinthians 8:1–13, where Paul addresses it, though in a slightly different way to how the author of Revelation does here. Paul argues that it is all right to eat food offered to idols so long as it doesn't act as a stumbling block to others. The 'Jezebel' leader of Thyatira seems to have agreed with the Pauline stance, but took it one step further and also allowed members of the church to be involved in 'fornication', which could mean temple prostitution or might simply refer to worshipping other gods and not sexual activity. Since Revelation was probably written towards the end of the first century AD, I have assumed that 'Jezebel', whoever she was, was not the leader of the church in the mid 50s.

All in all, the reference reveals the complexity of living in a world in which the worship of gods was so widespread and so all-encompassing that it was difficult to avoid, and required constant vigilance, as the earliest Christians sought to live out their devotion to Christ in a way that did not suck them back into old patterns of worship.

It is not clear where the Christian community came from in Thyatira. It is possible that Paul travelled through there briefly on one of his journeys through Asia Minor, though no direct reference is made to this in Acts. More likely is the possibility that people from elsewhere, like Ephesus, brought word of faith in Jesus Christ. It is this explanation that I chose to follow here.

For more on the Christian community in Thyatira from Revelation see D. Aune, *Revelation* (Thomas Nelson, 1997), 201–14.

JOHN IN EPHESUS

Early Christian tradition locates John in the city of Ephesus. Irenaeus, writing in the late second century, said that his teacher, Polycarp, told the story that John the Apostle rushed out of a bathhouse in Ephesus – refusing to bathe there when he saw that a notorious heretic (Cerinthus) was present (Against Heresies 3:3–4). Tertullian (also late second century) also claimed that Polycarp was appointed Bishop of nearby Smyrna by John (*The Prescription against Heretics*, 32).

While it is impossible to be confident that John was in Ephesus, the tradition about his living there is comparatively early and therefore on balance may be more rather than less likely.

PAUL'S MISSIONARY JOURNEYS

It is common to split Paul's travels proclaiming the Gospel into 'missionary journeys'. This is something suggested, though not named as such, by Luke's telling of the travels in Acts. In Acts 13:3, Paul and Barnabas are sent off by the church in Antioch (the 'first missionary journey'); in Acts 15:40 Paul took Silas with him, and the believers commended them to the grace of the Lord (the 'second missionary journey'). The start of the 'third missionary journey' (Acts 18:23) is less clear, as it simply says that 'he departed and went from place to place through the region of Galatia and Phrygia, strengthening all the disciples'. While describing Paul's travel as 'missionary journeys' makes it clearer (and easier to delineate on a map), it lends it a sense of planning that is not revealed in Acts itself. Paul travelled around a lot and, we can tell from epistles like 1 and 2 Corinthians, he looped back on himself for additional visits that are not mentioned in Acts.

As a result, I prefer to refer to Paul criss-crossing his way through the Mediterranean. This description seems to fit the narrative in Luke more accurately than three deliberately planned and executed journeys with a beginning, middle and end. It also means that Paul may have passed through somewhere like Thyatira even though it is not mentioned in Acts or the epistles.

STORIES OF JESUS' MIRACLES
The Infancy Gospel of Thomas tells a number of stories about Jesus' childhood, and contains twelve miracles in all, including the two I mention in this chapter. I have stretched the dating to use them here. The first person to quote from the Infancy Gospel of Thomas was Irenaeus, who lived in the late second century AD. What I am trying to illustrate, however, is the complexity of living as a Christian in the first century and of not knowing whether something was authoritative or not. We can often see in Paul's letters his attempt to combat views fed to his communities by passers-by, and indeed, especially in 2 Corinthians, a querying of Paul's own authority by the communities he founded. The question of who and what to believe was a lively one in the first century, and indeed many of the centuries that followed.

VARIETY AND CHURCH STRUCTURE
One of the reasons why it is hard to trace church structure in the New Testament period is because there does not seem to be

consistency across contexts. Overseers are mentioned in Philippians, but not elsewhere; elders are mentioned elsewhere, but not here. Frequent mention is made of people in certain contexts who have churches meeting in their houses, with the implication that they were the leaders of the gatherings (see for example Prisca and Aquila in Romans 16:5); whereas in Philippians it appears that the 'overseers' were the leaders. It would hardly be surprising if 'church order' grew up differently in different places, with models of leadership arising out of local contexts such as synagogue worship, trading guilds, or philosophical societies. Frustrating though this may be to those of us who are trying to reconstruct a picture of early Christian worship and structure that can be used and possibly replicated in a modern context, it is important not to force the New Testament to say something that it does not. There does seem to be great variety in this early period, so that what happened in Philippi was not, necessarily, what happened in Corinth or Rome.

For an interesting exploration of the ways in which synagogue worship might have shaped church structure see J. Burtchaell, *From Synagogue to Church: Public Services and Offices in the Earliest Christian Communities* (Cambridge University Press, 2008).

Chapter 8

ANCIENT ROMAN STREET FOOD

Street food was a Roman invention. Although the well-off could afford a kitchen in their own home, the majority of people ate from the many food stalls that would be found in any Roman city. A *taberna* was the most common place to buy food: a takeaway stall selling a particular kind of food. In addition there were *thermapolia*, where there were long tables at which people could sit to eat. People would also sell food from carts or baskets along the side of the road.

For more on this see https://medium.com/exploring-history/
the-street-foods-of-ancient-rome-7f3d7e27d45d

HADES
Greeks believed that souls travelled to Hades after death. It is
described variously as being beyond the sea or beneath the
world. Hades was believed to be solely for the dead, and invis-
ible to the living. Hades was ruled by the Greek God 'Hades',
in Roman mythology called Pluto. In Greek mythology 'souls'
were insubstantial shades that existed in Hades, but with no
knowledge or purpose. They were also frozen in time and took
the form that they had at the moment of death.

New Testament ideas about life after death are, therefore,
radically different to Greek ideas involving real bodies and
resurrection and especially hope. It is worth noting that, in the
New Testament, the Greek word Hades was often translated as
'hell'. As a result, readers from the Greek and Roman world
would have understood it very differently to how we might
understand hell.

For more on this see P. Gooder, *Heaven* (SPCK Publishing,
2011), 94–96.

Chapter 9

BREAKING BREAD
One of the earliest descriptions of Christian worship can be
found in Acts 2:43–47. Following the coming of the Holy Spirit
at Pentecost, Luke describes the life of the earliest Christians as
having everything in common (2:44); spending time in the
temple (2:45); breaking bread at home, and sharing food with
joy and simplicity (2:45).

FOLLOWERS OF THE WAY

One of the descriptions of the Christian faith in Acts is 'The Way' (see Acts 18:25–6; 19:9; 22:4; 24:14). Indeed, it appears to have been the way in which the earliest Christians talked about themselves. Acts itself observes that the label 'Christian' was first used in Antioch (Acts 11:26, 'it was in Antioch that the disciples were first called "Christians"'), but implies that this was a description used of them by those who were not Christian, and was not a self-designation. Indeed, some wonder whether it was a derogatory title. The Greek word *christianoi* is made up of the Greek word for Messiah (*Christ*) and the Latin ending '*ianus*' meaning belonging to. A similar ending was used for those with allegiance to Herod (*Herodianoi*) and to Augustus (*Augustianoi*). *Herodianoi* appears to have been used with pride as a self-designation, and *Augustianoi* in a far more derogatory way. The fact that the earliest Christians did not appear to use the word to describe themselves suggests that perhaps it might have meant something like 'those Messiah types'.

Given this, while I have used the word Christian in the notes as an easy shorthand, I have avoided it in the story itself, as those in Lydia's community and beyond might not have used it of themselves.

DEACON

One of the complexities of understanding 'church order' in the earliest communities is working out what the titles actually meant. As noted above (page 257), the two words *episkopoi* and *diakonoi* appear to be being used by Paul in Philippians 1:1 as titles, but precisely what they meant remains unclear.

The title *diakonos* would have sounded particularly odd to the first-century ear. It was the usual word for servant, so to use it in an honorific way would have sounded strange. In a way it sums up the counter-cultural emphasis of Christianity in this period. In a world that cared only about status and honour, to have, as a title of respect, a word like *diakonos* that referred to some of the lowest status people within society would have been surprising and dislocating, and in being so would have conveyed something vital about what Christians believed.

For more on this see J. N. Collins, *Diakonia*, and A. C. Stewart, *Original Bishops*.

TENEMENT BUILDINGS

Although when we imagine Roman houses we imagine the kind of Roman domus I have described Lydia living in, the majority of the Roman world lived in different kinds of housing. In Roman colonies such as Philippi, houses would have been a more affordable option than they were in Rome, where, due to the shortage of space, houses were prohibitively expensive. Nevertheless, most people lived in tenement buildings, or *insulae*. Archaeologists estimate that 90–95 per cent of the population of Ostia (the coastal town near Rome) lived in tenement buildings. *Insulae* were often four or five storeys high, with wealthier occupants living on the lower floors and the poorest people living on the top, where is was harder to escape if the building crumbled or a fire broke out. *Insulae* were designed to accommodate the maximum number of people and so were often cramped and unsanitary.

For more on buildings and social status see P. Oakes, *Reading Romans in Pompeii: Paul's Letter at Ground Level* (SPCK Publishing, 2009).

EKKLĒSIA

The Greek word *ekklēsia* was used relatively early by both Paul and Matthew to describe the gathering of followers of the Way. This was an interesting choice. In the Old Testament, the assembly of God's people was called in Hebrew the *qahal*. When this word was translated into Greek sometimes it was translated most of the time by the word *synagōgē* from which we get the word synagogue, and the rest of the time it was translated by the word *ekklēsia*.

The word, however, did not just have a Jewish background. It also had a meaning in Greek cities, referring to citizens (not Roman citizens, but Greek citizens of the city who had voting rights). The power of Greek city states waned during the Roman empire, but the memory of the significance of the *ekklēsia* remained. In Greek city states those included were people wealthy enough and with sufficient status to be citizens; in the Old Testament the *qahal* – or gathering – was limited to men, but also, according to Deuteronomy 23:1–4, excluded the descendants of Ammonites or Moabites, illegitimate children, and eunuchs.

The resonance of the *ekklēsia* being a gathering open to women and men, adults and children, slave and free, rich and poor, was significant. I have left the word in Greek in the text because no English word communicates the extent of this resonance sufficiently. Our English word 'church' contains other echoes more focussed around buildings.

Chapter 10

PAUL AND SPAIN

My previous book, *Phoebe*, explored Paul's hopes of going to Spain as expressed in Romans 15:24 and 28, and how that all fitted with his arrest and imprisonment, first in Jerusalem and then in Rome.

What does become clear from both Acts and Romans is that although Paul's arrest in Jerusalem was not in his plan – he simply went to deliver the collection that he had made from Greek churches like the one in Philippi to the church in Jerusalem, which was struggling as a result of a famine – going to Rome to speak to the emperor about the good news of Jesus

Christ was always his aim. His ambition was to preach to the ends of the earth, but also to what he saw as its centre – Rome. Indeed, the story of Acts is really the story of how the good news spread from one centre of the world (Jerusalem) to another (Rome), though Luke made it clear throughout that in his view the real centre of the world was to be found in neither Jerusalem nor Rome, but in heaven.

THE EMPERORS CLAUDIUS AND NERO

Claudius (full name: Tiberius Claudius Caesar Augustus Germanicus) was born in 10 BC in Lyon, Gaul, into an ancient aristocratic family. His uncle was the Emperor Tiberius (42 BC to AD 37). Claudius was born with a limp, was slightly deaf, and was, as a result, considered by his contemporaries to be clumsy and coarse (for a long time it was thought that Claudius might have had polio, but modern theories point more to cerebral palsy as the origin of his symptoms). It is thought that this is why he escaped the killings of so many other nobles (including his father, his mother, and his two older brothers) that took place during the reigns of Tiberius and Caligula. It is certainly the reason that he became so well educated. Written off by his family, he spent a lot of time alone and wrote twenty-eight history books in Greek, as well as an autobiography, and a treatise on the Roman alphabet in which he argued for the addition of three extra letters to the alphabet (although none of these works now remain). After the murder of the Emperor Caligula (his older brother's son) he was found in the imperial palace trembling by the praetorian guard, and made emperor the next day. His learning meant that he was a good administrator and effected a number of significant changes in the workings of the empire.

Claudius's marriages were the subject of much comment. He married four times, after two failed betrothals. Claudius's final marriage was to his niece, Agrippina the younger, who spent a long time plotting to make her son, Nero (full name: Nero Claudius Caesar Augustus Germanicus), emperor at the expense of Claudius's natural born sons. Ancient historians believed that Claudius was poisoned by Agrippina, though some modern historians wonder whether he died naturally of old age.

In many ways Nero's accession to the throne was hailed by his contemporaries as the start of a golden age. The senate had been widely opposed to Claudius's reign, and was behind a number of attempted coups that occurred, which led to Claudius executing a large number of senators. Claudius was also renowned for having a viciously bad temper, which he took out on all those close to him. Nero was a handsome and charismatic young man. He was made emperor in AD 54 at the age of sixteen, and promised, in a speech written by his tutor the Roman philosopher Seneca, to restore the glory of the senate during his reign. His early years as emperor went well, and people's optimism about him appeared to be well founded.

This changed in AD 59 when Nero murdered his mother, Agrippina the Younger. From then on Nero's personal excesses and mood swings dominated his reign, and also led to the murder of Octavia, his first wife, in AD 62. This story is set in the early 60s, when Nero's reputation was beginning to turn and the stories of his lifestyle and brutality were becoming known. The fears I present of Christians coming to the attention of the Romans and suffering as a result began to come true after the great fire in AD 64.

For more on the reign of Claudius see J. Osgood, *Claudius Caesar: Image and Power in the Early Roman Empire* (Cambridge University Press, 2010).

And on Nero see D. Shotter, *Nero Caesar Augustus: Emperor of Rome* (Longman, 2008).

THE EXPULSION OF THE JEWS FROM ROME

The Roman historian Dio Cassius reported that, in AD 41, the emperor Claudius issued an edict that forbade Jews from holding meetings (*Roman History* 60:6.6). This may well have been because of 'Christian agitation in the synagogues resulting in violent conflicts' (Jewett, *Romans*, 18–19), which so worried the Romans that they forbade Jews from meeting together at all. A different Roman historian, Suetonius, reported that Claudius later expelled from Rome 'the Jews constantly making disturbances at the instigation of Chrestus's (Life of Claudius, 25) in around AD 49. This seems to imply that a little over ten years before the setting of this story the Romans were unable to distinguish between Jews and followers of Christ, so they expelled everyone. This would seem very likely from what we know of the Romans. We know from the Jewish historian Josephus that Romans regarded Jews as suspicious and untrustworthy in any case, and they would have seen adherents of, what was to them, a strange religion that found its roots in Jerusalem fighting among themselves and expelled them all.

For more, see R. Jewett, *Romans: A Commentary* (Augsburg Fortress, 2006), 18–20.

EUODIA AND SYNTYCHE

The disagreement between Euodia and Syntyche is infamous even though we know very little about it. All that Paul says in Philippians 4:2 is, 'I urge Euodia and I urge Syntyche to be of the same mind in the Lord.' The implication of this is that they were not 'of the same mind' at the time of writing. From this simple statement have arisen some eye-watering judgements and sweeping statements about women and their natural ability to fall out with each other.

What we actually know about Euodia and Syntyche is relatively little. Their names are Greek, meaning 'Good Journey' and 'Good luck' respectively. Their names stand in contrast

Notes: Chapter 10

to Clement, mentioned alongside them, whose name was Latin and of Roman origin. Paul's mention of them by name and as 'co-workers' with him indicates their status alongside him as missionaries. It is this that suggests they might legitimately be viewed as two of the overseers Paul addresses in 1:1 (see the argument in C. Osiek, *Abingdon New Testament Commentary – Philippians & Philemon* (Abingdon Press, 2000), 111–112). Others have argued that they were the deacons also mentioned in 1:1 (see D. Peterlin, *Paul's Letter to the Philippians in the Light of Disunity in the Church: 79* (Brill, 1995)), but, given that Paul calls them 'co-workers', overseers seems marginally more likely. John Chrysostom also appeared to consider them to be of importance within the Philippian church, saying:

> These women seem to me to be the chief of the Church which was there, and he commendeth them to some notable man whom he calls his 'yokefellow,' to whom perchance he was wont to commend them, as to a fellow-worker, and fellow-soldier, and brother, and companion, as he doth in the Epistle to the Romans, when he saith, 'I commend unto you Phebe our sister, who is a servant of the Church that is at Cenchrea.'
>
> St John Chrysostom, Homilies on Philippians 13

This brings us to the source of their disagreement. One explanation, which I have found persuasive, is that they disagreed over whether to support Paul or not. In Philippians 4:10 Paul alludes to the Philippians having stopped supporting him ('I rejoice in the Lord greatly that now at last you have revived your thought for me'), but the letter was shaped around Epaphroditus's visit and delivery of gifts ('I am fully satisfied, now that I have received from Epaphroditus the things from you', 4:18). This suggests that although they had stopped supporting Paul, they then began again. A reasonable scenario seems to be that Epaphroditus updated Paul on a disagreement between Syntyche and Euodia about whether to support him or not, and he decided to address it head on in 4:1–18.

See the argument in M. A. Jennings, *The Price of Partnership in the Letter of Paul to the Philippians: 'Make My Joy Complete'* (T&T Clark, 2018), 154.

PAUL'S IMPRISONMENT IN ROME

As noted above (page 252), it was unusual for prisoners to be kept in prison for very long, since Roman prisons only kept people awaiting trial or awaiting execution, and not usually for punishment. Acts 28:16 notes that Paul's Roman imprisonment was not in a prison, but in a house by himself which he paid for at his own expense (28:30). If we accept Rome as the location for Paul's imprisonment, it makes sense of the Philippians' gift to him to help him offset expenses in what would have been a very expensive location, though the same would have been true in Ephesus as well.

There is an ancient tradition that the house in which Paul lived, awaiting trial before the emperor, was a house under Santa Maria in Via Lata, on the site of the Palazzo Doria Pamphilj, where the Anglican Centre in Rome is now housed. Recent archaeological investigation has confirmed that the location is of the right date and could have been the place of his imprisonment. For discussion of this see https://romanchurches .fandom.com/wiki/Santa_Maria_in_Via_Lata and http://www. matthewcowden.com/2016/10/23/pauls-house-arrest-apart- ments-discovered/.

As Paul's imprisonment was in a private house, he seems to have been allowed to have various companions. We know that Epaphroditus was with him because Paul made reference to this in Philippians 2:25–30, and that Timothy was also there, as the letter to the Philippians comes from both him and Paul. The question is, who else might have been there? Given Luke's knowledge of this part of Paul's life, it is commonly assumed that he accompanied Paul to Rome (though at this point we should note that the accounts of Paul's sea journey and shipwreck have such a different style it is often assumed that these were not written by Luke himself). Others who may have been there include Aristarchus (mentioned in Colossians 4:10–11), Tychicus (also mentioned in Colossians 4:7–9 and Ephesians 6:21–22), Onesimus (mentioned in Colossians 4:9 and Philemon 10), Mark (mentioned in Philemon 24 and Colossians 4:10), Jesus Justus (mentioned in Colossians 4:10), Epaphras (Colossians 4:12), and Demas (Colossians 4:14 and Philemon 24). The key question is whether Paul wrote Colossians and, if he did, whether he wrote it at a similar time to Philippians and during the same period of imprisonment or not. If he did, then we can construct a considerable group of companions for him; if not, then only Timothy and Epaphroditus were there. Paul's apparent reluctance to lose Epaphroditus does suggest that he had only a few companions, not the numbers of people indicated by Colossians and Philemon, but it is hard to be certain on this front.

THE JOURNEY FROM PHILIPPI TO ROME

The excellent website https://orbis.stanford.edu/ makes it possible to calculate journey times and routes across the Roman empire, using different modes of transport (on foot, on a horse, on an ox cart, and even military march) including the difference made if travelling in winter or summer. The summer route to Rome would be by ship from Neapolis to Puteoli or Ostia using the Corinthian *diolkos* (a road that spanned the Isthmia between the ports of Cenchreai and Lechaion and avoided the dangerous tides that flowed around the south of Greece) and would have taken around twenty days; the winter route would have been by the Via Egnatia with a short section by ship between Dyrrhachium and Brundisium, and would have taken around thirty-seven days.

Epaphroditus

Epaphroditus is mentioned only in Philippians: once in 2:25–30 and then at the end in 4:18. A similar name – Epaphras – is mentioned in Colossians (1:7 and 4:12) and in Philemon (23). This would be the shorter version of Epaphroditus, but since Epaphroditus is clearly from Philippi and Epaphras from Colossae, and because the name is very common, they are unlikely to be the same person.

Epaphroditus is mentioned very fondly by Paul. He is called his brother (*adelphos*), co-worker (*sunergos*), fellow soldier (*sustratiotēs*), apostle (*apostolos*) and minister (*leitourgos*). In addition to this, we learn from 4:18 that he went to Paul to deliver the churches' gifts and aid, then he fell dangerously ill and nearly died. He then recovered, but was homesick and worried for all those he'd left behind (2:26–27).

As noted in the body of the story in Chapter 3, the name Epaphroditus comes from the name for the Greek goddess Aphrodite. It was common, especially in Greek culture, to name people after gods and goddesses even if this meant giving a man the name of a female goddess.

The discovery of purple

A mythical explanation of the discovery of purple was provided by the little known philosopher and grammarian Julius Pollux, from Naucratis in Ancient Egypt. Although Pollux was writing in the second century AD, it is likely that the story he told stretched back for many centuries, passed on through oral tradition. His *Onomasticon* was a thesaurus, ten books long, organised by theme, and contained, alongside grammar and words and phrases, a range of fascinating stories and insights into life in the Roman world. One of these stories – the story of Hercules and his dog – was the story told by Rufus in this chapter. It was made famous in the modern world by the artist Peter Paul Rubens (1577–1640).

Chapter 11

BEING UN-ROMAN

In some ways, the concept of 'being Roman' was inclusive. The spread of the empire across the then known world meant that becoming Roman was comparatively easy, and Roman citizenship could be earned in a number of ways (in particular it was often given to soldiers and aristocrats who came from the provinces). In other ways, however, being Roman was very exclusive, and it was easy to fall outside the brackets of acceptability. Conventional behaviour fell within strict parameters, and those that fell outside those bounds, for a wide range of reasons from dress to sexuality, from religion to banditry, were at best vilified and at worst persecuted. Being 'Roman' involved, above all, allegiance to the emperor. Christians who swore their allegiance to 'Jesus Christ as Lord' were automatically at odds with Rome. It is these dynamics that led in some instances to full blown persecutions, but in others to Christians feeling simply ill at ease in Roman society.

See on this S. McElduff, *UnRoman Romans*, https://pressbooks.bccampus.ca/unromantest/ (accessed 19 July 2021).

What is harder to identify is how and to what extent the Romans pursued those they considered to be un-Roman. The picture is varied and unsystematic and seems to have depended on circumstance and the identity of those deemed 'un-Roman'. The higher a position someone held in society the more their Roman-ness mattered: Roman citizens mattered more than non-citizens; aristocrats more than those with low status, and so on.

For an interesting exploration of Christian persecution see C. Moss, *The Myth of Persecution* (HarperCollins, 2013).

THE DEPOSING OF HEROD ARCHELAUS

One of the most significant historical events in Judea happened in AD 6. Herod Archelaus was one of the sons of Herod the Great and, on Herod's death, was granted half of the kingdom to rule – the regions of Samaria, Judea and Idumea. The rest of the kingdom was split between two other sons, Herod Antipas (who governed Galilee and Perea), and Philip (who governed Iturea and Trachonitis).

Archelaus came to the throne in the middle of a crisis. His father, Herod the Great, had erected the image of a golden eagle over the gate of the temple. Two teachers – Judas and Matthias – incited around forty of their pupils to hack the eagle to the ground with axes because they saw the act as blasphemous. Herod had had them arrested and burnt to death. When Archelaus came to the throne the people of Judea pleaded with him to avenge the death of the forty – something he refused to do and a riot ensued, in the course of which around three thousand people were killed.

Archelaus's bad start continued, and the Jews and Samaritans united in their opposition to him and repeatedly petitioned the Romans to remove him. This came to a head in AD 6 after another revolt by Judas the Galilean. At this point the Romans removed Archelaus from the throne and ruled Judea, Samaria and Idumea directly through a prefect. The most famous of these prefects was Pontius Pilate, who was prefect from approximately AD 26 to 36.

For more on the Herodians see N. Kokkinos, *The Herodian Dynasty: Origins, Role in Society and Eclipse* (Spink Books, 2010).

ROMAN SOLDIERS IN JUDEA

There were two key types of soldier in the Roman empire: legionaries and auxiliaries. Legionaries were employed directly by Rome and their allegiance was to the emperor. They were

Roman citizens when they were recruited, and earned around three times as much as the auxiliaries. Most legionaries were infantry. Auxiliaries, in contrast, were equally divided between infantry and cavalry, and were often made up of local, non-Roman citizens who would be granted Roman citizenship as a reward for their service. Alongside them were soldiers who served the local king, or, as in the case of the temple, the temple authorities.

There were no legionaries posted in Judea until after the Jewish war (in AD 66–73) when the Legio X Fretensis was located in Judea. Before then the Roman soldiers in the region were auxiliaries, and thought to be made up of Archelaus's soldiers who had been incorporated into Roman forces after Archelaus had been deposed as king in AD 6. The Roman centurion at Jesus' crucifixion, therefore, was probably not a Roman citizen, but would likely have been made one after he left the army. The soldiers referred to in the Gospels would have been a mixture of Roman auxiliary forces, the soldiers of Herod Antipas from Galilee, and the temple soldiers.

As a result, the centurion at the crucifixion would almost certainly have been an auxiliary, and used to speaking in Greek rather than Latin, and maybe also would have been even more comfortable with Aramaic than either of the other two languages.

For more on this see C. B. Zeichmann, 'Military Forces in Judaea 6–130 CE: The Status Quaestionis and Relevance for New Testament Studies' *Currents in Biblical Research* 17, 1, (2018), 86–120: https://doi.org/10.1177/1476993X18791425 (accessed 19 July 2021)

THE SCARLET/PURPLE CLOAK AT JESUS' CRUCIFIXION
The details of the cloak put on Jesus differ from gospel to gospel. Mark's Gospel (15:7) says that they put 'purple' on him; Matthew's (27:28) that they put a 'scarlet cloak' on him, i.e. a

soldier's cloak; Luke's Gospel does not contain the detail, and John's Gospel makes reference to a 'purple robe'. The point of the action (including putting a crown of thorns on his head) was to parody the dress of a Hellenistic king, like the Herodians or the Hasmoneans (the descendants of the Maccabees). Exactly what they used to mimic this attire has got lost in the retelling of what happened.

Since the cheaper form of purple, made from the madder root, is a shade known today as 'Turkey red' then the scarlet robe could have been a more accurate description of the colour of whatever was used, as the chances of them using the expensive true 'Tyrian purple' would be slim.

Chapter 12

GOD'S SON

The question of what the centurion meant when he said in Mark 15:39 'Truly this man was God's Son' has intrigued scholars for many years. The problem is that the construction is unclear in Greek, because it uses the verb 'to be', which removes the need for the definite or indefinite article ('the' or 'a'), so could mean the Son of the God; the son of a god; a son of the God; or a son of a god. While it's a small, picky point, the answer given really affects what the centurion meant when he said it – was it a declaration of faith or a statement that Jesus was clearly someone special?

The key feature to notice is, perhaps, that what the centurion meant was not as important as what Mark understood it to mean. For Mark this statement recalls two key events – the baptism and the transfiguration – in which God spoke from heaven declaring Jesus to be his Son. This third statement this time by a human being moves the statement from heaven to earth, from God to a Roman solider, and is therefore significant in the structure of Mark's Gospel.

CHURCH ORDER AND SYNAGOGUE WORSHIP

James Burtchaell argues in his book *From Synagogue to Church* that the lack of archaeological evidence for distinctive Christian identifiers before the fourth to fifth centuries AD suggests that it was probable Christian communities grew up in or alongside Jewish synagogues. Not only that, but the 'roles' of *'episkopos'* (bishop or overseer) and *'diakonos'* (deacon) map onto the leadership roles found in various synagogues around the ancient world – the leader of the synagogue (*archisynagogos*) and the assistant (*hyperetes*). I have imagined here that, as the Christian community in Philippi emerged from the place of prayer, the two roles of *episkopos* and *diakonos* mentioned in Philippians 1:1 emerged out of these two roles: leader of the synagogue and assistant. Jonathan and Akiva – the two named members of the synagogue community in the body of the story – I am imagining to be leader (Jonathan) and assistant (Akiva).

For more see J. Burtchaell, *From Synagogue to Church: Public Services and Offices in the Earliest Christian Communities* (Cambridge University Press, 2008).

FRINGES

For more on fringes see page 240.

ANCIENT SYNAGOGUES

For many years it was assumed that while the second temple stood, before its destruction in AD 70, synagogues were unnecessary and took place in the temple and only the temple. Despite mention of synagogues in the Gospels, it was assumed that these had been included by a later community, after the fall of the temple, once synagogues were more widespread, or that they referred to a few unusual synagogues which were not typical in the period. Archaeological discoveries, however, have indicated that this assumption was inaccurate. There are large numbers of synagogues, including a good number in the Holy Land itself, which all pre-date the fall of the temple.

This then leads on to the question of what synagogues were used for. Some argue that they were used solely as a community gathering space, and not for worship at all. Evidence from the Gospels, however, suggests that this too is inaccurate and that people would gather to hear the scriptures read and expounded in the synagogues even before the temple fell. There is no doubt that synagogue worship expanded and became far more significant and elaborate after the fall of the temple, but there is clear evidence that it existed even before then.

I have deliberately left open the question of whether the place of prayer in Philippi had become a full synagogue in this story, but wanted to note the importance of the space to the Jewish Christian community, who I have imagined took it over.

For more on ancient synagogues see L. Levine, *The Ancient Synagogue: The First Thousand Years,* 2nd edn (Yale University Press, 2005).

The other detail I have included in the description of the place of prayer is paintings. This is anachronistic, since the most striking paintings found in a synagogue come from the Dura-Europos synagogue dated to the third century AD, but the paintings found there are so significant I couldn't resist imagining similar ones in Philippi. What is striking about the paintings, which cover the walls of that synagogue, is the vibrancy of their colours and the way in which they tell the story of God's people from the time of Moses onwards. Pictures of the paintings can be found easily from a Google search, and are well worth a look.

For more on artwork in synagogues of this period see R. Hachlili, *Ancient Jewish Art and Archaeology in the Diaspora* (Brill, 1998).

Chapter 13

SENECA AND GALLIO

Seneca – Lucius Annaeus Seneca the Younger – was the younger son of Seneca the Elder, an aristocrat, writer and rhetorician. He was a stoic philosopher, dramatist and politician. Although he was born in Corduba in the Roman province of Baetica in Hispania (now Spain), he grew up in Rome. He was elected to be a Roman quaestor (whose primary role was investigating murders) and as a result joined the Roman Senate in the late 30s AD, where he was well known for his rousing speeches. Dio Cassius notes that the Emperor Caligula was so offended by his oratory that he commanded Seneca to commit suicide. Seneca only escaped because he was at the time so ill that Caligula was informed he would die soon.

In AD 41, after Claudius had become emperor, Claudius's wife Messalina maliciously – and probably incorrectly – accused Seneca of having an affair with Julia Livia (Caligula's sister). The Senate condemned Seneca to death, but Claudius commuted his sentence to exile and he lived for the next eight years on the island of Corsica. In AD 49, Agrippina became Claudius's fourth wife and persuaded her new husband to allow Seneca to return from exile and become the tutor of her son Nero. When Nero became emperor Seneca acted as his advisor from AD 54 to around AD 62 (the approximate setting of this story) when his influence began to wane. In AD 65 he was caught up in an unsuccessful plot to kill Nero, and was ordered to kill himself. This he did by cutting his veins and slowly bleeding to death which, according to the historian Tacitus, was a long and painful death.

Seneca's elder brother Gallio – Lucius Junius Gallio Annaeanus – was also a rhetorician, though much less well known than his brother. He was probably exiled with Seneca on Corsica, and returned to Rome with him in AD 49. He was appointed proconsul of Achaea (which included Corinth) in AD 51, but ill-health meant he resigned from that post a year later. He is mentioned in Acts 18:12–17 in this role which conveniently dates Paul's first visit to Corinth as AD 51–52.

CRASSUS
The other historical figure mentioned in this chapter is Crassus – Marcus Licinius Crassus – who was a highly successful Roman general in the first century BC. He built a fortune through buying a large number of slaves who were builders and architects, and then buying and rebuilding houses that had burnt down. Plutarch estimates that his wealth increased from 300 talents to 7,100 talents, which represented around two hundred and twenty-nine tonnes of gold. Crassus was particularly famous for quashing the slave rebellion led by Spartacus. He was a great rival of Pompey and of Caesar, and eventually died in a skirmish with the Parthians. It is said that the Parthians poured molten gold into his mouth to mock him for his relentless yearning for riches.

The Crassus featured in this story is an imagined descendant of the famous Crassus from Roman history.

Chapter 14

RELATIONSHIPS BETWEEN JEWISH AND GENTILE CHRISTIANS
One of the features of Paul's letters is the ongoing difficulty of the relationships between Jewish and Gentile Christians. It is clear both from the New Testament itself and from accounts following the New Testament period, that the demands of the law on Jewish Christians led to unintended but regular conflict with Gentile Christians. It is this that lies behind a number of key passages in the Pauline letters. Even in Philippians (see 3:7 and 3:19) Paul hits out at Jewish attitudes that have led them to consider their heritage as contributing to an innate superiority

or to an expectation of certain ways of behaving (for more on this see page 97).

One of the challenges we face today is that Jewish Christianity is no longer as common or as widespread as when Paul was writing. As a result, we end up putting together the worst of Paul's criticisms with the worst of Jesus' critiques of the Pharisees, and assuming that all Jewish Christians in the first century were arrogant, petty and judgemental. The Gentile Christians of Paul's day would have known that this was not true because they knew the Jewish Christians. One of the blights of the Christian tradition has been the assumption that the worst criticisms of the worst excesses of Judaism and/or Jewish Christianity are true of all Jews. I have tried to present some of the complexity of this dynamic in this and subsequent chapters, and to suggest that many Jewish Christians were nothing like the stereotype we have of them in our minds.

For a fascinating insight into Jewish attitudes to Christianity and to the New Testament read A-J. Levine, and M. Z. Brettler, *The Jewish Annotated New Testament* (OUP, 2017).

FELLOWSHIP

One of the key theological words in Philippians is the Greek word *koinōnia*, which is found in 1:5; 2:1, and 3:10. The word can be variously translated as fellowship, sharing, participation and partnership. Although it only occurs three times, referring to the Philippians's 'sharing in the Gospel' (1:5); their 'sharing in the Spirit' (2:1), and Paul's own sharing in the sufferings of Christ (3:10) it underpins the whole epistle. The word has a vertical as well as a horizontal aspect: *koinōnia* between people takes them deeper into *koinōnia* with God in Christ Jesus, and vice versa. *Koinōnia* with God in Christ Jesus demands a *koinōnia* with those who are in Christ. You cannot have one without the other. Paul's vision is that *koinōnia* in the Gospel leads to a deeper *koinōnia* between people. He is thankful for the Philippians's willingness to share with and support him in prison, and prays that this will lead to their own deeper sharing of a life together. At various points in the letter he was also critical of the disunity that had broken out in the community, which manifested particularly in the breakdown of the relationship between Euodia and Syntyche (4:2). For Paul, participation in Christ had a real and tangible impact on human relationships in every aspect of life.

The word *koinōnia* and its use in Philippians has become particularly important in world mission for understanding how partnerships between people can be fully mutual. For an excellent outline of this theology see J. Price, *World-Shaped Mission: Reimagining Mission Today* (Church House Publishing, 2012).

RABBI SHAMMAI
The quotation I have put on the lips of Jonathan (in my own translation) comes from *Pirkei Avot* (1:15) which is a compilation of sayings from the rabbis that was included in the Mishnah as *Avoth*, but which also existed independently with an additional section known as *Pirkei Avot*. Although the Mishnah dates from the second century AD, the rabbinic sayings it contains are thought to have originated much earlier. Rabbi Shammai is thought to have lived between around 50 BC and AD 30. It is, therefore, quite possible that one of his sayings – particularly something like this – would have been discussed by Jews in this period.

Chapter 15

CRITICS AND PERSECUTORS OF THE PHILIPPIAN CHRISTIANS
A mention in Philippians 1:28 of 'your opponents' has generated considerable discussion about their identity. It is widely agreed among scholars that these 'opponents' were Romans. Although it is clear that later in the letter (3:4–11 and 3:17–4:1)

Paul is raising concerns about Jewish Christians and their attitudes, at the start of the letter most understand 'your opponents' to mean Roman opposition to followers of the Way. Judaism and Christianity were both regarded as a perversion of Roman-ness and often appear to be confused with each other (see page 271 for a discussion of the expulsion of Jews and Christians from Rome). Key to being a 'good Roman' was fitting in, following the customs and, most importantly, worshipping Romans gods, including the emperor (see page 276 for a first discussion of un-Roman-ness). Those who did not fit in with Rome could be accused of *maiestas* or treason. References like Philippians 1:27–28: 'I will know that you are standing firm in one spirit, striving side by side with one mind for the faith of the gospel, and are in no way intimidated by your opponents', suggest that the Philippians were experiencing low grade harassment from the Romans in their everyday lives. This might have been all the more likely in a Roman colony like Philippi, which sought to be as Roman as possible and even to excel in its Roman-ness because it was so far away from Rome itself. The storyline I have imagined with Aurelia here reflects on the impact of living through this kind of experience.

For more on the opponents mentioned in Philippi generally see B. J. Oropeza, *Jews, Gentiles, and the Opponents of Paul: Apostasy in the New Testament Communities, Volume 2: The Pauline Letters* (Cascade Books, 2012).

Chapter 16

THESSALONICA

The city of Thessalonica, around a hundred miles west of Philippi along the Via Egnatia, was founded in 315 BC by King Cassander of Macedon. In 148 BC it became the capital of the Roman province of Macedonia so, although not a colony, it was a more important city than neighbouring Philippi. There was a thriving Christian community there and it was the recipient of two letters from Paul.

Chapter 17

GAUL

Roman Gaul refers to the area of Western Europe that includes modern day France, Luxembourg and Belgium, as well as much of Switzerland, the Netherlands and Germany. For many years the Roman republic fought against the Celtic and Aquitaine tribes who inhabited the land. Under Julius Caesar a series of campaigns led to Gaul falling to Roman control (around 58 BC), which allowed Caesar to continue onwards to Britain even though he captured little on his first campaign. The Gauls did not accept Roman rule easily, and battles against the Romans continued until probably as late as AD 70. Gaul became a part of the Roman empire during the reign of Emperor Augustus. The regular battles and skirmishes meant that there were a large number of Gallic slaves who were taken as spoil by the Romans and were therefore later to be found elsewhere in the empire.

The name Aculia is a name from Gaul that means quick or fast.

For more on Roman Gaul see J. Drinkwater, *Roman Gaul: The Three Provinces, 58 BC–AD 260* (Routledge, 2013).

WRITING TOOLS IN THE ROMAN WORLD

Everyday jottings have been found on a wide range of artefacts. Wax tablets (which could be erased and used again) or thin pieces of wood were particularly popular, but writing has been found on many other objects too – especially broken pots, which were often repurposed, a little as scrap paper would be today.

Letters were largely sent on either clay tablets or papyrus scrolls. Given the length of letters like Philippians it is most likely that they would have been written on short papyrus scrolls that would then have been rolled up and sealed. Sometimes the seals were made out of wax, as we would expect, but often they were no more sophisticated than a few lines drawn across the join in the paper. In other words, a line would have been drawn around the scroll that would join up only if it was rolled exactly as it had been when first sent. A letter written from prison was unlikely to have a wax seal on it simply because it would have been harder to source the necessary materials for this.

EPAPHRODITUS'S ILLNESS

In Philippians 2:25–30, Paul talks about sending Epaphroditus back with the letter to the Philippians. In this passage he clearly feels the need to explain why he did this. Although some think it is because the Philippians were expecting Timothy to return first (M. Silva, *Philippians*, 159), others think the explanation is necessary because they expected Epaphroditus to stay with Paul longer (Bird and Gupta, *Philippians*, p. 106), i.e. until his trial and release or until his sentencing and death. What is clear is that the letter explains why Epaphroditus is bearing the letter even though the Philippians might not have expected him to do so.

Whatever the reason for the explanation that Paul felt the need to give, the details he provides give us insight into both Paul's own relationship with Epaphroditus and that of Epaphroditus with the Philippians themselves. The words he used to describe Epaphroditus's desire to return to the Philippians are heartfelt: he yearned for them (NRSV says longing for) and was in anguish (NRSV says distressed) because the Philippians had heard of his illness. Also significant is the tense used for both verbs. Paul used the present participle, which communicates not a single one-off 'pang', but ongoing experience: he kept on yearning for them and was continually anguished. He also talked of Epaphroditus being so ill that he nearly died (literally the Greek says 'approaching death').

All of this implies that Paul was concerned for Epaphroditus's wellbeing and as a result decided to send him back to the Philippians for his own welfare as well as theirs. I have imagined a relapse of Epaphroditus's illness on his return journey. There is no evidence of this in the text, but if his original illness was an infection caught on the way to visit Paul, or indeed in the prison cell, a relapse would not be unlikely.

Cantor/lector

In modern Judaism a *hazzan* or cantor leads the congregation in the singing of their worship. The term *hazzan* was first used to refer to a leader of singing only in the sixth century AD. Before then the *hazzan* was an official of the synagogue who looked after the building and other practical matters more generally. It is not known how early this role existed in synagogue worship, but it is not impossible that such duties as I have imagined for Akiva in this story would have included reading the Scripture and other texts in worship. Early Christianity certainly had the role of *lector*, though again evidence for this comes from the fourth century AD onwards. Nevertheless in a largely illiterate culture it is likely that there would be someone or some people whose role was to read the Scripture or other texts to those gathered together.

For more on public reading in early Christianity see D. Nässelqvist, *Public Reading in Early Christianity: Lectors, Manuscripts, and Sound in the Oral Delivery of John 1–4* (Brill, 2015), 163.

Skubalon or excrement

There is a debate among scholars about whether the word *skubalon*, which I've rendered as excrement ('I regard them as rubbish,' NRSV), was a vulgarity or not. Some argue that it should be translated as 'crap' or 'shit' to indicate that it was really a swear word; others, including myself, argue that the word itself was not that vulgar (and in any case the Romans swore by using the name of a god not by talking about human waste) and referred simply to something that needed disposing of.

This is one of those passages that would have been shocking to its first hearers, but not for the reasons we might imagine. *Skubalon* referred to something disposable, something that was of such little value it should be thrown away, but it wasn't really a swear word, and its impact rested more in what it was saying than how it was said. The really shocking part of Paul's statement here was his view that his Jewish heritage – the one thing that in the past he thought granted him high status in God's plan for the world – was not only worth very little, but was of such little value that it was worthy of being sent to the rubbish heap in comparison with his identity in Christ.

For more on obscene speech and its usage see this fascinating study: J. F. Hultin, *The Ethics of Obscene Speech in Early Christianity and Its Environment* (Brill, 2008), 128.

Chapter 18

TRADE ROUTES IN THE ROMAN WORLD
One of the questions that emerges in this period is why the Jewish diaspora spread so far throughout the Roman world. There were Jews spread across a large part of the Roman empire and it is estimated that around five million Jews lived outside of Judea and Galilee in the first century AD. There are numerous possible answers to this question (the causes behind the spread of economic migrants are varied), but one of them is trade and trading routes: merchants who would buy goods in one part of the world and sell them in another were vital for local

economies. The Via Egnatia, as we noted above (page 220), ran from Dyrrhachium on the Adriatic sea to Byzantium (later called Constantinople and now Istanbul) in Asia Minor (modern Turkey). The Via Maris ran through Capernaum from Egypt to Syria. These trade routes were key to everyday life as well as to the economy, and their existence explains some aspects of population movement throughout the empire.

The presence of Jewish merchants moving from west to east and back again was well documented from around AD 500. Our period is obviously much earlier than this, but the widespread presence of Jewish communities in cities and towns across the Roman empire is best explained, at least in part, by trade and trading routes.

GALILEAN FISHING BOATS AND HOUSES

An ancient fishing boat from the first century AD was discovered in the 1980s on the north-west shore of Galilee (i.e. very close to Capernaum). The boat was shallow and flat-bottomed, clearly to counteract the many storms that were suddenly whipped up on the sea. This construction meant that the boat could get close to the shore for fishing (or indeed, as in the case of Jesus, to sit in while he addressed the crowd – Matthew 13:1–2).

For more on the discovery of the so-called 'Jesus boat' see D. Peterson, 'The Jesus Boat', *History by the Slice* (blog, 26 July 2019): https://www.disappearingman.com/archaeology/the-jesus-boat/.

Many houses in Galilee were built simply from dark volcanic rock or basalt rocks, wedged together a little like a dry-stone wall. If people could afford to, they would plaster the walls with mud and straw. Since space was at a premium, guest rooms or extra spaces were often located on the roof (see 2 Kings 4:10) and external steps were used to reach it. Roofs themselves were often constructed from beams, covered with tree branches and clay. It was therefore quite easy to make a hole in the roof if required.

PAUL'S OPPONENTS IN PHILIPPI

From the nineteenth century onwards, one of the key issues in Pauline scholarship has been the identity of Paul's opponents in his epistles, but especially in 2 Corinthians, Galatians, Philippians, Colossians and the Pastoral epistles.

For general discussion about this see S. E. Porter (ed.), *Paul and His Opponents (Pauline Studies)* (Brill, 2005), and B. J. Oropeza, *Jews, Gentiles, and the Opponents of Paul* (Cascade Books, 2012).

In Philippians there are four mentions of opponents, which have led scholars to attempt to identify them. In 1:15–18 Paul mentions those who 'proclaim Christ from envy and rivalry', though he also here mentions those who proclaim him 'from goodwill'. It is unlikely that Paul has in mind anyone from Philippi here, since he is talking in this passage of the way in which his imprisonment has allowed him to proclaim the Gospel to the whole imperial guard (1:12). This suggests that the opponents he has in view are opponents to his ministry throughout his life. The next opponents mentioned in the letter are clearly in Philippi because in 1:28 he instructs the Philippians not to be 'intimidated by your opponents'. As noted above, these opponents appear to be Romans who opposed Christians for their 'un-Roman-ness' (see page 286).

The final two mentions both fall in chapter 3 ('Beware of the dogs', 3:2 and 'their end is their destruction . . .' 3:19). While some think that Paul's reference here is to Jews generally (see G. F. Hawthorne, *Philippians* (Zondervan, 2015), 124), many modern scholars see these as Jewish Christians who are enforcing circumcision on Gentile Christians (see for example M. F. Birdand N. K. Gupta, *Philippians*, 17–18). There is no evidence that such people lived in Philippi. They may have done, but it is just as possible that Paul is warning the Philippian Christians to be on their guard lest someone like that tries to persuade them to live differently. What I have tried to suggest in this account is that Paul's opponents have as much – if not more – to do with people Paul has fought with in the past in places other than Philippi than actual Jewish Christians in Philippi. Paul's mention of these people in chapter 3 is so generic and so warning in its tone, it is unlikely that he was speaking about people who were actually to be found in Philippi when he sent the letter. In any case, if Acts 16 is to be believed, the Jewish population in Philippi had been so small at Paul's first visit (small enough to have a place of prayer rather than a synagogue) that he was unlikely to have anyone particular in mind. Much more likely is that Paul had developed a concern during his ministry about those Jewish Christians who aggressively sought to make all followers of Christ convert to Judaism. As a result, the people Paul probably has in mind are a type of person, not actual groups of people known to him in Philippi. Nevertheless, the tone of his tirade would have been bruising to any Jewish Christians who heard it.

For more on Paul's opponents see N. Nikki, *Opponents and Identity in Philippians* (Brill, 2018).

'THEIR GOD IS THE BELLY'
One of the oddest of Paul's descriptions in his outburst at the end of chapter 3 ('Their end point is destruction; their god is the belly; and their glory is in their shame; those who think about earthly things,' 3:19) is the accusation that 'their god is the belly'. There is extensive discussion among scholars as to precisely what Paul might be talking about in this description, and his language is metaphorical enough to make it quite hard to be sure exactly what he means. He could be referring to self-indulgence in a parallel with 1 Corinthians 6:13 ('"Food is for the stomach and the stomach for food," and God will wipe out both this and that. The body is not for un-chastity but for the Lord, and the Lord for the body'), or he might have been

reflecting on a more general love of self that stands in contrast to Christ's self-giving love as laid out in Philippians 2:5–11.

For more on these descriptions see the helpful account in K. O. Sandnes, *Belly and Body in the Pauline Epistles* (Cambridge University Press, 2002).

AN OUTLINE OF PHILIPPIANS
In this chapter I tried to give a brief outline of the letter to the Philippians with the key features of Paul's argument. For a clearer sense of how the letter works as a whole see the excellent introduction to Philippians from the Bible Project, which gives a very accessible but thorough introduction to the whole letter in a little over nine minutes: https://bibleproject.com/explore/video/philippians/.

Chapter 19

'HAVING THE SAME MIND/THINKING THE SAME THING'
One of the key phrases from Philippians that is repeated, though in a slightly different form in the introduction to the Christ Hymn in Philippians 2:2 and 5 and in an instruction to Euodia and Syntyche in 4:2, is translated in the NRSV as having 'the same mind'. In fact, the Greek doesn't use the word mind at all and uses a verb instead – *phroneō*. This verb has a wide range of meaning, from think, to understand or comprehend; from feel by experience, to being wise or prudent. Philippians 2:2 reads 'top up my joy by thinking the same thing' (for more on this phrase see page 313), and 2:5 reads literally 'think (or ponder) this among you which was also in Christ Jesus'. Likewise, 4:2 reads literally 'I encourage Euodia and I encourage Syntyche to think the same in the Lord.' In other words, it's a more dynamic construction than simply 'to have the same mind': it implies both action and decisiveness. It also implies that 'thoughts' won't simply stay in the mind, but will affect

how people act towards one another. It is also worth noting that what is being encouraged here is not simple agreement or unanimity, but seeing the world through a similar lens – the lens of Christ – and living in the light of that.

One of the major areas of discussion about Philippians 2:5–11 (known widely as the Christ Hymn) is whether the hymn itself is an invitation to be imitated or whether it is simply a description of Christ and who he is, with an invitation to live in the knowledge of this. Various scholars from the twentieth century, such as E. Käsemann, argued vehemently that it was impossible for Christians to imitate Christ and that this could not be meant in this hymn. This view is less widespread today, and, although scholars acknowledge that Christ's exaltation at the end of the hymn is not promised to the Philippians, it is generally understood that 'think this among you which was also in Christ Jesus' is an invitation to see the world as Christ did, a vision that involves humble living and not grasping at status, and that while it is not quite possible to mimic Jesus in every aspect, 'living his story' is a key part of Paul's argument here.

For a helpful discussion of these options see Bird and Gupta, *Philippians*, 76–77.

THE PHILIPPIAN CHRIST HYMN
One of the most famous passages from Philippians is the so-called 'Christ Hymn'. This name, given to the passage by scholars, tells you something about the discussions that have swirled around the passage. Throughout the twentieth century, scholars debated whether verses 6–11 pre-existed the writing of Philippians, and in particular whether it was 'pre-Pauline'. In other words, was it a 'hymn' that existed in the early church that was borrowed by Paul and used here? The problem with this discussion is that the hymn fits perfectly in Philippians. Indeed, there is an argument that verses 6–11 are the core of the

book around which the rest of Paul's letter is fitted. While this does not mean that it would be impossible for Paul to have borrowed the hymn and written his letter around it, the theology, the language, and the style of the hymn are so thoroughly Pauline that a more obvious solution is to conclude that Paul himself wrote it.

A key observation made by many scholars about the structure of verses 6–11 is that it forms a V-shape, beginning with Christ in heaven with God, then taking the form of a slave, then going even lower to death on a cross, before being exalted back to heaven again. It is worth noting that it is not quite a V-shape, in that the slow descent is not matched by the rapid ascent to exaltation. Nevertheless, the movement in the statement – downwards and then up again – is noticeable.

This then leads into what it is. Is it, in fact, a hymn, an early creedal statement, or a piece of theological poetry? In other words, was it sung, recited or simply read by the Philippians? The answer is that we can't know. As it appears in Philippians it was a form of theological poetry, but whether it had an afterlife as a hymn or creedal statement is impossible to know. All we can do is guess. My guess is that a poetic statement as powerful and beautiful as this, and which remains as evocative in the modern church as this passage is, would probably have been used by the Philippians in one way or another, whether in speech or singing. In the story, I have imagined Clement picking it up and singing it, and that this was how its message was embedded in the minds of the Philippians.

Two words, in particular, have been especially important in this hymn. The first from verse 6 is translated by the NRSV as 'exploited' (the NIV translates it 'used to his own advantage', and the ESV 'a thing to be grasped'). The word *harpazō* has a range of meanings in the general area of seize, snatch, steal, grasp or plunder. The problem of translating it directly like that is that it implies that Christ was 'grasping' equality with God and did not naturally have it by right. This is why the NRSV opts for 'exploit' rather than the more literal 'grasp'. I have long wondered whether 'cling to' is an even better solution, as it still has the grasping element, but implies that he had it all along.

The other word of vast importance is *kenoō* (translated by the NRSV as 'emptied himself'). This word has traditionally been translated as 'empty' and has led into some hugely important theology known as kenotic theology or a theology of self-emptying. The idea that lies behind this theology is that as Christians we are called to empty ourselves as Christ did. The conundrum of this is of what do we empty ourselves? Unless we are very careful, this can push us towards a 'theology of burn-out' in which Christians pour themselves out again and again until they are completely empty and unable to do anything at all. This is, self-evidently, not what the passage means. Jesus emptied himself of status, but not of the Godhead; of exaltation, but not of life. His self-emptying did not lead to him being less of himself. He willingly refused to cling to those things that gave him status in the world, and instead embraced those things – like slavery – that most people shunned. This is not a counsel of self-harm, but of a full, generous embracing of those who were least in the world.

Whatever conclusions you draw on where Philippians 2:5–11 came from, its form and significance and the words that it uses, the passage remains one of the richest, most profound and significant in the whole of the New Testament. It is worthy of much reflection and thought. To prompt you into further reflection I have given it again below:

> *Think this among you, which was also in Christ Jesus,*
> *who though he existed in the form of God did not regard*
> *equality with God as something to cling to, but he poured*
> *himself out taking the form of a slave, becoming just like*
> *humans and, being found in human form, he lowered*

*himself and became someone who obeyed orders even to
the point of death, the death of a cross.*
*Therefore, God exalted him extraordinarily and graced him
with the name that is above every name, so that at the name
of Jesus every knee, whether in heaven, on earth or under
the earth, would bend and every tongue acknowledge that
Jesus Christ is Lord to the glory of God the Father.*

For a particularly helpful discussion of Philippians 2:5–11 see
T. D. Still, *Philippians & Philemon* (Smyth & Helwys, 2011),
62–67. And for a taste of Kenotic Christology and what it
entails see S. J. Youngs, *The Way of the Kenotic Christ* (Cascade
Books, 2019).

Chapter 20

SLAVERY IN THE ROMAN EMPIRE

The Roman empire was in many ways built on slavery. Slaves
were seen not just as essential to the functioning of the empire,
but as a part of Roman identity. The first century BC historian
Dionysius of Halicarnassus identified the start of slavery in the
Roman empire with its founder Romulus, who gave fathers the
right to sell their own children into slavery if they needed to
(*Roman Antiquities*, book 2). This may or may not be true, but
it reveals a belief that slavery was a fundamental part of the
Roman self-identity, at least in the mind of Dionysius.

Although slavery had always been a part of the Roman
republic, it rapidly grew as a result of the expansion of the
empire. As the army conquered new lands, they forced new
people into slavery. The greater the victory the greater the
number of slaves captured. For example, after the destruction
of Carthage at the end of the Third Punic war in 146 BC, it is
estimated that 250,000 people were enslaved. This debased the
'slave currency' for a period, as so many new slaves flooded

onto the market. Warfare was not the only means by which people became slaves. As the reference to Dionysius above indicates, people in financial hardship might sell members of their family into slavery to free themselves from debt. Slavery was so normal in the Roman empire that it was very rarely questioned. The three so-called servile wars (the third of which featured Spartacus' slave rebellion) were regarded with a certain level of bemusement by Roman citizens. This may be why Paul is so silent on the subject of the freeing of slaves, to the surprise – and understandable outrage – of modern readers.

It is estimated that in the first century BC there were about 5 million slaves across the Roman empire as a whole making up about 10–15 per cent of the whole population. This proportion rose to 30–40 per cent of the population of Italy where the concentration of slaves was higher. It is also worth noting that only 49 per cent of slaves were owned by the aristocratic elite. The rest were owned by the less wealthy, indicating how widespread and 'normal' the practice of slave owning was.

There is a discussion in Roman literature about the treatment of slaves. There were some, like Seneca, who argued that a slave who was well looked after would work better than those who were abused, but it was only in the sixth century AD with the Code of Justinian that slaves were declared to be people rather than property, and, therefore, should be treated with dignity. However, others treated their slaves brutally. A particularly chilling account comes from this period, during the reign of Nero. A well-known senator was murdered by someone in his household, and Nero upheld the senate's decision to execute every slave in the household in retribution.

One of the intriguing features of Roman slave ownership was the expectation that at least some slaves would be freed during their lifetime. Some bought their freedom with money accrued during their time as a slave. Others were freed by their owners. This often took place when someone died and they left provision for the freedom in their will. Indeed, this practice was so common that the Emperor Augustus ruled that no one could free more than 100 slaves in any one will. The process of freeing a slave – known as manumission – was carefully laid down in Roman law. It was done before a magistrate, and a formal ceremony enacted the freedom. In Rome this led to the slave receiving citizenship rights within the empire. Of course this process only happened where the owners of the slaves were themselves citizens. In a city like Philippi, where Lydia was unlikely to have been a citizen, the manumission would have taken a more informal form as described in the story here. I am aware that I have inserted a modern sensibility into this story by having Lydia free the three boys out of a sense of guilt. This is unlikely to have featured in the mind of someone in the first century, but the joy of writing a story is that your characters can behave as you would like them to, even if you acknowledge that they are unlikely to have done this in practice.

For more on slavery in the Roman world see G. S. Aldrete, *Daily Life in the Roman City: Rome, Pompeii and Ostia* (Greenwood Publishing Group, 2004), 65–68, and J. Toner, *How to Manage Your Slaves by Marcus Sidonius Falx* (Profile Books Ltd, 2015).

It is hard to convey to a modern audience the shock that would have been caused to early Christian communities by Paul's language about being 'slaves of Christ' (a phrase sometimes obscured in English translations, which often render it 'servant of Christ') and his exhortation in Philippians 2:5–11 to follow in the footsteps of Christ by taking the form of a slave. The suggestion would have been abhorrent to anyone living in the Roman world, where the goal would have been to avoid slavery at all costs. Slavery was normal, but no one would have chosen it willingly. For this to have been one of the key pillars of Christian life and practice would have felt, at the least, very strange to a first-century audience.

For a fascinating study on Paul's slave language see Dale B. Martin, *Slavery as Salvation: The Metaphor of Slavery in Pauline Christianity* (Yale University Press, 1990).

Chapter 21

No notes.

Chapter 22

THE ROMAN JUDICIAL SYSTEM

During the period of the Roman republic, the Roman legal system focused primarily around civil cases under a process known as *Legis Actiones*. A plaintiff would make an accusation against someone else, who would then be summoned to trial first in front of a magistrate, then in front of a judge. The trial often consisted of oral statements given alternately by two advocates, after which the judge would pronounce his decision. In most cases the judgement would consist of financial penalties against the unsuccessful party, which the victorious person was obliged to pursue themselves. Although the system had changed a little in the period of the early empire, the period in which this story is set followed the formulary system, which was still a very similar situation: a plaintiff and defendant put their case before a judge, and a verdict was declared.

Most of the evidence for the Roman legal system, however, applies to Rome and to Roman citizens. Non-Roman citizens in the provinces had a much more varied experience, and far fewer rights. Unlike Paul, who appeared to be able to appeal to the emperor for a fair hearing, a non-citizen had no real rights and had to accept the verdict of the judge no matter how unjust it was. Provincial governors and magistrates could try people for any reason they chose, and could inflict any kind of penalty they wanted to on defendants. There was an expectation, however, that a governor would behave with honour. Although much earlier than this setting, the Roman lawyer Cicero prosecuted Gaius Verres in one of his most famous trials, for crimes he committed while governor of Sicily. He was renowned for extorting money illegally from local citizens and plundering treasures from temples across the island. Although it was clear that Verres believed he could get away with this because Sicily was not Rome, Cicero's moral outrage at his actions led to his exile from Rome.

A fascinating exploration of the evidence for the implementation of law in the Roman provinces can be found in K. Czajkowski, B. Eckhardt, and M. Strothmann (eds), *Law in the Roman Provinces* (Oxford University Press, 2020).

It is also worth noting that prisoners awaiting trial had more freedom than those awaiting execution. The evidence of Acts and, indeed, Philippians, indicates that they would have been allowed visitors to bring financial and food aid.

ROMAN PORRIDGE
A meal such as Tertius might have taken to the prison would probably have consisted of 'wheat pap', a recipe for which was provided by Cato the Elder in *De Agricultura, 86*.

Recipe for wheat pap: Pour ½ pound of clean wheat into a clean bowl, wash well, remove the husk thoroughly, and clean well. Pour into a pot with pure water and boil. When done, add milk slowly until it makes a thick cream.

Into this might have been added meat and/or vegetables as funds allowed.

See Aldrete, *Daily Life*, 111–113 for more on this.

Notes: Chapter 22

'DON'T FRET'

The verse I translated as 'don't fret about anything, but in everything in prayer and entreaty with thanksgiving let your requests be known to God,' comes from Philippians 4:6 and is translated in the NRSV as 'Do not worry about anything, but in everything by prayer and supplication with thanksgiving let your requests be made known to God.' The key word here is 'worry' or 'fret'. The idea of the word is of going over and over something and worrying about it and so 'fret' seems quite a good translation. It isn't just a command against 'worrying', but against unhealthy patterns of dwelling on something and picking at it so it gets worse. This sense is enhanced by the form of the verb (a present imperative) which implies to keep on doing something over and over again.

Sometimes this verb is translated as 'do not be anxious'. This can be misinterpreted, and we should be careful about it. Anxiety is a recognised medical condition that cannot be allayed by a command to stop doing it. Paul's command here is not a command against anxiety, and should not be confused with it. What Paul is addressing here is the common human tendency to worry away at things; this is not the same as experiencing long-term and debilitating anxiety.

There is a movement today that recognises the importance of the practice of gratitude for establishing and maintaining good mental health. I am fascinated to find evidence of it in Paul's letter to the Philippians, written as it was from a prison cell. There seems to be a clear connection here between prayer with thanksgiving and the peace that Paul goes on to talk about.

THE PEACE OF GOD

It is widely accepted that lying behind Paul's use of the word 'peace' (in Greek *eirēnē*) is the Hebrew concept of *shalom*. As indicated in the story, *shalom* is a much bigger word than peace, certainly in the way that the concept of peace was used in the Roman empire.

Pax Romana, sometimes known as *Pax Augusta* as it was declared by the Emperor Augustus, was a key phrase used in the Roman empire between the defeat of Mark Anthony and Cleopatra in 31 BC and the death of Marcus Aurelius in AD 180. The *Pax Romana* was more propaganda than reality, but sought to establish the principle that the Romans had brought peace and prosperity across their empire. By binding military leaders together in loyalty, the *Pax Romana* attempted to rule out the possibility of civil war and local unrest. The reality was that hints of unrest were brutally put down through military aggression.

The peace that Paul is talking about in Philippians is of an entirely different register, and this will have been felt deeply by Paul's Philippian audience. As we noted above, Philippi was a Roman colony in which large numbers of veterans lived, whose role when they were soldiers would have been to enforce the *Pax Romana*. Their vision of peace and the vision presented in Philippians 4:7 couldn't have been more different. Paul's understanding of peace was a sense of wholeness and completeness; not just a lack of conflict, but a sense of community and togetherness, a harmony that had no room within it for the brutality of the Roman army. It is interesting that Paul calls it a peace that goes beyond or surpasses all human thought or understanding.

For more on the *Pax Romana* and its importance for Roman self-definition see A. K. Goldsworthy, *Pax Romana: War, Peace and Conquest in the Roman World* (Weidenfeld & Nicolson, 2016).

Chapter 23

The discussion in this section of the notes focusses on Philippians 3:4b–10. It would be worth reading this passage before continuing with these notes. Chapter 3 of Philippians contains some of the most important verses in Philippians (after the Christ Hymn in 2:5–11).

CONFIDENCE IN THE FLESH

If anyone else considers themselves to have reason to put their confidence in the flesh, I have more: ⁵ circumcised on the eighth day, from the people of Israel, of the tribe of Benjamin, a Hebrew of Hebrews; according to the law, a Pharisee; ⁶ according to zeal, a persecutor of the church; according to righteousness in the law, without reproach.

One of the most striking features of the early verses of Philippians 3 is Paul's description of his heritage and the confidence that his background lends him. Paul's use of the word flesh (in Greek *sarx*) stands in stark contrast to his use of the word body (in Greek *sōma*). Flesh is most often used more negatively to refer to that which will come to an end, and body more positively to refer to the whole of ourselves that will rise from the dead at the end of all times. Although Paul's description of his heritage appears positive here, it is striking that he calls it confidence in the flesh, indicating that this is something that is transient and will pass away. For more on Paul's use of flesh see P. Gooder, *Body: Biblical Spirituality for the Whole Person* (SPCK Publishing, 2016), 62–71.

However, the oddest item in Paul's list of reasons to be confident is his reference to his persecution of Christians. All the rest can easily be seen as a 'boast', but this, in a letter to largely Gentile Christians, seems, at best, odd. In the first instance it raises the question of why Saul of Tarsus (later known as Paul) should think that persecuting Christians was a good thing to do. It is important to note that at this point, Christianity was not a religion in its own right entirely separate from Judaism. What is known as 'the parting of the ways' between Judaism and Christianity did begin with the events surrounding the death of Stephen (reported in Acts 7) and the ministry of Paul, but escalated when the temple was destroyed in Jerusalem in AD 70 (around ten years after the setting of this story). Even then the two were not entirely separate. Another key date for a parting between the two was the Bar Kochba rebellion in AD 130–35, but there is evidence that there remained a strong connection between Judaism and Christianity well into the third century AD.

For more on the parting of the ways see J. D. G. Dunn, *Parting of the Ways: Between Christianity and Judaism and Their Significance for the Character of Christianity* (SCM Press, 2006).

In the first century there were a wide range of different forms of Judaism – Pharisees, Sadducees, the community at Qumran, and those who followed wandering prophets in the desert to mention but a few – there were many different beliefs and expressions of devotion. It has, therefore, long been a conundrum as to why the particular expression of Judaism that involved following Jesus Christ was worthy of persecution where others were not. Some suggest that it was because they followed someone whose mode of death – on a cross – was abhorrent; some argue that it was because the early Christians worshipped Jesus, which raised questions about whether they were monotheistic or not; others, still, maintain that the problem lay in their attitude to Gentiles and their willingness to eat with them. The reality is that it was probably a mixture of all these reasons that made those who followed Christ particularly upsetting to their Jewish compatriots.

What is fascinating here, however, is that Paul should list it as something of which to boast about to an audience that would probably have been shocked by it. It suggests that Paul was doing a similar thing in this list to what he did in 2 Corinthians 11:21–29, where he turned a list of boasts in strengths into a list of weaknesses. In my view, Paul's persecution of Christians is deliberately thrown into an otherwise positive list to signal that Paul is all too aware that his virtues are not what they might appear at first glance.

RIGHTEOUSNESS AND FAITH

. . . not having my righteousness – righteousness from the law – but righteousness through the faith of Christ, the righteousness from God based on faith.

The climax of Paul's list can be found in verse 9. What Paul really cares about is not his heritage or what happened in the past, but that he has a righteousness that comes, not from the law, but from faith in Christ. This verse in Philippians is a crucial one for understanding Pauline theology – and some of the debates that surround it – and is worth us pausing with for a while.

There are two words/phrases here that lie at the heart of Pauline theology: righteousness/justification and faith in Christ/faith of Christ. These two help us to understand the central core of what Paul believed about himself and his relationship with God in Christ Jesus, but are, almost inevitably, mired in extensive debate and discussion among Pauline scholars.

First, righteousness. The Greek work *dikaiosunē* can be translated into English using either the word justification or righteousness (although both words are close in meaning, justification comes into modern English from Norman French, and righteousness from Anglo Saxon – modern English translations choose one or the other of these words to translate this same Greek word depending on the context). The word *dikaiosunē* is crucial to Paul's theology, but can have different shades of meaning depending on the way in which it is used. Bird and Gupta, *Philippians*, 138, helpfully identify three main uses of the word:

- To refer to a characteristic or action of God. God is righteous in that he always keeps his promises.
- To refer to the entirety of God's saving action in the world.
- To refer to someone who believes in Jesus Christ – no matter what has happened in the past they receive the gift of 'righteous status' before God.

It is clear that Philippians 3:9 is using the third main use of the word, and Paul is talking about his own righteous status before God (and by extension that of anyone who believes).

This is an all too brief description of the many debates about justification and righteousness in Paul. For a more thorough exploration of the many issues see T. Wright, *Justification – God's Plan & Paul's Vision* (SPCK Publishing, 2009).

Second, faith. The Greek word *pistis* can be translated as belief, faith and even faithfulness (for similar reasons to justification and righteousness – belief comes from Norman French, and faith from Anglo Saxon). The question that has raged among Pauline scholars for years, is whose faith is it? Does the righteousness that Paul talks about in 3:9 come from his faith in Christ or Christ's own faithfulness? In other words, do we receive the gift of righteous status before God because we believe, or because Christ was faithful to his calling? It may not surprise you to know that there is very little agreement on this question and ultimately you will need to make the decision for yourself. However, in my opinion, this verse reveals to us that it is possible Paul meant both. In Philippians 3:9 Paul talks about faith twice:

not having my righteousness – righteousness from the law – but righteousness through the faith of Christ, the righteousness from God based on faith.

The second use of faith does appear to refer to the faith of the believer, so either Paul said the same thing twice or he was using 'faith of Christ' the first time to talk about Christ's faithfulness to death, even death on a cross, and the second time to refer to his own faith. In other words, it is Christ's own faithfulness to fulfil his calling that makes the gift of righteousness possible. When we believe in Christ we join in with his faithfulness throughout our own faith/faithfulness to Christ. In the context of Philippians, which has declared Jesus' obedience to the point of death (i.e. his faithfulness) in only the previous chapter, this seems to me to make the best sense. It is therefore not an either/or scenario, but a both/and one, and this explains why scholars find it so hard to come down definitively on one side or another. Our faith in Christ allows us to join with Christ's faithfulness, and through that to receive the gift of righteousness before God.

For a very helpful collection of essays arguing both sides of this debate see M. F. Bird and M. P. Sprinkle (eds), *The Faith of Jesus Christ: Exegetical, Biblical and Theological Studies* (Paternoster, 2009).

Chapter 24

No notes.

Chapter 25

ROMAN USAGE OF THE WORD BARBARIAN
The word barbarian comes from the Greek word *barbaros* and in Latin *barbarous*. In Greek it meant 'babbler' and was a

reference to how other tongues sounded to the Greek – and subsequently Roman – ear, and then to how Greek sounded when spoken by non native speakers. The Greeks used the word to describe anyone who had not been 'civilised' by Hellenic culture, and this is how Paul uses the word in Romans 1:14 ('I am a debtor both to Greeks and to barbarians, both to the wise and to the foolish') and in Colossians 3:11 ('In that renewal there is no longer Greek and Jew, circumcised and uncircumcised, barbarian, Scythian, slave and free; but Christ is all and in all!'). He also used it in its more etymological sense in 1 Corinthians 14:11: 'If then I do not know the meaning of a sound, I will be a foreigner (*barbaros*) to the speaker and the speaker a foreigner (*barbaros*) to me.'

The Romans used the word similarly, but to refer to everything that was non-Roman. It referred especially to those tribes, like the Celts, who seemed mysterious and unconquerable. While it was more often used to describe those who lay outside the 'civilising effect' of Rome, it was used, on occasion, to describe those who lived within the empire, but who were not citizens. The problem for non-Roman citizens was that they had very few rights at all. The advantage was that they were not subject to the same expectations of behaviour as the citizens were. The charge of *majestas* (see page 286) was much harder to level at those who were not Roman citizens, barbarians or not.

THE PATRON/CLIENT SYSTEM AND SALUTATIO

The Roman patron/client system was the bedrock of many relationships throughout the Roman empire. The wealthy patron helped to take care of the client – often financially, but also in terms of introductions to influential people and other such support. In exchange, the client would show deference to the patron, voting as the patron instructed, supporting causes, and so on. Part of the deference shown by the client to the patron included a morning '*salutatio*'. Clients would line up outside their patron's house each morning to greet them, and then would run any errands that the patron wanted or would offer any other help as it was needed. Patrons would normally meet their clients in the atrium, while sitting on a formal seat in the centre of the space. It was a sociable time, and relationships were built not just between patron and client, but also between clients of the same patron.

Chapter 26

WOMEN AND THE ROMAN WORLD

It is often said that women had no status at all in the Roman world. While on one level this may be true, studies reveal that the situation was far more complex than that. Women could be Roman citizens, but could not vote or hold political office. They could inherit money, own land and write wills. They could even appear in court, as Lydia does in this story. The key divide is often cited as the split between 'public' and 'private' spheres: women could occupy different roles in private than they could in public. The problem with this, as Cohick points out, is that the distinction between public and private has never been very easy to establish (L. Cohick, *Women in the World of the Earliest Christians: Illuminating Ancient Ways of Life* (Baker Academic, 2009), 285–320).

As a result, although some Roman writers, such as Plutarch, argue that women should not be seen in public without their husbands, there is archaeological evidence that women had a much wider influence than might at first be imagined. Among a range of other evidence, there are statues to women praising their public deeds, inscriptions indicating that they were generous patrons, and legal documents indicating that they were appointed to be patrons. What this reveals is that what some Roman writers thought ought to be the case was not universally so. Indeed, texts that prescribe the role of women are often written into contexts in which actual practice is different. A text that declares something should be so is often arguing against what was actually happening.

It is also worth noting that there were a large number of women who exercised influence through their husbands. Many wives and mothers of emperors, such as Livia Drusilla, wife of Augustus, and Agrippina the Younger, wife of Claudius and mother of Nero, had a huge impact on the shaping and life of Rome. In the character of Aurelia, I imagined a similar powerful woman who tried to use her status to shape public life, if only informally.

An interesting recent book that explores a range of questions about the role of women in this period is S. Parks, S. Sheinfeld, and M. J. C. Warren (eds), *Jewish and Christian Women in the Ancient Mediterranean* (Routledge, 2021). Read alongside L. Cohick, *Women in the World of the Earliest Christians*, it is possible to gain a much more nuanced picture of the situation than is often depicted.

Also fascinating is B. MacLachlan, *Women in Ancient Rome: A Sourcebook* (Bloomsbury Academic, 2013), which provides a helpful range of primary source texts to build a rich picture of the everyday lives of women in the Roman world.

Chapter 27

No notes.

Chapter 28

PHILIPPIANS 2:1–4

¹ *If there is any reassurance in Christ; if there is any comfort in love; if there is any companionship in the Spirit; if there is any compassion and kindness,* ² *top up my joy by thinking the same thing, by having the same love, being united, thinking a single*

thing. ³ (Do) nothing from selfish intrigue, nothing from conceited imagination, but in humility regarding one another as superior to you, ⁴ looking not to your own things, but to the things of each other.

Although much less well known than the verses that follow them, verses 1–4 of chapter 2 of Philippians are crucially important for understanding not just the Christ Hymn, but the whole of the epistle. There are a number of points to notice about the passage that help to make sense of it.

- Verse 2:1 hints at the Trinity, but falls shy of a full Trinitarian formulation. If you compare it with 2 Corinthians 13:13, you can see the similarities: 'The grace of the Lord Jesus Christ, the love of God, and the communion of the Holy Spirit be with all of you.' Notice the similarity of the phrases: grace, love and communion (or companionship/fellowship – the Greek word is the same as in Philippians 2:1). The difference in Philippians is that love is not directly attributed to God (though the hint hangs in the air), and following the threefold phrasing there are two more words, compassion and kindness, which don't appear to fit with the threefold phrasing that goes before them.
- The phrase normally translated 'the same mind' (see discussion on page 294) occurs twice in 2:1–4 and again in 2:5 in slightly different forms. In 2:2 it says 'think the same thing'; in 2:4 'thinking the one thing' and in 2:5 'think this . . .'. All this seems to point to the 'same' 'one' thing that they were to all think, which was to think what Christ thought, or more likely, to view the world in the same way that Christ did . . . 'not considering equality with God a thing to be clung to . . .'.
- The word that I translated as 'being united' and which the NRSV has as 'being in full accord' is the word 'sumpsuchoi'. This form of the word only occurs here in the New Testament, and might be translated as 'be co-souled'. The prefix *sum* in

Greek means together with, and *psuchē* can be translated as soul or life-force (for more on 'soul' in Paul see my previous book *Body* (SPCK, 2016)).

- The words in verse 3 are equally interesting. *Eritheia* (selfish intrigue) and *kenodoxia* (vanity or conceited imagination) appear to be a direct criticism of the values of the Roman world, which were based on appearances and honour. Living with *eritheia* and *kenodoxia* involved precisely living with an eye to increasing your own honour, usually at the expense of someone else's. These stand as the direct opposite of the values presented in the Christ Hymn.

If there was ever a summary of the key principles of Christian living, Philippians 2:1–4 is surely one of the clearest. In short, it says if there is any substance to what you believe, you must allow it to change how you live. Live in unity with those around you, not looking out for what benefits you, but taking care of what benefits them. Paul's vision here runs counter to the principles of honour and shame that were at the centre of Roman society, principles that called for the protection of your own or your family's honour at the expense of those around you. Paul's words here are a clarion call to a different way of living and are as relevant today as they were then.

CHRIST'S GLORIOUS BODY
In Philippians 3:20 Paul states:

> For our citizen rights are in the heavens, from where we eagerly await a saviour, Lord Jesus Christ, who will change the form of our humble bodies to be like his glorious body according to the power that makes him able to subject everything to himself.

This, along with 1 Corinthians 15, has been a key part of discussions about what happens after death. The focus of the debate about this verse is the question of whether if our citizen rights are in heaven, our existence after death will also be there. Although traditionally this passage has been seen as pointing to a heavenly existence after death, many modern scholars argue that this passage like 1 Corinthians 15 points to a physical resurrection on a renewed earth. Tom Wright argued, famously, that this passage should not be interpreted as a belief that Christians go to heaven when they die (see T. Wright, *Surprised by Hope: Rethinking Heaven, the Resurrection, and the Mission of the Church* (SPCK Publishing, 2007), 164). Using the analogy of a fridge he claims that if we say we have a beer for a friend in a fridge we do not expect them to climb into the fridge to drink it. In the same way the fact that our rights as citizens are in the heavens does not mean that we need to be in heaven to inherit them. Rather, our citizen rights are kept safe in the heavenly realms ready for us at the moment of bodily resurrection. I take a similar view. Paul's understanding of life after death is clearly articulated in terms of the resurrection of the body on earth, not an ethereal existence in heaven. This is also true here. Our humble bodies will be changed in form to be like Christ's glorious body, one assumes at the moment of resurrection, but they will still be bodies.

Our citizen rights are those things that, like Roman citizen rights, govern not only identity, but action. Being a Roman citizen meant that a person would behave in a certain way, but would also gain certain advantages in their lives. Paul's point here is that having citizen rights in heaven had a similar effect. It required people to act in certain ways and came with certain advantages. The key difference being that the advantages – those from having our humble bodies transformed into the form of Christ's glorious body – will happen not now, but in the future.

For more discussion of Paul's expectations of life after death see P. Gooder, *Body*.

Chapter 29

No notes.

Chapter 30

WHATEVER IS TRUE . . .

Paul's 'virtue list' in 4:8 is unlike any of the other lists in his writings. In many ways it feels like a summary of the letter's command to live Christ's story as our own story. In answer to the question, 'Yes, but what does that mean in practice?', you could respond: 'Whatever is true, whatever is honourable, whatever is just, whatever is pure, whatever is agreeable, whatever is praiseworthy, if there is any goodness, if there is anything worthy of approval, ponder these things' . . . and then do them.

For more on Paul's virtue lists see S. Porter, 'Paul, Virtues, Vices, and Household Codes' in J. P. Sampley (ed.), *Paul in The Greco-Roman World: A Handbook Volume II* (Bloomsbury T&T Clark, 2016), 369–90.

REJOICE

Paul's emphasis on joy runs through Philippians. He rejoices that Christ is proclaimed even while he is in prison (1:18); he rejoices in the Philippians and their faith (2:17) and asks them also to rejoice with him (2:18). He sends Epaphroditus so that they can rejoice at seeing him, but most of all towards the end of the letter he tells them to rejoice in the Lord (3:1; 4:4 and 4:10). This seems to fit with his advice towards the end of the letter not to 'fret', but to let their requests be known before God (4:6) and that they should ponder what is true, honourable etc . . . (4:8).

It is interesting to notice that the verb *chairō*, translated 'rejoice' here, could also be translated 'delight in'. This offers a helpful lens through which to view Paul's exhortation. A deliberate and focussed decision on what we take delight in as a spiritual discipline feels a little easier than the command to 'rejoice' when we feel no shred of joy at all.

Epilogue

WHAT HAPPENED TO PAUL?

The end of Paul's imprisonment

One of the great mysteries about Paul is what happened to him after his imprisonment. The problem is that there is very little clear evidence at all about what happened. Church tradition has Paul martyred in Rome and buried beneath the Basilica of St Paul Outside the Walls in Rome. There is a tradition that states that Paul was executed by decapitation at the Aquae Salviae, on the Via Laurentina, and that his head bounced three times, which produced three fountains, hence the place became known as St Paul at the Three Fountains.

The strong association of Paul's death with the city of Rome certainly makes it possible – and even likely – that he died there. What is unclear, however, is how or when he died. Was he killed by Emperor Nero? Did he die in prison? Did he leave prison and travel onwards to Spain, returning later to die, either naturally or by martyrdom, at a later date? As we do not know the answers to these questions it seemed sensible to me to leave the story there, with both Lydia and Timothy as uncertain as we are.

Select Bibliography

Adams, Edward, *The Earliest Christian Meeting Places: Almost Exclusively Houses?* (London: T&T Clark, 2015).

Aldrete, Gregory S., *Daily Life in the Roman City: Rome, Pompeii and Ostia* (Connecticut: Greenwood Publishing Group, 2004).

Ascough, Richard S., *Lydia: Paul's Cosmopolitan Hostess* (Minnesota: Liturgical Press, 2009).

Aune, David E., *Revelation* (Nashville: Thomas Nelson, 1997).

BibleProject, 'Honor-Shame Culture and the Gospel Podcast | BibleProject™', accessed 10 May 2021: https://bibleproject. com/podcast/honor-shame-culture-and-gospel/

Bird, Michael F., and Gupta, Nijay K., *Philippians* (Cambridge: Cambridge University Press, 2020).

—and Sprinkle, Preston M (eds), *The Faith of Jesus Christ: Exegetical, Biblical and Theological Studies* (Milton Keynes: Paternoster, 2009).

Bockmuehl, Markus, *The Epistle to the Philippians* (London: Continuum, 2006).

Brooten, Bernadette J., *Women Leaders in the Ancient Synagogue: 36* (Providence: Brown Judaic Studies, 1982).

Burtchaell, James, *From Synagogue to Church: Public Services and Offices in the Earliest Christian Communities* (Cambridge: Cambridge University Press, 2008).

Collins, John N., *Diakonia: The Sources and Their Interpretation* (Oxford: Oxford University Press, 1990).

Czajkowski, Kimberley, Eckhardt, Benedikt, and Strothmann, Meret (eds), *Law in the Roman Provinces* (Oxford: Oxford University Press, 2020).

Drinkwater, John, *Roman Gaul (Routledge Revivals): The Three Provinces, 58 BC–AD 260* (Abingdon: Routledge, 2013).

Dunn, James D. G., *The Parting of the Ways: Between Christianity and Judaism and Their Significance for the Character of Christianity* (London: SCM Press, 2006).

Fee, Gordon D., *Paul's Letter to the Philippians: The New International Commentary on the New Testament* (Michigan: William B. Eerdmans Publishing Co., 1995).

Ferguson, Everett, *Demonology of the Early Christian World* (New York: E. Mellen Press, 1984).

Fitzmyer, Joseph A., *The Acts of the Apostles* (New Haven: Yale University Press, 2007).

Goldsworthy, Adrian, *Pax Romana: War, Peace and Conquest in the Roman World* (London: Weidenfeld & Nicolson, 2016).

Gooder, Paula, *Body: Biblical Spirituality for the Whole Person* (London: SPCK Publishing, 2016).

—'Diakonia in the New Testament: A Dialogue with John N. Collins', *Ecclesiology*, 3, no. 1, 2006, 33–56.

—*Heaven* (London: SPCK Publishing, 2011).

Graves, David E., 'What Is the Madder with Lydia's Purple? A Reexamination of the Purpurarii in Thyatira and Philippi', *Near East Archaeological Society Bulletin*, 2017, 3–29.

Gruca-Macaulay, Alexandra, *Lydia as a Rhetorical Construct in Acts* (Atlanta: SBL Press, 2016).

Hachlili, Rachel, *Ancient Jewish Art and Archaeology in the Diaspora* (Leiden: Brill, 1998).

Hawthorne, Gerald F., *Philippians, Volume 43: Revised Edition* (Michigan: Zondervan, 2015).

Hemer, Colin J., *The Book of Acts in the Setting of Hellenistic History* (Indiana: Mohr Siebeck, 1989).

Hengel, Martin, *Acts and the History of Earliest Christianity* (Minneapolis: Fortress Press, 1979).

Holmberg, Bengt, *Paul and Power: The Structure of Authority in the Primitive Church as Reflected in the Pauline Epistles* (Oregon: Wipf and Stock Publishers, 2004).

Hultin, Jeremy F., *The Ethics of Obscene Speech in Early Christianity and Its Environment* (Leiden: Brill, 2008).

Jennings, Mark A., *The Price of Partnership in the Letter of Paul to the Philippians: 'Make My Joy Complete'* (London: T&T Clark, 2018).

Jewett, Robert, *Romans: A Commentary* (Minneapolis: Fortress Press, 2006).

Keener, Craig S., *Acts: An Exegetical Commentary: Volume 3: 15:1–23:35* (Michigan: Baker Academic, 2014).

Kokkinos, Nikos, *The Herodian Dynasty: Origins, Role in Society and Eclipse* (London: Spink Books, 2010).

Kraabel, Alfred T., 'The Disappearance of the "God-Fearers"', *Numen* 28, no. 2, 1981, 113–26. https://doi.org/10.2307/3270014.

—*Judaism in Western Asia Minor Under the Roman Empire: With a Preliminary Study of the Jewish Community at Sardis, Lydia* (Cambridge: Harvard University Press, 1968).

Lentz Jr, John C., *Luke's Portrait of Paul*, 1st edn (Cambridge: Cambridge University Press, 1993).

Levine, Amy-Jill, and Brettler, Marc Z (eds), *The Jewish Annotated New Testament* (Oxford: Oxford University Press, 2017).

Levine, Lee I., *The Ancient Synagogue: The First Thousand Years*, 2nd edn (New Haven: Yale University Press, 2005).

MacLachlan, Bonnie, *Women in Ancient Rome: A Sourcebook* (London: Bloomsbury Academic, 2013).

Malina, Bruce J., *Timothy: Paul's Closest Associate* (Collegeville: Liturgical Press, 2008).

Martin, Ralph P., *A Hymn of Christ: Philippians 2:5-11 in Recent Interpretation in the Setting of Early Christian Worship*, 3rd edn (London: Inter-Varsity Press, 1997).

Matthews, Shelly, *First Converts: Rich Pagan Women and the Rhetoric of Mission in Early Judaism and Christianity* (Stanford: Stanford University Press, 2002).

McElduff, Siobhán, *UnRoman Romans,* accessed 19 July 2021: https://pressbooks.bccampus.ca/unromantest/

Milgrom, Jacob, 'Of Hems and Tassels', *Biblical Archaeology Review 9*, no. 3, 1983, 61–65.

Murphy-O'Connor, Jerome, *St. Paul's Corinth: Texts and Archaeology*, 3rd edn (Collegeville: Michael Glazier Books, 2002).

Nässelqvist, Dan, *Public Reading in Early Christianity: Lectors, Manuscripts, and Sound in the Oral Delivery of John 1-4* (Leiden: Brill, 2015).

Nikki, Nina, *Opponents and Identity in Philippians*, vol. 173 (Leiden: Brill, 2018).

Oakes, Peter, *Philippians: From People to Letter,* vol. 110 (Cambridge: Cambridge University Press, 2000).

—*Reading Romans in Pompeii: Paul's Letter at Ground Level* (London: SPCK Publishing, 2009).

Oropeza, B. J., *Jews, Gentiles, and the Opponents of Paul: Apostasy in the New Testament Communities, Volume 2: The Pauline Letters* (Oregon: Cascade Books, 2012).

Osgood, Josiah, *Claudius Caesar: Image and Power in the Early Roman Empire* (Cambridge: Cambridge University Press, 2010).

Osiek, Carolyn, *Philippians & Philemon* (Nashville: Abingdon Press, 2000).

Parks, Sara, Sheinfeld, Shayna and Warren, Meredith J. C., *Jewish and Christian Women in the Ancient Mediterranean* (Abingdon: Routledge, 2021).

Peterlin, Davorin, *Paul's Letter to the Philippians in the Light of Disunity in the Church*, vol. 79 (Leiden: Brill, 1995).

Peterson, Doug, 'The Jesus Boat', *History by the Slice* (blog), 26 July 2019: https://www.disappearingman.com/archaeology/the-jesus-boat/

Porter, Stanley E., ed., *Paul and His Opponents*, Pauline Studies, vol. 2 (Leiden: Brill, 2005).

—'Paul, Virtues, Vices, and Household Codes' in J. P. Sampley (ed.), *Paul In The Greco-Roman World: A Handbook*, vol. II (London: Bloomsbury T&T Clark, 2016).

Price, Janice, *World-Shaped Mission: Reimagining Mission Today* (London: Church House Publishing, 2012).

Rapske, Brian, *The Book of Acts and Paul in Roman Custody*, vol. 3 (Michigan: William B. Eerdmans Publishing Co., 1994).

Reimer, Ivoni Richter, *Women in the Acts of the Apostles: A Feminist Liberation Perspective*, Linda M. Maloney, trs. (Minneapolis: Augsburg Fortress, 1995).

—'Women in the Acts of the Apostles. Ch. 3', Interpret Scripture Correctly, 16 May 2017: http://www.interpretingscripturecorrectly.com/women-in-the-acts-of-the-apostles-chapter-3-lydia-reimer/

Richards, E. Randolph, *Paul and First-Century Letter Writing: Secretaries, Composition and Collection* (Nottingham: Apollos, 2005).

Sandnes, Karl Olav, *Belly and Body in the Pauline Epistles* (Cambridge: Cambridge University Press, 2002).

Schottroff, Luise, *Let the Oppressed Go Free: Feminist Perspectives on the New Testament*, Annemarie S. Kidder, trs. (Louisville: Westminster John Knox Press, 1993).

—*Lydia's Impatient Sisters: Feminist Social History of Early Christianity*, Barbara Rumscheidt and Martin Rumscheidt, trs. (London: SCM Press, 1995).

Shotter, David, *Nero Caesar Augustus: Emperor of Rome* (Harlow: Longman, 2008).

Silva, Moisés, *Philippians* (Michigan: Baker Academic, 2005).

Stewart, Alistair C., *The Original Bishops: Office and Order in the First Christian Communities* (Michigan: Baker Academic, 2014).

Still, Todd D., *Philippians & Philemon* (Macon: Smyth & Helwys, 2011).

Toner, Jerry, *How to Manage Your Slaves by Marcus Sidonius Falx* (London: Profile Books Ltd, 2015).

Verhoef, Eduard, *Philippi: How Christianity Began in Europe:*

The Epistle to the Philippians and the Excavations at Philippi (London: T&T Clark, 2013).

Witherington, Ben, *Conflict and Community in Corinth: A Socio-Rhetorical Commentary on 1 and 2 Corinthians* (Michigan: William B. Eerdmans Publishing Co., 1996).

Wright, Tom, *Justification – God's Plan & Paul's Vision* (London: SPCK Publishing, 2009).

—*Surprised by Hope: Rethinking Heaven, the Resurrection, and the Mission of the Church* (London: SPCK Publishing, 2007).

Youngs, Samuel J., *The Way of the Kenotic Christ* (Oregon: Cascade Books, 2019).

Zeichmann, Christopher B., 'Military Forces in Judaea 6–130 ce: The *status quaestionis* and Relevance for New Testament Studies', *Currents in Biblical Research* 17, no. 1, 1 October 2018, 86–120: https://doi.org/10.1177/1476993X18791425